Praise for *Bit Player* by Janet

"Delightful… In flashbacks, Dawson does a fine job bringing World War II–era Los Angeles to life."

—*Publishers Weekly*

"For anyone in the old movie scene, *Bit Player* is a treasure trove. For mystery lovers, *Bit Player* is another in a long line of get-your-teeth-into mysteries by Janet Dawson…. A tightly woven plot keeps Jeri on the trail…. She is very likable and I admire her doggedness. A good read once again. Never expect less with a Janet Dawson novel."

—*Bookloons*

"The arc moves back and forth between past and present very smoothly…. Great fun and well done. And especially interesting for folks who like Hollywood history."

—*I Love a Mystery*

"The best thing about a Jeri Howard book is that the author gets *everything* right: characters, dialogue, setting, pacing, plenty of twists and turns, with a well-plotted storyline."

—*Over My Dead Body*

"This is everything I enjoy in a mystery: the family involvement, a murder from the past, and the progression of clues obtained from interviews and research."

—*Mystery Scene*

"Fans of Jeri Howard will be delighted with her newest mystery, and fans of historical fiction will enjoy the nostalgia of old Hollywood and pre–World War II America."

—*Historical Novels Review*

What You Wish For

What You Wish For

A novel of suspense

Janet Dawson

2012 · Perseverance Press / John Daniel & Company
Palo Alto / McKinleyville, California

JBR

A Perseverance Press Book
Published by John Daniel & Company
A division of Daniel & Daniel, Publishers, Inc.
Post Office Box 2790
McKinleyville, California 95519
www.danielpublishing.com/perseverance

Distributed by SCB Distributors (800) 729-6423

Book design by Studio E Books, Santa Barbara, www.studio-e-books.com

Cover painting by Mary Proenza, *Buena Vista*

10 9 8 7 6 5 4 3 2 1

LIBRARY OF CONGRESS CATALOGING-IN-PUBLICATION DATA
What you wish for : a novel of suspense / by Janet Dawson.
    p. cm.
ISBN 978-1-56474-518-7 (pbk. : alk. paper)
I. Title.
PS3554.A949W37 2012
813'.54--dc23
                        2012014304

To my mother, Thelma Dawson,

and to friends of long standing,
Dawn Zinser Church and Barbara Heep

Many thanks to Rhys Bowen and Shelley Singer
for their insights and input. And thanks also to
Meredith Phillips and John and Susan Daniel of
Perseverance Press for publishing this novel.

What You Wish For

1

THEY WERE GOOD FRIENDS, sisters that Lindsey Page had acquired through chance rather than birth. She knew these women well—or so she thought.

April sun poured light from a blue sky as Lindsey walked through San Francisco's Financial District. The scent of flowers from a nearby stand vied with the pungent stench of urine from the doorway of a shuttered business. On her first visit in 1967, the Summer of Love, the city had looked magical to Lindsey, full of wonder and promise. It hadn't looked that way for a long time. The city was dirtier, the streets meaner.

I am getting old and cynical, Lindsey thought.

She walked up Montgomery Street past a homeless man muttering to himself, his hair and beard matted, clothes ragged and filthy. Other people on the sidewalk ignored him. They muttered, too, into cell phones or headsets, or pressed tiny keys, connected to their devices rather than the people around them.

Gretchen Segal was already at the café, sipping white wine. She looked at her watch. "Claire's late, as usual."

"Me, too. I lost track of time." Lindsey ordered iced tea and glanced at the menu.

A few minutes later, Claire Megarris arrived, carrying a shopping bag sporting the red-and-blue logo of Dunlin Coffee Roasteries. She sat down next to Gretchen and pulled out two bags. "I brought goodies. Sumatra for Gretchen, Costa Rica for Lindsey."

Lindsey held the bag to her face and breathed in the aroma. "Thanks. We coffee junkies appreciate having you as a source."

"As we say over at the Dunlin Building, life's too short to drink bad coffee." Claire glanced at the menu. "I'll have iced tea and the salad with smoked trout. No wine for me. I need a clear head for an afternoon meeting."

"Linguine carbonara," Gretchen said. "Never met a plate of pasta I didn't like."

"Crab cakes, blue cheese dressing on the salad." Lindsey handed the menu to the server. "Lunch with just the three of us feels strange." After all, Annabel had originally brought them together. But today she would not be joining them.

Claire sighed. "Yes, it does. She could be in rehab for months. She tries to talk. It's hard to understand her, with that aphasia. Her left side is partially paralyzed. What if she has permanent disability?"

"Give it time," Lindsey said. "It's only been six weeks since the stroke. She could make a full recovery. With all the therapy, I think she's better."

Gretchen looked stricken. "If only we hadn't played that last set of tennis…"

"It's not your fault," Lindsey said. "It didn't happen because you and Annabel were playing tennis. She could have had that stroke any time. You might as well hold yourself responsible for the last earthquake."

ANNABEL and Gretchen had a tennis date that Saturday, at the Claremont Hotel in Berkeley. Lindsey and Claire were joining them for lunch and an afternoon luxuriating at the hotel spa, treating themselves to massages and facials.

The hotel, a white confection surrounded by manicured grounds and tennis courts, rose at the base of the Berkeley hills, where a major earthquake fault lay beneath wooded slopes and canyons. Like a snake slithering from its den to bite the unwary, the fault sometimes made its presence felt with a shake that rattled the animate and knocked the inanimate from shelves. Then the ground would still. The damage would be catalogued, the broken glass swept up and discarded. Until next time. There was always a next time, one that might bring a fatal bite.

At the courts, Lindsey sat on a bench and watched Annabel and Gretchen play tennis. They finished the set and walked to the side-line where they'd left their gear. Both reached for their water bottles. Then Gretchen waved. "Claire! Over here."

"I'm ready for lunch and an afternoon of pampering," Claire said as she joined them. "First we have to get these two aging Wimbledon rejects off the court. Come on, let's eat."

"The reservation's at one," Annabel said.

Claire grimaced in mock frustration. "You told me noon."

"You're always late, so I compensate." Annabel tucked her bottle into her tennis bag.

"Now she's a poet," Claire shot back.

"We'll play one more set." Annabel stretched, working the kinks out of her back and shoulders. She walked back to the service line, tossed the ball into the air and swung the racquet high above her head. But she never made her downswing. She froze. The ball dropped and rolled toward the net. Her racquet clattered onto the court. Annabel pressed both hands to her temples, face crumpling with pain. She took a step, then collapsed and fell like a broken doll, blue eyes wide with confusion, saliva dribbling from her mouth as she tried to speak. Claire shouted into her cell phone. Sirens wailed, lights flashed, paramedics ran toward the tennis courts.

"YOU haven't played tennis since then, have you?" Lindsey asked now.

Gretchen shook her head. "No. I can't even bear the sight of my tennis gear. Doug hid it."

"If I knew where your tennis gear was, I'd haul it out and plop it down in front of you. I might even volley a few balls with you."

"Lindsey on a tennis court?" Gretchen smiled. "Now that's scary."

Lindsey squeezed Gretchen's hand. "Annabel will recover. You once told me she had a will of iron. Now Dr. Page prescribes a good meal." She glanced at Claire. "How are Hal and the kids?" Annabel and Hal had two daughters, Tess and Sharon, and a son, Adam.

"Being upbeat and positive," Claire said. "Hal goes to the rehab place every day. He takes lunch for both of them and talks to her.

I know he's worried. At the office I'm shouldering as much of the burden as I can. But he's the CEO. We have a board meeting later this month, with important decisions to make. Some people are using Hal's preoccupation with personal matters to put forth their own agendas. The corporate world is so damned cutthroat."

"Yeah, and you love it," Gretchen said.

"It shows?" Claire laughed. "Oh, you know me too well."

Lindsey smiled. "The only difference between academic politics and office politics is that the corporate types are more plain-spoken than professors. Maybe less stodgy and hidebound."

"Hidebound? Stodgy? It's worse than that," Claire said. "Max Brinker is a sexist old dinosaur. He drives me crazy."

"You have to take Max as he is," Lindsey said.

"I don't want him, period." Claire scowled. "I'm tired of hearing how things were done in the good old days when Uncle George ran the company. I wish Max would retire. He's way past his sell-by date. But he just keeps hanging on. As if I didn't have enough on my plate, my assistant's pregnant, going on maternity leave. I don't know what I'm going to do without her." The server brought their orders. Claire picked up her fork. "How goes it with you?"

Lindsey took a bite of her crab cake. "I'm doing interviews for my book. Next week I'm going to the Oregon Shakespeare Festival. I'm glad I retired, so I can do what I want to do."

Claire shuddered. "Retirement would bore me silly."

"You'd be surprised what crops up to fill the time." Gretchen twirled linguine on her fork. "I'm gardening, volunteering."

"Are you still working with that adoptive parents organization?" Lindsey asked.

Gretchen nodded. "This is my last term on the board, though. I want to keep my summer free to spend time with Doug and the kids. Nat graduates from high school this spring. Can you believe that?"

"Where did the time go?" Claire asked. "That sweet little toddler, all grown up."

"He's grown, all right," Gretchen said. "He was so small when we adopted him. Now he's almost as tall as his dad. He goes off to college in the fall. I'll probably be glad to have him out of the house." The misty look in Gretchen's eyes belied her words. "We'll still have Amy at home. She'll be thirteen in September. Another teenager."

Claire turned to Lindsey. "How's Nina? Does she like living in Texas?"

"I haven't heard from her lately." Lindsey sipped iced tea. She hadn't communicated with her daughter in months. Daughters—a dangerous subject.

Fork in hand, Claire reached across the table and excised a bite from one of Lindsey's crab cakes. Taking people's food was an old habit of Claire's. Lindsey had gotten used to it over the years.

They all shared a decadent chocolate dessert, then paid for their lunches. Claire headed back to work, Lindsey and Gretchen to BART. As they walked home from the downtown Berkeley station, they passed the empty shell of the UC Theatre on University Avenue. A scrap of song went through Lindsey's mind, Fred Astaire singing of danger ahead, as he and Ginger Rogers twirled and dipped through the last frames of *Follow the Fleet*. The old movie house's marquee lights were out, the box office was boarded up, and the display cases that once held movie posters were empty. Fred and Ginger no longer danced here.

"It seems strange not to see the names of the latest double feature," Lindsey said. "Old movies. Film noir and screwball comedies. Or musicals. I could always count on Fred and Ginger to cheer me up."

"The *Rocky Horror Picture Show* on Friday nights." Gretchen grinned. "Yeah, I was sorry to see it go. But these days, with cable and DVDs, I'm not surprised. The last time Doug and I took the kids to a movie, dinner and tickets for four added up to an expensive evening."

"I remember when I could get into a movie for a buck and a quarter," Lindsey said, "back when I was in high school. Watching a DVD at home isn't the same as seeing a movie in the theater. Sitting in the dark gazing up at the big screen, with all those people. You came here on your first date with Doug."

"You remember?" Gretchen laughed. "He spilled buttered popcorn in my lap. I never did get the stain out."

"I seem to be on the nostalgia train lately," Lindsey said. "Thinking about the past, all of us living together in that house. But we're not in college anymore. We're middle-aged."

"Don't remind me," Gretchen said. "You never talk about Nina. That must have been some argument."

Lindsey sighed. "It was. Same damn thing. Just different words."

They walked north on Milvia Street. The neighborhood segued from commercial to residential. Houses mostly, though there were plenty of apartment buildings and houses divided into flats. They said good-bye in front of the Segals' house. Lindsey lived a block away. She'd returned to Berkeley last year after retiring from California Polytechnic University in San Luis Obispo, moving into this house where she'd lived while finishing grad school. Now she'd inherited the house from Aunt Emma.

The one-story brown-shingled bungalow was larger than it looked, added onto several times since it was built in 1910. It sat on a narrow corner lot at Milvia and Vine Streets, its yard full of plants and flowers—dark green rosemary, pale green succulents, tall stalks of red-and-yellow alstroemeria, fringed white Shasta daisies, and or-ange California poppies. A dark red clematis vine climbed a trellis and rosebushes lined the fence. Lindsey pushed through the gate and stopped to inhale the fragrance of a lush coral rose, its extravagant bloom the size of a plate.

A woman sat on the wide porch railing. Short dark hair framed her face and her left eyebrow was pierced with a gold stud. Multiple earrings decorated both lobes and her right forearm had a pink rose tattoo. Dark circles under her blue eyes, drawn by fatigue, looked like bruises.

Daughters—the dangerous subject had come home.

2

LINDSEY FOUND HER VOICE. "Nina. What are you doing here?"

Nina stood and sighed. "You could say you're glad to see me."

"I'm always glad to see you," Lindsey said. "But…"

At Nina's feet were a zipped red nylon tote and a black backpack with wheels and a handle, airline tags attached to both. "They say home is the place that when you have to go there, they have to take you in."

"That bad?" Lindsey asked.

"Yeah. Can I come in?"

Lindsey climbed the steps and put her arms around her daughter. At first there was no responding pressure. Then Nina's arms moved and her cheek brushed against Lindsey's head. Awkward, after those harsh words months ago.

I'm leaving. I don't want to see you, ever again.

Sticks and stones can break my bones but words can never hurt me. Not true. Words hurt worst of all.

"Can I stay here for a couple of nights?" Nina asked.

"Do you have anywhere to go after a couple of nights?" When Nina shook her head, Lindsey pulled out her keys and unlocked the front door. "You can stay here as long as you like. Have you eaten?"

"Not unless you consider pretzels food," Nina said, as they took her bags to the guestroom. "You can't even get peanuts anymore."

"Let's get you something to eat."

"Be right there." Nina shed her jacket and went into the bathroom.

Lindsey headed for the kitchen, wondering what had prompted Nina to swallow her pride and come home from Texas, four months after that horrible argument. She opened cabinets and drawers, setting the table. From the refrigerator she took a pitcher of iced tea and a container of chicken left over from last night's dinner.

"I've already had lunch," Lindsey said when Nina joined her in the kitchen. "But you can make a sandwich. Here's some chicken and cheese bread."

Nina reached for the cutting board and a serrated knife. The cats appeared, their unerring feline instinct telling them food was in the vicinity and the humans could be persuaded to share. Clementine, the calico cat, wound around Lindsey's legs. Lola Montez, the fluffy white cat with crossed blue eyes, sat in the doorway and meowed. Lindsey put a handful of chicken into each cat bowl, on opposite sides of the kitchen. The cats moved quickly to their respective bowls and began to eat.

"They still don't get along," Nina said.

"They're learning to tolerate each other, after all these years." Lindsey filled two glasses with iced tea. "At least Clementine doesn't pounce on Lola as much as she used to. It just takes time, or they're getting older."

"You cats have it lucky." Nina knelt and stroked Clementine's sleek back. "Sleep all day, plenty to eat, not a care in the world, except that other cat. What a life." She straightened, then washed and dried her hands.

Lindsey took a jar from a cabinet. "No pretzels. But I have peanuts."

"Thanks, Mom." Nina managed a tired smile as she ate a handful of peanuts. She layered chicken and cranberry chutney on the bread. Lindsey joined Nina at the table, sipping iced tea as she watched her daughter. Nina ate quickly, hungry after a day of traveling.

"There's ice cream in the freezer," Lindsey said. "Chocolate chip."

"Later. I need a shower. And some sleep." Nina put her plate and cutlery in the dishwasher.

"The bed's already made up," Lindsey said, following Nina to the guestroom. Nina unzipped the backpack and took out a toiletry bag and an emerald silk robe. She drew the blinds and stripped off her jeans, then pulled her T-shirt over her head. She unfastened her bra and reached for the robe.

"What's that on your arm?" Lindsey asked. "A new tattoo?" The mark was a faded patch of yellow-green on Nina's left upper arm. Not a tattoo. A bruise.

Nina slipped her arms into the silk robe, reached under it and removed her panties. As she tied the belt of the robe she said, "You were right about Chad."

Anger welled up. But Lindsey kept her voice even. "I didn't want to be right. Take your shower and lie down. We'll talk later, if you want."

Nina carried her toiletry bag into the bathroom and shut the door. A moment later, Lindsey heard water raining down in the shower, reminding her of the last time she'd seen her daughter. That awful day in December, as the old year spun to its end. A gray day, full of rain.

"BUT what about Christmas?" Lindsey asked. "We always spend Christmas together."

December was a set of rituals, evolved over time. She and Nina decorated the tree and listened to Christmas music, baked cookies and fragrant loaves of pumpkin bread, searched for special gifts, and wrapped packages with paper and ribbons. No matter who else was involved, family and friends, on other days, in other places, Christmas morning was the two of them, mother and daughter together, lingering over coffee, unwrapping presents. Lindsey was looking forward to the holiday, the first in this house since she'd moved back to Berkeley.

"Chad starts a new job in Austin on January second," Nina said. "We have to find a place to live."

"Why leave before Christmas? Can't you join him after the holidays?"

"We're driving to Texas, Mom. With the two of us spelling each other we can make it in a few days. Chad thinks that's the best thing to do."

He would. "Have you thought this through?"

"Of course I have," Nina said. "Give me some credit. I know you don't like Chad. You've never even tried."

"Have I ever said I don't like him?"

"You don't have to. It's obvious from the way you treat him. You look at him like he was a bug that crawled out from under a rock."

No, Lindsey didn't like Chad. Nina met him at a Pink Slip Party in San Francisco, where people between jobs or seeking employment in the tech industry gathered for drinks and networking. Job-hopping was the norm. Since graduating from San Francisco State University, Nina had changed jobs every year, using her technical writing skills to leverage her way through a succession of software firms in Silicon Valley, salary and perks increasing with each new position. She worked at an Internet start-up in San Francisco, sharing an apartment with a coworker. But they were hardly ever at home. They worked sixty or eighty hours a week. Nina loved her work, the fat paychecks sweetened with stock options and the conspicuous-consumption lifestyle.

Lindsey had suspected for some time that all this New Economy stuff would face some Old Economy realities. So it had. Nina and her roommate showed up at their office one morning to find the doors locked. They were allowed into their cubicles long enough to clean out their desks. Their final paychecks bounced. Nina wasn't worried, confident she could get another job. But it was the beginning of the long plunge. She and her roommate stuck it out for a while, drawing unemployment insurance, looking for work, taking contract assignments. Nina sold the sports car, the electronic gadgets, the furniture, and took much of her wardrobe to a resale shop. Her roommate packed up and left California. Nina moved in with Chad.

Lindsey couldn't understand what Nina saw in him. He was a tall, blond Texan, with attitude and ego to spare. He was also manipulative, with a mean streak. Lindsey had nothing to go on but her gut feeling about Chad, and the few times she'd seen him verbally upbraid Nina. She hoped she was wrong. It was Nina's life, she'd have to bump into her own brick walls as she figured out her own path. Lindsey just hoped her daughter wouldn't get in the way of Chad's fist.

Now Chad had decided to return to Texas, and Nina was going with him. She wasn't interested in cautionary words about suddenly pulling up stakes and heading for a town she'd never visited before, with a man her mother didn't trust.

"It's selfish of Chad to insist that you go with him right before the holidays." Even as she said the words, Lindsey knew she'd added fuel to the fire.

"It's selfish of you to want me to stay," Nina snapped, "so you won't be alone at Christmas."

"I was looking forward to spending the holidays with you. It's always been just the two of us."

"And whose fault is that?" Acid etched Nina's words. "If you'd married my father, you wouldn't be alone."

It always came back to that, the same argument they'd been

having ever since Nina was old enough to feel the sting of being the child of a single mother, a child who, according to the dictates of conventional society, didn't have a father. He existed, but his name wasn't on the birth certificate. He wasn't a presence in Nina's life. Lindsey had done it all, teaching her daughter how to tie shoes and ride a bicycle, providing food, shelter and the pleasant accoutrements of middle-class life. But in the midst of what Lindsey called abundance, Nina felt lack. Over the years she had built up a powerful reservoir of resentment.

The argument had really started when Nina was still in the womb, as Lindsey debated with herself. Should she terminate this unplanned pregnancy? Should she have the baby? What would raising this unexpected child do to her plans, her dreams, her life? Once she'd made that decision, Lindsey had made a second—that she would not reveal the identity of the father to anyone, not even her child.

Lindsey felt she'd made the right choice. She loved her daughter. It had been difficult, finishing her course work and her doctoral dissertation, putting her dreams on hold, finding work, supporting herself and her daughter. But she sometimes questioned the wisdom of her second decision. As Nina grew older, she wondered why other little girls had daddies at home and she didn't.

Lindsey had never told the man that he'd fathered her child. It was late in the game for such revelations. There were other reasons, people, consequences to consider. As the years with no answers passed, Nina's questions became more infrequent. Lindsey was relieved of the burden of not answering them. But Nina's resentment simmered under the surface, sometimes bubbling up in harsh words. Like now. Why wasn't it good enough for Nina to have a mother who loved her?

"This isn't about me, or your father. It's about you and Chad." Lindsey voiced her concerns about Chad and the possibility of abuse: verbal, emotional and physical.

Nina shook her head in disbelief. "You're crazy. You're projecting it on Chad and trying to control me."

It was as though Lindsey had pulled on the end of a piece of yarn, causing a carefully constructed garment to unravel. Nina lashed her with harsh, bitter, ugly words that spouted like a geyser from her well of resentment. Then she headed for the door.

"Don't leave." Lindsey reached for her daughter. Nina pushed Lindsey away. Her hand struck one of the Christmas decorations on the hall table, a small plaster-of-Paris angel, painted silver, gold, and blue. Nina had made it for Lindsey when she was in third grade. Now the angel flew off the table, crashing onto the hardwood floor, breaking into several pieces. Lindsey cried out, knelt to pick up the pieces.

Nina wrenched open the front door and stormed out into the rain, tossing words that hurt at her mother.

I'm leaving. I don't want to see you, ever again.

NOW Nina was back, asleep in the guestroom, hair dark against the white pillow, her discarded green robe on the floor. Lindsey picked up the robe and draped it over a chair, her fingers brushing her daughter's cheek. The older she got, the more Nina looked like her father.

Lindsey shut the door. She got the mail and sifted through the envelopes, separating junk from bills, finding a letter from her mother. There were two bedrooms at the back of the house. The smaller of these was her office, walls crowded with bookshelves. An ergonomic desk held her computer and printer. The calico cat was curled into a ball in the office chair, nose tucked under paws.

Lindsey tossed the junk mail into a recycling bin and opened the other envelopes, glancing at the bills before filing them in a basket on her desk. Then she took out the digital recorder that contained that morning's interview. She needed to upload the audio file on the recorder to the computer and then transcribe the interview. But Nina's unexpected appearance on her doorstep had taken precedence over work. The transcription would keep until tomorrow.

LINDSEY woke on Friday morning, nose-to-whiskers with Lola. The white cat pushed her head under Lindsey's hand. Lindsey stroked the cat. Sleep tugged. Her eyes grew heavy and her hand stilled. A paw, claws sheathed, batted Lindsey on the cheek.

"All right." Lindsey threw back the covers and got up, putting on robe and slippers. Both cats jumped to the floor and headed for the kitchen to stand purring by their bowls.

It was chilly this April morning, a gray sky hinting rain. Lindsey ground coffee beans and poured water into the drip coffeemaker. The coffee perfumed the kitchen with its aroma. She filled a mug with dark brew, lightened it with milk, and carried the mug back to her bedroom. After she'd showered and dressed, she looked in on Nina, who was still asleep.

Lindsey retrieved the *San Francisco Chronicle* from the porch, glancing at headlines that heralded war, a stumbling economy, climate change, another murder. May you live in interesting times, she thought. She'd been living in interesting times her whole life. Right now she could go for some boring times. In the kitchen she ate a scone while she read the paper. Then she refilled her coffee mug and walked back to her office. Time to get to work. She turned on the computer, connected the digital recorder to its cradle, and uploaded the audio file of yesterday's interview with the woman from El Salvador.

The book-in-progress was a study of Latin American women who'd immigrated to the United States as a result of wars and upheaval. Through her interviews, Lindsey had collected firsthand accounts, a catalogue of horror, evidence of the human cost of political unrest and civil war, tales of the powerless exploited, and frequently murdered, by the powerful. Many women found it difficult to talk about their experiences. War, deprivation—and in some cases torture—had traumatized them.

Lindsey had been meeting Flor Cooper for two months, at a *panadería*, a Mexican bakery, on Fruitvale Avenue. At first Lindsey did most of the talking, filling silences, gaining the Salvadoran woman's confidence. Then Flor began to talk, about her husband and children, their home, and her husband's large extended family. She talked of the immediate past, but she skirted the story of her life in El Salvador, before she came to *El Norte*, the United States. It was as though her life began the day she crossed *la frontera*. But yesterday Flor had opened the long-shut door and talked. What came out disturbed Lindsey. How could she do what Flor asked?

The researcher should remain detached from the subject. But what if the interviewee asked the interviewer for a favor? Lindsey the mother wanted to help Flor. Lindsey the historian countered with a reasoned argument for remaining detached, uninvolved.

But I am involved, Lindsey thought, ever since I got that woman to trust me. This is real life, with real people and real emotions.

It was a simple request. Flor wanted Lindsey to meet her Saturday morning at the Berkeley Farmers Market, so she could prove that what she'd told Lindsey was true. Lindsey looked at the calendar. Saturday was free—or did it have a cost?

Yesterday Flor's hands had been busy with her needlework. Her wooden embroidery hoop held a length of crisp white fabric, stretched tight, as Flor pushed a needle and a strand of crimson thread through the fabric, creating a border of flowers—roses and pansies and daffodils, meticulously stitched in jewel-bright red, purple and yellow. She was making pillowcases, Flor said, a gift for a friend.

Flor set aside her embroidery and reached into the canvas bag at her feet, producing an envelope containing recent snapshots of her children. After Lindsey admired these, Flor took another photograph from her bag, this one in a plain wooden frame. Her smile faded, like the colors in the picture. The image showed a man and a woman in front of an adobe building, a church with a crucifix above the door. To the man's right was a second building, with a sign that read MERCADO, Spanish for market. The woman was a much-younger Flor, wearing a printed blouse and a long skirt. In her arms she held a sturdy little boy, perhaps eighteen months old.

"This is me," Flor said. "My husband, Atenacio. My son, Efraín."

"You were married before? In El Salvador?"

Flor nodded. "I was sixteen. Atenacio was eighteen. We had another child before Efraín. A little girl. She died when she was a baby. Then Efraín was born. A strong little boy. *Mi corazón, mi precioso.*"

My heart, my precious one. Something terrible must have happened to Flor's husband and son. Surely she wouldn't have left them behind in El Salvador if she'd had a choice. Lindsey handed the photograph back to Flor, who put the picture into her bag and pushed her chair away from the table. Outside they walked to a nearby park, an oasis of green in the urban neighborhood, and sat on a bench near the children's play area, where a young woman pushed a little boy on a swing.

Now, in her office, Lindsey started the recording, hands poised over her keyboard, ready to transcribe the spoken into the written. First she heard traffic noise and a child's laughter. Then came Flor's voice.

"I was born on a *finca* in Ahuachapán department in western El Salvador. Department means province. *Finca* means plantation, estate. My family moved from one *finca* to another. My husband Atenacio and I did the same. That's the way it is, with coffee. The work is seasonal. The workers come and go. The last place we lived was a *finca* in Chalatenango department, in a village called San Blas. You won't find it on a map. It isn't there anymore."

3

San Blas, Chalatenango Department, El Salvador, April 1989

"NO, M'IJO," FLOR GUZMÁN SAID as her son neared the fire. Efraín was hungry, lured by the beans simmering in the iron pot and the grill full of *pupusas*, small thick cornmeal patties filled with *queso*, soft white cheese. Flor tore a piece from a *pupusa* and gave it to Efraín, who crammed the morsel into his mouth.

"*Mi precioso.*" She smiled and brushed dust and crumbs from Efraín's mouth. Her first baby, a girl, had died at three months, too soon buried in the churchyard of another village near another *finca*. A year later, Flor gave birth to this healthy boy, with his father's round face and good humor. Efraín was strong and smart. He would learn to read and do sums. Maybe he would go out in the world and do something besides pick coffee cherries.

Be careful what you wish for, her neighbor Prudencia told her. You might discover it isn't what you want after all. Don't tempt fate by trying to change it. Besides, what else would the boy do? He was a *campesino*, a peasant, like his parents, following generations of peasants who roamed the countryside, working ranches and *fincas*, hands stained, gnarled and callused from hard labor.

It's good for a mother to dream for her son, Flor thought. She saw Atenacio climbing the hill. How handsome he was, how strong and gentle. She was lucky to have such a good husband.

That morning, Flor and Atenacio, carrying Efraín, walked down to the little adobe church. Father Bartolomeo, the priest from Texistepeque, came once a month, to celebrate Mass and hear confessions. Afterwards, the men of the village gathered outside, while the women went home to prepare the midday meal.

Atenacio was with Nazario Robles, who wore a uniform and carried a rifle. Nazario's mother and sister lived here, in a house by the earthen dam that bisected the little valley where San Blas lay. The family came from Morazán department, to the east, where the Salvadoran army fought the rebels. They'd fled, fearful of being killed, like those in the terrible massacre in a village called El Mozote, where hundreds were murdered by the army.

It wasn't the first time Flor had heard of such horrors. Death squads and the army sowed fear everywhere. Even Archbishop Romero had been murdered in a chapel in San Salvador, shot down as he celebrated Mass. And the old ones told stories of la Matanza, the great killing of 1932, when tens of thousands of peasants had died in an insurrection, put down with swift and brutal slaughter. Nothing changed, they said. There was unrest and peasants died.

While Nazario and his *compadres* fought the army, his mother, sister and brother-in-law had joined the tattered throng of peasants moving around the countryside, from one department to the next, seeking work. They came to San Blas at the same time Atenacio and Flor arrived at this huge *finca* owned by Don Humberto.

When Nazario visited his family, his presence—and the gun he carried—made some *campesinos* uneasy, especially Tránsito Vigil, the man who ran the market. Flor had overheard the two men arguing that morning, when she and Atenacio left the church to find Nazario in the plaza, waiting for his mother.

"Why are you here?" Tránsito demanded. "You bring danger. Don

Humberto will be angry to know you are on his *finca*. We don't want that. He has been good to us."

Nazario snorted his derision. "He exploits you. All of you." He looked around, his eyes taking in the ramshackle houses on the slopes above the plaza, the threadbare clothing worn by his mother and sister. "You work from dawn far into the night and he pays you a pittance. You live in miserable shacks and pay rent money to that rich bloodsucker. When the work is gone, you move on to another *finca*, where another rich man exploits you. This will go on, unless we break the backs of these landowners."

"Our lives are as God meant them to be," Tránsito said. "You rebels bring trouble, blowing up bridges, burning *fincas*. Then the army comes and attacks villages."

"You're a fool." Nazario moved toward Tránsito, but Father Bartolomeo separated the two men. Atenacio told Flor to take Efraín and go home.

Flor didn't know what to think. She lived in a small, familiar world, caring for her family, working. She and Atenacio picked coffee cherries from trees covering the hillsides and worked in the processing plant that separated the outer skin of the coffee berries from the thick pulp that covered the beans. Atenacio ran machinery, Flor filled sacks with roasted beans.

Maybe Nazario was right. Flor wasn't sure she understood everything he said. But she and Atenacio had moved many times, with nothing more than their clothing, some blankets, and Flor's iron pot. When there was no work, the *campesinos* migrated, and there were always others seeking the same jobs. In her grandfather's day the *campesinos* stayed on the land, worked it, and were paid with food and a place to live. Now landowners like Don Humberto moved the people off the land and planted crops that didn't need as many *campesinos* to work them, or ran cattle in the cleared fields. *Campesinos* came and went, struggling to survive, sometimes desperate for work.

They had been in San Blas two years, longer than they'd stayed in the last village. But she didn't know how much longer they would be here. Times were hard. That meant moving on.

Nazario's words outside the church were true. Don Humberto paid his peasants barely enough to buy food from Tránsito's store, where prices were high. Most of them had small gardens, like the one Flor had dug into the rocky soil of the hillside and nourished with water she carried from the nearby creek. Atenacio paid a portion of his wages back to the landowner, so they could live in this one-room house, the roof in need of constant mending. Efraín was barefoot, wearing a faded shirt and ragged shorts. Flor herself had only a few skirts and blouses and she kept Atenacio's few clothing items cleaned and mended.

The rest of the village looked as mean and makeshift as their clothes. Maybe Nazario was right. Things should be better, Flor thought. She wanted more for her son.

Atenacio picked up Efraín and raised him high, laughing as his son squealed with glee. Then he set the boy on the ground. "I asked Nazario to share our meal."

Nazario shook his head. "You're kind, but I won't take your food. I'm expected at my mother's house. I wanted to give you this." He leaned his rifle against a tree and opened his knapsack, pulling out a pasteboard folder—a color photograph. On a Christmas visit to his family, Nazario had brought a camera and taken pictures, including this one, showing Flor, Atenacio and Efraín outside the church. "The boy has grown so much in four months."

"He'll be two in September. Thank you. We will treasure this." Flor and Atenacio admired the photograph. Then she carried it into the house and put it on the shelf next to her mother's rosary.

Outside, Atenacio drank from the tin dipper in the water jar. "We hear of fighting to the north. But it's been quiet here."

"Humberto wants quiet," Nazario said. "Nothing must interfere with his crop. He needs money for his *finca*, his son's army commission, and his son-in-law's political schemes. The army and the politicians will pay. We'll march into San Salvador and kill them all."

"I don't like to hear talk of killing." Flor reached for Efraín.

"You aren't safe here," Nazario said. "Humberto knows the rebels are coming. He's hired men with guns."

"Like that brute Cruz," Atenacio said.

"I told my family to leave," Nazario said. "I tell you the same. Leave soon, before the rains start next month. We control the north, and we're moving south, into this part of Chalatenango. Soon we'll control the whole department. Come north to Los Árboles. It's a rebel town. There are jobs in the sawmill."

Atenacio frowned. "I'll think about it."

"Don't wait too long." Nazario picked up his rifle and walked down the hill.

Flor spooned beans into a bowl, took a *pupusa* from the grill, and handed the food to Atenacio. Then she served herself and sat cross-legged on the ground, feeding Efraín from her own bowl. "Should we go?"

"I don't know," Atenacio said.

THE men with guns came that afternoon, when the village was quiet and the people were taking siesta after their Sunday meal. Jeeps drove over the hill from the coffee processing plant and disgorged men in uniforms, men with hard faces who carried rifles and guns in holsters at their hips, sharp machetes tucked into their belts. The men dispersed through San Blas, rounding up *campesinos*, herding them to the plaza.

Flor held Efraín and stood at Atenacio's side in the plaza. The people around her looked frightened. The man Atenacio had called a brute, Cruz, had an ugly, scarred face, massive shoulders like a bull, and thick hands, fingers decorated with big gold rings. Father Bartolomeo tried to speak to Cruz but he swatted the priest away as though he were a troublesome insect. Cruz's hand snaked out and seized Nazario's mother, pulling her roughly to face him.

"Where is the rebel?" Cruz barked. "I know you're hiding him."

"I don't know what you mean," Señora Robles said.

Cruz slapped her. She fell back against her daughter and son-in-law, mouth bleeding where Cruz's rings had torn her flesh. "*Puta.* I know your son's with the rebels. Where is he? Where's your bastard? Tell me, or I'll kill you and all the rest of these traitors."

"These people aren't rebels," Father Bartolomeo said. "They are simple *campesinos*."

Cruz pulled the machete from his belt. "This village is a nest of rebels and Communists. We should have cleaned you out long ago. Give up the rebel." He drew the machete along Señora Robles's throat and a thin line of blood appeared.

"He's gone," Atenacio said. "He only comes to see his mother, like a good son."

Cruz raised the machete and struck. Blood splashed over Flor. Atenacio fell lifeless to the dust. Nazario's mother screamed. Cruz cut her throat and silenced her forever, then he shot the priest.

La Matanza. The slaughter. A dam had burst. A river of blood surged over the village. Flor held Efraín tight and ran like the other *campesinos*, screaming with fright as the men with guns attacked like ravening beasts. They shot at everything that moved. Men, women and children fell under the volley.

Flor was halfway up the hillside when she stumbled and fell. She hit the ground hard, trying to protect Efraín. At first she thought Atenacio's blood stained Efraín's chin, but it was a cut. Jagged bits of glass glittered on the path where they lay. She used her blouse to stanch the boy's blood and scrambled to her feet, running up the hill to hide behind a rough pile of logs that separated her house from that of Prudencia.

Efraín cried with pain. Flor put her hand over her son's mouth. He must not make any noise and give them away. She stared in horror at the nightmare below in the plaza. Bodies lay crumpled outside the church. The men with guns clubbed those who hadn't died from the bullets. The men with guns took women and girls, some as old as Prudencia, some barely older than Efraín, tore off their dresses and held their legs apart. Right there in the plaza they raped them over and over. Then they cut the throats of their victims. Finally the men with guns rounded up the people they had not yet killed and shut them inside the church, along with the bodies. They poured gasoline on the walls and roof and set the building on fire. Flames licked the building. The people inside screamed.

Efraín whimpered. Get away, she must get away. Flor slipped from behind the log pile and ran toward her house. Rough hands caught her and seized Efraín. Two men with guns, faces like demons. Flor cried with anguish as Efraín wailed.

"Here's a fine one," the man who held Efraín said.

"This is a fine one, too." The other man pushed Flor against the house. He squeezed her breasts, pulled up her skirt, and unzipped his trousers. She didn't care what happened to her. All she cared about was her son, struggling as the other man carried him down the hill.

An iron cooking pot thunked against the man's head. Prudencia was behind him, a grim smile on her face as she swung the pot, striking again and again. He fell sideways, his head bloody. Prudencia dropped the pot. "He's dead. The pig."

Flor looked down to the plaza, frantic, searching for Efraín. She saw three children in a Jeep—a little girl, a baby, and her son. She took a step forward, but Prudencia pulled her back. "No. They will kill you and still take the boy. You must live, so you can find him again."

"I can't leave him," Flor cried. Prudencia wouldn't let go of her arm. The Jeep with the children drove away.

Prudencia spat on the man's body. "They'll come looking for this piece of shit. We must be far away when they do."

THE wind keened through the trees at the top of the ridge. Flor and Prudencia stopped at a rushing creek, washing away dirt and blood. They walked along the narrow dirt track that followed the creek. Eventually this path joined a wider gravel road that wound north, over the mountains to Los Árboles, the rebel town. But they didn't take the road, afraid the men with guns would find them. Back toward San Blas, black smoke rose, the afternoon sun a red sore glowing through the pall. The men with guns had burned the church and the people locked inside it. Now they were burning the rest of the village.

As the sun lowered behind the mountains, they found a cave in some rocks, the entrance hidden from view by bushes and a fallen tree. Flor pulled branches from the bushes and spread them on the rock-strewn earth. Then she and Prudencia lay down on the makeshift bed and huddled together for warmth, blanketed only by gloom.

Prudencia fell asleep. Flor stared out at the night. Tears rolled down her face until she was sure she had no more. She felt the dull moan of hunger, but that was dwarfed by the shrieking pain in her heart. She had nothing left, not even the photograph of Atenacio and Efraín, only their images burned on her brain. She might as well be dead. Sleep came, fitful and fragmented. She woke several times during the night as she heard sounds in the distance, growling engines, tires crunching on gravel, the ominous rattle of gunfire.

The women crawled from the cave as soon as the sun appeared. Flor's throat was parched. They found a spot where the creek was deep and clear, cupped their hands and drank, thankful for the water. But hunger gnawed their bellies. Prudencia scrabbled in the plants growing near the creek and pulled out some roots, declaring them safe to eat. The roots were hard and bitter, but filled their stomachs.

They resumed their journey, leaving the creek and climbing a footpath higher into the mountains. Wind rustled leaves in the trees. Then Flor smelled sulfur. They found a hot spring feeding into another creek, barely a trickle, careening down a rocky hillside. They splashed warm water on their aching feet, found colder water farther downstream and drank again. They followed this creek as it tumbled through valleys and ravines. Finally they came to the edge of a bluff where the creek cascaded over the edge in a waterfall. They looked down into a mountain valley, buildings clustered on either side of the creek.

A gravel road, half-hidden by trees, wound down the slope in a series of switchbacks, widening on the valley floor. Los Árboles, high in the mountains where timber was plentiful, had a sawmill, a long low building with a corrugated tin roof, in a yard surrounded by logs and boards. A big truck was parked in the yard outside the mill. As Flor watched, three men began loading lumber into the truck bed. In the plaza a church tower rose, surrounded by buildings.

"Is it safe?" Prudencia clung to Flor for support.

"Is anywhere safe?" Flor asked. This rebel town was a target for the army. But today she saw no sign of the men with guns, like those who had destroyed her life.

They made their way down the bluff. At the first house they

came to, a woman at an open fire fried *pupusas* for the midday meal. When Flor and Prudencia left the shelter of the trees and appeared in the yard, the woman gasped. Flor leaned against a tree, weariness enveloping her as she described what had happened. The woman gave them the *pupusas* and sent her daughter to the sawmill to fetch her father. When the men from the mill arrived, Flor told the story again. Each time she thought of San Blas, or forced the words from her mouth, it hurt. This pain would never go away.

Nazario Robles appeared later that afternoon, fury in his red-rimmed eyes. With him were Beatriz, a woman who wore a uniform and carried a rifle, and an American named Merle Sefton, tall, with blond curls visible under her cap. She turned on a tape recorder, listening intently as Flor and Prudencia told how the village of San Blas died.

"We saw the smoke yesterday," Nazario said. "This morning we went to San Blas. I feared everyone was dead. Then I heard you were here." He reached into his shirt pocket and pulled out the photograph he'd given her the day before. "We found this in your house."

Flor looked at the photograph that Nazario had given her the day before, the one that he'd taken of her, Atenacio and Efraín. She took the picture and clutched it to her heart. In Spanish, the American woman asked permission to take photographs. Flor nodded and looked down as the camera flashed. Someone handed her a handkerchief and she wiped her eyes.

"We must write down everything that happened," Nazario said to the American woman, "the names of the people who died. With the pictures you took this morning and these eyewitness accounts, you will write a powerful story."

Prudencia shivered. A woman standing nearby took off her shawl and draped it over the old woman's shoulders. A bell tolled the hour. "My husband, Leonardo Muñoz, a man of sixty-one years. He was a good man. We were married forty years. My son Pedro, thirty-nine years. His wife, Edita, thirty-six. Their children, my grandchildren. Five of them." Prudencia stopped. Her lips quivered. Then she went on. "Félix, twelve. Vilma, ten. Servando, seven. Narcisa, four. And the baby, a year old. His name was Tomás."

"Lucita Robles, my mother," Nazario said. "Forty-seven. My sister Victorina López and her husband, Perfecto, both twenty-six. My nephew Santos, six, and my niece Cresencia, seven."

"Atenacio Guzmán." Flor looked at the photograph. She blinked, trying to blot out the picture of her husband's death. "A good, kind man, twenty-five."

"Efraín?" Nazario asked.

Tears rolled down Flor's cheeks. "They took Efraín and two other children, a baby and a little girl. Where do they take the children? Where can I find my boy?"

Beatriz frowned. "We've heard of this. The army kills almost everyone, but takes the children. No one knows where."

"This wasn't the army," Nazario said. "This was Humberto's hired thugs."

"They knew you had been to the village yesterday," Prudencia said. "Cruz singled out your mother. But Lucita was brave to the end. She would not tell them anything. The leader beat her, and Atenacio tried to help her."

Nazario swore. "I've caused their deaths—my family, the people in the village."

"Stop it," Beatriz told him. "You've visited the village before."

"How did they know I had been there?" Nazario asked. "Did someone tell Humberto?"

"Tránsito Vigil, I think," Prudencia said. "He thought he was better than the *campesinos*, because he was a storekeeper."

"Humberto is a dead man," Nazario said. "Some day I will kill him."

"Perhaps you will," Prudencia said. "But now we must make the list of names. So no one forgets. Tránsito Vigil, his wife Aurelia, their daughter Marisella."

"Father Bartolomeo, the priest from Texistepeque," Flor said. "Ofelia and Juan Izalco."

When they finished, the list of the dead of San Blas numbered one hundred and seven people. They weren't sure of all the names, because several families had just arrived in the village a few days before the attack. As far as they knew, only five people had survived—Flor, Prudencia and the three missing children.

Nazario told her later that the American journalist took many more pictures at San Blas and wrote a story that appeared in American newspapers. He showed her a copy. Flor couldn't read the English words, but she recognized the photograph of her own tearstained face. Flor and Prudencia stayed in Los Árboles until the tide of war turned and the town was no longer safe. They crossed the border into Honduras, to a camp for displaced Salvadorans.

But no one knew what happened to the three children taken from San Blas. Weeks passed, then months, and finally a year. There was no word, no information. Flor's hopes of finding her son seeped away, like water from a creek parched by the sun. The years went by like the bell that had tolled as she and Prudencia recited the names of the dead.

4

TO LOSE A CHILD, Lindsey thought, that was the worst.

She looked at the words she'd transcribed, struggling to maintain her researcher's detachment. It was one thing to read old documents and letters about events of a century ago, but this was different. The civil war ravaging El Salvador in the 1980s and 1990s had been widely reported, a litany of horrors inflicted on the population, revealing the human capacity for evil, and the determination and spirit that allowed people to survive.

Flor's story of the destruction of San Blas and the son who had been snatched from her arms was harrowing. Lindsey thought about her own daughter, remembering Nina as a toddler, recalled holding that plump and trusting little burden.

Yesterday, as Flor held the photograph rescued from the ruins of San Blas, her face held a faraway look that crossed time and geography.

"I survived," Flor said. "As Prudencia told me to do. She died a year later, still in that camp. Don Humberto died in his bed, or so I heard. Nazario helped me come to the United States. We stay in touch. Letters first, then e-mail. He put his guns away, married, had children. He is part of the government now, in Chalatenango department. Who would have thought it, to hear him talk back then? He has been a good friend to me, searching for information on Efraín and other children who disappeared during the civil war. There is an organization working to locate them. Some have been found."

"Why have you decided to tell me this now?" Lindsey asked.

"I need your help." Flor smiled, face full of joy and hope. "For so many years this picture was all I had left of Atenacio and Efraín. But now, a miracle! My prayers are answered. Efraín is alive. Here, in Berkeley. I've seen him. He looks just like his father. He has a scar on his chin, from the cut he got that day."

Kids always have scrapes and scratches. How could Flor be certain that the boy she'd seen was Efraín? "Where did you see him?" Lindsey asked.

"At the Berkeley Farmers Market, three weeks ago. Please help me. You write books and know many things. I must find out what name Efraín has now, where he lives and who he lives with, so I can get my son back." Flor sensed Lindsey's hesitation. "He is my son. I know this. His face is burned into my memory. It doesn't matter how long ago it was. To me it was like yesterday. I think of him every day. Come to the market with me on Saturday. If he's there, you can see for yourself."

LINDSEY reread the transcript. The pain of the Salvadoran woman's loss leapt off the pages. But now it was more than just another research interview. It had moved from that realm when Flor told Lindsey that her kidnapped son was alive and living in the Bay Area—and she wanted to reclaim him.

Flor said the American reporter, Merle Sefton, wrote a story about San Blas. Flor had seen a copy of the article, with her own picture. Lindsey set aside the printed transcript and did an Internet search on the reporter, garnering pages of hits. As Lindsey clicked through hyperlinks, she found a photograph of a tall middle-aged woman with tousled blond hair, dressed in khaki slacks and shirt, a battered camera bag slung over one shoulder.

Sefton was a Navy veteran who'd worked as a photojournalist after retiring from the service, building an extensive body of work. An Oklahoma native, she'd been visiting family in Oklahoma City the day a powerful bomb destroyed the federal building and was on the scene taking photographs shortly after the explosion. She'd interviewed and photographed concentration camp survivors who'd attended the opening of the Holocaust Memorial Museum in Washington D.C. Lindsey found a photo essay about Amelia Earhart's last flight. Sefton had taken pictures of the stops along the route, finishing up with two photos that illustrated the question marks surrounding Earhart's fate. The first was a shot of the old Japanese jail on the island of Saipan where local rumors placed the aviator, the second a photo of her last known coordinates, showing a surging ocean and a stormy sky.

Lindsey worked her way through several electronic databases and periodical indexes, refining search terms until she located the full text—no photos—of Sefton's article about the San Blas massacre. She printed out the story and looked for follow-up articles. What she found was depressingly familiar, reminding her of the 1981 massacre at El Mozote and several nearby villages by troops of the Atlacatl Battalion of the Salvadoran army. The press in El Salvador had ignored the killings, but the incident had been reported in the *Washington Post* and the *New York Times*. Both the Salvadoran government and its primary source of funding, the Reagan administration, had denied the El Mozote massacre had ever occurred. The incident was restructured into a story of a friendly, ostensibly democratic ally, no matter what its human rights record, versus Communist rebels who were not to be trusted and not above manipulating reporters. The callous mass murder of several hundred civilians, many of them children and old people, evolved into a battle, where the deaths were regrettable but understandable casualties of war resulting from clashes between rebels and government forces. Those who had reported El Mozote were vilified as dupes of the Salvadoran rebels. Despite the presence of survivors still living nearby, witnesses who had told the story to reporters, it wasn't until 1992 that the reports gained credence, as forensic anthropologists began exhuming skeletons in the ruins.

There were similarities between El Mozote and San Blas, but also differences. The death toll in El Mozote and surrounding villages had been seven or eight hundred, depending on who did the counting and how many villages were included in the tally. According to Flor, one hundred and seven people had died in San Blas, a small hamlet, a collection of workers' huts located on private property, the *finca* owned by a man Flor called Don Humberto. The perpetrators weren't Salvadoran army troops, but the landowner's paramilitaries. Unlike the survivors of El Mozote, who still lived in the vicinity, the two adult survivors of San Blas—Flor and Prudencia—had disappeared.

The reaction to the San Blas story was similar to El Mozote. Merle Sefton had been denounced as a naïve reporter being fed lies by the rebels. The landowner, Humberto Aragón, claimed there had never been a village at the site of San Blas. There was a valley by that name, where a creek widened into a lake behind an earthen dam near Aragón's coffee processing plant. Aragón claimed the lake had been there for years, saying his father had constructed the dam in the 1930s. He was wealthy and influential, and he'd gotten Sefton kicked out of El Salvador. She'd been apprehended on his property two days after the incident, escorted to the airport in San Salvador, and stripped of her visa and press credential.

Back in the United States, Sefton found herself on the receiving end of disbelieving comments by elected officials and State Department staffers—and a sneering, condescending editorial in the *Wall Street Journal*, which had also, Lindsey recalled, denied there had ever been a massacre at El Mozote. No proof and no witnesses, the editorial said, ignoring Sefton's interview with the two survivors and calling her San Blas story preposterous.

But there must be proof San Blas had existed. What about area maps? Would they include a workers' village on private property? What about Flor's photograph? The fading color snapshot showed Flor, her first husband, Atenacio, and her son Efraín, standing near the little church in San Blas, with the sign from the village store visible in the background. But the photo would have been dismissed by those who wanted to discount Sefton's article as another plaza, another market, in another village.

What had happened to Merle Sefton in the intervening years? In 1989 she'd worked for an independent news service in Los Angeles. After that her name appeared most frequently in newspapers in Seattle and Portland. Finally a hyperlink led Lindsey to the website of Southern Oregon University in Ashland. Sefton taught there, in the communications department.

Ashland. Talk about serendipity. Lindsey's tickets for her visit to the Oregon Shakespeare Festival in Ashland were in her desk drawer. She jotted Merle Sefton's e-mail address and phone number on a pad, composed a message and sent it off. A moment later she received an automatic reply indicating Sefton was unavailable and would respond to messages upon her return to the office on Monday. Lindsey called Sefton's office number and left a voicemail, underscoring her need to talk with the journalist.

Lindsey went to the kitchen for another cup of coffee, just as Nina appeared from the guestroom, wrapped in her emerald robe. "I was wondering when you'd get up. Did you have a good sleep?"

"Like I was drugged." Nina yawned and raked a hand through her untidy hair, peering at the kitchen clock. "What time is it? Holy cow, that late? I need coffee." She opened the cupboard and grabbed a mug. She filled it with coffee, inhaled the aroma and drank. "Oh, that's good." She swallowed another mouthful. "Okay, I feel human now." She sat down and sifted through the newspaper.

"For future reference, I keep the coffee beans in that red tin next to the grinder." Lindsey poured herself another mug of coffee. "You want some breakfast?"

"Yeah. I'll get it. A bowl of cereal or something. That's usually all I have." Nina opened the classified ad section from the *Chronicle* and scanned the page as she drank her coffee. Then she sighed and closed the newspaper. She got up, poured herself more coffee, and opened cupboards, taking a bowl from one and examining Lindsey's supply of cereal in another. As she lifted her arm to pull out a box, the sleeve of her robe fell and revealed the fading bruise.

Lindsey's mouth tightened at the sight. With an effort, she bit down the impulse to voice her anger at Chad, to ask Nina what had happened. It's like a damned elephant sitting in the kitchen. We both know it's there and at some point we'll have to talk about it.

Nina filled a bowl with cereal, strawberries and yogurt, then returned to the table and sat down. "I need to boot up my laptop to check my e-mail. And make some calls. See what I can do about finding a job."

"I'm sure you'll be able to find work."

Nina shrugged, the corners of her mouth pulling down. "I know you mean to be reassuring, Mother." She gestured at the newspaper headlines. "We're embroiled in this damn war, the economy's in the toilet. Things just keep getting worse."

"It helps to have a positive attitude." Bite my tongue, Lindsey thought. I sound just like my mother. Is that what happens when you get older?

Nina sighed. "I think I have a clearer picture of the job market than you do. There aren't that many jobs out there, at least not in my field. I know people who have been out of work for a year or more."

"I'm your mother. It's my job to be the cheerleader." This isn't going to be easy. Did you think your prickly daughter was going to lose all her thorns overnight? Particularly when her life is a mess and she feels lousy about it? Fat chance.

She walked back to her office and returned to the kitchen with a small flat object in her palm. "Here's the extra house key."

Nina looked at the key for a moment before taking it. "This is only temporary. I'll be out of your hair as soon as I can."

Lindsey smiled. "Let's do that one-day-at-a-time thing, okay?"

"Okay." Nina finished her cereal and put the bowl and spoon in the dishwasher. "So how are the girls—Claire, Gretchen and Annabel?"

Nina didn't know about Annabel. Of course, she couldn't, since mother and daughter had had no contact while Nina was in Texas. "Annabel had a stroke, a bad one, six weeks ago. We were all going to have lunch after she and Gretchen played tennis. She collapsed right there on the court. It was awful."

Nina looked shocked. "My God, she's not that old. How is she? Will she recover?"

"It's affected her speech and motor skills," Lindsey said. "She has aphasia, slurred speech, and difficulty walking. She's in rehab in the city, getting therapy. I visit her once or twice a week. I see improvement. But it's slow."

"Annabel's a fighter," Nina said. "She'll get better. You've known her a long time."

"More than half my life. I met her when I moved into that house near the campus." Lindsey raised her coffee mug, remembering. The past, choices made—or avoided. And that's a choice, too. One thing leads to another, like stones tossed into a pond, ripples moving inexorably outward, becoming consequences.

5

Berkeley, California, June 1972

JANIS JOPLIN'S GRAVELLY VOICE exhorted the Lord to buy her a Mercedes-Benz. The music came from a portable radio on the patio, where a young woman with short blond hair stretched out on a chaise longue, the top of her red bikini unfastened, baring her back.

"That's Claire," Annabel Dunlin said. "She lives upstairs."

Lindsey turned from the window and looked around the bedroom of the furnished apartment. The rent was higher than she'd planned on spending, but the apartment was much nicer than the others she'd looked at today.

She liked the house on Hillegass Street the moment she saw it, two stories, green stucco with white trim. The wide front porch held four honey-colored rattan chairs with cushions. Metal wind chimes hung from a hook at the end of the porch. Colorful petunias, velvety pansies, white Shasta daisies and golden California poppies grew in clay pots on the porch, and rosebushes, heavy with blooms, ranged along the front of the house.

Inside, the rooms had been turned into apartments. The available unit—first floor, on the right of the stairs—consisted of a living room and bedroom, with a kitchen and bathroom tucked in between. The apartment had hardwood floors, high ceilings and tall windows in each room, letting in plenty of light.

The bedroom furniture included a double bed, a nightstand and a dresser with a mirror. Lindsey examined the walk-in closet, with built-in shelves on one wall. The bathroom was small. So was the kitchen, but it had adequate counter and cupboard space, plus new appliances.

Back in the living room Lindsey mentally set the square table with her own placemats, dishes and flatware, saw her books in the bookcase, her typewriter on the desk. The blue-and-yellow rug she'd bought in a Mexico City *mercado* would go in front of the sofa, her rocking chair near the front window, where she could wrap herself in her crocheted afghan and look out at the roses.

"You were wise to come up early," Annabel said. "Spring semester's over and students are moving out. Apartments go fast, particularly this close to campus."

"So I've heard," Lindsey said. "I just got my master's at Santa Barbara and I'm starting my doctorate in history here at Cal. First priority is a place to live."

She was staying temporarily with Aunt Emma. But Lindsey wanted her own apartment. She'd looked at several before seeing the flyer in the women's restroom at Doe Library, advertising a furnished one-bedroom apartment south of campus. Lindsey grabbed the flyer and found a pay phone.

"This is a great location," Lindsey said now.

"Close enough to People's Park to catch the occasional whiff of tear gas," Annabel said. "Though the south side of campus isn't as crazy now as it was a couple of years ago."

"Is the neighborhood safe?"

Annabel smiled. "The house is safe. I can't vouch for your welfare out in the world at large. There's a grocery store within walking distance, on Telegraph Avenue. Let me show you the other amenities."

They left the apartment and walked down the central hallway to the rear of the house, where the back door led out to the porch and patio. A set of metal stairs had been attached to the building exterior, serving double duty as access to the upper apartments and a fire escape. Beyond the patio the deep backyard held a swath of green lawn, more roses, an oak tree, and a vegetable garden. The detached garage was used for storage, Annabel told her. There were wind chimes here, too, above a bedroom window. Annabel reached for the metal tubes. They rang together in a deep melodious sound.

Back inside the house Annabel showed Lindsey the walk-in closet under the stairs, with shelves and a pegboard with hooks. "More storage. Tools, if you need them. Vacuum cleaner, ladder. The ceilings are so high you'll need a ladder to change light bulbs." She shut the closet and led the way to another, near the back entrance. "Last but certainly not least…"

Lindsey felt as though she'd died and gone to heaven when she saw the matched Maytags. "A washer and dryer. Hallelujah. I hate hauling everything to the Laundromat."

"So do I." Annabel closed the door. "Do you want the apartment?"

Lindsey did the math in her head, calculating the monthly rent and the estimated cost of utilities, groceries and other expenses. She had some money saved, plus her student loan, and the promise of work as a researcher in the fall. The rent was a stretch. But she didn't want to be penny-wise and pound-foolish. It was worth it to pay more for a safe, comfortable place to live.

"I want it," Lindsey said. "What do I have to do? Fill out an application, leave a deposit? Promise to hand over my firstborn child?"

"Nothing as drastic as that," Annabel said. "It's yours. You'll fit right in."

"But what about the landlord?" Lindsey asked.

"I am the landlord," Annabel said. "I decide who lives here. Fill out an application and give me a check for the first month's rent."

When Lindsey entered Annabel's apartment, it dawned on her that her new housemate had money. A real, honest-to-God Persian rug lay on the floor, deep reds and blues glowing like jewels. The living room had a fireplace and a mantel with an ornate gold-and-glass clock. There were no posters tacked up on the walls here; Annabel had framed silkscreen prints. The tables, polished dark wood, looked as though they came from an antique store or the old family manse. In the front corner of the room stood a desk, an old wooden office chair, and a small table holding a portable electric typewriter.

Barrister's bookcases, the kind with glass covers, stood on both sides of the front window. Lindsey glanced at the titles of the books on the nearest shelves. Shakespeare, Keats, Shelley, Austen, Dickens. Poetry and literature. Annabel must be an English major. A music box, a carousel, with plunging black-and-white horses under a red-and-yellow canopy, sat on top of one bookcase.

"That's beautiful," Lindsey said.

"A gift from my mother," Annabel said.

"What does it play?"

Annabel lifted the box and turned the key on the underside. The lilting waltz from Rodgers and Hammerstein's *Carousel* began to play. "Appropriately enough." She pulled a form from a folder on the desk. "Have a seat and fill that out."

Lindsey sat down in the office chair and began filling out the application. "When was the house built?"

"The Twenties," Annabel said. "Converted to apartments in the late Fifties. I have the original living room, with the fireplace. My bedroom was the dining room, and my kitchen is the original. Your apartment must have been a parlor and a study. The four bedrooms upstairs were turned into two apartments with kitchens and bedrooms added."

"How did you come to be the landlord?"

Annabel sat down in the armchair, picked up a pen and doodled on a yellow pad. "Housing for students is always tight in Berkeley. My father's solution was to buy a house for me to live in while I attend college. His only caveat is that my fellow tenants be female and they fill out that application."

Lindsey wrote out a check for the rent, feeling a twinge as she subtracted and saw the dip in her bank balance. "Your father must have a lot of money." She looked up, embarrassed. "I'm sorry. I shouldn't have said that."

Annabel laughed. "It's okay. He has piles of money. He solves problems by spreading it around. I've lived here since I started my freshman year. It's the first time I've ever been out on my own. If you can call living in a house with three other people being out on your own. One of these days I would like to live alone."

"Plenty of time for that." Lindsey handed the check and the form to Annabel.

"I wonder." Annabel glanced at the application. "I should warn you. My father has this assistant, Max Brinker, who runs background checks on people who live here. So if you had any part in burning the Bank of America building while you were at UC Santa Barbara, you should 'fess up now. I do have the final say-so. I've overruled him before."

"Never been arrested," Lindsey said. "Marched in my share of antiwar demonstrations. But I haven't torched any buildings. No scandals in my past. I'm just a hick from Paso Robles."

Annabel chuckled and held out her hand. "Welcome to Berkeley, Lindsey. If you can't be scandalous here, you're not trying."

Lindsey shook Annabel's hand. "I'm going to enjoy living here."

"I'm sure you will." Annabel pulled a typewritten sheet of paper from the manila folder, wrote Lindsey's name and the date at the top, and signed her own name at the bottom. "I don't bother with leases or anything like that, but you'll need some sort of verification that you've rented the place, so I wrote up what passes for a rental agreement. The electricity's still on and the phone is connected. I had the girl who moved out transfer those accounts to my name. Easier that way. All you have to do is go downtown and fill out paperwork at Pacific Gas and Electric and Ma Bell." Annabel opened one of the desk drawers and took out a ring holding two brass keys. "The big one fits in the front and back doors. Which we do keep locked at night. The little one is to your apartment. It's official."

Someone opened Annabel's door. The blonde in the red bikini strolled in, a twinkle in her sharp blue eyes. "Well?"

"We have a new housemate," Annabel said. "Lindsey Page, this is Claire Megarris."

"Welcome to the gilded cage," Claire said. "You're no freshman. Transfer student?"

"Grad student, history. Got my bachelor's and master's at UC Santa Barbara."

"Undergrad," Claire said. "Business and econ."

"Also undergrad," Annabel said. "English major, history minor."

"I guessed that from your bookcases," Lindsey said.

Annabel laughed. "Keats is a dead giveaway."

"And the fourth tenant?" Lindsey asked.

The house's outer door opened, admitting a tall, big-boned woman with long sandy curls, brown eyes in a square freckled face. Her cotton shirt sported a McGovern button and her faded jeans were decorated with beads. She stopped in the doorway of Annabel's apartment. "Hey."

"Hey, yourself," Annabel said. "This is Gretchen Kohl. Grad student, sociology."

Lindsey smiled. "Lindsey Page. Grad student, history."

"Glad to meet you," Gretchen said. "When are you moving in?"

"As soon as I can," Lindsey said. "I've been staying with my aunt in North Berkeley."

"If there's anything you need," Annabel said, "like sheets, towels, kitchen stuff, to tide you over until you get the rest of your things, just ask."

Gretchen looked at her watch. "Gotta run and make myself gorgeous."

"Got a date?" Claire asked. "Who with?"

"That guy I told you about, Doug Segal. He's a first-year law student up at Boalt Hall." Gretchen shook her finger. "But no poaching. I saw him first."

"I'll be too busy to have much of a social life," Lindsey said.

"We'll see about that." Claire winked and turned to Gretchen. "I expect a full report when you return. If you return."

Gretchen blushed. "Claire! It's dinner and a movie, not a life-long commitment."

Claire laughed. "Who says there has to be a commitment? Shall I wait up?"

"If you feel like waiting up, be my guest. Now I have to get ready. Nice to meet you, Lindsey." Gretchen raced up the stairs.

"Go collect your things," Annabel told Lindsey. "We'll have dinner later. We'll pool our resources and have scintillating mealtime
conversation. Which makes up for the fact that Claire can't cook
worth a damn."

"I don't need to cook," Claire said. "As long as there are restaurants and takeout. Or salads. I'm really good at tearing lettuce."

"I could make a run over to that grocery store you mentioned,"
Lindsey said.

"That's okay," Annabel said. "We'll pick your brain instead. If
you're going to be living here we have to know all about you. Details,
the gorier the better."

"Same here," Lindsey said.

Claire laughed. "Are you sure? Could be dangerous." She struck a
pose at the foot of the stairs and trilled in an English accent just like
Deborah Kerr, "Getting to know you, getting to know all about you."

Lindsey retrieved her green VW and drove to downtown Berkeley, where she had the power switched to her name and arranged for
phone service. Then she drove back to her aunt's house, packed her
belongings, and loaded them into the VW.

Serendipity provided Lindsey with a parking place in front of her
new home on Hillegass Street. Claire, in skin-tight jeans and a lacy
blouse, was on the sidewalk talking with a lanky, long-haired guy. As
Lindsey got out of the VW, Claire peered through the car's windows.
"Is this all you've got?" Claire beckoned to the guy. "Hey, Jody, this is
Lindsey. She's moving in. Give us a hand."

Jody acknowledged Lindsey with a nod and opened the passen-
ger-side door. "Where d'you want this stuff?"

"First door on the right, thanks." Lindsey picked up her type-
writer and started up the walk. Annabel opened the front door.

"Welcome home," Annabel said. "Need some help?"

When Lindsey's possessions were inside the apartment, she hung
towels in the bathroom and made the bed. Claire appeared with an
armful of pots and pans and piled them on the kitchen counter. "As
Annabel pointed out, my cooking skills are minimal. I have no desire
to improve them. I haven't boiled, broiled, or baked anything in ages.
You might as well have these."

"Thanks," Lindsey said.

"You're welcome. You two are on your own for dinner. Jody and I are going out."

"I thought you were going to tear lettuce," Annabel said. "No matter. I've got salad fixings in the fridge and chicken in the oven."

"I could at least contribute some coffee," Lindsey said, unpacking a tin of Folger's from a box of foodstuffs her aunt had provided.

Claire laughed. "Coffee we've got. Courtesy of Dunlin Corporation."

"What's Dunlin Corporation?" Lindsey asked.

"Coffee," Annabel said. "They import it, roast it, sell it. Anything to do with coffee."

"Also tea and spices," Claire added. "My father started the company. Now Annabel's father runs it. Annabel and I are cousins. My mother is her father's sister."

"We'll get acquainted while we fix dinner," Annabel said.

"Catch you later." Claire stepped out into the hall and glanced up. "Well, look at you."

Lindsey and Annabel crowded into the doorway. Gretchen posed on the landing, wearing a floral print dress with a scooped neck and a gauzy skirt. Her unruly curls were tied back with a scarf, and multicolored beads dangled from her neck and earlobes. She twirled and the skirt swirled around her hips. "What do you think?"

"You look gorgeous," Claire said. "He won't be able to keep his hands off you."

"At this point I just want to get to know him," Gretchen said, "not have a wrestling match." They heard footsteps on the porch steps. "That's him now."

6

THE DAY SHE'D HAD THE STROKE kept playing in Annabel's mind like an old movie, the film broken in the middle of the reel, then inexpertly spliced together, in fragments, without continuity. She heard Claire's teasing voice—"...aging Wimbledon rejects..."

She saw herself lying on the tennis court, body jerking as horrified faces stared down at her. The ambulance screamed down the hill to the hospital. In the emergency room people hovered over her, bright lights contrasting with darkness as voices clamored and machines beeped.

Another room, with muted light, doctors, nurses. Her husband, Hal, slumped in a chair next to her bed, exhaustion and anxiety painting his face. She tried to speak and instead croaked like a frog. She tried to reach for Hal. Her hand was frozen. The confusion gave way to realization, panic, despair. Her body didn't work properly. The pathways from brain to fingers had been interrupted. She was trapped, unable to speak or move.

Days blurred into weeks. They brought her from the hospital to this place, a private room with round-the-clock care, more nurses and doctors and therapists. She'd been here several weeks now, speech and movement gradually returning as the therapists worked with her.

Memories of the past, many unwelcome, crowded into her head. Memories she'd kept at bay for years lurked in the shadows at the edge of her mind, waiting to torment her again.

Annabel shook her head, coming back to the present. It was early afternoon. She'd had an exhausting physical therapy session that morning. Forcing her limbs to move according to the therapist's regimen left her tired and wrung out. Hal arrived at noon, bringing lunch from a nearby deli. They ate while Hal talked and she was content to listen. After Hal left, she thought she would nap. Instead the memories came, pushing unbidden into her head.

Annabel at fifteen on Haight Street, in 1967, the Summer of Love—the day she found Lily again, after losing her for so many years.

She and Claire had cut class to come to the Haight that day. They wandered along the street, poking around in the shops, looking at clothes, watching the people. Annabel felt transported, exhilarated. In front of a shop, a man puffed on a joint. Annabel sneezed. She didn't like the smell of pot or patchouli oil.

At the end of Haight Street they crossed to Golden Gate Park and Hippie Hill, where hordes of people, fish moving with the school, pooled on the gentle slope, swimming lazily to music. The air was redolent with marijuana. Annabel sneezed again, then stretched out on the grass. On a nearby radio Grace Slick's mesmerizing voice spun out the lyrics to "Somebody to Love." Then Claire went off with some guy. Angry at being abandoned, Annabel scrambled to her feet and walked back down Haight Street. She talked to one of the hippies, resplendent in a tie-dyed T-shirt and paisley pants. He laughed as he crowned her head with daisies. "If you come to San Francisco," Annabel sang in a sweet, clear soprano, smiling as she saw herself mirrored in the store window. Now she was one of the gentle people with flowers in their hair.

But the man and the woman who suddenly stumbled in front of her weren't gentle. They were damned scary. The woman's long blond hair made her look like an angel, but she cursed and hit the man with her balled-up fist. The man struck back, a hard blow to her stomach, knocking the woman against the building. She slid down the wall and landed with a thump, vomiting onto the sidewalk. The man grabbed her wrist and wrenched open her fist, prying money from her fingers. He stuck the greenbacks into his jeans and strode away. The woman struggled to her feet, wiping vomit from her chin with her purple gauze sleeve.

Annabel shrank back, eyes wide, nose assailed by the stench behind the cloying incense of Haight Street. She saw past the colorful clothes on the people around her, saw unwashed bodies and dirty fingernails.

Then Annabel saw Lily, coming out of a corner market. She gasped, then ran to catch up with the older woman who had worked for the Dunlins for so many years.

Lily had gone away after the fire. She'd put a pot roast in a pressure cooker on the gas range in the kitchen, and turned the flame down low while she went out for half an hour, to have a cup of tea with the housekeeper next door. But the flame burned higher, not lower. Liquid evaporated, meat and vegetables shriveled into dry tinder and burned. The flames ignited the cabinets and fire spread through the kitchen, filling the house with smoke. When Annabel came home from school, a red fire truck blocked the sidewalk in front of the house and smoke filled the air, gray like fog. But it stank of burn and char, unlike the fresh salty mist off the ocean.

That's why they made Lily go away. Because of the fire. Because Lily was careless. At least, that's what they said.

Now Annabel shuffled the memories like cards, trying to put them in order. She reached for the television remote. Maybe there was a movie she could watch, one that didn't star her.

Her older daughter Tess entered the room, carrying a bouquet of flowers. She was tall and slender, with intense blue eyes. Dark hair framed her face.

She looks like her father, Annabel thought.

"How are you feeling today?" Tess kissed Annabel on the fore-head. "I'm between appointments. So I thought I'd come and see you." Tess discarded the wilting flowers from the old arrangement on the bedside table. She filled the vase with water and began arranging the mixture of iris, freesia, Shasta daisies, and baby's breath.

"If you come to San Francisco," Annabel sang, her voice almost a whisper.

"Be sure to wear some flowers in your hair. That's an old song." Tess plucked a daisy from the bouquet and tucked it behind her mother's ear. "There. Flowers in your hair." She sat down next to the bed. "That's not the only reason I came to see you."

Annabel frowned. "Why?"

Tess took a deep breath. "I know Hal isn't my father. I had a blood test. The whole family went to donate blood after you had the stroke. We had tests to type our blood. My blood type doesn't match yours. Or his. So he's not my father. You could have told me. I'm past thirty. Who is my father?"

Silence. Annabel reeled away from memories long suppressed. Her mouth opened, but she couldn't speak. It wasn't due to the apha-sia. She'd spent a lifetime keeping secrets, glossing over the truth. She wasn't ready to have this conversation. Not now. Maybe not ever. But eventually she must. Just as Lily had finally answered An-nabel's question, so many years ago.

Tell me how my mother died, Annabel asked. Tell me what you saw. Maybe later, Lily said, a closed look on her face. Later, when you're older.

Tess's jaw tightened. "At first I was angry. I'm still upset. It's taken me weeks to work up to this. I don't want to hurt you, Mother. But I have to know about my father. I can't have this question mark hanging over me."

Annabel closed her eyes, unable to face her daughter. She knew that look. Her daughter had a will of iron. Tess wouldn't be deterred. The truth was there, for anyone who wanted to root it out. She opened her eyes.

Tess sighed. "I know you don't want to talk about this now. But I have to know, Mother. If you won't tell me, or you can't, I'll ask Lindsey. Surely she knows. Or she can help me." Tess sighed and glanced at her watch. "I need to get back to work. I'm meeting a client in Berkeley. Maybe I'll see Lindsey afterwards."

But Lindsey has secrets of her own to keep, Annabel thought.

"Tess," Annabel said finally, the sibilance like hissing snakes, a tangle of lies threatening to slither from their hiding place. "I love you."

"I know." Tess fingered her necklace. Annabel hadn't seen it before. It was a tiny silver pineapple swinging from a silver chain.

A silver pineapple... Annabel's heart pounded. Here was a memory she would never be free of, etched in her brain, as though it had happened yesterday. A Friday afternoon in April. Mother's eyes had been open, but they'd stared unblinking at the ceiling. She looked as though she'd awakened from a nightmare and found the goblins still there to greet her.

7

San Francisco, California, April 1961

ANNABEL THUMPED HER SHOES against the wooden chair in the principal's office. "My tummy hurts. I want to go home."

Miss Simpson compressed her lips and drummed her fingers on

her desk. "I've called your house. There's no answer. You can't go home by yourself. You must wait until someone comes to get you."

"I might throw up," Annabel declared.

Miss Simpson looked dismayed at the prospect. She consulted her address book and reached for the telephone. "I'll call your aunt."

Miss Simpson was a dried-up prune, her face all wrinkly, with mean eyes and a wispy moustache above her thin mouth. She hated the sound of Annabel's feet thumping against the chair. So Annabel swung her legs faster and harder, enjoying the *thump-thump-thump* of her shoes against the wood and the sour look on Miss Simpson's face.

"Annabel! Please stop making that noise. It's most annoying."

That's why I'm doing it, Annabel thought. Old Prune Face stuck a finger into the telephone dial and rotated it, rearranging her expression so she could suck up to Aunt Rebecca. That was stupid. Aunt Rebecca couldn't see her on the phone. Miss Simpson didn't believe the story about the tummy ache. Annabel had used that excuse once too often. But she didn't care. She hated school—this one, anyway.

Annabel wanted to go to the public school, like her friend Sally who lived across the street. Both girls were the same age—nine—but Sally got to do whatever she wanted. She played softball in the park, roller-skated in the street, wore dungarees like a boy, and even rode the bus all by herself, downtown to Union Square or Chinatown or the Ferry Building, out to Golden Gate Park and Playland at the Beach.

But Annabel never got to do anything or go anywhere by herself. She had to go to Miss Simpson's private school for girls and wear white blouses, green plaid skirts and Mary Janes, enduring stupid rules and dull classes, so boring that more than once Annabel had been reprimanded for reading a book on the sly rather than paying attention to lessons. She had to take a class in something called deportment, which involved manners and stupid tea parties. And there was a rumor that next year—when she started fifth grade—she'd have to take dancing. With boys.

Annabel's stomach clenched. She might actually throw up. Sometimes her tummy aches were real. She wanted to go home and be with Lily, who would make tea and almond cookies. Annabel would snuggle into a nest made of pillows with a pile of Nancy Drews, reading until her eyes got heavy and she went to sleep.

Since Lily wasn't home yet, Annabel would just have to go home by herself. She wriggled in the hard wooden chair and reached for the glass candy dish on the table next to her. The lid made a satisfying *clink-clink-clink* as she toyed with it.

"Annabel, don't fidget." Old Prune Face hung up the phone. "The line is busy. Your aunt is on the telephone."

I know what it means, you stupid old prune. Annabel thumped her shoes against the chair and knocked the lid from the candy dish.

"Please wait in the outer office," Miss Simpson snapped. "I'll try your aunt's number again in a few minutes."

In that office, Annabel sat in a chair near the hallway door and thumped her shoes against the chair leg. The secretary gave her the evil eye, glaring at Annabel over the newspaper she was reading when she was supposed to be working. Annabel looked at the headlines, about that man John Glenn, orbiting in a space capsule. She'd like to strap Miss Simpson onto a rocket and shoot her into outer space.

When she wanted to, Annabel could be quiet as a whisper. The secretary got up and went into the supply closet. Annabel slipped out and hurried down the corridor, out the front door, and down the steps to the street. Fog moved through the Golden Gate and crept up the hills to Pacific Heights. Spread out before her was San Francisco, where Father had a big office in a tall building, and Chinatown, where Lily lived. The Bay Bridge stretched across the water to Treasure Island and Oakland.

The house where she lived—big, old, and gray like the fog—was on the corner of Octavia and Washington, near Lafayette Park. The garage door was open. Lily must have forgotten to close it when she went to the grocery store. Annabel walked through the detached garage and across the backyard. She found the extra key Lily kept on a ledge under the steps, unlocked the back door, and entered the house.

Lily had been baking. The big kitchen smelled of almonds and vanilla. The dish drainer held a cookie sheet and baking utensils. Annabel pried the lid from the round tin on the table, revealing plump golden-brown cookies topped with almonds. She popped one in her mouth and savored the sweet buttery flavor. She couldn't make tea because she wasn't supposed to turn on the stove. Instead she used a chair to climb onto the counter. She took a glass from a cupboard and poured milk from the bottle in the refrigerator, careful not to spill any. She sat at the table, drinking milk and eating cookies. Then she left the glass and tin on the table and left the kitchen, heading to her room upstairs to read until Lily got home.

On the hallway floor was a silver pineapple. Annabel picked it up and held it in the palm of her hand. It should have been on the half-moon table at the bottom of the stairs. Mother said the pineapple was a symbol of hospitality, of welcoming people. She had a collection of pineapples on that table, different sizes, made of china, wood, ceramic, glass. Fragments of glass and china now crunched under Annabel's shoes. Broken glass glittered near the front door. The pineapples, some in pieces, were scattered across the floor. Annabel picked up a crystal fragment and tucked it into her skirt pocket, along with the silver pineapple. Her heart thumped as she inched forward. The newel post at the end of the polished stair rail was carved to look like a pineapple, and it was smeared with red.

"Mother?" she whispered.

Mother was past hearing, sprawled on her back at the bottom of the stairs, eyes open. Blood pooled under her head, stained her shiny black hair and clothes. Annabel leaned over and touched her mother's face, careful to avoid the blood. She heard steps on the front porch. That wouldn't be Lily. She'd use the back door. A key turned in the lock, the front door opened, and Aunt Rebecca walked in. She looked strange in her black raincoat and gloves, carrying a key ring in one hand and a shopping bag with handles in the other. Aunt Rebecca stared, her mouth a wide, shocked O. She dropped the shopping bag and more bags spilled out, along with her purse. She grabbed Annabel's arm and pulled her through the living room to the study, pushing her into a leather chair.

"What are you doing here? Why aren't you in school?" Annabel didn't answer. Aunt Rebecca picked up the telephone. "Miss Simpson has some explaining to do."

But it wasn't Miss Simpson that Aunt Rebecca called. "This is

Mrs. Megarris, Mr. Dunlin's sister. I need to speak to him immediately." Aunt Rebecca listened for a few seconds, then she snapped, "Get him out of the meeting. It's urgent." She fiddled with a strand of blond hair that had escaped from her bun. A moment later she said, "It looks like she fell. How do you know? What the hell do you expect? Lily? No. Annabel's here. She seems to be in shock. I said I would. You owe me, George." Aunt Rebecca slammed the phone receiver back into its cradle. She stared down at Annabel. "What the hell am I going to do with you?"

She looks really mad, Annabel thought. I wish she'd go away. I want Lily to come back. She'll hug me and feed me tea and cookies.

Aunt Rebecca took a deep breath and a muscle twitched in her jaw as she shook her index finger at Annabel's nose. "You stay right here in this chair. Don't move an inch."

Aunt Rebecca walked back through the living room and gathered up the shopping bags. She went upstairs. Floorboards creaked above the living room as Aunt Rebecca moved around the bedroom Annabel's parents shared. Then Annabel heard water running. What was Aunt Rebecca doing in the bathroom? Curiosity drove Annabel from the chair to the hall. She avoided looking at Mother's body and stared up the stairs. The water stopped running and the floorboards creaked again.

Annabel retreated to her mother's desk, in the alcove formed by the bay window at the front of the house. A pink envelope lay on the blotter next to the phone. The spikes and swirls of black ink resolved themselves into a name, Father's name. George Dunlin. Annabel reached for the envelope.

"I told you to stay in the study."

Annabel dropped the envelope and turned around, tears pricking her eyes. Aunt Rebecca looked different. She'd removed her black raincoat, revealing a green suit, and she carried two big shopping bags. She set the bags by the front door, picked up the envelope, and tucked it into one of the bags, dangling her key ring from one finger. "Go to the study, Annabel."

When Annabel complied, Aunt Rebecca opened the front door and went outside. Annabel ran to the bay window and looked out.

Aunt Rebecca was putting the bags in the trunk of her car. By the time she returned to the house, Annabel was back in the study. Aunt Rebecca tucked her keys into her pocket and smoothed her hair. "I'm sorry I snapped at you. I know it's awful for you to see your mother like that. But we have to be brave." The phone rang. Aunt Rebecca jumped and reached for the receiver. "Dunlin residence." She listened for a moment, then her mouth twisted as though she'd bit into a sour pickle. She spoke sharply into the mouthpiece.

"Yes, this is Mrs. Megarris. Annabel's here, Miss Simpson. I'm quite upset that you let her leave school and come home by herself. You shouldn't have let her out of your sight. We will discuss this later, Miss Simpson. Now is not the time." She banged down the receiver. "There. I hung up on her. The dried-up old bitch."

Aunt Rebecca took a deep breath and picked up the telephone. "Operator, get me the police… This is an emergency, an accident. My sister-in-law fell down the stairs. I think she's dead. No, I just found her. I'm Mrs. Lawrence Megarris, at the home of my brother and sister-in-law, Mr. and Mrs. George Dunlin, in Pacific Heights."

Aunt Rebecca recited the address. Soon the doorbell rang and Aunt Rebecca opened the front door. Now the house seemed crowded with people. Some wore uniforms and some didn't. There were loud voices and strange noises and flashes of light from the hallway.

Two men—one short, the other tall—told Aunt Rebecca they were inspectors from the San Francisco Police Department. Annabel thought inspectors were supposed to look like men in the old Sherlock Holmes movies she and Lily watched on television, with pipes and funny English accents. But these inspectors looked and talked like ordinary men. They wore suits and hats, like her father.

"The principal called me to let me know Annabel wasn't feeling well," Aunt Rebecca said. "Before I got to the school, Annabel left and walked home on her own. I came over here to check on her and found my sister-in-law dead. I called the police and my brother."

Annabel wondered why Aunt Rebecca messed up the order of things. Miss Simpson hadn't been able to get through to Aunt Rebecca, because the phone was busy. She'd called Father before she called the police, not the other way around. And she didn't tell the inspector about going upstairs and running water in the bathroom, or putting the bags in her car. Was that supposed to be a secret?

Father came, and the grown-ups talked, their voices a jumble. Then Lily rushed to the study, took Annabel in her arms, and talked in Chinese. Annabel didn't know what Lily was saying, but she felt safe and comfortable. Her father's voice, like a cold splash of water, told Lily to pack a suitcase, because Annabel was going home with Aunt Rebecca. No! She didn't want to go home with Aunt Rebecca. She wanted to stay here with Lily.

The inspector told Lily to take Annabel to the kitchen, so he could talk with her. Her father and aunt didn't like that. While the grown-ups argued, Lily took Annabel's hand and led her to the kitchen. She sat Annabel at the table and told her that things would be all right. Annabel took cookies from the tin and stacked them on the table, in a row, like a wall.

The inspectors came back to the kitchen and talked with Lily. Then the tall inspector turned to Annabel. "My name's Gary. I'm a policeman. Will you answer some questions?" Annabel ate a cookie and decided to trust him. She nodded.

8

"I'M GOING UP TO ASHLAND next week, to the Shakespeare Festival," Lindsey told Nina on Friday afternoon.

Nina was at the kitchen table, with her laptop and cell phone, looking at job listings. "I've never been to Ashland. Can I go with you?"

Given their prickly relationship, Lindsey was surprised Nina wanted to join her. Even if it was just the enforced togetherness of the day-long drive up to Oregon and they went their separate ways in Ashland, it was a splash of mother-daughter time after a long drought, so she'd take it.

"Sure. I'm leaving early next Thursday, coming back the following Monday. I'll show you the schedule." Lindsey retrieved the brochure from her office, and handed it to Nina, pointing out the red ink circles she'd drawn on several pages. "These are the plays I plan to see."

While Nina leafed through the brochure Lindsey called the bed-and-breakfast inn and changed her reservation to a room with two beds. Then she opened the refrigerator, picked up pen and paper, and started a grocery list, moving from the refrigerator to the kitchen cupboards. "I need groceries. Anything special you want?"

Nina glanced at the list. "I'll eat whatever's here. No fruit or veggies?"

"I'm going to the Farmers Market tomorrow."

Nina's cell phone rang and she answered it, walking into the living room. When she finished the call she returned to the kitchen. "That was a friend of mine who works in downtown Berkeley. We're going to meet for coffee. She knows about some job openings here in the East Bay. Give me the grocery list and I'll stop at the store on the way back."

"Thanks. The shopping bags are in the hall closet. I'll get some money."

"I've got cash," Nina said. "I'll pitch in while I'm staying here."

Since Nina was without a job and a place to live, Lindsey assumed her daughter was in financial straits. But pointing that out might be construed as meddling. Besides, she was picking up the tab for the Ashland trip.

Nina collected several canvas bags and opened the front door just as Gretchen came up the steps, looking as surprised as Lindsey had yesterday when Nina arrived. "Hi, Gretchen," she said, heading down the front steps.

"You can close your mouth now," Lindsey said. "Come in. I'll make tea."

"When did this happen?" Gretchen asked, following Lindsey to the kitchen.

Lindsey poured water into the kettle and set it on the stove. "Yesterday. She split up with Chad." She scowled. "There's a bruise on her arm. Fading now, but it must have been ugly when it was new. Other than telling me I was right about him, she hasn't said anything."

Gretchen frowned. "He hit her?"

"I'm sure he did. I'd like to wring his damn neck. I suppose even-tually she'll tell me what happened. In the meantime, it looks like I have a houseguest for the foreseeable future. She's out of a job. She's been underemployed for the past couple of years. Her career choices haven't worked out the way she'd hoped. I know how that feels."

"Much as we'd like to protect our children from every possible harm, we can't put guards around them," Gretchen said. "It will be interesting for you, having her home. You've lived alone for so long."

"The nest is never really empty. Nina and I lived with Mom and Dad in Paso Robles when I took the job at Cal Poly, until I bought my house in San Luis Obispo. We'll manage." The teakettle whistled. Lindsey got up and made a pot of Earl Grey tea. "What brings you to my doorstep this afternoon?"

"I'm here to invite you—and Nina—to brunch on Sunday." Gretchen added sugar to her tea. "Come over about ten."

"Thanks. What would you like me to bring? I'm going to the Farmers Market tomorrow morning. I'll pick up some fruit."

"I'll be at the market, too," Gretchen said. "It's too early for peaches and apricots. But they should have strawberries."

The doorbell rang and Lindsey went to answer it. Another sur-prise, this time Annabel's older daughter. "I hope you don't mind my dropping by without calling," Tess said.

"You're always welcome. Come in. Gretchen's here. We're hav-ing tea."

"Good. That's just as well," Tess said. "I want to talk with both of you."

"Is Annabel all right?" Lindsey asked, worried.

"Yes, she's better. It's just that..." Tess sighed. "I don't know where to begin."

Lindsey waved her toward the living room. "Have a seat. I'll be right back." She walked back to the kitchen. "It's Tess. She says Annabel is fine, but she wants to talk with us about something. She's in the living room. You grab the cups, I'll get the rest."

"I hope nothing's wrong," Gretchen said.

When they were settled in the living room, Lindsey asked, "Now, what's this all about?"

Tess sipped tea. "I asked Mother a question, but she won't—or can't—answer it. I thought you might be able to." She took a deep breath and plunged on. "Who is my father?"

Mothers and daughters—and fathers, a dangerous subject.

Not this again, Lindsey thought. And from a different, unexpected source.

Gretchen looked stunned. "What makes you think Hal isn't your father?"

Tess set her cup on an end table. "He can't be. I found out after Mother had her stroke. It's taken me weeks to process that information. After Mother's stroke, we—me, Sharon, Adam, Dad…" Tess stopped, as though the word had suddenly become alien, at least with respect to Hal Norwood. "We thought it would be a nice gesture to donate blood. We were so appreciative of the people at the hospital and how marvelous they'd been. We went to a blood bank in the city and they typed all of us. That's how I found out what blood types we are. My blood type is B positive, and neither Mother nor…Hal… have that type. He can't be my father. No matter what it says on my birth certificate. My real father has type-B blood."

"Your real father," Lindsey echoed, the phrase replete with snares and booby traps. Just what was a real father? Merely biology, the provision of the sperm to fertilize the egg? Or was it something less tangible? A memory came, Hal shepherding the children down the stairs at the Point Reyes lighthouse, pointing out the whales breaching offshore.

Words tumbled from Tess's mouth. "I saw Mother earlier this afternoon. I finally screwed up my courage and asked her. She just closed her eyes and ignored me."

Gretchen shook her head. "Your mother is ill. This isn't a good time."

"Will there ever be a good time?" Tess countered.

"Why does it matter so much?" Lindsey had never gotten a satisfactory answer from Nina, during their acrimonious discussions about her own daughter's paternity. Maybe Tess had formulated a better response. Maybe it was easier dealing with someone else's conundrum, rather than her own.

"Hal is not my father," Tess said.

"He raised you," Gretchen said. "In every respect but one, he's your father."

"Yes. But…" Tess hesitated. "I don't know whether he knows I'm not his child. But now I know. It's eating me up inside. I have to know the truth."

Careful what you wish for, Lindsey thought. "Sometimes the truth isn't pleasant. Are you sure you want to go there?"

"I've asked myself that question, over and over," Tess said. "I have to know. I'm a person who has to know things, the where, the why, the how."

Lindsey sighed. "All these years I've thought Hal was your father. I don't know the answer to your question."

"You were her closest friends," Tess said. "You two, and Claire. You must know something. You all lived together in college."

"Hal was around on a regular basis that year," Gretchen said. "They had an understanding. When Annabel told us they were getting married, I wasn't surprised."

I was, Lindsey thought. But I was too preoccupied by my own life to notice what was going on with Annabel.

"Mother must have been involved with someone else that spring," Tess said. "I thought surely you'd know. You have to help me. I've collected Mother's keepsakes in a box. There are some envelopes I haven't opened yet. Before I do, I thought maybe the two of you could take a look, a fresh pair of eyes, or two."

Gretchen shook her head. "I couldn't invade your mother's privacy."

Isn't that what historians do? Lindsey thought. Invade the privacy of others? Poke around in diaries, journals, correspondence, scribbled notes, and business records? Historians prized such sources, because they were close to the grain of life. But it was usually the relics of the deceased that historians examined. Annabel wasn't dead.

A crack appeared in Tess's controlled façade, revealing turmoil underneath. "How do you think this makes me feel? A bomb, right in front of me, ripping apart everything I thought was certain. A mother, a father. Now I'm the odd one out. I don't have a place in my family anymore. I can't go back to the way things were. I have to find out who my father is." Tess stood, ready to leave. "Please think it over."

After Tess left, Gretchen shook her head. "That was unexpected. Annabel and Hal have been married for such a long time. They've had a good marriage."

"Have they?" Lindsey studied the contents of her cup, as though she might find answers there. "Tess was born seven months after the wedding."

"Hell's bells, it's not like any of us were virgins," Gretchen said. "Doug and I lived together before we finally got married. So Annabel was pregnant when she walked down the aisle. I figured she and Hal were sleeping together. They saw a lot of each other that spring. Her father was pushing the relationship, grooming Hal to take over the company eventually."

"They were dating other people. I don't know who else Annabel was seeing."

"Neither do I. That was about the time of my split with Doug. I was wrapped up in my own problems until we got back together. I don't know anything about Annabel's love life at the time. I wouldn't tell Tess if I did. Annabel wouldn't want us prying into her life, especially at a time like this. The past is past. Leave it that way."

The past has a penchant for getting in the way of the present. Lindsey thought about Nina's resentment at not knowing the identity of her father. She wished she could wrap both Nina and Tess in cotton wool, like delicate ornaments, never to face dings, scratches and breakage. But she couldn't. They were adults, forging paths for themselves in the larger world. She recalled what Gretchen had said earlier, about not being able to put guards around their children. Sometimes people did, to no avail.

9

Berkeley, California, February 1974

LINDSEY SET HER BOOK BAG and the metal pan on the bottom step and turned to lock her apartment door. As she tucked her keys into her jacket pocket, Claire came down the stairs, buttoning a tweed coat over sweater and slacks.

"What have you got there?" Claire picked up the pan and lifted the aluminum foil covering the contents. "Brownies? You made brownies and didn't tell me? Ooh, you bad girl." She stuck her fingers into the pan and pulled out a brownie, eating it with relish.

Lindsey grabbed the pan. "Leave it to you to help yourself."

Claire licked frosting from her fingers. "You weren't going to eat all of them."

"Neither are you. I'm taking them over to Art's place. He's fixing dinner."

"I remember him. Tall, wears glasses. Do I smell romance?"

Lindsey shrugged. "Not really. We're research assistants for a project in the history department. Art volunteered to cook dinner, so I made dessert. Where are you off to?"

"Dinner with a friend. Sure I can't talk you out of more brownies?"

Lindsey hid the pan behind her back. "I'll bake another batch, just for you. I promise."

"I'll count on it," Claire said. "Have a good evening, sweetie."

Outside, Claire got into her red Mustang and headed south toward Derby Street. Lindsey walked north, turned right on Parker Street and right again onto Benvenue, which paralleled Hillegass. A blue Volkswagen Bug, engine running, was parked under a street lamp just past the corner. The two people inside had their heads together, but they quickly drew apart when Lindsey glanced at them. The passenger was a woman. Lindsey couldn't see the driver.

Art Smithers lived in a ramshackle house converted into student apartments. A Rolling Stones number boomed from one of the units. She climbed the stairs to the second floor and knocked on Art's door. When he opened it, a rich aroma of garlic and tomatoes seeped out into the hallway. "Smells wonderful, whatever it is."

"Spaghetti with meat sauce." Art pushed his glasses up his nose. "You do eat meat, don't you? I forgot to ask if you were a vegetarian."

Lindsey draped her jacket over the back of a chair. "I'm an omnivore. I brought brownies. There's one missing. I had to wrestle Claire for them."

"All I have left to do is cook the spaghetti." Art poured glasses of red wine. The table was set for two and a bowl held a salad. Art put the spaghetti into the pot of boiling water and stood over it while Lindsey tossed the salad with dressing. Then Art heaped spaghetti and sauce on plates. They ate, mopping up sauce with hunks of garlic bread.

After washing up, Art made coffee to go with the brownies. They went over their notes, identifying gaps in their research as they worked on the latest draft of the report they were writing. It was after nine when they stopped. Lindsey stuffed books and papers into her bag, declined Art's offer of leftover spaghetti sauce, shifted the remaining brownies to a plate, and left with her bag and the empty pan.

In the downstairs apartment, the Rolling Stones sang about standing in the shadow. The street was dark, pierced here and there by porch lights and street lamps. As she walked toward the corner, Lindsey saw the blue Volkswagen Bug, its engine still running. That was odd. She'd arrived at Art's apartment sometime between six-thirty and seven and it was after nine. Had that car been sitting there all this time? When she got closer to the VW she noticed something else that didn't seem right. The front license plate was covered with mud, obscuring the numbers. The rest of the car looked clean, and it had been days since the last rainfall.

They're waiting for someone, Lindsey thought. For more than two hours, with the motor running? Maybe they had splashed through a puddle somewhere. A puddle that only got mud on one little rectangle in the front of the car?

The woman in the VW was looking across the street. Lindsey looked in the same direction, seeing another car, a white convertible, in the driveway of an apartment building directly across from the VW. The convertible faced the street and its engine was running, too. Was that a car backfiring? No. That was gunfire.

A woman screamed. Three figures dragged a woman toward the white convertible. She struggled, screaming all the while. She wore nothing but a robe. It slipped from her shoulders, revealing bare flesh. "Let me go!" the woman cried. One of her captors opened the trunk of the white convertible as the other two lifted the struggling woman off her feet. They shoved her into the trunk and shut the lid.

Lindsey didn't realize she was moving until she stepped out into the street. She didn't realize she had dropped the things she was carrying until the metal pan clattered on the pavement. One of the kidnappers swung toward her, raising a rifle. Lindsey fell to her knees, onto something sharp, but she ignored the pain as she scuttled between two parked cars. Shots whined over her head like angry bees. She trembled, heart pounding, gasping for breath. The gunfire continued but it seemed to have shifted direction. She raised her head so she could see what was happening across the street. The people who'd run out onto the porch of a nearby rooming house scattered as the kidnappers fired at them. The white convertible screamed out of the driveway onto Benvenue, then around the corner onto Parker. Another car, a station wagon, streaked by, someone inside the car firing a gun. The blue Volkswagen Bug peeled away from the curb.

The people from the rooming house shouted, all talking at once, joined by others who lived on Benvenue Street. Lindsey sat on the curb and scrabbled inside her bag for pen and paper, writing down everything she could remember. White convertible. Three kidnappers, one smaller than the other two—a woman? What color was that station wagon? White and something else, blue or green maybe. Blue VW Bug with the muddied license plate, parked outside for more than two hours, engine running. The woman in the passenger seat had short blond hair partly masked by a scarf.

Someone loomed over her. She gasped.

"Lindsey?" Art knelt beside her. "I'm sorry I scared you. What the hell happened? I heard guns. Are you all right?"

"I'm fine. Call the police."

"Somebody already did."

Sirens screamed, getting closer, as Lindsey got to her feet. Her slacks were torn at the left knee. She reached down, felt dampness, then lifted her fingers and saw red. "I'm bleeding."

"There's glass all over the pavement," Art said. "Looks like a broken beer bottle. Let's go to my place. I'll doctor that."

Lindsey shook her head. "I'm a witness. I have to give my statement to the police."

Police cars turned onto Benvenue Street, lights flashing. Art took Lindsey's hand and stayed with her while she talked with one of the police officers. She overheard the police talking. The woman who'd been kidnapped was a fellow student, Patricia Hearst. She was the granddaughter of famed newspaper magnate William Randolph Hearst. Her father, Randolph, was the publisher of the *San Francisco Examiner* and her mother, Catherine, was a conservative member of the University of California Board of Regents.

Art stuffed the pan into Lindsey's bag and walked her home, holding her arm as she limped along beside him. The cut on her knee had stopped bleeding but now her knee ached. Claire had just returned. She unlocked the front door as Art set down Lindsey's bag, said good night, and left.

Claire smiled. "He walked you home? How chivalrous. Say, what's happening on the next block? There are flashing lights and sirens everywhere."

Lindsey's voice sounded as though it came from someone else, far away. "A kidnapping. I saw it."

Claire grabbed Lindsey's arm and pounded on Annabel's door. "Gretchen! Annabel!"

Annabel opened her door. "What?"

Gretchen appeared on the landing. "You yelled? Say, there's something going down on Benvenue. I can see cop cars from my bedroom window."

"A kidnapping," Claire told them. "Lindsey saw it."

"Oh, my God." Gretchen hurried downstairs. "What did you see?"

Annabel propelled Lindsey into her apartment and made room on the book-piled sofa. "Lindsey, you're hurt."

Lindsey looked down at the angry-looking cut on her knee. "I fell on some glass."

"Where's your first-aid kit?" Claire demanded.

"In the medicine cabinet," Annabel said. "Peroxide and iodine, too."

The housemates spun away, then returned. Gretchen set a small basin of water and a handful of washcloths on the coffee table. Annabel uncapped the peroxide, poured some into the water, and dropped in one of the cloths.

Claire sat in the desk chair, tilting the table lamp, casting a harsh spotlight on the injured knee. She took scissors from the first-aid kit and cut away the torn fabric, then she bathed the wound with a damp cloth. "It looks clean," Claire said. "I don't see any glass. It's a nasty cut, though. You might need stitches. I'll wrap it really well but just to be safe you'd better get this checked out in the morning." She dabbed iodine on the cut, then bandaged it.

The knee hurt like hell. Lindsey took four aspirin and washed them down with a glass of water Gretchen fetched from Annabel's kitchen. "You've got something on the stove, starting to boil," Gretchen told Annabel.

"I was making cocoa. I hope it's not burnt." Annabel went back to the kitchen and returned with a tray, handing out mugs of cocoa. "Now, tell us what happened."

Lindsey fought back tears. She held the mug with both hands, taking comfort in its warmth, and the strong, sweet taste of cocoa.

THE Hearst kidnapping—the news was filled with little else, particularly after the missive received on Thursday from some group calling themselves the Symbionese Liberation Army. The communication declared that Patricia Hearst was a prisoner of war, and made demands in exchange for her release.

The following day, Friday, Lindsey started her first load of laundry and went outside to check the mailbox, but the postman hadn't delivered yet. A large black Cadillac pulled into the driveway. The driver's-side door opened and a big man got out—Max Brinker, Mr. Dunlin's assistant. Then Mr. Dunlin got out of the Cadillac. Annabel's father was tall, bulky through the middle, though his well-cut gray suit hid it well. His face was lined under his thinning iron gray hair. Mrs. Megarris, Claire's mother, emerged from the car's backseat. In her navy blue suit, gloves, and hat, she looked completely out of place in this south-of-campus neighborhood.

"Hello, Lindsey. I hope your knee is healing. Claire told us what happened Monday night. How dreadful for you." Mrs. Megarris seemed genuinely concerned. Mr. Dunlin, on the other hand, looked through her with frosty blue eyes.

"Thanks. I'm fine." Lindsey had gone to the campus clinic Tuesday morning. Now the stitches in the cut tugged and itched under the bandage.

"Claire and Annabel are expecting us," Mrs. Megarris said as she and Mr. Dunlin came up the front walk to the porch, followed by Max Brinker.

"Indeed we are," Claire said from the front door. She looked solemn, but a smile played around her lips. "Come in."

"Wait for us outside, Max," Mr. Dunlin said as he and Mrs. Megarris entered the house and went into Annabel's apartment.

Lindsey stole a sidelong glance at Max Brinker, then she went inside. Gretchen sat on the top step of the stair landing, her knees drawn up, arms folded over the front of her blue-and-gold Cal sweatshirt. Lindsey joined her. "What's going on? Annabel's father and Claire's mother are here, and that man Brinker is outside."

"Claire told me her mother and uncle are spooked by the Hearst kidnapping," Gretchen said, an edge to her voice. "They know they're targets. Dunlin's rich, a classic ruthless robber baron, like Jay Gould and Andrew Carnegie."

"At least Carnegie built libraries."

"He also locked out his workers and had people killed during the Haymarket Riots. Anyway, they want Annabel and Claire to leave school. Either permanently, or at least until this whole kidnapping thing blows over."

"What?" Lindsey's first thought was purely selfish. What if she had to leave her nice cozy apartment and find another place to live? Then she considered what leaving school would mean for Annabel and Claire. "That's crazy. They graduate in May. They can't put that on hold."

"That's what Claire and Annabel said. The phone calls have been flying across the bay for days," Gretchen said. "Annabel has a will of iron, when she wants to. When she was ready to start college, her father wanted her to go to one of those fancy women's colleges back east. She insisted on Cal. But her father manipulates whatever he can, which is why we're living in such a cushy place. No residence hall for Annabel. Claire wanted to go to Stanford. But her uncle said no, she had to go to Cal, with Annabel. Since he's paying for it, he had the last word. Claire's mother doesn't have much money, even if she is a company director. Dunlin pays, so he calls the shots." A phone rang in one of the upstairs apartments. Gretchen got to her feet. "That's mine. See you later."

Lindsey went back down the stairs to her apartment. She looked out the window. Max Brinker was at the curb, talking with a young man with a dark handlebar moustache. Lindsey realized she'd seen the man before, standing at the window of his second-floor apartment in the old house next door. That window faced Claire's windows, with a good view of this house and the backyard. Suddenly it hit her. The man worked for Brinker. He was a guard, watching the house. It felt creepy, somehow, to know that he'd been keeping an eye on them.

She headed to her bedroom, scooped towels into the wicker basket and carried it to the laundry room at the back of the house. The washer was still in its spin cycle. Then it shut off. As Lindsey transferred her wet clothes from washer to dryer, she heard voices and looked up. A wire mesh rectangle covered the opening to an air duct near the ceiling, where the dryer was vented. The laundry room shared a wall with Annabel's kitchen. Lindsey knew she shouldn't be eavesdropping, but she couldn't stop herself.

"It's three months till graduation," Annabel said. "I'm not leaving school."

"You're overreacting," Claire said. "We're perfectly safe here."

"I'm sure that's what the Hearsts thought," Mrs. Megarris said. "The things that go on in Berkeley make me wonder if anyone is safe living here."

"How about the Zebra killings in San Francisco?" Claire countered. "It's a dangerous world, everywhere."

Mr. Dunlin spoke, his voice cold, demanding. "I want you to leave school at once. I didn't want you here in the first place."

"I know that," Annabel said. "But I'm here, and I'm staying."

Now they argued, all talking at once. Lindsey strained to differ-

entiate words, her hands moving automatically as she scooped detergent into the now-empty washer and dumped in the towels. Then she
heard Annabel's voice. "I know you've got men watching the house.
I've seen them."

"How could we not?" Claire said. "Their apartment window is
about ten feet from mine. The guy with the moustache is cute. My
compliments to Max Brinker."

Now Mr. Dunlin spoke again. "Since you won't leave school, I've
had Max put on two more bodyguards. They'll watch the house and
escort you everywhere."

"Oh, for God's sake," Claire said. "Does that include when we go
to the john? That's overkill. We won't have any privacy."

"Take it or leave it," Mr. Dunlin snapped.

"We'll take it," Annabel said. "But I don't want them to look like
bodyguards."

"I'll leave that to Max," Mr. Dunlin said. "This will have to do,
for the time being. But if anything else happens, we'll revisit this."

Lindsey felt ashamed of herself for listening. She started the
washer. Water whooshed, drowning out the voices. She went back to
her apartment, thinking about bodyguards and change.

10

IT WAS TOO EARLY for peaches and apricots, but there were
plump ripe strawberries at the Berkeley Farmers Market. On this sunny April Saturday, people crowded Center Street. Lindsey tasted a
strawberry offered by a vendor, then chose three baskets, counted out
bills, and tucked the berries and her wallet into her tote bag.

She glanced at her watch. Five minutes to eleven, when she was
due to meet Flor.

She'd reread the transcript this morning. Flor's words leapt from
the page, describing her husband's murder, her son's abduction, the
massacre at her village. It was such a small favor, a simple request. All
Flor wanted Lindsey to do was look at a boy who bore a resemblance
to her son. But Lindsey was having second thoughts.

She bought lemons from one vendor, broccoli and squash from another, then joined Nina at another booth. "I got strawberries. I'll make shortcake."

"Real shortcake? Not that icky spongy stuff the supermarkets try to pass off as shortcake."

Lindsey chuckled. "I wouldn't let that icky spongy stuff pass my lips. Real shortcake from scratch. With real whipped cream. Just add another layer to my hips."

Nina glanced at her mother. "You look great for a woman your age."

"My age? You make me sound ancient."

"Oh, you know what I mean."

Over half my life, Lindsey thought, looking at her daughter. She wouldn't be that age again for all the tea in—wherever. She saw herself, a frazzled single mother, tussling day-to-day with Nina, the willful toddler from hell. That time had been hard, as Lindsey struggled to pay the bills, finish her dissertation, and raise her child. It had taken her years to build her financial security. The willful toddler was now an adult, but that particular struggle hadn't gotten any easier. Just for today, they had a truce. It was good to stroll through the market together.

Eleven o'clock. Lindsey scanned the street leading toward the downtown Berkeley BART station. No sign of Flor.

"Who are you meeting?" Nina asked.

"A woman I interviewed for the book. She's from El Salvador."

"Do we need salad stuff?" Nina asked. They walked to a nearby booth where vegetables were displayed like jewels. Lindsey selected bell peppers in red, yellow and orange, while Nina chose a cucumber and a head of romaine lettuce.

Lindsey looked at her watch again. Five after eleven. Then she saw Flor, face flushed, her children's hands clasped firmly in her own. "I am sorry to keep you waiting. There was some difficulty getting away. I hoped to leave the children with Tony. But…" Her eyes moved to Lindsey's right, taking in Nina.

"This is Flor Cooper," Lindsey said. "And her children, Michael and Antonia."

Flor smiled. "You are Lindsey's beautiful daughter."

Nina looked surprised. "Is that what she calls me?"

Flor nodded. "Oh, yes. She is very proud of you. She shows me your picture and tells me about you working in Texas. Have you come for a visit?"

Nina gave Lindsey a searching look. "Sort of."

"Mamá, can we look around?" Antonia asked.

Michael chimed in. "Yes, Mamá, please."

Flor frowned. "No. It's safer if you both stay with me."

"There's a guy over there selling cookies," Nina told the children. "I'll treat you, if it's okay with your mom." She glanced at Flor. "I won't let them out of my sight. I promise."

Flor hesitated. Then she nodded. Nina led the children toward the booth where cookies and other baked goods were being sold. "My husband, Tony, wanted to know why I wished to leave the children with him at the shop this morning. I told him about seeing Efraín at the market. We quarreled. He thinks I see ghosts where there are none to see."

"Do you?" Lindsey had wondered as well.

"See Efraín because I want to see him? No, I didn't make this up. I know my son. This boy is my son."

"Where did you see him?" Lindsey asked.

"There, on the grass." Flor pointed toward Civic Center Park, a square block of grass and trees. Center Street, site of the market, was on the north side of the park. The Berkeley High School campus sprawled to the south. "Three weeks ago my friend Carmen and I came to this market, late morning, like now, between eleven and noon. I saw this boy. At first I couldn't believe my eyes, but the longer I looked at him, the more I knew he was Efraín. He was with two other boys, acting silly, the way boys do. He wore a Berkeley High School T-shirt. I followed him and his friends to a movie theater on Shattuck Avenue. I thought about waiting until the movie was over so I could follow him to where he lives now. But I had to go home. I didn't see him the next Saturday. But last Saturday he was here, with the same boys. After they left the market they went to the BART station."

The women walked onto the park's grassy lawn. From here Lindsey could see most of the park, but the booths blocked her view of Center Street. A man sat on the grass nearby, wearing faded jeans and a tie-dyed T-shirt, long blond hair cascading down his back. He strummed a guitar and sang "Yellow Submarine" in a clear tenor. The children clustered around him joined in the chorus.

"There," Flor whispered as the song ended. "Those three boys. The dark one, in the middle, that's my son." She pointed toward Berkeley High as three teenagers crossed the street and cut through the park, heading toward the market. The short blond boy grabbed something from the dark-haired boy's back pocket, ran a few steps, then tossed the object to the tall redhead. Rectangular, shiny, about six inches long—a harmonica. The dark-haired boy intercepted the harmonica in mid-toss and stowed it in his pocket. The boys were about ten feet away when the dark-haired boy turned and Lindsey got a good look at his face.

"Are you sure, Flor?" Lindsey tried to sound detached. But she wasn't. Far from it. "It's been a long time. Are you sure this is Efraín?"

Flor's hungry gaze never left the boy. "Yes, I'm sure. It doesn't matter how long. Would I forget my own son? Never. Every detail of his face is burned into my brain. I think of him every day. Finally, my prayers are answered and I see him again, right here. He looks just like his father. You see the resemblance, don't you? From the picture I showed you. He has that scar on his chin, from the broken bottle."

Lindsey looked at the boy who teetered on the precipice between boyhood and manhood. Thick black hair curled around his ears and fell onto his forehead, over his dark brown eyes. The crescent-shaped scar near the cleft of the boy's chin stood out, pale against his brown skin. There were many ways a teenaged boy could acquire such a scar. It didn't necessarily mean that he was who Flor said he was. Flor's loss, what she felt, could make a woman see a resemblance where none existed.

"I know he is my son," Flor said. "I want him back. You must help me."

The boy smiled at Lindsey. Then he and his friends joined the throng on Center Street. Flor and Lindsey followed, locating Nina and the children. "*Mamá*, are you done?" Antonia asked. "I have to be at soccer practice at one."

"Yes, I'm done. For now." Flor took her children's hands and looked at Lindsey. "I will call you. We must talk about what to do." She turned and walked toward the BART station.

"What was that about?" Nina asked. "You look like you've seen a ghost."

A ghost, Lindsey thought. The past always comes back to haunt us.

"Let's go home," she said. "This tote bag is heavy."

"I knew we'd see you here." Gretchen called, walking toward them, with her daughter, Amy, at her side. "Did you get everything you came for?"

More than I bargained for. Lindsey nodded. "Yes, including strawberries."

"We're going to make shortcake," Nina said. "The real kind."

Amy grinned. "I love strawberry shortcake. I'll come over and help you eat it."

The man who'd been playing the guitar in the park now moved among the crowd, strumming the strings, singing the blues, Robert Johnson's "Love in Vain." A harmonica joined in, wailing along with the guitar. The harmonica player came up behind the man with the guitar. Then the song ended with a flourish and the listeners applauded.

Gretchen laughed. "Nat, love, please carry this bag."

Nathaniel Segal, soon to graduate from Berkeley High, took Gretchen's bag and slung the straps on his shoulder. He smiled at Lindsey, as he had earlier. The crescent-shaped scar near the cleft of his chin stood out like a beacon.

Lindsey had been in denial ever since Thursday morning. She knew the Segals had adopted Nat from a Salvadoran orphanage. But how and when had he arrived at the orphanage? What had happened to his birth parents? Was Nat really Efraín, Flor's lost son? Now Lindsey recalled how Gretchen found her son.

11

Berkeley, California, February 1988 and July 1989

THE OPENING BARS OF "You've Got a Friend" poured from the car's speakers as Lindsey took the University Avenue exit and headed into Berkeley. The sky was dark and full of clouds. Wind tossed tree branches. Friday night's storm brought rain and bluster into Saturday morning. Raindrops splattered the windshield and Lindsey upped the tempo of the wipers.

She'd gotten up at five that morning, filled a thermos with coffee, dropped thirteen-year-old Nina off at her parents' home in Paso Robles, and pointed her car north. All the way she listened to Carole King's *Tapestry*, singing along while the cassette tape cycled repeatedly through the player.

It wasn't the most convenient time for a visit. She had lectures to prepare and papers to grade for the history classes she taught at California Polytechnic University in San Luis Obispo. Friday, yesterday, was her catch-up day. She'd spread books and papers in front of her while eating the leftover casserole she'd brought for lunch. She'd already been interrupted twice when the phone rang. She sighed and picked up the receiver.

"Lindsey, can you come up?" Annabel asked. "We're having a wake."

"Who died?"

"Gretchen had another miscarriage."

"Oh, no. Not again."

"Yes. Please come. At a time like this, Gretchen needs her friends."

Lindsey glanced at her calendar. "I can't leave until tomorrow. Nina has a school thing tonight. I have to go. I missed the last one and she pitched a fit."

"Believe me, I understand," Annabel said. "Tess and Sharon fuss if I miss any of their school activities. Kids."

"Yeah, kids," Lindsey said. "If I can get on the road early I should be there by noon."

Lindsey called her mother, arranging for Nina to spend the weekend with Grandma. But it wasn't as easy for Lindsey to get away as she had anticipated. Nina objected to staying with her grandparents. She pouted all the way from San Luis Obispo to Paso Robles, and then threw a tantrum in Grandma's living room.

Now Lindsey turned off University Avenue and headed north. Gretchen's house was on Milvia, a block from Aunt Emma's place. When she and Doug bought it, the two-story Victorian was shabby and run-down. Over the years they'd dealt with the neglect, and their efforts showed in the pale blue exterior, the house's gingerbread trim decked out in contrasting dark blue with bright yellow highlights. Weeds and overgrown shrubs had given way to a front yard land-scaped with native grasses and flowers in all seasons.

How cozy and welcoming the house looked. All it lacked, as far as Gretchen was concerned, was a baby to occupy the bedroom she'd decorated as a nursery.

Annabel's Volvo and Claire's Porsche were in the driveway. Lindsey parked her Honda on the street. Claire met her on the porch. "I'm really glad you could make it."

"Me, too. How's Gretchen?"

"She'll be all right. She's resilient."

Lindsey stepped into the front hall, set her umbrella on the floor in the corner and removed her jacket, thinking of Annabel's three children—and her own unplanned, unexpected pregnancy. "Three miscarriages in four years. It's not fair."

"Nobody ever said life was fair." Claire led the way to the liv-ing room, where Annabel and Gretchen sat on the sofa. Red-gold flames danced in the fireplace, warming the cozy, comfortable room. Music played softly, from a stack of albums on the stereo system in the corner. Gretchen blotted her reddened eyes with a handkerchief. Lindsey sat down and put her arms around her friend.

"I'm so glad you're here." Gretchen rested her head on Lindsey's shoulder. Then she straightened and leaned back on the sofa. "I was five months along this time. I thought it was going to be all right. No morning sickness, nothing like that."

Lindsey squeezed Gretchen's hand. Three pregnancies. In Anna-bel's case, they had led to three healthy children. For Gretchen, each pregnancy, so promising at the start, ended in a too-early splash of blood, pain, unfulfilled hopes, an empty nursery, tears of loss.

Gretchen managed a crooked smile. "I'll be fine. I know. I got over the other miscarriages, I'll get through this one." Her eyes filled with tears again. "I remember back in high school and college, fumbling around with condoms and diaphragms and those damn gels and foams. That little edge of danger when I did have sex, because I was afraid of getting pregnant. And now, when I want to get pregnant and have a baby, I find out it's more difficult than I thought. I always figured I could have a baby. I have all the equipment. Who knew it wasn't functioning properly? Ironic, isn't it?"

Getting pregnant was something most women figured they could do, Lindsey reckoned, as inevitable as tempting fate by having sex without protection. Discovering that one was unable to conceive, unable to carry a pregnancy to term—yes, that was ironic.

Gretchen and Doug waited to start their family, wanting first to establish their home and careers. When they married in 1978, Doug was just a few years out of law school, working as an associate in a San Francisco law firm. Gretchen was an Alameda County social worker. By the early 1980s, Gretchen joked about feeling left out, as friends and relatives had children. Now they had the house and money in the bank. Now it was time to have babies. Out went the pills. In came the ovulation charts.

But nothing happened. The doctors said the problem wasn't his. It was hers, so Gretchen felt guilty. She and Doug began the infertility roundelay—artificial insemination, in vitro fertilization, and Gretchen's careening emotions and hormones. Finally she conceived, full of joy and excitement as she decorated the nursery. Then she wept when the pregnancy ended in a miscarriage at two months. Again she conceived and carried the fetus for three months before losing it to another miscarriage. Now this third miscarriage, five months into a heretofore untroubled pregnancy.

Gretchen sighed. "Well, this is supposed to be a wake. Let's have some wine. I haven't had any booze since I got pregnant and I could certainly use a drink."

"And something to eat," Annabel said. A wake meant food

and drink. Provisions covered the coffee table, an assortment of deli food—cold cuts, cheese, bread, potato salad and coleslaw—and a bottle of Chardonnay. Plates, cutlery and glasses crowded a side table. Annabel opened the wine, filled the glasses, and handed them around.

"I haven't eaten since breakfast, and that was very early this morning. That pastrami over there is calling to me." Lindsey picked up a plate and made herself a sandwich.

"Doug and I talked it over," Gretchen said, sipping wine as she spooned up potato salad. "Four years on this fertility roller coaster is enough. I can't do this anymore. I guess I wasn't meant to give birth to my children. We'll adopt."

"I'm glad you're taking such a positive attitude." Annabel raised her glass. "A toast. Here's to good friends."

Four glasses clinked together. "Good friends," Lindsey echoed. "Let nothing come between us."

"Another toast." Claire held her glass high. The others lifted their glasses again, waiting for Claire to speak. "Here's to the kids you'll have someday, Gretchen. I know you will, because you'll make a helluva good mom. You'll have your kids, by hook or crook, if I have anything to say about it. You deserve to have whatever you want."

"Thanks for being my friends," Gretchen said, wiping away tears. "I don't know what I'd do without you."

NEARLY eighteen months had passed since the friends gathered to comfort Gretchen after her miscarriage. Lindsey received second-hand reports on the adoption saga from Annabel. The Segals discovered the wait for a healthy white infant—and the bureaucracy of the American adoption system—was as daunting as the infertility treatments. They plugged into the private adoption network, willing to take an older child, a toddler, or a child from a foreign country. More than a year had passed since Gretchen's last miscarriage and several adoption prospects hadn't panned out.

Lindsey drove up again and now they gathered in the Segals' backyard, this time to celebrate. Gretchen, her face radiant, cradled a toddler in her lap, a sturdy little fellow with black hair and wide brown eyes, his dark skin contrasting with Gretchen's fair coloring. He sucked his thumb, solemnly taking in the sights around him.

"We named him Nathaniel." Gretchen hugged the little boy tighter. "After Doug's grandfather. Nathaniel Douglas Segal. Nat for short."

"The minute I saw him," Claire said, "I knew he was Gretchen's little boy." She kicked off her sandals and dug her toes into grass. "I was in El Salvador on business, staying with my friends, the Medranos. They're patrons of an orphanage. Cristina had some business there, so I went with her, and spotted this sweetie pie. I went right back to my hotel and called Gretchen."

"At the orphanage they said he was two, but I think he's younger," Gretchen said. "We don't know when he was born. So we decided his birthday is today, the Fourth of July. An all-American birthday." Her eyes brimmed with happiness. Nat was decked out in crisp blue shorts and a white shirt, with red sneakers on his feet.

"How did he wind up at that orphanage?" Lindsey asked.

"Lots of kids down there are abandoned or orphaned," Claire said. "Civil war plays hell with the coffee business, I can tell you."

"Leave it to Claire to reduce everything to business," Annabel said. She pulled the cork from a bottle of Chardonnay and refilled the glasses.

"The business supports you, dear cousin," Claire retorted, "in the manner to which you have become accustomed."

"The manner in which I've always lived. Yes, I know." Annabel leaned back in her chair. "I'm surprised Gretchen and Doug were able to adopt him so quickly. Claire saw him at the orphanage this spring, and he got here in time for the Fourth of July. I thought the paperwork took longer than that."

Gretchen nestled the little boy in the crook of her left arm. "Doug has a friend from law school who works in the State Department. That helped with the visa. As for the paperwork on the other end, Claire's friends in El Salvador smoothed the way."

"Of course. Cristina's husband is in the government and they give that orphanage lots of money, so everyone was eager to oblige."

Claire rubbed her fingers against her thumb. "When all else fails, there's *la mordida*. The bite."

"Bribery?" Lindsey asked.

"Let's not be squeamish, ladies," Claire said. "That's the way business is done in Latin America, and most of the world. You get used to it. Come now, Lindsey. The academic world has its share of tit-for-tat. You scratch my back, I'll scratch yours. I'll support your grant proposal if you'll give me tenure."

That hit home. Lindsey was in the middle of the tenure process herself, and it had caused her anxious moments during the past year. "Yes, academic politics can be fairly ruthless, even at a smaller school like Cal Poly."

"Just think how bad they'd be if you'd gotten that job at UC Berkeley," Claire said. "Anyway, what does it matter where he came from? He's an orphan. He needed a home. Gretchen needed a baby. Now he's got a home. Gretchen has a baby. Everyone's happy." Claire kissed the little boy on the forehead. He reached up and grabbed a handful of her blond hair. She laughed and pulled away.

Gretchen stroked the little boy's cheek. "The woman at the orphanage told me their children's parents get killed in the fighting, or kids are abandoned because their parents can't take care of them. She said he'd been left at the orphanage in April, and she acted as though it didn't really matter to her. She had so many children and she was glad to find a home for this little guy."

"In any case, he's lucky to be here." Lindsey smiled at the toddler. "He's very quiet. I don't think he's made a sound since I got here."

"He's really shy." Gretchen sipped her wine. "This must be overwhelming, all these people, speaking a strange language. He must miss his birth mother. I think about his mother sometimes. Maybe she's dead. Or she couldn't take care of him and that's why she left him at that orphanage. We saw so much poverty and strife down there."

"Give him plenty of love," Annabel said, "and he'll be just fine."

"I intend to. I've saved up lots of love for him." Nathaniel Douglas Segal took his thumb from his mouth and reached for Gretchen's wineglass. "No, Nat love. Mommy drinks wine. You have apple juice.

Here's your cup." Gretchen set the glass on the table and picked up a plastic child's cup with handles on either side. The little boy grasped the handles and drank, several drops of pale gold juice dribbling from the corners of his mouth. Gretchen pulled a crumpled paper napkin from her pocket and gently wiped his face.

Now that Nat's thumb was out of his mouth, Lindsey saw a crescent-shaped mark on the little boy's chin. "He has a scar. I hadn't noticed that before."

Gretchen nodded. "He had a bandage on it when we first saw him at the orphanage. The people at the orphanage said he fell and cut himself. My doctor says as he gets older the scar will be less visible."

"I can still see mine." Lindsey's fingers moved to her own forehead, where a childhood accident had left its mark.

Claire squinted. "I can't. All those wrinkles get in the way."

"Thank you very much," Lindsey said. "Is that a silver hair I see among the gold?"

She stretched her arms above her head, relishing the warm afternoon sun in the Segals' backyard. The mouthwatering aroma of barbecued meat wafted from the patio grill. Doug Segal used tongs to turn chicken and ribs. Hal Norwood sprawled on a lawn chair, beer bottle in one hand, his face in profile. The picnic table was loaded with food. Nina and Sharon hovered at one end, filching deviled eggs. Adam, telltale smears of avocado green on his face, had been at the guacamole and chips. Tess was holed up somewhere, Annabel said, with her nose in a book.

Gretchen called to her husband. "Hey, what's the story with the chicken and ribs? We've got hungry people over here."

"Grab a plate," Doug said. "It's ready. Of course there may not be any deviled eggs left."

Sharon giggled and dodged away from the picnic table, but Nina remained, licking egg yolk from her fingers, looking unrepentant. "If you didn't want me to eat them, you shouldn't have left them out."

"Did you leave any for the rest of us?" Lindsey glanced at the platter. Nearly half the deviled eggs were gone. "You're going to make yourself sick."

"Mom." Nina turned one syllable into two. "You sound like Grandma."

"God forbid I should sound like my mother," Lindsey said as Annabel came up behind her. "I've got to watch that."

"It goes with motherhood," Annabel said, and called, "Tess, wherever you are, we're eating."

Lindsey picked up a plate and claimed one of the remaining deviled eggs. Then she helped herself to everything else, including potato salad and baked beans. Doug had transferred the meat to a platter, setting it at one end of the picnic table. "What the heck, I'll have both." She took a rib and a drumstick.

"Been marinating in my special sauce for days," Doug boasted. "You'll be back for seconds and thirds."

Lindsey laughed. "Just let me get through the firsts." She carried her plate to one of the tables on the lawn. She gnawed on the rib, then wiped barbecue sauce from her hands and reached for her glass, smiling at Annabel. "Gretchen is over the moon. I haven't seen her this happy for a long time."

"I'm pleased for her." Annabel bit into a chicken breast.

"I hadn't been keeping up with the adoption saga," Lindsey said. "The past year has been hectic. I'm up for tenure."

"Don't worry, you'll get it. You've certainly published enough."

Tenure wasn't the only reason Lindsey hadn't been paying that much attention. Nina was a handful and it got worse when she became a teenager. Lindsey's father was growing older, getting more forgetful and irascible. He'd had a bout with pneumonia that spring. One of her brothers had separated from his wife. And Lindsey had extricated herself from a relationship that wasn't working.

"Serendipitous," Lindsey said, "that Claire should visit that orphanage and see that boy."

"Yes, she was in El Salvador right after my father's funeral."

"I was sorry to hear that he'd died. It was rather sudden." Lindsey hadn't really known Mr. Dunlin. Her concern was for Annabel, who'd lost her mother at an early age, and now her father. Annabel didn't say anything about missing him. Their relationship had been formal and distant, so different from Lindsey's own rambunctious family where emotions were warm and on the surface.

Annabel picked up her fork and drew a pattern in the baked beans on her plate. "The heart attack? He'd had warning signs—his cholesterol level, blood pressure, chest pains. He ignored them. Typical of him. Now he's gone. His birthday would have been next week." She smiled. "Remember, we went to his birthday party back in the Seventies, that fancy catered affair, with the pianist murdering pop tunes in the hotel ballroom. That's where we met Hal."

"The food was spectacular," Lindsey said with a smile. "And the people who were there. I had no idea your father was so connected. He left the Pacific Heights house to you?"

"Oh, yes." Annabel's smile disappeared. "He left it to me. Along with all the ghosts."

Lindsey looked at her curiously. "Is the house haunted?"

"In a manner of speaking." Annabel shivered, but it might have been the summer fog creeping across the bay from the Golden Gate, gray-white wisps now feathering across the blue sky like tendrils of ivy.

"Are you going to move?"

"I like our house in Noe Valley," Annabel said. "It's sunny in that part of town. Pacific Heights is cold and foggy. Hal wants to move. It would be closer to work for him. We could use more room. When Tess was a baby, our house seemed big enough, but with three kids, we're bursting at the seams. Now that Hal is CEO we'll need to do more entertaining." She made a face. "Not that I'm all that interested in playing hostess."

"But you're good at it," Lindsey said.

They talked about houses and children while they ate, going back, as Doug had predicted, for seconds. As the fog moved in they put on sweaters. Afternoon gave way to evening, the sky darkening. Doug went inside and changed the music, from the rock and jazz that he'd been playing all afternoon, to something more appropriate for the Fourth of July. Lindsey smiled as she heard the opening bars to "Stars and Stripes Forever."

The four friends pulled their chairs into a circle and sat, talking, drinking wine, nibbling brownies. Fireworks started in the distance, a few pops here and there, then rapid and loud, a constant barrage. Nathaniel Douglas Segal, sleepy and full of food from his first American Fourth of July, had been drowsing in Gretchen's lap. Now he woke up, eyes wide as he looked for the source of the bangs. Then he began to cry, his frightened wails drowning out John Philip Sousa and the fusillade of fireworks.

12

ELECTRIC GUITARS SCREAMED overhead. Gretchen called, "Nat!" The dark-haired teenager with the scar on his chin appeared on the stair landing. "We have guests. Crank down the volume on that noise, please."

Nat rolled his eyes. "Music, Mom."

"The jury's out on that. Your old mom's ears can't handle it." Gretchen smiled at Lindsey and Nina. "I miss the Beatles. Those were the days. Am I an old fogey?"

"It can't be helped," Lindsey said. "Happens to all of us. Hey, the Rolling Stones are still out there touring. Who would have thought Mick and Keith would be strutting their stuff for forty-plus years?"

Gretchen laughed. "Looking like forty-plus miles of bad road. Sex, drugs and rock and roll will do that to you."

The electric guitars abated and Nat returned to the stairs. "When do we eat? Remember, I'm a growing boy."

"Soon." Gretchen led the way through the living room. "That kid is a bottomless pit. You know the stereotype about the teenaged boy with his head in the refrigerator? You just met him."

"I brought strawberry shortcake," Lindsey said. "Not the usual Sunday brunch fare, but we love it."

In the kitchen Doug was assembling ingredients and utensils on the counter. He waved his whisk. "I'm making my killer buttermilk pancakes, renowned around the world. Very popular here in Berkeley, anyway."

"I've got a frittata and sausage warming in the oven. And I made a big fruit salad." Gretchen pointed at the glass bowl that held a mixture of bright red berries and melon. "Claire's late. We'll start without her. Coffee, juice, mimosas?"

"I'll have a mimosa," Lindsey said.

"Coffee for me." Nina filled a cup from the coffeemaker on the counter. Gretchen poured Champagne and orange juice into a glass for Lindsey.

There were too many people in the kitchen, so Lindsey went out to the backyard, site of that long-ago Fourth of July barbecue, when Nat was a toddler newly arrived in the United States. He'd cried when he heard the fireworks. At the time she thought it was because he was startled by the noise. Now she wondered. If Nat was Efraín, did he remember what happened at San Blas? Flor's son had been four months shy of his second birthday when he'd been kidnapped.

Lindsey's fingers moved to her own forehead, as they had the day of the barbecue. Her own scar was still there, very faint. She'd been two years old, jumping up and down on her bed, when she lost her balance and fell, forehead hitting the corner of the nightstand. She recalled her two-year-old self, looking back at her from the bathroom mirror. Mama, a cold, wet washcloth in hand, wiped away Lindsey's blood and tears. Daddy held her tightly, murmuring reassuring words in her ear, as he held up a square of Lindsey's favorite candy, the Hershey bar peeking from the waxy white wrapping on the bathroom counter.

Lindsey blinked and the image vanished. A child remembered, even if the trauma occurred at an early age. Efraín would remember San Blas—his father's murder, and being torn from his mother's arms.

Lindsey looked out at the yard. On the patio were a low round table, a chaise longue padded with faded floral fabric, and four metal chairs. Lindsey set her glass on the patio table and stepped onto the grass, walking toward the back fence, which was covered with abutilon, its bell-shaped flowers bright red, orange and yellow.

Twelve-year-old Amy Segal sat cross-legged on the grass near the vegetable garden, leafing through a book. Her glasses were perched on her nose and her straight black hair was pulled back in a ponytail.

Amy came from an orphanage in China, where infant girls were commonly abandoned.

It was Nat's story, though, that raised questions in Lindsey's mind. Yesterday, after returning from the Farmers Market, Lindsey had gone to the Internet, searching for the missing children of El Salvador, abandoned, orphaned, and stolen. She discovered an article about a woman whose infant son had been taken during "scorched-earth" counterinsurgency operations, when the army targeted villages suspected of being sympathetic to guerrillas. The frantic mother had been told that her child would now serve the government, not the rebels. The boy, along with other children, was loaded onto an army helicopter. He was found twelve years later in an orphanage near San Salvador.

The *Asociación Pro-Búsqueda de Niños y Niñas Desaparecidos*, the Association for the Search of Disappeared Children, was using DNA testing to aid Salvadoran parents in reclaiming children. The University of California at Berkeley had even gotten involved, as the Human Rights Center on campus worked with a state lab to create a DNA database. The association had dealt with hundreds of requests by parents for information on abducted children, and had resolved about a third of them. Some children were dead, others adopted by families in Europe, Latin America and the United States. Some lived with the families of Salvadoran army officers. Others were found in orphanages or in street gangs, still in El Salvador. Birth certificates were falsified, changing dates and places that might link the children to their real families. Selling babies and children who were purportedly abandoned or orphaned had proved lucrative.

How had the toddler with the cut on his chin arrived in that orphanage in El Salvador?

"Hello, Amy," Lindsey said now. "You have a big garden this spring."

"I picked out some of the herbs and veggies. Early Girl tomatoes, lemon cucumbers, chives and basil. But we really have to watch the basil. Snails love it. They just mow it down." Amy got to her feet. "Daddy's making buttermilk pancakes."

"I'm looking forward to a great big stack of those pancakes, with lots of butter and maple syrup." They walked back to the patio. Lindsey sat in one of the chairs and sipped her mimosa. "What are you reading?"

Amy showed Lindsey the paperback on birds of the San Francisco Bay Area. "We have finches and sparrows and Stellar's jays. Hummingbirds, too. They like red flowers. The kind we have are called Anna's hummingbirds. There's a picture right here." Amy held up the book so Lindsey could see the illustration.

"I've seen them at my hummingbird feeder," Lindsey said. The Segals' black-and-white tom ambled across the grass with his rolling, fat-cat gait, his tail straight up in the air and a placid look on his face. "Does Moby Cat try to catch the birds?"

"He's too fat to catch anything." Amy sat on the chaise and patted her lap. Displaying surprising agility for a big-bellied cat, Moby Cat wiggled his rear end and launched himself onto Amy's lap. He purred loudly as he butted his head against Amy's chest and kneaded his paws on her legs. "Oh, Moby Cat." Amy hugged the cat and stroked him under his chin. He purred even louder, tilting his head up for a better angle.

"This cat doesn't miss any meals," Lindsey said.

"Indeed," Gretchen said from the patio door. "His Rotundity loves to eat. Speaking of eating, it's pancake time. Get 'em while they're hot."

Lindsey and Amy joined the others in the dining room. Nat slathered his pancakes with butter, added syrup, and passed the pitcher to Lindsey. "Who was that lady you were with at the market?"

"Her name is Flor," Lindsey said. "I interviewed her for my book. Why do you ask?"

"Just curious." He lifted a forkful of pancake toward his mouth.

"Mom." Nina gestured at the pitcher. "If you're not going to use the syrup, pass it over."

Lindsey poured syrup on her pancakes and handed the pitcher to Nina. She served herself frittata and sausage. They ate, the only sounds the clink of forks on plates. Nina got up to get more coffee. "Refills, anyone?"

"Just bring the pot," Gretchen said as the doorbell rang. She pushed back her chair and headed for the front door, returning with Claire, who carried a square pink bakery box.

"I'll trade you these scones for a mimosa," Claire said. "Light on the orange juice, heavy on the Champagne."

Gretchen took the box. "One mimosa, coming right up."

Claire's eyes widened as Nina carried the coffeepot into the dining room. "Nina. What a surprise. Here for a visit?"

Nina filled Lindsey's cup, then her own. "I've moved back to the Bay Area."

"Welcome home, then. Staying with your mother?"

"Temporarily."

Gretchen returned, a brimming glass in one hand and a plate piled with scones in the other. She handed the glass to Claire and set the plate on the table.

"We've got fruit salad, sausage and frittata," Gretchen said. "Doug's going to make more pancakes. We inhaled the first batch."

"No pancakes for me. I'll have fruit salad and a sliver of frittata." Claire sipped her mimosa, then reached for the bowl.

"I'll have more pancakes," Nat said.

"That's a given, son." Doug grinned at the boy and headed for the kitchen.

When the last of the pancakes had been eaten, they lingered over coffee, talking. Then Gretchen said, "Nat and Amy, let's clear the table and help Dad clean up. Lindsey and Claire, I want to talk with you, privately. Wait for me on the patio. I'll be there in a minute."

Lindsey and Claire went outside, where Moby Cat was curled up on the chaise, nose tucked under paws as he slept. "When I saw you Thursday you didn't mention Nina was back," Claire said.

"She showed up that afternoon," Lindsey said. "The move to Austin didn't work out. I'm curious about something. Nat, and that orphanage in El Salvador where you first saw him."

Claire pulled petals from a rose and dropped them. "Why do you ask?"

"Research for my book. I came across some articles about missing children in Central America, taken from their parents during the war down there. It seems a lot of children wound up in orphanages. It made me wonder where Nat came from."

Claire shrugged. "An orphanage in San Salvador. Gretchen and Doug adopted him. He has a wonderful home with people who love him. End of story."

"What if Nat has family somewhere?"

"His family is here," Claire said.

"But his birth parents—"

"His birth parents are dead, I assume. The little guy was left in the orphanage where I saw him. I don't know how he got there. He's lucky to have been adopted." Claire looked up as Gretchen came outside. "On the phone you were terribly mysterious. You said you wanted some girl talk, just the three of us, about Annabel. So talk."

Gretchen pulled up a chair. "Sit down. Just shoo Moby Cat off that chaise."

"Oh, I wouldn't disturb Moby Cat for the world. It's best to let sleeping cats lie. Don't you agree, Lindsey?" Claire laughed, her eyes twinkling.

"Tess showed up on Lindsey's doorstep Friday afternoon, with the damnedest announcement." Gretchen described the conversation that had followed.

"So the blood test shows Hal isn't Tess's biological father," Claire said. "That's a surprise. But he's been her father in every other sense of the word since she was born. Why poke around in Annabel's past, dragging the two of you with her?"

"She has questions and she's looking for answers," Lindsey said. "So am I."

"Careful what you wish for, Lindsey. You might get it. And you might not be happy with the answers." Claire shrugged. "Sorry. I'm not much help, am I? Things are topsy-turvy since Annabel's stroke. Hal's mind isn't on business. He's been so distracted that I've had to take over much of the day-to-day company operations. The quarterly board meeting is coming up and all the functional meetings before that. Tess going off half-cocked on some windmill-tilting expedition is the last thing the family needs."

Gretchen nodded. "I agree. I'm staying out of it."

"Then we're all agreed," Claire said. "I'll have a word with Tess."

I haven't agreed to anything, Lindsey thought. She opened her mouth, then closed it as Nat and Amy came out onto the patio. They bore trays holding bowls of strawberry shortcake, sweet crumbly golden-brown biscuits covered with sliced strawberries and whipped cream. Doug followed with more bowls. Nina brought up the rear, carrying a tray of coffee mugs.

"I thought we just ate," Gretchen said.

"Our son and daughter were agitating for shortcake now," Doug said as he and Nina set the trays on the picnic table and began handing out bowls. "After all those pancakes I don't know how they have room."

"I would love some. I didn't have all those pancakes." Claire took a bowl and spooned up a strawberry covered with whipped cream. "Nina, what's next? I know you're a technical writer, but the job market's tight now."

"I have feelers out with people I know," Nina said. "I picked up some leads from a friend. I'll take a temporary assignment, just to bring in some money. Anything I can find. I'm flexible."

"I've just had a brainstorm." Claire waved her spoon. "The perfect solution. My assistant had the nerve to get pregnant on me. She goes on maternity leave in a couple of weeks. I don't know how I'm going to manage without her. None of the temps I've seen can handle the job. I need someone who can do more than just answer the phone. Nina, you'd be terrific. I could certainly use your writing and editing skills."

"You could work for Claire while you look for a more permanent job in your field," Gretchen said.

"Who knows, a job might turn up at Dunlin," Claire said. "There's a flock of writers in public affairs. Maybe you could do some temporary assignments for them as well. Although I warn you, I am a challenging boss. Are you interested?"

Nina smiled. "Yes, I am. I'd like to discuss the job, just one-on-one with you."

"Of course. So would I. Let me check my calendar." Claire went into the house, returning a moment later with her purse. She pulled out a smartphone and looked at the display. "Monday is busy. But I have some time at four. Can you come over then?"

"Sure. Four o'clock it is."

Claire's job offer was certainly out-of-the-blue, Lindsey thought. Even if it was temporary, it might be just what Nina needed.

"Lindsey and I are visiting Annabel tomorrow evening," Gretchen said. "Come with us."

"I'm having drinks with someone after work," Claire said. "Then dinner with Mother. She's going to visit Annabel, too. I'll see you at the rehab place."

"Drinks after work, huh? Business or pleasure?" Gretchen asked. "Are you still dating that venture capitalist from Palo Alto?"

"No, I'm seeing a new guy."

Gretchen laughed. "Claire, the only thing that's consistent about you and men is the revolving door. Every time I see you there's a new guy."

"Claire has been consistent, in her fashion. What about the Latin lover? We met him at Mr. Dunlin's birthday party back in the Seventies. Severino…" Lindsey stopped as she recalled the man's last name. "Aragón, right? Annabel's cousin from El Salvador."

13

CONNECTION, OR merely coincidence?

Lindsey reread the transcript of Flor's recording, then Merle Sefton's article about the massacre. Flor referred to the landowner as Don Humberto, no last name. Sefton was more specific. The men who slaughtered the inhabitants of San Blas, left the village in ruins, and took Efraín were a private security force hired by coffee planter Humberto Aragón.

Was this the same genial man Lindsey met at Mr. Dunlin's birthday party in the summer of 1973?

Lindsey pushed away the papers. This morning at Gretchen's brunch, when she'd brought up Severino Aragón, Claire said, "Him? Ancient history." But there *was* history.

Annabel called the party a command performance, having less to do with her father's birthday and more to do with the twenty-fifth anniversary of the company. She and Claire, commanded to attend, swore that if they had to dress up and spend an evening in a Nob Hill hotel with people in suits and fancy dresses, Lindsey and Gretchen must come, too.

Lindsey, feeling like a hick in her thrift shop dress, had been introduced to Humberto Aragón, Mr. Dunlin's brother-in-law from El Salvador. With him were his wife, Nella, and their three offspring. Handsome, mustachioed Severino and his sulky teenaged brother, Roberto, were both dark, with their father's sturdy frame. Cristina, a slender blonde, resembled her mother.

Claire spent the evening flirting with Severino. The relationship came later, after she graduated from Berkeley and obtained her MBA from Stanford. She worked for the Dunlin Corporation, procuring the commodities—coffee, tea, cocoa, spices, nuts—the company imported, processed and sold. At times Claire went to Central America on business, to El Salvador, where she'd encountered Severino again. Their relationship moved past flirtation. Marriage had been mentioned, but nothing ever came of it.

Not surprising. Claire's love affairs waxed and waned, like the inconstant moon, or burned out quickly, going from hot flames to dead ash. Sometimes the embers rekindled, though. Severino was an off-and-on relationship Claire resumed when she had a whim to do so. How ancient was that history? Besides, Claire was friends with Severino's sister Cristina, now married to a politician named Medrano, and the patron of that San Salvador orphanage where Claire first saw Nat, the abandoned toddler.

Sunday morning's warm sun and clear blue sky had disappeared behind the afternoon's scudding gray clouds. Lindsey left her office and went to the kitchen. She filled the teakettle with water and set it on the stove. The doorbell rang. Tess stood on the porch, holding a white banker's box with a lid. Lindsey wondered what sort of snakes lurked beneath the lid.

Nina, who'd been reading the newspaper, jumped up from the sofa. "Tess! It's great to see you. I left a message on your cell phone."

"I was planning to call," Tess said. "Then I decided to show up in person."

"Come in," Lindsey said. "I've just put the kettle on for tea."

Tess set the box on the floor in the entry hall. "It's been ages since I saw you, Nina. I thought you moved to Austin with your boyfriend."

"I moved back. Alone. I'll fill you in later. Sorry to hear about your mom," Nina said. "I hope she's improving."

"She seems to be," Tess said. "She's better, thanks to the therapy. But it's slow and takes a lot out of her. She gets frustrated when her body won't work properly. The aphasia, that slurred speech, is worse when she's stressed."

"Gretchen and I plan to visit her tomorrow evening," Lindsey said. When the teakettle whistled, she went to the kitchen and returned with a tray bearing a teapot of Earl Grey, fragrant with bergamot, and all the accoutrements. She set the tray on the coffee table, poured tea and handed cups to Tess and Nina.

"It's nice of Claire to offer you a temporary job," Tess said. "It could work into something permanent."

"That would be great," Nina said. "Though I don't even know what the job entails. I'm going over to Claire's office tomorrow afternoon to talk about it. Even if I work just a few months while Claire's assistant is on maternity leave, I'll have some money coming in. I could certainly use a paycheck."

"Are you still with the insurance company, Tess?" Lindsey asked. "Your mother said you are an ergonomic evaluator."

"I do workplace assessments," Tess said, "to make sure computer equipment is placed correctly in work stations. In the past, people used typewriters and they didn't think about where they put them. When computers came along, employees plopped them down on existing desks. They still do, which means keyboards and monitors are positioned awkwardly or too high. That leads to eyestrain and repetitive stress injuries in the hands and arms. Then come the workers' compensation cases. I'm the ounce of prevention, so to speak." Tess stirred milk and sugar into her tea, then turned to Nina. "Will you live here for the time being?"

"Temporarily," Nina said. "Until I can get my own place. When I have a paycheck, I can cross that bridge."

"Speaking of crossing the bridge—the Bay Bridge—I have an ulterior motive for asking," Tess said. "My flat in Noe Valley has two bedrooms and my roommate's leaving at the end of June. Maybe you could move in."

Nina brightened. "Great idea. I love that neighborhood."

"So do I," Tess said. "We lived there from the time I was a baby until we moved into the Pacific Heights house. It's an easy commute downtown. I live on Twenty-sixth Street, two blocks west of the J Church streetcar line, near Twenty-fourth, where the shops and restaurants are."

Nina crossed her fingers. "Let's see what happens. I don't even have the temporary job yet, much less a permanent position."

"I'm sure you will. Claire believes in taking care of family. And you are family," Tess said, her blue eyes piercing Lindsey like an X-ray machine. "You four—Mother, Lindsey, Gretchen and Claire—you've been like sisters ever since college."

"We're almost like sisters, too," Nina said. "Twins. We look alike, but you're two weeks older than I am."

Lindsey changed the subject. "Has Sharon set the date for her wedding? And how's your brother?"

"It's an August wedding," Tess said. "Adam graduates from Stanford this spring. He says he's going to do as little as possible this summer, before looking for a job."

"How's your dad holding up?" Nina asked.

"I don't know." Tess paused. "Lindsey, there's something I want to discuss with you."

"I'll give you some privacy." Nina got to her feet, gathered up the newspaper, and left the living room.

"What's in the box?"

"Mother's things," Tess said. "I went to the house this afternoon and took them from her desk. I haven't looked through them yet. I want you to do that, with your researcher's eye. Mother always kept old address books, no matter how tattered they got, full of crossed-out addresses and phone numbers. She said she never knew when she might need to unearth someone's last known whereabouts. There are bits and pieces, and some folders she kept in a hidden drawer I found when I was a little girl. She told me they were keepsakes, special things from the past, but she didn't say what made them special. Mother is secretive. Now I know why. The things in that box are clues to Mother's past. Maybe you'll figure out why they were important, why she kept them. Maybe my father's name is in one of those address books."

"You don't know where this will lead. You may find you don't want to go there."

"But I do know where it will lead, to my real father. I do want to go there."

"Do you know the story of Pandora's Box?" Lindsey asked.

Tess nodded. "The gods gave Pandora a box full of all the world's evils and told her never to open it. But she had a curious nature. She opened the box."

"And let out sorrow and misfortune. Is that what you want to do?"

Tess's eyes glittered, with tears—and anger. "How about the myth that Hal Norwood is my father? He isn't. My whole life is based on a lie."

We all live on lies, Lindsey thought. It's just a matter of degree. "When—or if—you discover the answer, you may not like the truth any better than you like the myth."

"You're saying it's better not to know. How can you make that decision for me?"

"I'm not making it for you," Lindsey said. "But you've chosen to involve me. You've asked for my help, my blessing even. I'm not sure I can give either."

"You've known Mother far longer, far better. I don't think I know her at all. If you won't help me, I'll have to ask Hal myself."

"No. Please don't do that."

"What else am I to do? This is really important to me."

"I will think about it," Lindsey said. "Take the box home with you."

"I'll leave the box here. Just in case."

"I wish you wouldn't. I'm not going to open it."

Tess smiled as she got up from the sofa. "There was something else in Pandora's Box. Hope, the only thing that helps us deal with sorrow and misfortune. That's why we visit Mother, hoping she'll get well and be herself again. So I hope you will open the box."

She's so sure she's right, Lindsey thought as she watched Tess leave.

"What did Tess want?" Nina asked, returning to the living room.

"Something I'm not sure I can give."

"It's about that box, right?"

"Yes. But I can't discuss it. Do you want any dinner?"

Nina shook her head as she gathered cups onto the tray. "After that brunch? I don't think so. If I get hungry I'll fix something."

Lindsey carried the tray into the kitchen and loaded cups into the dishwasher. Then she poured out the remaining tea and washed the pot.

Ironic, to think of helping Tess identify her biological father, while denying her own daughter the same knowledge. Nina had the same anger. It had affected their relationship for years. But it was easier to deal with someone else's demons.

Annabel and Hal were *supposed* to get married. Her father kept pushing eligible bachelors in her path. Hal Norwood, with an MBA from the Wharton School of Business, had the proper credentials. He was personable, attractive, and he worked with the chief financial officer at the Dunlin Corporation. So Hal was what Annabel called the latest designated suitor.

The irony was that after Annabel's initial resistance, she and Hal had dated during the following months. And they did get married in June of 1974. Hastily, seven months before Tess's birth. Lindsey assumed they'd consummated the relationship before the ceremony. It was the Seventies, those heady days of sexual freedom, of doing whatever you felt like, when you felt like doing it, before the chilly specter of AIDS showed up to haunt the Eighties. But there was more to the story. Premarital sex, but not with Hal. Who, then, if not Hal?

At the time, Lindsey had been consumed by her own problems—

her own unexpected pregnancy, the decision to have the baby. She worried about how she'd support herself and the child, whether she'd be able to finish her doctorate and get an assistant professorship at Berkeley. Those had been difficult years. She'd managed to accomplish most of her goals. The Berkeley professorship, long sought, had almost been within her grasp. She'd been short-listed for a position in the History Department. But life intervened. She withdrew from consideration for the Berkeley position, taking instead the Cal Poly job in San Luis Obispo.

At the time, Lindsey told herself she had to do it, to be close to her aging parents in nearby Paso Robles. Her father had begun his slow descent into the tangle of Alzheimer's disease. Then her mother had a heart attack. She'd always felt as though her two brothers hadn't contributed as much time and energy as she had to caring for their parents. That task fell to the sacrificial daughter, as Emma put it when Lindsey informed her aunt of her decision to uproot herself and her child from the place she loved, to return to the place where she grew up.

Lindsey sighed. Road not taken, in life, and in love, wondering what it would have been like if she had followed one path, and not the other. Regrets were pointless, a waste of time. You just have to make the best hand possible out of the cards you're dealt, she told herself.

AT midnight, Clementine and Lola had a growling, hissing altercation at the foot of the bed. Both cats hit the floor and raced out of the bedroom. Lindsey switched on the bedside lamp when she heard something crash to the floor. She threw back the covers, stuck her feet into her slippers, and walked through the kitchen and dining room in the dark, finding her way through habit and the faint illumination from the street lamp outside. An indignant yowl and another crash came from the living room. Lindsey yelped as her shin encountered something. She stumbled, groped her way along the wall, and turned on the overhead light. She'd tripped over the box Tess had left in the hall. It was on its side and the lid was off, spilling the contents onto the floor.

I said I wouldn't open that damned box. Now I have. Is it too late to put everything back?

More hisses from the living room. Lindsey sidestepped the box and switched on another light. Clementine had chased Lola to the top of the shelves that held the TV and stereo equipment, knocking over a lamp and scattering CDs and DVDs to the floor. Lindsey shooed Clementine away, and rescued Lola, who dug her claws into Lindsey's arm and leapt to the floor. Lindsey examined the red scratches on her arm, then set the lamp back in place. In the hall, she scooped spilled items back into Pandora's Box. Something glittered. Glass? No, crystal, smooth on one side, jagged on the other.

Why would Annabel save a piece of broken crystal? And a little silver pineapple, tarnished black?

Lindsey reached under the hall table and picked up two items that had fallen from the box. The first was a snapshot showing two people—Annabel, about eight years old, and an Asian woman, probably in her thirties, arm wrapped protectively around Annabel's shoulder. The second was a book, pages open to the flyleaf, with an inscription in a foreign language.

Deus ex machina. The machine of the gods, in the physical aspect of a couple of quarreling cats and a middle-aged woman stumbling around in the dark.

14

THE CLANG OF a cable car bell always meant San Francisco to him.

The cable car rumbled through the intersection of Powell and Post streets. Rod Llewellyn glanced at his reflection in a store window and was startled to see his grandfather's face looking back at him. The old man was long dead. But Rod was much like him—tall frame, blue eyes, narrow face and sharp nose, hair now more silver than black.

Why should he be surprised? He was past sixty.

The light changed and he crossed Powell, walking down Post

Street. He'd debated about whether he needed the jacket he wore with his open-necked shirt and crisp khaki slacks. With San Francisco you never knew. When he'd arrived yesterday afternoon it had been raining. Now the Dewey monument in the middle of Union Square pointed up at Monday's cloudless blue sky.

He walked past a Dunlin coffee bar and saw people inside. The place wasn't as busy as the Starbucks across the street. The green-and-white logo of the ubiquitous Seattle-based company sprouted all over the city, like toadstools after rain, far outnumbering the red-and-blue Dunlin signs.

Post Street ended at Montgomery Street in the heart of the Financial District. Rod crossed Market Street, weaving through crowds of office workers. He passed a ragged homeless man, muttering to himself, stinking of urine, dirt and booze.

Stevenson Street was more of an alley, sandwiched between Mission and Market streets. Max Brinker waited outside a café called Neetos, his big frame in a gray suit. He was past seventy now. What remained of his hair was white. Max took one final puff on his cigarette, ground it out in a nearby planter, and headed for the café.

"Bad for you, that." Rod indicated the discarded cigarette.

"That's what my doctor says," Max said in his gruff bass. "He feels the same way about red meat. I don't pay any attention to him. Let's get some lunch."

Neetos was a breakfast-and-lunch place catering to office workers from the Financial District and the neighborhood south of Market. The café had one line for take-out, another for patrons wanting tables. The two men queued up in the second line. Rod scanned the menu offerings on the board above the counter. Max didn't bother. When he got to the head of the line he ordered a bacon cheeseburger, rare, with grilled onions, fries, and a soda. Rod opted for a bowl of chicken-and-sausage gumbo.

"Soup. That's how you stay so damn skinny." Max led the way to a table at the back.

Rod smiled. "All in the genes. Tall and thin, that's my lot."

"Crowded in here most of the time," Max said as they sat down and unloaded their trays. "The food's good. That's why it's busy."

"Away from your usual track, isn't it?" Rod flashed a good-humored grin. "I thought you favored Sam's."

"Thank God it's still there. Sam's is old San Francisco. When I got here in nineteen sixty this town was something, but not anymore. It's sure as hell changed, and not for the better. The whole city's filthy. It would take a month of Sundays to clean the grime off the pavement. Beggars everywhere, sleeping in doorways, hands out on street corners. The mayor and the Board of Supervisors posture and make speeches. In the meantime, people have to step over crap in the streets. *Bon appétit.*" Max picked up his cheeseburger. "Now to business. Tell me what you're going to tell the board next week."

Rod spooned up soup. "Hurricanes in Mexico and Central America last year caused a hell of a lot of damage to coffee plantations. The crop loss is significant."

"Weather and politics," Max said. "If it's not storms or drought, it's war and some damn politician with his hand out."

As they ate their lunch, they talked more about weather, war, and politics, and their volatile effect on tea in Sri Lanka, coffee in Kenya and the cashew crop in Brazil. When Rod finished his soup, he took a sip of his iced tea and set down the glass.

"Now Max, you didn't need to hear that report today. Yes, you're the chief operations officer and I'm the senior vice president who buys product and ships it to the States. But you asked me to come to San Francisco early. Then you called me last night and set up this lunch date in a restaurant south of Market where it's unlikely we'll be seen together. Why?"

Max chuckled and wiped his hands on a napkin. "You were always sharp. That's why I hired you, way back when."

A smile played at the corners of Rod's mouth. "I thought you hired me because of my youth, strength, and manly good looks."

"Well, that, too." Max laughed, then his face turned serious. "I trust you."

"I'm glad you have such faith in me."

"I always have." Max reached for his soda. "You've been away from San Francisco a long time. It's time you came home."

"Home?" Rod shrugged. "Like the song says, anywhere I hang

my hat is home. I have an apartment in Houston but I might as well move into the warehouse at the port. I spend most of my time there, when I'm in town. The rest of the time I live in hotel rooms all over the world. You want me to come back to work at corporate head-quarters?"

"I need you," Max said. "Chuck Caldwell is retiring."

"I knew he was thinking about it," Rod said. Caldwell was ex-ecutive vice president of operations, Rod's immediate superior, and a member of the Dunlin board of directors. "But I didn't know he'd made up his mind. He's not that much older than I am."

"He says he wants to enjoy his retirement while he's still young enough," Max said. "Retirement, hell. If I retired, I'd be bored out of my frigging mind. I've been working too long to sit around twiddling my damn thumbs."

Rod smiled at the thought of Max ever retiring. Leisure would never suit the old man. "You'll keep working until they carry you out."

"Damn straight," Max said, a fierce expression on his wrinkled face.

"When is Chuck retiring?" There's more to this, Rod thought.

"It's official at the end of the month," Max said. "The board of directors will vote on his replacement at the board meeting on Wednesday of next week. If I have anything to say about it, that will be you. I want you on the board."

Rod sat back in his chair. "Me? You say you need me. Why? What's going on?"

"Claire's up to something."

"Claire." Rod sipped his tea. It didn't alleviate the distaste he always felt when he heard Claire Megarris's name. "That means trou-ble."

"Right. She doesn't like me. The feeling's mutual," Max said. "She thinks I'm an old fart. You bet I am. I've been with the company a long time. I had a great deal of respect and admiration for George Dunlin. He built this company into what it is today, one of the big-gest specialty food brokerages in the country. I won't let her grind his legacy into the ground."

"You saved George's life, or so the story goes."

"I was doing a hitch in the Army," Max said. "George was in Nicaragua buying coffee. Nineteen fifty-nine, when the Somozas were in power. My outfit was on a joint operations exercise teaching the local military how to behave like soldiers instead of thugs—not that it took. We were out at some godforsaken coffee plantation and the shooting started. I knocked George down a second before one of those slugs hit the wall where he'd been standing. He'd have been dead and we wouldn't be sitting here listening to me tell the tale."

"So he hired you."

Max nodded. "George was grateful. He never was very demonstrative, but he shook my hand and told me to come see him when my hitch was up, said there'd be a job waiting for me. I'd already decided I didn't want to make the army a career. When I got out of the service the next year I came to San Francisco and took him up on his offer. He made me his personal assistant. Through the years I had my fingers in lots of pies. Security, then overseeing all the administrative operations at corporate. That's how I wound up as chief operations officer, even if I don't know beans about coffee. George trusted me the way I trust you. I consider you my protégé, Rod. And a friend."

"Likewise, on the friend part." Rod was touched by Max's faith in him. He liked Max, and always had. Once you got used to the old man's abrasive exterior, he had a good heart. "What's Claire planning? Or do you know?"

"Oh, I know." Anger reddened Max's face. "Claire is planning an internal takeover of Dunlin Corporation."

Rod frowned. "Can she do it?"

"She can if she packs the board, since Dunlin's a privately held corporation. George never would go public, never wanted shareholders mucking around in company decisions. No stock, so Claire can't buy herself a majority share. But she can control the board if she has the votes."

"There are seven people on the board," Rod said. "Four internal, three from outside. So she needs four votes. Lots of companies have bigger boards. More votes needed for a majority."

"George believed in keeping the board small, for better control.

That worked to his advantage in the past. Unfortunately, now it works to Claire's advantage. She's got three votes and she's working on the fourth." Max ticked off the numbers on his thick fingers. "The company directors are Hal as chief executive officer, me as chief operations officer, and two executive vice presidents, Caldwell and Claire. The outsiders are the general counsel, who's a lawyer from that firm where we farm out the legal work, and two family members."

"Annabel Norwood and Rebecca Megarris," Rod said.

"Right," Max said. "Rebecca will back her daughter no matter what. Annabel would back Hal, except she's incapacitated because of that stroke. Hal holds her proxy. Until last year the general counsel was Bert Farnsworth, an old fart like me. He and I agreed on things. I could count on his vote. Then in October he got hit by a car."

Rod shook his head. "And died in January. Unfortunate accident."

"Unfortunate is right. According to the bylaws, the board can replace a member who's incapacitated for more than eight weeks. Claire started agitating to replace Farnsworth as soon as we hit that mark. We had to pick a new general counsel. And she had just the candidate, a lawyer in Farnsworth's firm, her pal from Stanford. Marissa Tybalt." Max spat the words out as though they tasted bad. "Four women on the board, three of 'em in Claire's camp. I argue with some half-assed idea Claire proposes, I'm a hidebound old sexist."

Rod chuckled. "Max, you *are* a hidebound old sexist."

"Damn right I am. So was George. Claire calls me a dinosaur."

"You've never liked her," Rod said. "I remember that tussle over the coffee bars."

"Goddamn coffee bars are losing money hand over fist," Max snarled. "I said they would. I argued until I was blue in the face, but Claire ramrodded it through the board. She's got brass balls, but she's not as bright as she thinks. We import commodities. We process, package and sell them wholesale to restaurants and grocery stores. Getting into retail was a mistake. Starbucks owns that market. Claire won't listen to reason. Those coffee bars were her idea, and she doesn't care how much red ink the company bleeds to keep them going."

"Why do you figure she's planning a board takeover? Something she did?"

"No single incident," Max said. "A pattern of behavior, one that smells like empire-building. She moved into a high-level position way too fast, because she's family. Now she's invading other people's turf. The coffee bars should rightly be an operations project, not hers. She convinced the board to move public affairs from admin to marketing, so now she controls that, too. She gets involved in hiring and human resources, which is supposed to be the bailiwick of the VP for admin, who just lets Claire meddle. Then Claire gets Tybalt elected general counsel. She's got three votes on that board of directors— hers, her mother's and Tybalt's. Caldwell's retirement is her chance to make it four."

"She must have her own candidate," Rod said.

"Graham from Marketing. One of her bright young protégés. Wouldn't be surprised if she's sleeping with him."

"That's the sort of remark that gets you the sexist label."

"Except in Claire's case, I'm probably right," Max said. "She's a manipulative, predatory bitch. The only reason she's in a high-level position is because she's a relative. She's after power. It's all about her."

"So you want to throw me into the lion's den. Thanks a lot, Max."

"You're the logical choice. Someone who goes out in the field and gets his hands dirty. You're a senior vice president, with the company more than thirty years."

"How does Hal feel about all this?" Rod asked.

"I mentioned your name and he reacted favorably. He likes you."

"But he hasn't given his whole-hearted support."

"Claire is lobbying hard for her candidate. Besides, Hal has a lot on his mind."

"Annabel's stroke."

"Yeah. Can't blame him, with her sick like that. He's distracted. Claire sees an opportunity and she's moving in. Hal's an easygoing guy, sometimes too much so. Claire takes advantage of that. So does her mother." Max narrowed his eyes. "They're a pair, those two. Cut from the same cloth."

"You don't like Rebecca Megarris either. How long has she been a director?"

"Since 'sixty-one," Max said. "She'd been lobbying George for a board seat ever since her husband, Lawrence, died. She figured she was entitled to his director slot and a share of the company, too, since her husband started it."

"I thought he and George both started it, after World War Two."

Max shook his head. "Not exactly. Lawrence started importing coffee after the war. But he was no businessman. That's why he brought in George, who was an excellent businessman. George built up the company under his own name during the Fifties, expanding the product lines. Lawrence, on the other hand, was fond of booze. He sucked up the sauce, came to work hungover, or drunk. George put up with it for a while, but when Lawrence started drinking at the office, George bought him out. Lawrence drank himself to death. George put most of Lawrence's payoff money in Rebecca's hands and a trust for Claire, so they'd be taken care of. But Rebecca figured George owed her a directorship. You need to know this stuff if you're going to be on the board."

"I haven't agreed to it yet," Rod said. "Can you get me elected? Claire got Marissa Tybalt elected general counsel over your objections."

"Hal will vote with me," Max said. "With Annabel's proxy that's three."

"And Claire's got three. What about the fourth vote?"

"Caldwell himself. The way the bylaws are set up, he votes on a replacement director before his resignation is effective. He likes you. I've already got him convinced you're the man for the job. And you are. I know that, and so do you. Are you with me?"

Rod thought about it. Max had always done well by him. "Seeing as it's you who's asking, Max, yes. But I won't be in your pocket. I have an independent streak of my own."

"Fair enough." Max grinned. "I told you when I hired you there would be a future for you with the company. In the meantime, there's a rumor going around that the Dunlin Building and the south-of-Market warehouse are for sale. They're not. I want to know where that rumor originated."

"I'll see what I can find out."

As Max headed back to the Dunlin Building, Rod walked to Grant Street, where massive pillars bracketed the street, the gates to Chinatown, a neighborhood he'd often explored when he first came to San Francisco. That was a long time ago. Half his life. Good years, for the most part, spent on the Dunlin Corporation payroll. He'd done well, financially and professionally—promotions, raises, responsibilities, respect. Yet he hadn't put down any roots in his private life. No wife, no children. He lived in apartments or hotels, without so much as a cat for companionship. This lack of personal ties sometimes weighed on him. He always thought that eventually he'd get married and have a family. But eventually never came.

Regrets... Waste of time to think about that now. He'd been dealt a hand of solitaire, and he'd played his cards as well as he could. He'd come a long way and Max Brinker had set him on the path to where he was now.

He walked up Grant to California Street and saw the cable car rumbling through the intersection, down the hill toward the bay. The bell clanged, bringing memories.

15

San Francisco, California, February 1974

THE GRIPMAN CLANGED the bell as the California Street cable car moved up the steep slope toward Nob Hill. Rod Llewellyn sipped coffee and reread his mother's letter. His grandfather had died. The old man had lived a full life, but Rod was sorry he wouldn't hear Granddad's voice again, except in his head.

His grandfather's passing had Rod thinking about the future. Was he meant to be a rambler and rover all his life?

He could stay in San Francisco, put down roots. He liked his one-bedroom flat above an Italian delicatessen in North Beach, a base for his exploration of the city. He read about its history and sampled its views and food. Coffee and pasta in North Beach, then up to Chinatown, where he filled up on the little dumplings called *dim sum* and poked through shops looking for exotic and inexpensive gifts for his family. At Fisherman's Wharf he watched tourists as he ate crab cocktails or freshly baked sourdough bread. And he rode the cable cars, marveling at the view as the car descended toward the bay. At Ocean Beach he walked the long sandy stretch where the land ended, with San Francisco spread out at the edge of the continent and nothing to the west but the vast gray expanse of the Pacific Ocean.

When he'd turned eighteen there were no jobs in the little mountain town where he was born and grew up. He left, moving from city to city, job to job. He'd landed in New York City first. But he wanted to see more of the country, so he caught a train to Philadelphia. From there he headed west—Pittsburgh, Detroit, Chicago, then Denver and Los Angeles. He was willing to do any kind of work as long as it suited him. He moved on when he got restless.

He arrived in San Francisco in September 1973, checked into a cheap downtown hotel, and scanned the classified ads, applying for any job that looked like a good prospect. He soon found work as a security guard at the Wells Fargo Bank here in the Financial District. He'd worked security before, most recently in Los Angeles. Patrolling the bank lobby was easy and the pay was good. He wasn't sure if this was permanent. Pleasant as the city was, he might just be a rambler and a rover.

His coffee break was over. He tossed the cup into a nearby trash can and slipped his mother's letter back into his pocket. The wind from the bay was damp and cool, flavored with salt and brine. He was glad it was Friday, a weekend ahead of him. At the bank entrance he held open the door for a man he recognized as a regular customer.

"Thanks," the man said. "Llewellyn, isn't it?"

"Yes," Rod said, surprised. "How did you know?"

"I make it my business to know what's going on around me, and who's doing it."

The man was older than Rod, broad-shouldered and well-dressed, with dark brown hair and a pair of hazel eyes that didn't miss much.

When he'd finished his business at the teller window, he walked to-ward Rod and handed him a business card. "I'm Max Brinker. How much do they pay you to watch the lobby? If you don't mind my asking."

"I don't mind." Rod named the figure. Brinker looked like he had a proposition to make and Rod was always open to an opportunity.

"I've got a job for you. It's a bit unusual, but I think you'd be good at it. I'm prepared to offer a better salary." Brinker glanced at his watch. "Do you go to lunch at noon? Good. Come to my office, in the Dunlin headquarters across the street."

The Dunlin Building at the corner of California and Montgom-ery rose six stories, with a façade of rosy brown brick and ornate cor-nices around the windows and along the roof lines. It wasn't as tall as some of the neighboring buildings but it had an elegance those postwar skyscrapers lacked, a style harking back to the Art Moderne Twenties.

The double front doors were edged in bronze and the marble tile on the lobby floor was shot with white and brown. Bronze also framed interior doors, display cases, and the elevators at the rear of the lobby. Rod didn't know anything about the company or its busi-ness, but judging from the photographs displayed on the walls, it had something to do with coffee and tea.

The counter in front of the elevators was staffed by a uniformed security guard and a woman with a headset over her gray hair. She answered the phone in a perky voice that seemed at odds with her matronly appearance. "Good afternoon, Dunlin Corporation. How may I direct your call?"

Rod approached the guard. "Rod Llewellyn to see Mr. Brinker. He's expecting me."

The guard checked Rod's name against a list. Then he nodded, handing Rod a clipboard and a pen. Rod signed in. "Security, fifth floor. Go left when you get off the elevator."

The corner office had a view of the bay, looking north towards Alcatraz. After Rod sat down, the older man settled into the worn leather chair behind his desk. "Tell me about yourself. Where you're from, where you worked before the bank." After Rod did so, Brinker said, "You strike me as a young man who intends to get somewhere in this world. If you take this job, and do it well, there's a good chance of something else with the company. Does that interest you?"

"Very much," Rod said.

"This assignment is unusual, as I told you earlier. Hear me out before you give an answer." Brinker described the job.

Rod frowned. "You want me to baby-sit a bunch of college girls?"

Brinker laughed. "That's what I thought you'd say. I noticed you when you started working at the bank, so I've had my eye on you for some time now, thinking I'd bring you on board if the right assignment came along. This is it. I need someone who can blend into that Berkeley scene. You're young enough to be a college student yourself. With some modifications in your appearance you'll fit right in."

"These girls are past eighteen, old enough to look after themselves."

"Normally I'd agree with you," Brinker said. "But these aren't normal times. Berkeley's not a normal place. You've heard about the Hearst kidnapping?"

As though anyone could escape the front-page headlines in the newspapers, the lead story on local television and radio stations. First came the sensational Monday night kidnapping. Then came the dramatic message from the kidnappers, evidently the same people who'd murdered a school official in Oakland the previous November. They called themselves the Symbionese Liberation Army and referred to their captive, Patricia Hearst, as a prisoner of war.

"George Dunlin, the man who owns this company, is a wealthy man," Brinker said. "He's had threats against him in the past. This Hearst kidnapping hits close to home. He's a widower, with a daughter named Annabel. She and her cousin Claire are seniors at the university. With these crackpots kidnapping the children of wealthy people, he's concerned that his daughter and niece might be targets. He'd like them to leave school for a while. But they graduate at the end of the semester and don't want to interrupt their last term. However, they are spooked by this Hearst business. It happened close by and one of Annabel's housemates witnessed the kidnapping."

"Where do they live?" Rod asked. "Who owns the property?"

"Hillegass Street, south of campus," Brinker said. "When Annabel started college she wanted to live in Berkeley, near the campus, rather than commute from San Francisco. Mr. Dunlin bought this house with four flats. Annabel lives on the first floor, Claire on the second. As for the other two apartments, Annabel decides who lives there, but I do background checks on the renters."

This Dunlin fellow sounded like a man who liked to control everyone and everything, Rod thought. "He doesn't leave anything to chance, does he?"

"No, he doesn't," Brinker said. "Neither do I. Ever since Annabel and her cousin Claire started college, I've had two guards keeping an eye on them, from a rooming house next door. I'm doubling that to four guards, and changing the routine. The guards will continue to watch the house. They'll also escort Annabel and Claire everywhere they go. I need people who'll look inconspicuous in a classroom or on Telegraph Avenue. I also need someone who knows how to use a gun. Which you do, based on your job history. You had a carry permit when you worked that warehouse security job in Los Angeles."

"Yes, I know how to use a gun. You've already done a background check on me?"

Brinker smiled. "Of course. Still interested?"

Rod considered. Now that Brinker had explained the situation, the job made sense. Rod understood the reason for haste and the need for someone who would blend into the Berkeley scene. Brinker was focused, thorough. He knew exactly who and what he wanted. Rod liked that. Come right down to it, he liked Brinker.

"Count me in," Rod said. "When do I start?"

"Now," Brinker said. "I need you in Berkeley tomorrow. Quit the bank job, come back over here and we'll get things started."

When Rod returned to the Dunlin Building later that afternoon, Brinker's secretary had the paperwork waiting for him. He filled out the forms making him an employee of the Dunlin Corporation. His old permit had expired, so he filled out a new application to carry a concealed weapon. Then he was photographed and fingerprinted. "I'll use some of my contacts in Sacramento to expedite this permit," Brinker said, handing Rod his brand-new employee identification card. "Now go over to the Haight and find some clothes. And don't shave."

"I look like a damned convict with stubble. And it itches."

Brinker chuckled. "Come back tomorrow morning. It's Saturday but I'll be here at eight to brief you. And come in character. I want to see how you look before you go to Berkeley."

Rod caught a bus to the Haight-Ashbury neighborhood, east of Golden Gate Park. He ate a bowl of soup in a café, watching people. Then he prowled through the shops, buying clothes and accessories, all the while studying people on the street, how they moved and talked, then finally emulating them, trying on different roles. Like a chameleon on a wall, he took on the protective coloration of those around him.

When he showed up at the Dunlin Building the next morning, he walked with a cocky don't-give-a-shit slouch, as though he had a chip on his shoulder. He'd dragged his fingers through his thick black hair instead of combing it, and stubble prickled his skin. He wore faded, patched blue jeans and an old tie-dyed T-shirt. Scuffed leather boots and a soft leather jacket decorated with fringe and political buttons finished his ensemble. He looked so disreputable the security guard wouldn't admit him to the lobby until Rod flashed his employee ID.

"Perfect," Brinker said when Rod walked into his office. He poured two cups of coffee from the carafe on his desk. "There are three other men on the job. Carl Axelrod, Tom Pulaski and Mike Standish. I'm teaming you with Carl. I've arranged for a car. Go over to Berkeley this morning, take a look at the house, and meet Carl. Here's what you need to know."

Rod opened the file folder. It contained typed pages on the right and a five-by-seven-inch color photograph clipped to the left. The photo, an enlargement made from a snapshot, showed four young women, two blondes and two brunettes, standing on the deck of a sailboat, in shorts, T-shirts and tennis shoes, arms linked as they posed for the camera. On the bottom border of the photograph, someone had inked a date and sets of initials.

"This is Annabel Dunlin." Brinker pointed at the brunette on the right. A pretty girl, Rod thought, with brown hair combed back from her forehead and falling to her shoulders. She was medium height, about five-six, he guessed, slender, with a good figure, nipped in at the waist and curving gently where it should. She looked quiet and self-contained.

"Claire Megarris, Annabel's cousin." Brinker indicated the young woman with short blond hair, head tilted to one side as she smiled. "Her mother is Mr. Dunlin's sister, married to Mr. Dunlin's late partner."

"The reports on the others are in the folder." Brinker pointed at the woman with long sandy curls. "Gretchen Kohl, first-year graduate student in sociology, born and raised in Oakland. She moved into the house in the summer of nineteen seventy-one. A couple of arrests for protests. She almost didn't make the cut after Mr. Dunlin saw the report, but Annabel really likes her."

Brinker's finger moved to the fourth woman in the photograph, her long dark hair tied back in a ponytail, strands escaping and curling around her ears, brown eyes looking straight at the camera. "Lindsey Page, from Paso Robles, working on her Ph.D. in history. She moved into the house in June of 'seventy-two. She was on Benvenue Street Monday night and saw those thugs kidnap Miss Hearst. She got her bachelor's and master's down at UC Santa Barbara. They've had their share of radical activity on that campus. But Lindsey was too busy studying and working to get involved."

Suddenly Rod felt like a voyeur peeping through a keyhole. Four young women, a pleasant-looking group of friends sharing a house near the university, out for a sail on a sunny summer day when this photo was taken. Now he knew something about each of them. But they didn't even know he existed. In a short time they would, but he'd be just a presence, outside the door, off to the side, watching.

Rod left Brinker's office and walked to a garage south of Market Street. He picked up a Chevy Impala, an older model with an engine that belied its beat-up exterior, and drove across the Bay Bridge to Berkeley, where his future waited.

16

THE CONVALESCENT HOSPITAL where Annabel was in rehab was north of Golden Gate Park, in a mixed-use neighborhood of shops, offices and apartments. The hospital was expanding, a new wing under construction, pushing deep into the next lot to form an L. The driveway slanting down to the building's basement level promised much-needed parking. The construction workers had finished for the day, leaving the site secured by a high chain-link fence and a locked gate.

Gretchen dropped Lindsey off at the curb in front of the hospital and went in search of street parking. Lindsey glanced at the park's canopy of trees. She was a few blocks and a lifetime away from Hippie Hill and the Haight. Decades had passed since Monterey and the Summer of Love.

In June 1967, she and two friends, newly graduated from high school, crammed themselves into Lindsey's green VW, accompanied by sleeping bags, a cooler of provisions, and the worried admonitions of Lindsey's mother. They drove over to the coast and up the winding, cliff-hugging curl of Highway 1 to Monterey and the International Pop Festival. Excited about the lineup of bands, they'd gotten tickets soon after news of the festival went out. In Monterey they joined the throng of concertgoers, reveling in the music for three days.

After the festival ended, Lindsey and her companions had continued their journey north, to San Francisco. Her cousin, a student at the University of San Francisco, lived on Fulton Street near Golden Gate Park. The young women camped out in his living room while they spent the next week exploring their newfound freedom and the terrain of the Summer of Love. Lindsey still had photos of that time, in a box of things she kept telling herself she should toss. A box like Annabel's, the one Tess had delivered the day before.

On the fifth floor, a thick sheet of clear plastic covered the fire door between the existing building and the new wing, intended to keep out construction dust and noise. The door to Annabel's room was open. Hal sat next to the bed, holding his wife's hand, stroking it tenderly with gentle fingers, talking to her in a low voice that only he and Annabel could hear, sharing the intimacy of a long marriage. They'd raised three children, Lindsey thought, even if Tess wasn't Hal's biological child. Some kind of glue held them together all these years—love or habit, perhaps, an emotional connection, certainly the children.

Hal and Annabel had dated sporadically during the year between their meeting and their wedding. But Lindsey had never seen any sign that Annabel loved him. She'd been shocked to learn that Annabel was going to marry the designated suitor.

What happened? Lindsey thought, looking at them now. Why did you marry him? Did I misread the signals? Was it because he loved you all along and wore down your resistance? Because you weren't strong enough to reject the staid, structured life your domineering father had planned for you? Because you were pregnant and you needed a nice, presentable husband, someone who was already there, ready and waiting?

Hal looked tired. The handsome young man was now in his sixties. His body had thickened and lines crisscrossed his face. Gray hair had overtaken brown. He greeted Lindsey. Then Gretchen bustled into the room, crowing about finding a parking place down the block. "You look exhausted," Gretchen told him. "I hope you're not going to the office every day."

"I have to be there," he said. "The quarterly board meeting's coming up. It's hard to concentrate while I'm worrying about Annabel. I've got people covering for me. Max, of course."

"And Claire," Gretchen said. "You can always count on her to watch your back."

"She's been very supportive." Hal smiled. "She looks after things, whether at the office or out in the field, when we're traveling."

"You go on business trips," Lindsey said, as Gretchen moved to Annabel's bed.

"All the time," he said. "Conventions, trade shows, and trips overseas. Before I took over as CEO and Claire became the head of marketing, we traveled a lot, visiting growers and brokers. Tea in India, cocoa in Africa, and coffee all over the map."

"Growers like the Aragóns," Lindsey said. "Annabel's relations in El Salvador."

Hal nodded. "We'd always go to their estate. On these trips we'd visit the plantations to look at crops and processing plants. Going out to the countryside got scary in El Salvador back in the Eighties, during the civil war. Fortunately that's over. Humberto's dead now. Severino runs the estate. He's gone into politics, too. Cristina and her husband live in San Salvador. Roberto has a cattle ranch. I haven't done much traveling lately. I'd rather stay home with my family and leave the traveling to Claire. I don't think I've been to El Salvador since 'eighty-nine, the year George died."

The same year Claire saw Nat in the orphanage, Lindsey thought, and facilitated his adoption. Now she wondered if Hal had accompanied Claire on that trip.

"Here are my girls." Hal smiled as the two Norwood daughters appeared in the hallway. Sharon flung her arms around her father, while Tess hung back, her doubts about Hal visible to Lindsey's eyes.

Lindsey examined the two young women, gauging differences and similarities, looking for clues. Both had dark brown hair and blue eyes, as did Hal and Annabel. Lindsey saw echoes of Hal in Sharon's face. Tess looked more like Annabel, with her oval face and small, sculpted features. Maybe she also looked like the man who was her biological father, Lindsey thought. But who?

Tess walked to the bed, leaned over and kissed her mother's forehead, then said hello to Gretchen. Then she drew Lindsey out to the hallway. "Have you given any more thought to my request?" Tess asked, her voice low.

Pandora's Box, Lindsey thought. Curious things had spilled out the night before. "Strange as it sounds, I'd like to talk it over with your mother first."

"I talk to her all the time," Tess said. "I even asked her who my father was. She didn't answer. I don't know if it was because she doesn't want to, or because of the aphasia. When she gets stressed, it's hard to understand her. Go ahead and ask her, if it makes you feel better. But I hope you'll help me."

The elevator door opened and Nina stepped out. Lindsey wasn't sure her daughter even owned a skirt these days, but Nina had dressed up for her meeting with Claire, wearing navy blue slacks, an ivory shirt, and a tweed blazer she'd borrowed from her mother. Despite the purple streak in her hair she wouldn't look out of place in the Financial District. Nina smiled as she greeted her mother. "I got the job. Claire wants me to start next week, after you and I come back from Ashland, so I'll learn the ropes before her assistant goes on maternity leave."

"That's good news." Lindsey was glad to hear the cheerful note in her daughter's voice.

"Terrific," Tess said. "My roommate's leaving earlier than planned, end of April."

"I won't see a paycheck until the first of May," Nina said. "It'll be a short one at that."

Lindsey sighed, mostly for effect. "I imagine the First National Bank of Mom can help with rent, just to get you started."

"Thanks, Mom," Nina said with a grin.

"If it's really what you want to do." Lindsey added a few notes of motherly caution. "You haven't even looked at the flat yet. And this job is temporary. Claire's assistant will be back from maternity leave in four months."

"So come Labor Day I'll look for another job," Nina said. "But this gives me four months to tune up my résumé and make some contacts. I've been a tech writer and a project manager, but if an admin assistant job gets my toe in the door, that's okay. Besides, Claire says if she likes my work she'll keep her eyes peeled for a more permanent slot at Dunlin."

"I'm sure she will," Gretchen said from the doorway. "Claire will find something. She's on top of everything."

Lindsey visualized Claire as puppeteer, pulling the strings. She liked to be in charge, in control. Most of the time she was subtle about it. You didn't know Claire was running the show until she reminded you by tugging on the cords.

"Want to look at the flat tomorrow?" Tess asked. "Meet me at my office, we'll go to Noe Valley and I can show you the place. Then we'll have dinner."

"Tomorrow works," Nina said. "Where's your office?"

The elevator door opened again, and Rebecca Megarris walked toward them. Annabel's aunt was in her eighties, her white hair lacquered into submission. On this April evening she wore a mauve linen suit with a matching hat. She removed her gloves and tucked them into her handbag as she greeted Tess. "How is your mother, dear?"

"Improving every day," Tess said.

Mrs. Megarris sniffed. "I'll be the judge of that. Where's Claire? We're having dinner tonight. I must say, she's so busy at work I hardly see her."

"I saw her earlier this afternoon," Nina said. "She had another meeting afterwards. I imagine she's on her way."

"Nina? I thought you were in Texas. I can't keep up with you young people. So many changes." Mrs. Megarris walked into Annabel's room and gave her niece a critical once-over. "She looks the same. I'll have to speak to the doctor."

That was just like Mrs. Megarris, the grande dame, sure her words to the doctor would immediately improve Annabel's condition, like words to a sales clerk would improve the service. How Annabel joked about her bossy aunt, with her pretensions and imperious ways. Even now, Annabel regarded her aunt with amusement and exasperation. That's the old Annabel, Lindsey thought, the one I want to see again. What if this is all a colossal joke? What if everything is all right and Annabel is really just fine, having a vacation from all of us, laughing inside at all our concerns, alarms and diversions?

Mrs. Megarris returned to the corridor a few minutes later, chatting with Hal. Lindsey and Gretchen stayed with Annabel. Gretchen did most of the talking. Lindsey didn't say much, chiming in at the appropriate times, as the others moved in and out of the room. Visiting Annabel wasn't so much about seeing the patient as it was gathering at a village square, a time for the people in Annabel's life to check in with one another.

When Claire arrived, she kissed her mother and said, "Sorry I'm late. Business meeting. Getting my ducks in a row before the board meeting next week." Her short blond hair looked tousled, her face flushed, and her eyes were bright with some sort of excitement. She stepped into Annabel's room, waved at her cousin, then took Hal's arm. "I've been trying to catch a moment with you all day. I have the perfect candidate for Caldwell's position on the board."

Hal shook his head. "This isn't the time or place to talk business. Right now I'm taking my girls to dinner." He put his arms around Sharon and Tess. Sharon leaned into his embrace, but Tess held back, emotions warring on her face.

Annoyance flickered over Claire's face. Then she smiled. "Of course. Tomorrow at the office. Mother and I have dinner plans, too. We should be going." She and Mrs. Megarris walked toward the elevator.

"We should go," Gretchen told Lindsey. "Riding back with us, Nina?"

"Sure. But I need to find the rest room."

"Me, too," Tess said. "It's down this way."

"Let me say good-bye to Annabel." Lindsey left Gretchen in the hallway, talking with Hal and Sharon. Back in Annabel's room she sat down in the chair next to the bed.

"Lindsey," Annabel said. "Alone at last."

"Yes, it was a bit crowded in here."

"I appreciate the company. Hope to go home soon."

"I must talk with you," Lindsey said. "I'll be quick about it, before we get interrupted. Tess knows Hal isn't her father. She asked me to help her find out who her father is."

"I know. She told me."

"That's the kind of conversation a daughter should have with her mother."

"You haven't."

"No, I haven't," Lindsey admitted. "Maybe now I will. How can I answer Tess's questions if I don't do the same for my own daughter?"

"Too hard for me to explain right now." Annabel slurred her words as she spoke. Maybe she was tired. Or, as Tess had said earlier, stress made the aphasia worse.

Lindsey took Annabel's hand. "Yesterday Tess brought me a box of your things. Clues, she said, to help me find out about her father.

I told her I wasn't going to open it but last night I knocked over the box and things came tumbling out. Like Pandora's Box. I didn't mean to invade your privacy. But I couldn't stop myself from looking. There were all sorts of things you saved because they were important to you. Old address books and datebooks. Letters. A picture of you and an Asian woman, taken back when you were a little girl. A silver pineapple and a piece of crystal. I don't know why you kept those, but they must have some meaning for you."

Annabel squeezed Lindsey's hand, surprisingly strong. "Go ahead and look. Doesn't matter now. Please do me a favor."

"I'll do anything for you, you know that."

"Lily." Then Annabel said, almost as an afterthought, "Shoe."

"Shoe?" Lindsey glanced down at her own footwear. Then she got it. "Lily. The Asian woman in the picture. Her last name is Shu?"

"Yes. Call Lily. She doesn't know about the stroke, or where I am."

"Of course I'll call her," Lindsey said. "Her number's in the address books?" Annabel nodded. "How do you spell her last name?"

But before Annabel could answer, Tess and Nina returned from the rest room, and an orderly arrived with Annabel's dinner.

17

ON TUESDAY, AS SHE HAD every week for two months, Lindsey met Flor Cooper in a *panadería* on Fruitvale Avenue. They found a table in the corner, sipped coffee and nibbled on pastries as Flor did needlework. Music came from a CD player behind the counter, *corridos*, traditional Mexican ballads. A woman sang in Spanish, her alto voice counterpoint to a simple melody plucked on the strings of a guitar, a sad little waltz in three-quarter time. The song was called "*La Llorona*," the weeping woman, and it told the story of a woman who wandered and wailed, mourning the loss of her children.

Flor finished stitching a petal on the pillowcase she was embroidering, then carefully folded the fabric over the hoop. She put the needlework into the tote bag at her feet and pulled out the photograph taken in front of the church in the now-dead village of San Blas, showing Flor, her first husband, and Efraín, the child who'd been taken from her. She pointed at the boy. "You see how much he looks like his father. When I saw Efraín at the Farmers Market, I saw Atenacio at the same age. He was such a strong, handsome boy. *Mi corazón, mi precioso.*"

But Efraín Guzmán was now Nat Segal, the adopted son of Doug and Gretchen Segal. Lindsey found it difficult to acknowledge the fact. No good deed, she thought, goes unpunished. Why did I agree to go to the Farmers Market with Flor? But it was too late now to take back what she'd seen with her own eyes.

"Now that I have found Efraín," Flor said, "after all these years, my son will return to me. But this will be difficult. He believes his real mother and father are dead. He has been adopted. He was near the high school and he wore a T-shirt that said Berkeley High, so he probably goes to school there. I must find out what name he has now, and where he lives. But if I go to the school, I'm sure they won't tell me what I need to know. Privacy is a good thing, but in this case I need to get around it. Please, do you have ideas? What should I do?"

"I don't know," Lindsey said.

Flor looked at her curiously, as though she could see the struggle going on inside Lindsey's head. "Then I will go to the Farmers Market again on Saturday. If Efraín is there, I will follow him home and find out where he lives and what his name is now."

Lindsey shook her head. "You should wait."

"Wait? Why? I've waited so long. I can't wait any longer. I never gave up hoping I would find Efraín, and now I have. I want my son. I want to hold him in my arms."

"But he doesn't know you're his mother," Lindsey said. "As you say, he was adopted. He has different parents now. He may not remember you, or what happened in the village."

Flor conceded this with a nod. "That's possible. He was very young. Perhaps the mind blocks out terrible things seen by children, like his father's murder. For his sake, I hope so. What is the best way to approach this?"

"I'm going to Ashland on Thursday," Lindsey said. "To the

Oregon Shakespeare Festival. Merle Sefton, the reporter, teaches at the university up there. I will talk with her about San Blas and the story she wrote. I'll be back on Monday. I'll meet you here on Tuesday."

"How will this help?" Flor asked. "The reporter wrote what Prudencia and I told her. She knows nothing of the children who were taken from the village. This boy is my son, Efraín. A mother knows. I've read about this DNA testing. That would prove I'm his mother."

"It would," Lindsey said. "But you need the boy's cooperation, and that of his adoptive parents, to get a sample to test. Please, give me some time to think. My trip to Ashland was already planned. It was just by chance I found out the reporter is there. Perhaps she remembers some detail that's important."

Flor sighed. "Very well. I'll wait until you return. Tuesday morning, then. Right here."

Lindsey had bought herself a little time, but not much. She had to tell Gretchen and Doug about Nat, about Flor's claim on their adopted son. But how? And then what? Various scenarios disturbed her sleep that night, and she could settle on none of them.

LINDSEY sat at the kitchen table on Wednesday morning, drinking coffee and reading the *San Francisco Chronicle*, a column on the front page of the business section about the Dunlin Corporation. The company's first-quarter earnings were down and there was a pending vacancy on the board of directors. The numbers meant little to Lindsey, but the name Caldwell did. He was a director, retiring in June, and his replacement would be chosen at next week's board meeting. Caldwell was the name Claire mentioned Monday evening. She'd told Hal she had a candidate for Caldwell's board position.

There usually wasn't much turnover on the Dunlin board, but this was the second vacancy this year. The first had occurred when a longtime board member had died, the result of a traffic accident. Now Caldwell's position was available. Of the seven directors, four—Annabel, Hal, Claire, and Mrs. Megarris—were related by blood or marriage. The other three directors were company executives—Tybalt the general counsel, Caldwell, and Max Brinker. Four votes out of seven. It wouldn't take much to control that board. Perhaps Hal had someone else in mind, or Brinker had a candidate waiting in the wings.

The business columnist had frank opinions about Dunlin's current state of affairs. The coffee bars—the pet project of Dunlin marketing chief Claire Megarris, daughter of company co-founder Lawrence Megarris—were bleeding red ink, losing money hand over fist. Why was the company, with its history in imports and wholesale, involved in this misguided retail enterprise?

The columnist summarized the company's history, adding that Dunlin Corporation's fortunes had slipped since George Dunlin died in 1989, leaving his son-in-law and hand-picked successor Hal Norwood in charge. Things had changed since then—globalization, the market for the commodities the company imported. An unsubstantiated rumor said the board was considering the sale of its San Francisco real estate holdings. The area around the old waterfront warehouse had changed over the past few years, especially after construction of the Giants' ballpark, with real estate developers turning old industrial buildings into high-priced lofts. If Dunlin sold the warehouse and the Financial District building and moved all its operations to the more modern Port of Oakland, the company would gain much-needed cash, but remove the firm from San Francisco's tax base.

The Dunlin board was set in its ways and slow to change, the columnist added, and higher management had lately been prone to some internal bickering. If it was to survive, the company needed new blood, both on the board and in the upper levels of its chain of command.

Internal bickering, Lindsey thought. Discord among those in higher management. Claire always complained about Max Brinker, calling him a dinosaur, a rigid old sexist who resisted change and fought her every suggestion, wanting to run the company just the way Uncle George had. According to Claire, she was the one with the new ideas, the advocate for modernization and progress. But the company's money-losing coffee bars, an effort to move into the retail market, had been Claire's idea. Maybe the stakes were a lot higher than just a seat on the Dunlin board.

A power struggle? Was the person elected to replace the director who had died allied with Claire or Brinker? Lindsey pictured Hal in the middle, making peace, making compromises. Annabel, temporarily incapacitated due to her stroke, couldn't participate. But Hal probably held Annabel's proxy. Indefinitely? Or did that proxy have an expiration date, through some mechanism providing a third vacancy?

On Monday evening, Hal said he was distracted and worried about his wife. He could count on Claire, Gretchen had said, to watch his back. But what if Claire wasn't just watching Hal's back? What if Claire was looking for a spot to drive the knife home?

Claire always pointed out that her father started the firm and brought in George Dunlin later. Based on that history, she had as much right to run the company as Hal did. The official, public version was that Lawrence Megarris died of a heart attack. But Lindsey knew Megarris was an alcoholic whose descent into the bottle cost him his company and his life.

Nina shuffled into the kitchen, green silk robe cinched around her waist, purple-streaked hair rumpled. She moved like a heat-seeking missile toward the coffeepot and filled a mug, leaning against the counter as she took her first sip. She took a scone from a sack on the counter, heated it in the microwave, and sat down at the table, slathering it with butter and jam.

"Come next week you're a working girl," Lindsey said. "You'll have to get up earlier."

"It isn't next week yet."

"Did you like Tess's flat?" Lindsey asked. Nina had looked at the place Tuesday evening.

"It's great," Nina said. "Second floor, roomy, lots of light. I love the neighborhood."

"Are you thinking about moving in, once Tess's roommate leaves?"

"Not just thinking," Nina said. "I told Tess I would."

Lindsey felt that old familiar twinge. The advice she couldn't help giving would be misconstrued as meddling. "This job is temporary, no guarantees. You said yourself you could be looking for work again in September. I'm just concerned about your financial situation."

Nina sighed. "I know you are. So am I. Thank you for letting me stay, Mom. I appreciate it. But I can't live here indefinitely. It's an imposition on you."

"It's not." But it was. Lindsey was used to living alone, the freedom of not having to consider the wants and needs of another human being in her day-to-day activities. When confronting Nina as an adult, Lindsey sometimes told herself things had been easier when Nina was a child. But that wasn't true either. She and her daughter had traveled a rough road. Nina had been stubborn, willful and independent since the day she took her first step. But dealing with Nina during the terrible twos and threes was simpler than contending with the fifth-grader who pushed the envelope, or the sulky teenager who'd hit puberty like hell on wheels. To be honest, Lindsey had been relieved when Nina went away to college.

Now Nina was back. It wasn't easy to move back home as an adult. Lindsey knew that firsthand. The financial burden of being a single mother—pregnancy, childbirth and caring for Nina—coupled with the long hard slog of finishing her dissertation, had forced her to move in with Aunt Emma for several years, until she got her first teaching job at San Francisco State and moved to the city. When she'd accepted the position at Cal Poly in San Luis Obispo, she'd lived with her parents in Paso Robles until she bought a house. Lindsey remembered the arguments she'd had with her own mother during that time. It was hard to insist she was a grown woman when she had to move back home. Nina felt same way. Her daughter had accused her of not treating her as an adult. Lindsey had thrown the same words at her mother years ago.

"It is an imposition." Nina finished her scone, got up, and put her dishes in the dishwasher. "Besides, we don't get along, never have. It's better if we don't push it."

Even if it was true, hearing her daughter say it made it hurt more. Lindsey always figured it was her fault. Why was her relationship with her daughter so difficult? She felt as though she was teetering on a tightrope, trying not to say the wrong thing, trying to be supportive, yet trying to let Nina be her own person. She didn't want to open another skirmish in the ongoing mother–daughter war. "I'm sorry you feel that way. You're welcome to stay as long as you like. But it sounds as though your mind is made up."

"It is. I'm moving in with Tess. Right now I'm going to take a shower."

Lindsey remembered the words Nina had thrown at her during their big blowout back in December. "I try to be honest with you and you won't return the favor," Nina had shouted. "When do we ever get to relate to each other like a couple of adults?"

When indeed? Yes, Nina was an adult. But your kid is always your kid, Lindsey thought. I carried her in my belly for nine months and looked after her for all those years afterward. She's still my little girl. It's hard to let go of that. And what will happen if…when…I finally tell her about her father?

In her office, Lindsey switched on her computer and checked her e-mail, pleased to see a message from Merle Sefton, saying she could meet with Lindsey Friday morning in her office at Southern Oregon University. Lindsey replied, confirming date and time.

The banker's box sat in the middle of the office, full of promise and dread, its white cardboard exterior concealing Annabel's secrets. Lindsey sat cross-legged on the rug and pulled the lid from the box. Light glinted on the crystal shard and the tarnished silver pineapple. She reached for the snapshot of Annabel and Lily "Shoe," as Annabel had called her. Where was Lily now? Where had she lived then?

Lily was probably Chinese American, so Chinatown was a place to start. Away from Grant Street, which drew tourists to shops and restaurants, that part of the city had many narrow, hidden streets, alleys really. Was Lily at one of these addresses, apartments stacked on top of each other in narrow, old buildings, glimpsed from cross-streets on Chinatown's steep hills? Perhaps Lily had migrated to another part of the city. Chinatown had fluid borders, moving out to the Richmond and Sunset Districts of San Francisco. Lily may have moved to another town in the Bay Area, such as Oakland, which had its own Chinatown. Lily might live anywhere.

Surely Annabel had put Lily's phone number in her address

book. Or books. Tess said Annabel saved old address books, just in case. Lindsey did the same, though she herself had recently migrated to an electronic organizer. What would happen to old addresses now, if they only existed on a computer chip?

Not all the books in the box contained addresses. There were volumes of poetry, novels, and children's books, *Anne of Green Gables* and *The Secret Garden*. Lindsey smiled as she found a handful of small volumes in blue cloth bindings chronicling the adventures of that intrepid sleuth, Nancy Drew. She set these aside and concentrated on the address books, six in all, in varying styles and sizes.

This can't be that hard, she thought. Look through the addresses, find Lily. But Lindsey's conversation with Annabel had been interrupted before Annabel could tell her how to spell Lily's last name. Shu was an obvious choice. But there could be variations that sounded like *shoe*, such as Hsu, Tsu, or Xu.

Lindsey opened a small volume covered in worn brown leather and flipped through pages filled with Annabel's small, precise handwriting, pages crowded with letters and numbers, scribbles and doodles. Annabel was always doodling, tiny sketches of birds, flowers, fish, cats. So many times over the years she'd seen Annabel at a desk or a table, pen or pencil constantly moving as she drew on whatever piece of paper was in front of her.

This address book was untidy, well-used, its pages covered with ink and pencil. Addresses had been written between the appropriate lines, then crossed out as people changed location, with new addresses written above, below, in between the lines and along the margins, anywhere there was space for Annabel to write. In some cases she'd written addresses on less-used pages, regardless of alphabetical order. If that wasn't confusing enough, some addresses had no names to go with them, just initials, while others had nothing at all to identify them. Was there a code, waiting to be cracked?

Annabel used this book until there was no more room on its pages for pictures and words. There was no date in the front, nor had Annabel written her own address. But what about Lindsey's address? She opened the book to the *P*s. She saw her own initials, *LP* for Lindsey Page, in the center of a wreath of doodles. There were two addresses for *LP*, one at the top of the page that had been crossed out, and another added below it. The first address was the apartment south of Golden Gate Park where Lindsey lived when she was teaching at San Francisco State. The second one was her parents' house in Paso Robles, where she'd lived for several months when she took the position at Cal Poly in San Luis Obispo. So Annabel had started this address book in the late 1970s, after Lindsey got the job at SFSU and before she'd bought her house in San Luis Obispo in the 1980s. In a way, the book was a time machine. Those old addresses filled Lindsey's mind with pictures and memories.

She didn't see a listing for anyone named Lily. Nor did she find any initials that would go with a Lily Hsu, Shu, Tsu, or Xu. Or in the *L* pages, for just plain Lily. She reached for another address book, this one newer. Claire had moved to her condo on Nob Hill in the early 1990s, and that address was in this book, under the initials CM. Lindsey went through the book page by page. Still no Lily. Lindsey examined a third address book, then a fourth and a fifth. I must be missing something, she thought. It's got to be here. She's hidden the name and address somehow. Maybe she didn't want anyone to know she was in contact with Lily, though I can't think why. But it's here. I've just got to find it.

She stretched, muscles cramped and feet tingling from sitting on the floor. There was one more address book to examine. Just inside the front cover Annabel had written her own address, that of the green stucco house on Hillegass Street. She had lived there the entire four years she was in college, so the earliest date for this address book would be the fall of 1970, when Annabel came to UC Berkeley as a freshman. Lindsey turned to the *P*s, but she didn't see her own initials. She had moved into the Hillegass Street house in June 1972. There was the Milvia Street address, this very house, where she'd lived with Aunt Emma starting in the summer of 1974. No initials. But there was a doodle.

Lindsey chuckled. Here was the key to Annabel's address book, a drawing of a book, with pages. On closer examination Lindsey saw the initials *LP* along the edge of the drawing. She flipped to the *K*s. Gretchen Kohl had moved in with Doug Segal that summer. At the top of the page, above the address of the apartment Gretchen and Doug had shared, Lindsey saw a tiny sketch, a lump of coal and a seagull perched on a piling, with tiny waves lapping at its base.

Was Lily here? And was Lily a flower or a shoe? Lindsey leafed through the pages again, looking carefully at the doodles she had dismissed as mere drawings. Then she saw a flower, a lily sketched in next to an address and a phone number. Lindsey squinted at the drawing, then examined the sketch with a magnifying glass. She discovered the initials *LH* at the side of the lily's stem. Lily's last name was Hsu.

Now that Lindsey had the key, she went back through Annabel's address books, tracking the drawing of the lily and the addresses and phone numbers that went with it. The earliest book, from Annabel's high school days in the late 1960s, placed Lily on Beulah Street, near Haight. In the 1970s, Lily lived in the Sunset District, then sometime in the early Nineties, in the Richmond District. An answering machine picked up Lindsey's phone call. She left a message, hoping Lily Hsu would respond.

The doorbell rang. It was Gretchen. "I'm reporting for cat-sitting duty. Here to pick up the key, anyway."

"Come have coffee." Lindsey led the way to the kitchen, filled two mugs and set them on the table. She fetched an extra house key and a slip of paper on which she'd written the name and phone number of the Ashland bed-and-breakfast inn. "Thanks for looking after the cats while I'm gone. Cat food in the cupboard next to the sink, litter next to the cat box. We're leaving early tomorrow morning, driving home on Monday. You can reach me on my cell phone."

Nina came out of the guestroom with her purse slung over her shoulder. "I'm going shopping. I need a few things for the trip."

When she had gone, Gretchen asked, "How is that working, with Nina living here?"

Lindsey circled her mug with her hands. "It's awkward. This morning she informed me that she's moving in with Tess. She doesn't want to impose on me any longer. We had another one of our mother–daughter discussions."

"In civil tones, I hope."

Lindsey shrugged. "No blows were exchanged. Or voices raised."

"Then what's the problem?"

"This job with Claire is temporary. I'm guessing Nina doesn't have much money, though we haven't discussed it. This economic downturn hit her hard. She's been underemployed or unemployed over the past few years. The Texas move was a mistake, and not just financially. Thank God she realized it and came home. Moving in with Tess isn't very practical right now. Why pay rent when she could be out of a job again in four months?"

"Because she's an adult and doesn't want to live with Mom," Gretchen said. "Remember how we were at that age? I couldn't wait to get out of the house, even if it meant renting a closet in some squalid rooming house. Which is where I lived before I lucked into that apartment on Hillegass Street. Given her work situation and the economy, she's jazzed about having any kind of job. She'll have a paycheck and some benefits, even if it's only temporary. I'll bet Nina won't be out of a job in four months. Claire will find her a permanent position."

Lindsey nodded, remembering that she'd rejected Aunt Emma's offer of a room in this house in favor of a place of her own, on Hillegass Street with the others. "I worry about her."

"Of course you do. You're her mother. That's your job. That's what we moms do." Gretchen sipped coffee. "I'll worry about my kids no matter how big they get. Until I get old and creaky and it's their turn to worry about me. If Nina lived here you'd be at each other's throats. She needs her own place. She'll be fine."

"I hope so. She's had some rocky years. First she lost her job and apartment. Then she got involved with Chad, that obnoxious, narcissistic twerp…"

Gretchen smiled. "Don't hold back. Tell me how you really feel."

"I wish things were easier between us," Lindsey said. "If I told her about…"

"Her father? You've been adamant about keeping that secret. And I respect your privacy. It's late in the game to tell Nina who her dad is. Why now?"

"Tess, wanting to know about her father."

"You know what I think about that," Gretchen said. "Bad idea where Tess is concerned, maybe bad for Nina as well. You've put off telling her for so long that coming clean could backfire on you. My opinion. Take it or leave it. You have to decide what you want to do."

"I know." Lindsey sipped her coffee and pointed at the discarded *Chronicle*. "Did you see the business section this morning?"

"With all that innuendo about the Dunlin Corporation? Did I ever! That column was a hit piece directed at Claire. I called her right away. She's really pissed off. She's had run-ins with that columnist before. She thinks Brinker's behind that column. He's been a thorn in her side for ages. He hates anything innovative and wants to do business just the way Annabel's father did back in the good old days. Claire has so much emotion and energy invested in the company. Her father started it, but he gets left out of the equation and her Uncle George gets all the credit."

Like so much revisionist history, it depended on who did the revising. Megarris's alcoholism was the reason Dunlin had airbrushed his partner from the picture. Lindsey sipped coffee. "Mr. Megarris died such a long time ago, it's not surprising that Mr. Dunlin is the one—and the name—everyone remembers."

"True, but it's a family business," Gretchen said. "Claire and Mrs. Megarris are part of the family. That columnist implied there's a power struggle going on, but Claire says it's more a case of modernization versus doing business the same old way, retooling the company's goals and mission. Brinker's a major impediment to change. And Claire's concerned about Hal."

"Why?" Lindsey asked. "He's been running the company for years. Dunlin groomed Hal to take over as chief executive officer."

"Yes, and Dunlin left Brinker looming over the company, like a gargoyle. Claire's words," Gretchen added. "She says Hal's indecisive, won't move without consulting Brinker."

"Max is the chief operating officer," Lindsey said. "Of course Hal consults him. Annabel, too. She's on the board. There's a board vacancy coming up. Claire has a candidate to replace the director who's resigning. She was trying to lobby Hal Monday evening but he told her it wasn't the time to discuss it. That column said something about real estate for sale. Surely they wouldn't sell the Dunlin Building."

"Selling the warehouse makes sense," Gretchen said. "The commodities are shipped into the Port of Oakland. Most of their operations are already over there. Claire says the headquarters building needs an earthquake retrofit, and upgrading in terms of plumbing, wiring, and security. But I doubt she would give up that short commute to her condo on Nob Hill."

"Straight uphill," Lindsey said.

Gretchen laughed. "Downhill for going to work, uphill for going home. She takes the cable car at the end of the day. Enough about this. I have a volunteer thing and if I don't hustle, I'll be late."

Lindsey watched from the front porch as Gretchen left, and then Nina returned from her shopping excursion. "I should pack. Will I need any dress-up clothes?"

"For Ashland?" Lindsey shook her head. "No, it's pretty casual up there. Listen about this morning, when we were talking about your moving in with Tess, I didn't mean to be…"

Nina raised her hand. "I know you're concerned about me, Mom. Don't worry. I'll be fine." She went into the house.

Lindsey picked up a pine cone, fallen from a nearby tree, and sat on the wide porch railing. Next to her, a potted geranium held buds fat with the promise of bright red flowers. Her relationship with her daughter was up and down, like a merry-go-round, circling through argument and truce.

18

THE OREGON MORNING was cool, but the blue sky held a promise of warmth. Tulips and daffodils splashed bright colors along the walk and rosebushes were covered with buds. Lindsey and Nina walked from their cottage to the inn's main house, where French doors led into a dining room with a long table set for breakfast. They helped themselves to coffee from the urn on a nearby counter.

The woman who ran the bed-and-breakfast inn emerged from the kitchen, bearing a large platter with slices of cantaloupe and honey-dew melon, fat red strawberries mounded in the middle. She set the platter on the sideboard. "Breakfast will be ready in five minutes."

Lindsey smiled. "Something smells good."

"It's my mushroom clafouti. I hope you like it." A man and wom-an descended the stairs between the dining room and parlor, intro-ducing themselves. More guests appeared, from upstairs and the other garden cottage, as the innkeeper added more food to the sideboard: the clafouti, a platter of sausages, and a coffee cake with crumb top-ping, just out of the oven. The guests filled their plates and sat down to eat breakfast, discussing the plays they'd seen the previous night.

After breakfast, Nina planned to take the backstage tour. Lind-sey walked south to Southern Oregon University, where campus buildings scattered the sloping hill west of Siskiyou Boulevard. She located the communications department and Professor Sefton's of-fice, where the walls were covered with framed photographs in black-and-white, strong images of light and shadow. Lindsey surmised they were taken by the woman who sat behind the desk, her hands mov-ing over a keyboard.

Merle Sefton pushed back her chair and stepped around the desk. She was tall, her blond hair streaked with gray. A network of fine lines vied with the faint dusting of freckles on her face. She had a firm handshake and a southwestern twang in her voice. "Dr. Page, it's good to meet you. Now that we've got the niceties out of the way, call me Merle."

"And I'm Lindsey. I like your pictures. Especially this one." She pointed at a photograph showing a corridor in a derelict building, concrete walls crumbled, revealing the iron framework within. The image was eerie and unsettling, with empty doorways and windows lined up along the deserted hallway.

"I took that when I was in the Navy, stationed on Guam," Merle said. "It's the old Japanese army hospital on the island of Saipan."

"I've seen some of your work on the Internet. I particularly liked the photo essay about Amelia Earhart's last flight, with the picture of the little jail surrounded by jungle, and the picture of the waves. That one made me seasick."

"Me, too," Merle said with a grin. "I shot that from the deck of a destroyer at the tail end of a typhoon, and I was damned queasy myself. The jail is on Saipan, not far from the military hospital. There's a persistent rumor in that neck of the woods that Earhart was captured and held in the jail before being executed by the Imperial Japanese Army. Back in the Seventies, there were people still alive on Saipan who claimed to have seen Amelia."

"No one will ever know for certain the answer to that riddle. That's what makes it so intriguing."

"Please, have a seat." Merle waved at the chair in front of her desk. "Your email said you have questions about what happened at San Blas."

"I read your story and some of the articles that followed. You took a lot of flak, especially from the *Wall Street Journal*. But you stood by what you wrote."

"The *Wall Street Journal* never met a right-wing despot it didn't like," Merle said. "Particularly in El Salvador. I stood by what I wrote because it was the truth. Humberto Aragón ordered that massacre, then tried to cover his tracks. Not as effectively as he would have liked, because I saw what he did."

"Humberto Aragón was a landowner, not a right-wing despot."

"In El Salvador it's the same thing. He was a big ARENA supporter," Merle said, using the acronym for the conservative Salvadoran political party *Alianza Republicana Nacionalista*. "So is his family. His daughter Cristina married Francisco Medrano, a party bigwig. Severino Aragón is a congressman now. My exposé led nowhere. It's enough to make one a cynic." Merle leaned back in her chair. "What's your interest in San Blas? I checked you out as well. You're a historian and you write about the nineteenth-century American West."

"Cowboys, Indians and outlaws," Lindsey said. "Usually something a bit more scholarly, like my book about the wives and daughters of frontier army officers. Not all my research involves the nineteenth century, though. My latest book deals with immigrant women from Latin America. I've been talking with a woman named Flor from El Salvador. She's one of the survivors of San Blas."

Interest sparked in Merle's eyes. "Really? There were only two.

Five if you count the three kids that were snatched. She must be the woman who lost her child. The other woman was much older. I wondered what happened to them."

"Flor was the younger woman," Lindsey said. "The older woman died. Flor lives in Oakland. She remarried and has two children."

"Did she ever find her little boy? There's an organization in El Salvador working to reunite parents with their missing children."

"She has a lead," Lindsey said. "I'd already planned this trip to Ashland, then I found out you teach here. I'd like to know more about San Blas, beyond what appeared in the article you wrote. Your impressions, your opinions."

"Would you like to see the photographs I took?" Merle asked. "They're at home. I warn you, they require a strong stomach."

Merle lived in a one-story frame house near the campus. A big orange tabby cat greeted them at the door. "That's Rascal. He guards the house when he's not sleeping twenty-three hours a day." She led the way through the kitchen to a den, where a sliding glass door led to the small backyard. "I'll make coffee. I got the habit in the Navy, so I've got to have my brew. French roast, the darker the better."

Rascal jumped onto the arm of a recliner and offered his head to be scratched. Lindsey obliged, glancing at a plaque holding a brass bell and an inscription to JOCM M. A. SEFTON. "What does the A stand for? And what's the significance of the bell?"

Merle started the coffee brewing. "The A is for Alice, my grandmother's name. As for Merle, my mother was a big Merle Oberon fan. She saw *Wuthering Heights* every night for a week when it first opened. It was her all-time favorite movie. If I'd been a boy, she'd have named me Heathcliff." She ran her index finger over the bell's polished brass. "A ship's bell is a standard gift given to people leaving a duty station or retiring from the Navy. I got this one when I retired as a master chief petty officer, the highest enlisted rank. My specialty was journalism. That's what the JOCM stands for. When I retired, I'd been in the Navy twenty-five years. I joined up in 'sixty-three, after Kennedy was assassinated."

"I was fourteen, in the ninth grade," Lindsey said, remembering that awful Friday.

"I was nineteen. Joining the Navy was what I could do for my country. It was also a good way to get an education. The University of Oklahoma has an excellent journalism school but my family didn't have any money for college and my grades weren't good enough for a scholarship. I enlisted, went to boot camp, and the Navy sent me to school. I worked in Navy public affairs offices, writing and editing stories for base publications, writing press releases, taking pictures. Got to be pretty good with a camera, and in the darkroom. The Navy had a school for photojournalists, a year-long course at Syracuse University in New York. When I left Guam I went there, then I did a tour of duty at *All Hands*, the Navy magazine, in Washington D.C."

"How did you wind up in the middle of a war in El Salvador?"

"I was only forty-four when I retired," Merle said. "Young enough for another career. There were lots of things I wanted to do. I hooked up with a small independent news service. They sent me to El Salvador, told me to connect with a rebel group and find out what was going on down there." She glanced at a silver-framed photograph of an older man. "Joe didn't want me to go. He tried to talk me out of it. He said it would be dangerous. Maybe I was trying to prove I was as tough as he was. His name was Joe Redfern and he was a hell of a writer."

"He was," Lindsey said. "I've read his books. He died recently, didn't he?"

"Yes. I miss him. We were together more than twenty-five years. He was almost that much older than I was. A different generation. Coffee's ready."

They settled into chairs in the den. "So off I went to El Salvador. In April of 'eighty-nine I was in Chalatenango department, up north in Los Árboles, a town in the mountains near the Honduran border. The town was rebel territory. By then I'd had my share of encounters with the army and civilian authorities. In fact, that weekend I had an unpleasant run-in with an army colonel outside the city of Santa Ana. The guy threatened to pull my credentials and boot me out of the country. Which is what happened two days later. I was already on somebody's list."

"Before that, you went to San Blas," Lindsey said.

Merle nodded. "Twice. The first time was the day after the killings, the second time the following day. That first morning the sun was just coming up. It was quiet as death."

19

Chalatenango Department, El Salvador, April 1989

IT WAS QUIET, much too quiet.

The sun had just risen. The *campesinos* who lived in San Blas should have been up as well. It was time for the men to rise from their beds and go to work. The women would have awakened long before their men, lighting cooking fires and stirring pots. There should be children, shouting and laughing as children did when they played.

"That was the church," Nazario Robles told Merle Sefton as they stood near a log pile on the slope overlooking San Blas. "The store. The house closest to the dam, my mother lived there, with my sister and her husband." He fired up a cigarette and exhaled curses with the smoke.

The earthen dam was above the village, forming a pond from the water running down the mountain valley. Below the dam the creek diminished to a trickle and hugged the far edge of the clearing where the village lay, near a dirt road winding over a hill.

The nearest house was barely more than a hut. An iron cooking pot lay near the door. Merle and Nazario entered the house. She saw pallets and blankets on bare ground, clothes hanging from pegs, a few dishes lined up on a shelf. Merle reached for a flat pasteboard wallet containing a color snapshot showing a man, a woman and a little boy, dressed in what were probably their best clothes. The man in the picture, barely into his twenties, was solemn-faced, but the woman, a teenager, smiled shyly. She held the little boy in the curve of her arms, a sturdy child perhaps a year old, with black hair and black eyes, a round face and a wide smile.

Merle held up the photograph. "Did you know them?"

Nazario's mouth tightened. He tucked the picture inside his shirt. "They were friends."

Merle raised her camera and snapped off a few shots. Outside she took more photos of the house. Near the iron pot she saw a scrap of cloth, blue-gray, a shiny metal button attached by a thread. As she reached for it, something moved in the nearby trees. Merle straightened, every nerve alert. Nazario tensed and swung his rifle in the direction of the sound. Then he relaxed. "It's Beatriz."

"Clear for now," Beatriz called.

"How far to the coffee processing plant?" Merle asked.

"Over that hill, about one kilometer." Nazario pointed at the road on the other side of San Blas. "From the plant to the house where the landowner lives, maybe five kilometers. That's why I sent Beatriz to check, to see if there's activity at the plant. We may not have much time." He turned his back on the abandoned house and led the way downhill.

A few days earlier Merle was sleeping in a comfortable bed at the Camino Real hotel in San Salvador, where her news service, like many others, was based. In the capital she'd made contact with Nazario, who invited her to Los Árboles, a town in the Sierra Madre mountains, the northern part of Chalatenango department. She drove her rented car north out of San Salvador, heading for the *Cinturón de Oro*, the golden belt of rich agricultural land, through Santa Ana department, with its graceful city of the same name. North of Santa Ana she had a run-in with that flaming asshole of an army colonel who didn't like reporters eschewing the ruling party's line and trying to get the rebels' side of the story. He threatened to toss her out of El Salvador before finally letting her go. She fumed about it. When she was stopped at a roadblock north of Texistepeque, she wondered if the colonel had made good on his threat. The soldiers took their time examining her news service credentials and her passport. She held her tongue, reminding herself that Joe had warned her not to come to El Salvador.

You don't know what it's like, Joe had said. You were peacetime Navy. You've never been in a war, or a war zone. Joe knew what he was talking about. He'd been on battlefields from Guadalcanal to Vietnam.

She figured Joe would have kept his mouth shut instead of trading sharp words with that brass hat, with good reason. The colonel she'd tangled with earlier that afternoon was fairly high in the food chain, in a position to do exactly what he'd threatened. How the hell could she write the story if she wasn't here? Come to think of it, getting the boot would be mild compared with what could happen—and had—in this country. She could wind up dead out here in the boonies, a bullet in her head, courtesy of some death squad, or these soldiers.

She arrived in Los Árboles late Sunday, had dinner, and planned to get some shut-eye. But Nazario found her as she walked back to the threadbare hotel, telling her she must go with him to a village called San Blas on the other side of the mountain. There had been reports of weapons fire, and black smoke smudged the sky, visible for miles.

They left at four o'clock Monday morning, in a battered Toyota pickup that had somehow migrated from a Japanese assembly line to a war zone in El Salvador. She and Nazario rode in the pickup bed, while Beatriz shared the cab with the driver, who now waited for them on the ridge above, high enough to see if anyone was approaching and give a warning signal.

They drove on secondary roads, away from the main highway over the mountains, at times without lights. The army wasn't the only danger. Many of the powerful landowners had private armies, paramilitaries. Nazario was impatient, in a hurry to get to San Blas as early as possible. Otherwise it would be too late, he'd said. Too late for what he didn't say, but Merle figured he was worried that whoever was responsible for that plume of smoke was planning to cover up the reason for the fire.

They arrived at first light. But it was already too late for the people who'd lived in San Blas. The church was a blackened ruin, smoke rising from the ashes. The stench of char and decay rode the wind.

Merle heard a steady buzz, and realized that the sound came from swarms of flies covering the bodies.

Oh, Lord. This is going to be bad.

She'd seen pictures through the years, grim photographs of horrors, everything from Nanking to the Warsaw Ghetto, from Auschwitz to My Lai. But pictures, powerful as they were, could never compare with the reality. Now she was the one taking the pictures that would shock the people who viewed them.

Merle gagged, glad she'd had nothing to eat this morning. The stench overwhelmed her. The corpses had been lying here since yesterday afternoon. She took a bandanna from her pocket and tied it over her nose and mouth. It didn't help.

Merle switched on the portable tape recorder hanging by a cord around her neck, then raised her camera and started shooting pictures. She spoke into the recorder, describing the location of the shots, noting landmarks. She reached the end of the film and put a fresh roll in her camera.

Nazario stared at the church ruins. "I came here yesterday to see my mother. Then I went to meet my *compadres* at another camp. We heard gunfire. From a distance we saw the smoke. I knew all the people who lived here were dead." He swore again, castigating himself for visiting his mother, bringing this fate down on her and the village.

"You're not to blame," Beatriz said. "You've visited your mother only a few times. If Humberto knew about you, it was already too late."

"Who's Humberto?" Merle asked.

"Aragón. He owns this *finca*," Beatriz said. "His son Severino is in the army."

"So who did this? The army? Or the Aragóns?"

"Could be either one," Nazario said. "The army's been though here. But the Aragóns have their own private army patrolling the *finca*."

Merle steeled herself to the carnage around her and took more pictures, driven by the need to document the results of this frenzied orgy of violence. Then they heard three short bleats from the pickup's horn, the driver warning them. They hurried up the slope. Merle looked back and saw Jeeps coming over the hump of the road that led to the coffee processing plant, with a bulldozer in the rear. She raised her camera and squeezed off a few more shots.

Merle longed to wash away the stench of San Blas. She wrote most of the story in her head on the way back to Los Árboles, where she stood under a stream of tepid water in her hotel bathroom, scrubbing away the dust and stink but not the memory of what she'd seen. She toweled herself dry, put on her robe, and sat at her portable type-writer, fingers pounding the keys as words poured from her brain to the paper. She put the story and the film rolls into an envelope and hid them in her bag.

Her stomach reminded her she hadn't eaten since the previous day. It was nearly three. No wonder she felt like hell, with no food and very little sleep on top of what she'd seen that morning. She dressed, shouldered the camera bag she always carried, and went downstairs to the café across the street from the hotel. She ordered a cold beer and worked her way through several *pupusas* and a bowl of *curtido*.

Nazario and Beatriz caught up with her as she left the café, tell-ing her that two women from San Blas were here in Los Árboles. Merle checked the batteries in her tape recorder, counted the films in the bag and the shots remaining on the roll in the camera. Nazario drove to a house near the sawmill, where two survivors sat near the front door. Dried blood stained their clothes. Nazario sighed. Merle guessed he'd hoped one of the women would be his mother or sister, but neither was. He smoothed sorrow from his face and replaced it with anger. He held out the photograph they'd found in San Blas. Merle realized the younger woman was the mother in the snapshot.

Tears streamed from the woman's ravaged eyes. She took the pic-ture, sobbing onto the older woman's shoulder. Merle fought back tears and pointed her camera, trying to look unobtrusive, though the people gathered nearby stared at the tall blond American woman.

"Her name is Flor Guzmán," Nazario said. "She lived with her husband and son in the house where we found the picture. The other woman is Prudencia Muñoz."

The survivors described what had happened in San Blas, the grim tale winding out, like the tape on Merle's recorder, an orgy of rape and slaughter. "They took Efraín," Flor cried, "snatched him from me. Others, too. A baby, and a little girl. They took them away."

"We've heard of the army taking children," Beatriz said.

Flor rubbed away the tears. "These were Don Humberto's men."

"Humberto Aragón is a dead man," Nazario snarled. "Some day I will kill him."

"We must list their names," Prudence said. "So no one forgets."

The bell in the Los Árboles church tower began to toll the hour. The tolling of the names of the dead of San Blas went on far longer.

EARLY next morning, Nazario rapped on the door of Merle's hotel room, identifying himself. She threw back the covers, instantly alert, belted her robe over her pajamas, and unlocked the door. "What's up?"

"I'm going back to San Blas. To see if I can find out something about the children. Will you come with me?"

Merle ran a hand through her sleep-tousled hair. She'd updated her article about San Blas and its survivors yesterday afternoon, in a burst of white-hot energy. The story was finished—or was it? San Blas nagged at her, needing a follow-up. Those children, kidnapped, when most of the other inhabitants had been slaughtered. "I'll go," she said.

She dressed quickly in faded jeans, T-shirt, khaki jacket, a blue bandanna around her neck. She took only the Minolta and the telephoto lens, both in leather cases with straps, and filled her jacket pockets with film canisters. Her waist pack held her passport, press credential, and money. The story she'd updated last night and the rolls of film she'd shot were in a manila envelope in her suitcase, tucked into the plastic sack that she used to collect soiled clothes.

When they stepped out of the trees above San Blas, Merle thought they'd wound up in the wrong valley. Everything was gone, scraped away by the bulldozer. The earthen dam above the village had been breached, another dam thrown up below. Water covered the site, its surface deceptively smooth, reflecting the morning sun. San Blas was now a lake.

"They buried the bodies," Nazario said, "then demolished the buildings, to make it look like there was never a village here. There's nothing left."

Merle began taking pictures, looking through the telephoto lens. "Yes, there is. I can see the church below the surface."

They walked down the slope, circling the shoreline of the new lake to the dam, a crude construct of dirt, rocks, lumber and gravel. Bulldozer tracks waffled the mud at its base. It must have taken most of Monday to knock down the rude huts that had housed the *campesi-*

nos, build this dam and destroy the other, erasing the memory of the people who had lived here. But there hadn't been enough time for the water to cover the church.

They scrambled to the top of the new dam and looked into the shallow water at the charred ghost of the church. Merle switched to her regular lens, then waded into the water, the camera's motor drive whirring. She reached the end of the roll and splashed back to shore. She changed rolls and tucked the spent film into a canister, shoving it into the front pocket of her fanny pack, separate from the unused film. She climbed back to the top of the new dam and began shooting pictures again.

Nazario grabbed her arm, startling her. "We must go, now."

They started up the hill. Just past the spot where the old dam had been, Merle looked back and saw a Jeep crest the hill. Two men leapt from the vehicle, shouting. She heard the crack of gunfire and stumbled, feeling as though someone had punched her in the thigh. Nazario hauled her to her feet. Merle took a step, but her leg wouldn't work. She sat down hard. Blood oozed from a hole above her left knee, bright red on blue denim. Merle felt a wave of nausea. Don't look, she told herself. The bullet wound didn't hurt much, not then. Shock, probably. The two men from the Jeep were gaining on them.

She pulled the film she'd just shot from her pack and handed it to Nazario. "Go." He shook his head. She grinned, with a bravado she didn't feel. "Hey, they can't kill me. I'm an American, I'm a reporter."

"They'll kill you because you're a reporter. Your American passport won't protect you."

"It has to. I can't climb that hill and you can't carry me. No point in both of us getting caught. They have to stop for me. That gives you time to get to the truck. Take the film and go. Get the story and pictures to my news service." She told him where to find the envelope, hidden in the laundry sack.

She reached into the pack and took out two business cards—Joe Redfern's and the news service in Los Angeles that was paying her for this adventure. "Call the Los Angeles people. They'll tell you what to do with the film and the story. Call this man. He'll get me out. Go now."

Maybe Joe was right. Maybe I shouldn't have come to El Salvador after all.

The bullet had gone through her thigh, leaving an exit wound at the back. She figured that was better than having the slug still in there. She hoped it hadn't hit anything important. Her leg throbbed with pain, as though she'd been stung by the biggest goddamned bee on the planet. She wrapped her bandanna tightly around the wound, tying the ends of the cloth to keep it in place.

Her captors were shockingly young to have perpetrated the massacre she'd seen yesterday. Not that the old had cornered the market on decency. One man stopped in front of her, pointing a gun at her head. The second man continued up the hill. Moments later he returned, reporting that the rebel got away. Nazario was on his way to Los Árboles. He'd make those calls.

The first man slung his weapon onto his shoulder and reached down, grabbing the cases that held the camera and lens. He opened the camera case and pulled out the Minolta, his fingers fumbling with the catch at the back. He tore open the camera and pulled out the film, exposing it to the light. Then he smashed the Minolta and the telephoto lens against a tree. Merle winced at the tangled mess of glass and metal. Damn, that was her best camera.

Joe always said the best defense was an offense. Might as well brazen it out. "Take me to Humberto Aragón," she demanded in Spanish. "I'm an American journalist."

The man who'd smashed her camera sneered. "I should kill you, *puta*."

"Aragón would be angry. Killing a journalist isn't very smart."

He glowered at her as he ripped her watch from her wrist and shoved it into his pocket. Then he dragged her to her feet, shoving her back against the log. He went through her jacket pockets, pulling out rolls of unused film. These he handed to the second man, telling him to expose it. While his companion ripped open the film canisters, the first man fumbled at her waist. For a panicked second she thought he was trying to unfasten her jeans. Instead, with a contemptuous glare, he released the buckle on the waist pack. He unzipped it and rifled through the contents, pocketing the money. Then he pulled out her passport and her press credential. He looked them over, comparing her passport photo with her face.

"I'm scheduled to interview the American ambassador in San Salvador tomorrow," she lied. "The embassy and my news service will ask questions if I don't show up."

The two men stared at the documents, conferring in whispers. Then they grabbed Merle's arms and dragged her to her feet. She gasped. Pain pounded like a sledgehammer. Her captors manhandled her down the hillside to their Jeep and boosted her up into the backseat. Merle leaned back against the grimy, worn upholstery. Sweat trickled down her face and she tried to slow her breathing.

The driver gunned the Jeep over the hill, past the coffee processing plant, through rolling, cultivated hills, acres and acres of coffee trees hung with green coffee berries, then up a driveway to a two-story house encircled by a wide veranda. Merle saw the bulldozer inside a nearby shed. Her captors parked and hauled Merle from the Jeep, quickly surrounded by uniformed men who stared at her as though she'd dropped from Mars.

Then they parted, making way for a bulky man with a hard brutal face. He listened impatiently to his men, as his thick fingers flipped through her passport and press credential. "You should have put a bullet in her head and left her in the mountains."

Merle stiffened her spine and her voice. "I want to see Humberto Aragón."

The big man hadn't expected her to speak Spanish. He slapped her. "Shut up, bitch."

The screen door at the back of the house opened. The man who stepped onto the veranda wore a short-sleeved yellow shirt and khakis. He had cropped black hair and a moustache. He lit a cigarette and shoved the pack and lighter back into his pocket. "What's this, Cruz?"

"An American reporter, Major," Cruz said, a shade of deference to his tone as he handed over Merle's passport and press credential. "My men found her and a rebel at San Blas. The coward ran off and left her. She speaks Spanish."

Major. Severino, the landowner's son, the one Nazario said was in the Salvadoran army. He examined the documents, then looked at Merle, exhaling a stream of smoke. "Trespassing on private property is a serious matter in El Salvador."

The wound in Merle's thigh throbbed. Perspiration beaded on her upper lip and she gnawed the inside of her cheek.

"Bring her inside. She's hurt." The woman in the doorway spoke crisp Spanish. She wore blue slacks and a blue shirt. She pulled a scarf from her pocket and used it to tie back her long blond hair.

Severino frowned. "That complicates matters. Take her to the office."

Cruz propelled Merle up the porch steps and into a big kitchen, past a frightened-looking middle-aged woman, then to a central hallway, where Merle saw the underside of a staircase. Then Cruz shoved her into a small square room and a hard wooden chair. A window opened onto the back veranda.

A tall dark-haired man appeared in the hallway outside the office. He stared at Merle and spoke in English. "What the hell is going on?"

The blond woman answered, her voice low so Merle couldn't hear. The middle-aged woman appeared, bearing a tray with a basin of water, cloth, and a first-aid kit. She set these on the desk.

"*Gracias,* Ana." The woman pulled up a stool and sat in front of Merle. She said in English, "Let's take a look." She opened the first-aid kit. With scissors she cut away the bandanna and the denim above the wound, then dampened a cloth and wiped away the blood. "The bullet went all the way through. Here's the exit wound." The woman took a brown bottle from the kit and tipped liquid onto gauze. Merle winced as the woman cleaned the entrance and exit wounds, then smeared them with antibiotic cream. She bandaged the thigh tightly with gauze and tape, and stood, wiping her hands on the damp cloth. She opened a bottle, shaking several tablets into the cap. "Aspirin. Take these." She filled a glass from a carafe of water on the desk and handed it to Merle, who swallowed the pills. The woman took the glass from her.

The woman's English was good, Merle thought. She must have been educated in the United States. Now what happens? A sound intruded. Was that a baby crying? Merle couldn't tell for sure whether the wail came from inside the house or somewhere outside.

Curses exploded in the air. A man loomed in the doorway, with iron-gray hair and a thickset body clad in khaki work clothes. Humberto Aragón, Merle guessed.

"I am surrounded by fools and idiots," the landowner bellowed in Spanish, scowling at Merle. "They should have put a bullet in her head."

"She speaks Spanish," Severino warned.

The woman in blue took Humberto's arm. "Let's go outside." She, Severino and the landowner left the office, followed by the tall dark man in the hallway. Cruz remained at the office door. As though I'm going to make a break for it with this leg, Merle thought.

Ana came into the office and picked up the tray, fear in her eyes. "I heard a baby crying," Merle whispered in Spanish. "Are there children here? Three children? From San Blas?"

Ana looked startled, then terrified as she glanced at Cruz. She nodded, a quick, brief movement of her chin.

So the children were here in the house, Merle thought as Ana left the office. She listened, hoping to hear something, anything that would help her assess the situation. She figured it was precarious. Then she heard Humberto's voice, unexpectedly loud, and realized that the landowner was on the veranda, near the office window. What she heard made her go cold.

"...kill her now and get it over with."

The woman spoke, from farther away. "...bad idea."

"...too late for that." Severino's voice came in and out, as though he were pacing along the veranda. "...broker from Dunlin..."

Merle couldn't hear all of the woman's reply. "...if she winds up dead or missing...you don't want...take her to San Salvador."

"Just let her go?" Humberto Aragón shouted.

The other voices were farther away now and Merle heard only fragments of the conversation, indistinct. "...Cristina, call Francisco..." Severino said, then he moved away.

A jumble of voices made it difficult to determine who was saying what. Then she heard Humberto say, "...dupe of the rebels."

Severino's voice chimed in, closer now. "...she has no proof."

Yes, I do, you smug bastard, Merle thought. Plenty of evidence. There were two eyewitnesses to the slaughter in San Blas. Merle had photos of the site, before and after it was flooded. She'd already written the story, including those eyewitness interviews. Nazario would make sure the story and the film got to her bureau office in San Salvador. Merle was already planning to write one hell of a follow-up story. People would believe. She'd make them believe.

If she got out of this mess alive.

20

MERLE RUBBED HER LEG, just above the left knee. "It bothers me sometimes, right here where the bullet went through. Particularly when it's cold and damp."

Lindsey closed the file folder in her lap and set it on the low table between them. Merle was right. Viewing the photographic evidence of the San Blas massacre took a strong stomach. "What happened after you left the *finca?*"

"Severino took me to the airport in San Salvador. A government official—Severino called him Francisco—met us at the airport, with two soldiers. He tore up my press credential, handed me my passport, and told me I was being tossed out of the country. As easy as that, because the Aragóns made their phone calls. The soldiers put me on the next flight to the United States. I wound up in Houston with the clothes I was wearing, my passport, and no money. I'd left everything in the hotel in Los Árboles and Humberto's thugs took my money."

Merle sipped coffee and set her mug on the end table. "When I got to Houston I called Joe and the news service. Joe told me Nazario had already called. He had collected the story, film and my luggage, took them to San Salvador, and gave them to a journalist colleague who was heading for Los Angeles. Joe bought me a plane ticket and met me at LAX with a suitcase full of clothes. I was never so glad to see anyone in my life."

"Then the story and pictures were published," Lindsey said.

"Yes. It created a minor sensation. But ultimately nobody believed me. Let's put it another way. My story had no effect. There was no justice for the people of San Blas. Those who believed my story already had their minds made up about El Salvador. The Aragóns denied the whole thing. Not just the massacre. They denied there had ever been a village called San Blas. They denied the very existence of the people who had lived there, who'd worked for them."

"But surely the village appeared on a map," Lindsey said.

"Yes, but that valley is called San Blas. So is the creek that runs through it, the creek they dammed to form the pond. The village was an afterthought, thrown up when the coffee plant was built, one of several company towns for the *campesinos* on the Aragón *finca*. San Blas was there, and then it wasn't. Bulldozed and flooded in late April, the end of the dry season. The rainy season started in May and the elements obliterated whatever evidence was left—just as the Aragóns hoped."

"You had eyewitnesses, Flor and Prudencia. The other people who lived there must have had relatives. What about the pictures of the bodies? And the buildings that were flooded?"

"The *campesinos* in El Salvador are rootless," Merle said. "They move from place to place, searching for work. That snapshot of Flor's family—just peasants in front of a church. It didn't prove that the village of San Blas ever existed. Who's to say who lived where, and when? The Aragóns claimed I took those pictures of bodies at some battle and made up the story. The photos of the flooded village could have been taken anywhere, certainly not on Aragón land. As for my eyewitnesses, Nazario was concerned they might wind up dead, so he got them out of Los Árboles. Beatriz was killed a few months later. Nazario was my only witness, a rebel with his own agenda. The Aragóns did a bang-up job with their cover-up. I was just another flaming left-wing journalist out to smear the Salvadoran government and the landowners. Humberto called me a dupe of the rebels, painted me with that brush, and it stuck.

"The massacre and the cover-up took place. I know what I saw. Those people were murdered. They deserve to have someone say they lived and died. But that's the way the story played out. After a while, Joe told me to let it go and move on. So I did."

Merle shrugged. "Truth is the first casualty of war. I found that out in El Salvador. Humberto Aragón always described himself as a hardworking self-made man, but he inherited his wealth from his father and grandfather. He and others like him boast about how they built El Salvador into the country it is today. The Aragóns are part of that twenty percent of the population that controls sixty percent of El Salvador's wealth. The peasants still live in desperate poverty. That's the country El Salvador is today, all right."

"What is the Aragón family history?" Lindsey asked.

"Humberto was born on the *finca*," Merle said. "Humberto's grandfather Ramón came over from Spain in the eighteen-eighties. That's when the coffee elite started building their dynasties and amassing huge estates. The Aragóns have owned a big chunk of Chalatenango department since then and kept adding to it. Ramón's son Agustín continued the tradition. The coffee growers in El Salvador ran the country until the Thirties. They still have enormous power. They call them the Fourteen Families. Agustín Aragón was a big political conservative back then. *La Matanza*, the bloodletting, that was in 'thirty-two. A peasant uprising was put down, brutally. Thousands of *campesinos* died, some on the Aragón *finca*. Lord knows how many peasants have died over the past hundred years so the Aragóns could be members of the coffee elite." Merle raised her coffee mug. "Makes me wonder sometimes how much blood and sweat went into growing and processing those beans so I can have freshly ground French roast."

"Some coffee beans are grown by cooperatives," Lindsey said.

"Yes, cooperatives are trying to give the small farmers a fair shake. Reform efforts in the early Eighties were supposed to redistribute land. The idea was to take parcels from landowners who owned more than twelve hundred acres and give them to the *campesinos* who'd been working the land for generations. But the landowners resisted. They hired private armies and dared the government to come and take their land. Humberto's thugs were better armed than some of the Salvadoran army outfits I saw."

"What about Humberto's wife and children?" Lindsey asked.

"His wife, Nella, died of cancer. She was from a coffee-growing family in Santa Ana department. They had three children—Severino, Cristina, and Roberto. Severino now runs the *finca*. Roberto's a rancher. Cristina married a politician named Francisco Medrano. I think the woman in blue at the *finca* that day was Cristina. I heard Severino tell her to call Francisco."

"And the dark-haired man in the hallway?"

"I didn't get a good look at him. Maybe he was the coffee broker they were talking about. He seemed upset by the whole thing. But he never stepped forward to support my story, or challenge it."

"You never saw the children?"

Merle shook her head. "I heard a baby cry. I assumed the children were in the house. But I can't be sure. All I had to go on was Ana, the servant. When I asked about the kids, I'm sure she nodded. But she didn't say anything. In my story I wrote that the children had been taken from the village and were missing. I didn't mention Ana. She would have been in danger. I wonder what happened to those kids."

So did Lindsey.

21

I SHOULD HAVE KEPT my mouth shut, Lindsey told herself, that Monday night after the long drive home from Ashland. It wouldn't have made our relationship any worse than it already is.

She'd finally told Nina who her father was. Now her daughter was angry.

There was never a right time for that revelation, she thought. Unless I was open about it from the start. But I couldn't. There were other people involved. I had my reasons, good reasons. The cat is out of the bag now. It has claws.

Nina was in the hall, her bags packed, her face hostile. "I'm moving in with Tess. She's on her way over to pick me up. I don't want to be here with you."

Lindsey felt her own ire rise. "Why are you so angry? I could have had an abortion. But I chose to be your mother. I walked the floor with you those nights when you had colic. I worked all these years to put food on the table and a roof over our heads. You're my child. I love you. Why isn't that enough, Nina? Why is it never enough? Why does it boil down to who donated the sperm that fertilized the egg?"

"I could deal with it easier if it *was* some anonymous donor," Nina snapped. "If you'd told me something, anything, instead of nothing. I appreciate the fact that you gave birth to me, Mother. Thanks for the food, the roof over my head, college. Yes, all of that was your choice. But you also chose to be dishonest with me, to lie, to deceive me. Why couldn't you answer the question before now? I have a father. I could have seen him now and then. I could have had a relationship with him. But you robbed me of that. Does he even know I'm his daughter? Were you ever going to tell him?"

"He doesn't know. I decided not to tell him," Lindsey said.

"You made a choice for me, too. One I had no say in. Why? Why couldn't you be up front about it, from the start?"

"I had my reasons. I didn't want to hurt other people."

"Other people are hurt," Nina cried. "Me. I'm hurt. And I'm pissed. I feel as though my whole identity has been stolen from me."

Lindsey's voice sharpened. "It's not always about you, Nina. Your identity does not depend on the man who fathered you. You are who you are. You're also my daughter. I love you. That should be enough."

"Well, it's not." Nina turned away as the doorbell rang, opening the front door.

"Hi," Tess said to Lindsey. "I'm here to pick up Nina. My roommate's moving out sooner than expected, at the end of the week. For now she can sleep on the sofa."

"Works for me," Nina said. She glanced at Lindsey. "I left your key on the dresser." She stepped past Tess onto the porch and went down the steps.

"I had a late appointment with a client in Oakland," Tess said. "I was leaving his office when Nina called my cell phone, so I came right over. She said you'd had a blow-up. I'm sorry. I hope you work it out."

"So do I." Lindsey smiled, a poor attempt to mask the turmoil she felt.

"I'll talk with her. Maybe I can help. Have you had a chance to…?"

"The banker's box?" Lindsey shook her head. "Not yet."

When Tess's car pulled away from the curb, Lindsey leaned against the porch column, the weather-roughened wood prickling her cheek. Tears came. She felt heartsick, the way she had last December when Nina left with her boyfriend. Had she finally lost her daughter for good?

I can't think about that now.

She went into the house, tired from the journey and this latest emotional battle. At least the cats were glad to see her. Clementine and Lola meowed as they circled her legs, telling tales of abandonment and imminent starvation. The note Gretchen had left on the kitchen counter belied their protestations. Lindsey washed and dried the cat bowls, then opened a can. The cats purred and happily consumed their dinner.

Lindsey took a half-full bottle of Chardonnay from the refrigerator and poured herself a glass of wine. Tears threatened again, but she fought them back. She couldn't think about Nina right now. She had to think about something else. She carried her wine back to her office, turned on her computer, and listened to the messages on the answering machine. A couple of hang-ups, two calls from friends. Nothing from Lily Hsu. She contemplated the banker's box she'd pushed against one wall. Pandora's Box, open now, already letting the evil escape. She sat cross-legged on the floor and pulled the box toward her. She had to know. Ever since she'd heard Merle Sefton's version of events in El Salvador, Lindsey had wondered about the tall, dark-haired man the reporter saw in the hallway at the Aragón house. Hal Norwood? What if he'd known about the San Blas massacre and cover-up? That wasn't like Hal, to keep quiet about something so horrible. Or was it? How well did she know him? How well did she know any of her friends? Lately they seemed like strangers.

Lindsey separated the box's contents into categories. The artifacts, as she thought of them, went to her left. There were the obvi-

ous keepsakes, gilded baby shoes for each of Annabel's three children, a small handprint on a round plaster plaque that Tess had made
in kindergarten, a wooden tray with Adam's name scratched on the
bottom, a painted china dish signed by Sharon. These were the trin-
kets mothers kept, treasured because they were made by little hands
in art class or wood shop, presented with great flourishes on Mother's
Day, birthdays, Christmas. Their intrinsic value was in who made
them, who wore them. Lindsey also had such keepsakes, lovingly pre-
served, including the bronzed baby shoes, a mosaic plaque created
from wooden sticks and the contents of Grandma's button jar, and a
plump little cat Nina had sculpted out of clay and painted in decid-
edly non-cat colors, blue and purple and green.

Tears welled again as she thought of Nina. She sipped wine and
examined Annabel's keepsakes. The oxidized metal wind chimes tinkled as she set them on the floor. She picked up the tarnished silver
pineapple and crystal fragment, then set them aside and peered into
the box. Here were the address books she'd looked at last week, trying
to locate Lily Hsu. And the book with the strange inscription, a slim
volume by Dylan Thomas, the Welsh poet. She looked at the words
written on the title page. Were they in Welsh? The name below the
inscription looked like Rhonda. Annabel must have felt some connection to the person who'd given her this book, because she'd kept
it with her other treasures. Lindsey put the book on her office chair.
She'd look up the words on the Internet.

Next were three brown accordion folders, each one numbered,
with a flap closing the top. Lindsey picked up a folder. The contents
spilled into an untidy pile in front of her. She picked up an old black-
and-white photograph showing a young woman dressed in a white
blouse and gray skirt with a hemline below the knee. Her dark hair
was arranged in a Forties style. Written on the back of the photograph was the legend INÉS MARGARITA ARAGÓN, SAN SALVADOR, 20TH
BIRTHDAY, 2 APRIL 1949. So this was Annabel's mother. George Dunlin had been seventy-five when he died in 1989, so he'd been fifteen
years older than the woman he married.

Lindsey sifted through the papers, photocopies from the *San
Francisco Chronicle* and *Examiner* of the 1950s, with dates written in

the margins. The society pages of both newspapers had noted the Dunlin wedding in June 1950, and Annabel's birth in January 1952. In subsequent years the newspapers had chronicled and examined, in articles and photos, the social life of the Dunlins, at parties and receptions, the opera, ballet, theater and symphony. Mr. Dunlin always looked the same. But Mrs. Dunlin had changed. She looked increasingly stylish, her sophistication growing with each passing year.

Lindsey picked up a news article with a headline announcing the death of Mrs. George Dunlin. The woman had stumbled on the stairs of the Pacific Heights house and plunged down, hitting her head on the newel post. The body had been found by her sister-in-law, Mrs. Lawrence Megarris. Police were investigating and an inquest was pending. The inquest gave the coroner's final ruling—accidental death. A private family service had been held at a funeral home a few days after Mrs. Dunlin died. Then Lindsey found an article dated September 1961, stating that Mrs. Rebecca Megarris, widow of the late Lawrence Megarris and George Dunlin's sister, had been elected to the board of directors of the Dunlin Corporation. How did Mrs. Megarris's election to the board fit into the story of Annabel's mother?

She straightened the papers and returned them to the file, ignoring the other two folders. She'd been sidetracked long enough. She wanted to find out where Hal Norwood had been in April 1989. She sorted through Annabel's datebooks and calendars until she found the datebook from 1989, the year of the massacre at San Blas. It was a spiral-bound book decorated with lush color reproductions of paintings by Georgia O'Keeffe. Annabel's handwriting crowded every page with the record of her life. January—SHARON/DENTIST/2 P.M. February—ADAM/DOCTOR/10 A.M. March brought TESS/SCHOOL PLAY/7 P.M. Annabel had attended the symphony, the opera, the ballet, and in March—LINDSEY/DINNER/PLAY.

She flipped through the calendar to the fourth week in April, where, on Wednesday, Annabel had written SFO/NYC and a series of numbers. Flight numbers, departure and arrival times, and a Manhattan hotel reservation. Annabel had gone to New York City—by herself, or with Hal? Lindsey scrutinized the other entries in the date-

book. Two Broadway shows, the Met, MOMA. Then on Saturday—
MEET HAL MAD SQ GDN/DINNER W/FRED & ROBIN.

Annabel had accompanied Hal to a trade show, Lindsey guessed. Sunday's entry in the datebook noted the number of their flight to San Francisco, and the departure and arrival times. Sunday was the day of the San Blas massacre. So the dark-haired man Merle had seen at the Aragón *finca* wasn't Hal. But the conversation Merle overheard indicated he had some connection with the Dunlin firm.

I need to talk with Max Brinker, Lindsey thought. He knows everything.

The phone rang. The voice on the other end belonged to Lily Hsu.

"I'm so glad you called," Lindsey said. "Annabel asked me to contact you. She had a stroke and she's in rehab. She really wants to see you." Lindsey gave Mrs. Hsu the address and phone number of the hospital. "Could we meet tomorrow? I'd like to talk about Annabel."

Silence, as though Lily Hsu were considering whether or not she wanted to have that conversation. Then she gave Lindsey the address of a restaurant on Clement Street in San Francisco's Richmond District. "I will meet you at one."

22

ON TUESDAY MORNING, Lindsey told Flor about her conversation with Merle Sefton. "She thought she heard a baby cry at the Aragón house. The woman who worked there seemed to confirm this. The reporter never saw the children. They were probably taken to an orphanage."

"That much I guessed," Flor said. "But this doesn't help me get Efraín back. I went to the Farmers Market on Saturday but he wasn't there. That leaves me with the high school. What else can I do?" She looked at Lindsey, her face full of hope and trust, seeking answers.

Confession is good for the soul, so goes the saying. Thus far, revealing secrets had left Lindsey's soul feeling bruised. But she couldn't keep the information from Flor any longer. She took a deep breath. "I know who he is. I know the people who adopted him."

Trust ebbed from Flor's face. "Why did you keep this from me?"

Lindsey faltered, her words awkward, excuses rather than explanations. "I didn't know he was Efraín until you pointed him out. I've known his adoptive parents for years. The orphanage in San Salvador said his parents were dead."

Flor was angry now. "I'm alive. I'm his mother. I want my son. Tell me where he is."

"Please give me some time. He doesn't have any idea you're alive. I've been waiting for the right moment to talk with my friends. Let me tell them. Then I'll arrange a meeting. Give me a few days."

Flor shook her head as she pushed back her chair. "I've waited weeks. I will give you a day. If I don't hear from you by noon tomorrow, I will go to the high school and stand outside until I see him, no matter how long it takes. Find a way to tell them."

"I will." But there would never be a good time to have that conversation with Gretchen and Doug. "Oh, Flor…I'm sorry."

"So am I."

THE Dunlin Building on the corner of Montgomery and California streets was a matronly dowager of graceful proportions, with decorative cornices on the roof and ledges and sensible sash windows that opened to let in breezes from the bay, unlike its towering neighbors with their sealed glass and air conditioning, their bland postmodern masks. The building harked back to a different San Francisco, when life was slower, more ordered, more elegant, and people wore gloves and hats when they went downtown. Now security guards staffed a barrier in front of the elevators, a sign this was no longer that gracious time. In an alcove off the lobby, an espresso bar and retail shop dispensed Dunlin coffee and tea.

Lindsey had called Max early this morning, before leaving to meet Flor. As long as she was going to be in San Francisco, she hoped to talk with him. He'd agreed to meet her in the lobby and talk on the way to his lunch appointment. How would she find out what she needed to know? Max could spot a concocted story a mile off. The truth, or a variation thereof, was best.

"Max. How are you?"

"Fine." For a man his age, Max looked good in his well-cut gray suit, still big and broad-shouldered, with more wrinkles on his face. What hair remained was white. He smiled at her. "Good to see you. I understand your daughter, Nina, is temping, as Claire's assistant."

Lindsey felt a pang as she thought about Nina. "Yes. She started this morning."

They walked out to California Street. Max cut through the lunch-hour crowds like a battleship followed by a tugboat. "What's on your mind, Lindsey?"

She chose her variation of the truth carefully, though her story sounded threadbare to her. "I'm working on a book. I need background detail about the coffee business in El Salvador during the civil war. Dunlin Corporation has connections there. I'd like to talk with someone who traveled to coffee plantations and may have observed the conflict. I've interviewed an immigrant who was there in the spring of nineteen eighty-nine, working on an estate in Chalatenango department. I thought I'd start with you. You're chief of operations and you've been with the company since—"

"Since Moses was an altar boy," Max finished as they walked up Montgomery Street.

"Hal has visited Salvadoran growers," Lindsey said. "But I don't want to bother him. What about you? Have you been there?"

"Not me. I don't travel much, never did." Max gave her a side-long glance that left her feeling as though he'd figured out there was more to her variation of the truth than book research. "El Salvador... Specifically 'eighty-nine?"

"Since my other source was there that year it would be good to get another viewpoint from the same period."

"I certainly remember the civil war," Max said. "The rebels targeted coffee growers, trying to shut down production and paralyze the economy. You should talk with Rod Llewellyn."

"There's a name from the past. He was one of the guards at the Berkeley house."

Max nodded. "He's now a senior vice president in Operations, based in Houston. I'm sure he visited El Salvador in 'eighty-nine."

They crossed Market Street at Third, stopping on the corner in front of the Rand-McNally store, its window displays full of maps and guidebooks about Latin America. "What's his phone number in Houston?" she asked.

"You can talk face-to-face," Max said. "Rod's in town on company business."

"The board meeting," Lindsey said. "Interesting column in the *Chronicle* business section last week."

"It should be an equally interesting board meeting," Max said. "I'll have Rod call you."

"I'd appreciate that. He can reach me at these numbers." Lindsey handed him her card.

23

INSIDE THE TRAVEL STORE, Rod looked at colorful guidebooks designed to lure travelers to the beaches of Rio de Janeiro, the lush jungles of Costa Rica, the antiquities of Yucatán.

He glanced out the window and saw Max with a woman whose dark hair was streaked with gray. Lindsey, after all these years, a link to that time in Berkeley, when things were simple, before life got complicated.

Lindsey and Max walked in different directions. Rod caught up with Max at Neetos, where they queued up and checked the menu board over the counter. "What did Lindsey want?"

"Background information on the coffee business in El Salvador, for a book she's writing. Or so she says. I'm curious about her reasons."

"Why? Your suspicious nature?"

"My suspicious nature has served me well through the years." Max stepped up to the counter. "A Reuben sandwich, fries, and a Coke." He turned to Rod. "What'll it be?"

"A Caesar salad, with grilled chicken."

Max snorted in derision. "Oh, live a little. Don't leave me out here in cholesterol city all by myself."

Rod grinned. "All right. Two Reubens, then. I'll have coleslaw and iced tea."

They found a vacant table. Rod squeezed lemon juice into his tea. "Why are you curious about Lindsey's reasons?"

"I don't think she was being completely straight with me. She interviewed an immigrant who was working in El Salvador in 'eighty-nine, on a coffee plantation in Chalatenango department. That's where the Aragón estate is located She wants to talk with someone at Dunlin who was there at the same time. That would be Hal, Chuck Caldwell, several others—and you. Talk with Lindsey. Find out if there's more to this. Here's her card."

Max put the card on the table. The server showed up with their Reubens. The contents oozed between the dark rye bread slices. Max picked up his sandwich and bit off a mouthful.

"Now let's talk about tomorrow's meeting," Max said. "Getting you elected to the board is the first salvo. Dealing with Claire is the battle. It's going to be a tough fight. Claire is trying to take over this company, and she won't give up after one skirmish. We need every bit of leverage we can use against her."

Rod looked down at his plate and felt queasy. Too much food. He forced himself to take a bite. "You're confident I'll get elected."

"I am." Max wiped greasy hands on his napkin. "Hal's in our corner. I planted the seed and watered it. You've got my vote, Hal's, and Annabel's proxy. Caldwell's vote makes it four to Claire's three. I'll talk with Caldwell again, point out your abilities and qualifications, and remind him that you've been with the company far longer than this guy, Graham, whom Claire wants to put on the board. Experience and expertise should win the day." Max upended the ketchup bottle over his fries. "That's just the beginning. Once you're on the board, Claire will still be a problem. We'll have to neutralize her. I'd like to get rid of her, but that will take some time."

"Get rid of her how?" Rod asked. The phrase had a certain finality to it. But surely that was just Rod's own flight of fancy. Or wishful thinking on Max's part.

"Dump her from the board. Oust her. What do you think I mean? Assassination?" Max popped a couple of French fries into his mouth and wiped a smear of red from his lips. "Don't think I haven't considered it, usually after I've had a few drinks."

"I'm relieved to hear you're not homicidal," Rod said, only half-joking. Max had probably countenanced all sorts of deeds in his years with the company.

"By the time I'm finished with Claire," Max said, with a wolfish smile, "she'll be history. The directors will boot her ass off the board, out of the company, too, if I have my way. Then I can work on getting rid of Rebecca. Maybe the old broad will save me the trouble and die. Now spare me the politically correct crap. I'm a sexist old toad. I call a spade a spade. Everybody knows it. That's part of my charm."

"I wouldn't exactly call it charm, Max. But you're an original."

"Thank God for that. The world's too full of cookie-cutter clones, people who don't say what they mean and are terrified of having opinions. With me, you know what you're getting."

"About eighty proof, I'd say. With a bite."

"Damn straight."

"You're devious, too." Rod took a bite of his sandwich. "That column in the *Chronicle* last Wednesday wasn't very complimentary to Claire and her money-losing coffee bars. Did the columnist get his information from you?"

Max chuckled. "Strictly confidential, of course, and not for attribution."

"Very underhanded of you."

"I use every weapon in my arsenal," Max said. "Claire doesn't fight fair. Neither do I. She's sticking her fingers where they don't belong, taking over more turf, amassing more power. Caldwell's retirement gives her an opportunity to put her protégé on the board, but it won't stop there. She has another chance to control the board. I expect her to bring it up at the meeting tomorrow, especially when you're elected to replace Caldwell instead of her boy. That will upset her apple cart but she's got a backup plan."

"Annabel?" It was the next logical choice, given the company bylaws governing incapacitated directors.

Max nodded. "Eight weeks. If a company director has been incapacitated for eight weeks, the board can replace that director. Come Saturday, it's eight weeks since Annabel's stroke."

"Replacing a board member who's incapacitated isn't a given,"

162 · Janet Dawson

Rod said. "I reviewed the bylaws. It's simply something that could be done at the board's discretion. It was one thing to replace Farnsworth after his car accident earlier this year. His injuries were life-threatening and he did die. But I don't think anyone will convince Hal to replace Annabel. There's every chance she'll recover. Besides, it was her father's company, a big psychological factor that argues against replacing Annabel."

"Claire will argue it was her father's company at one time. Rebecca will back her up. Those two are a poisonous pair."

"How is Annabel?" Rod asked.

Max shrugged. "Lots of therapy, physical and speech. Hal's concerned about her mental state, says she seems disoriented and depressed. Not surprising. She's got aphasia, due to the stroke, so when she talks it's hard to understand her. That must be frustrating for her. It will take time, but she'll recover. Annabel's one tough lady."

Rod took another bite of his sandwich. "You wanted me to check out the rumors about the company selling some of its real estate. Apparently the *Chronicle* columnist heard the same rumors."

Max nodded. "He asked me about it, when I was giving him the lowdown on Claire and her coffee bar debacle. I gave him a no-comment on the real estate angle. He went ahead and tossed that into his column. Of course he wouldn't tell me where he picked up the rumors. It's all one way with reporters. Did you find out anything?"

"I checked with a friend of mine who works in commercial real estate. Strictly confidential, of course, and not for attribution." Rod smiled. "That boutique hotel company definitely wants to buy the headquarters building. They're offering a big pile of money."

Max shook his head. "They made an offer last fall. The board shot 'em down. The vote was five to two, with Claire and Rebecca in favor, everyone else opposed."

"They're hoping the board will change its mind."

"Not a chance," Max declared. "There's a lot of history in that building, company history and personal history. We're not selling. Not while I'm on the board. I don't care how much money the hotel chain is offering. Why are they still sniffing around?"

"Because Claire, or someone supposedly representing her, has been talking to them," Rod said. "The hotel chain thinks their offer is still on the table."

Max savaged the rest of his sandwich. "If Claire gets a majority, she'll have carte blanche to do any damn thing she pleases. But she doesn't have the votes yet. The board rejected that hotel offer. Claire's talking out of turn. She has no authorization to sell company assets, whether it's the headquarters building or the warehouse. Any idea who her representative is?"

"I wondered if it might be Marissa Tybalt, the new general counsel. You said she was in Claire's corner. But it would be a conflict of interest."

"Not that I wouldn't put it past either of them. It could be Rebecca."

"I thought of that," Rod said. "Rebecca does whatever Claire wants her to do. As for the other real estate, the warehouse would also fetch a good price. Lots of development going on in that part of town, old commercial and industrial buildings being converted to residential use, with lofts and condos going in. Again, it appears that Claire, or her representative, has been talking with a developer about converting the warehouse into lofts."

Max glowered. "Again without the board's okay."

"It gets worse," Rod told him. "Or better, from your perspective, since you're looking for ammunition to use against Claire. I checked out the developer, the same one who's been active converting warehouses and plants to lofts all up and down the Oakland waterfront. If my informant is correct, Claire owns a piece of his company."

"Big conflict of interest," Max said. "Can we prove it?"

"I'm working on it," Rod said. "But the board meeting is tomorrow morning. I may not have anything substantive by then."

Max shoved his plate aside, wiping his hands on his napkin. "Once you're officially a director, we'll tackle this real estate situation and nail Claire to the wall."

"Caldwell's retirement is effective June first," Rod said. "A month away. I'll need to go back to Houston and tie up whatever loose ends I can, personal and business."

"Personal?" Max grinned. "I thought you were wedded to the job."

"Seems like it. But I do have a personal life, an apartment I'll have to give up, in addition to packing up and moving back to San Francisco." Rod frowned. "I've got to find a place to live here."

"Store your stuff and live in a hotel for a while." Max drank the rest of his Coke.

"Hotels get old," Rod said.

"You lived in North Beach before, didn't you?"

Rod nodded, remembering. "A one-bedroom flat, above an Italian deli, near Washington Square. It was cheap. And I liked the neighborhood."

"You've come up in the world," Max said. "Rents are sky-high these days, but you can afford to live anywhere you want. I'm on Nob Hill. Bought a condo years ago, because it's close to the office. I ride the California Street cable car to work." Max glanced at his watch. "I'd better get back to the office. Keep looking into what Claire is doing under the table. See if you can find something tangible that proves it. Call Lindsey and set up a meeting."

They walked together to the intersection of California and Montgomery streets and Max entered the Dunlin Building. Rod had always liked the Art Deco touches of a bygone era. It would be a shame to sell it. The building had been synonymous with the Dunlin Corporation for nearly fifty years, a landmark in the Financial District. If Max had his way, Rod would be working there in a few weeks. Living in San Francisco again—well, he'd always loved the city.

The clanging bell of the California Street cable car shook him out of his reverie. He walked north on Montgomery to the intersection where Columbus Avenue angled off to the northwest, into Chinatown and finally North Beach. The boundaries of the districts were fluid, and China was definitely encroaching on Italy. Trays of pork buns and dumplings beckoned from *dim sum* cafés. When he crossed Broadway, the flavors changed. In the trattorias and coffee shops people lingered over espresso and biscotti. On this sunny spring day a shop selling gelato did a brisk business.

He was there before he realized where he was headed, standing on the sidewalk outside a delicatessen on Union Street. The Powell Street cable car bell clanged as the car moved through the intersection. Inside the deli was a refrigerated case of the cannoli he'd once loved. He could almost taste the crisp light shells filled with creamy ricotta, studded with fruit and chocolate chips.

His eyes moved up to the open window of the apartment where he'd lived so many years ago. Still there, though everything else had changed. That window box hadn't been there before. It held geraniums—white, pink, red. A young woman with long dark hair appeared and tipped a watering can over the flowers.

Music poured from the apartment, the urgent thrum of guitars, the underlying bass, the rhythm of the accompanying drums. He recognized the opening bars immediately, even before the sweet piping soprano sang the first words. The young woman at the apartment window wasn't even born when that song came out. He took Lindsey's card from his pocket as Joni Mitchell sang about falling in love too fast.

24

Berkeley, California, February 1974

MUSIC POURED FROM the house. The two women on the porch, alto and soprano, chimed in as Joni Mitchell sang about falling in love too fast.

Though it was February, the weather had turned balmy. Spring flirted with the Bay Area as the first crocuses pushed through the soil to sunlight. Tulips and daffodils promised to follow, ignoring the possibility that March would roar like a lion, blustering with wind, rain and cold.

Their pictures didn't do them justice. They were both quite pretty, Rod thought. Dark-haired Lindsey was the down-to-earth peasant next to Annabel, the patrician, with her chestnut-brown hair and hazel eyes.

"You're new," Annabel said. "I haven't seen you before."

"Don't make assumptions," Lindsey said. "Maybe he stopped to ask for directions." She was in T-shirt and cutoffs, a large square bandage on her left knee. She carried a bag of potting soil across the sunny porch and began transplanting geraniums into a large clay pot.

Annabel smiled. "Shouldn't there be a password or a secret handshake?"

"Mr. Brinker sent me," Rod said. "I guess that's the password."

"Oh, yes, the password is definitely Brinker. I'm Annabel, this is Lindsey. But you know that. You've been thoroughly briefed."

Yes, he had. He'd read through Brinker's files. He knew which apartments the women lived in, what they were studying at the university, and their class schedules. He knew that Claire drove a red Mustang, while Gretchen didn't have a car, relying on buses and a bicycle. The green VW bug was Lindsey's. The blue AMC Gremlin with the denim seatcovers, parked in the driveway to his left, belonged to Annabel. Lindsey had gotten that injury to her knee Monday night during the Hearst kidnapping.

The four young women who lived in the house knew about the guards, because their cooperation was essential to make the security arrangements work. Rod's job was to hang out in the neighborhood, keeping an eye on the house from the rooms Brinker had rented in the ramshackle rooming house next door, discreetly, inconspicuously, but there, ever-vigilant. The other part was to accompany Annabel Dunlin or Claire Megarris wherever they went.

Rod was conscious of his scruffy, unkempt appearance. He was usually more presentable, especially in the presence of two such attractive young women. Now dark stubble covered the lower half of his face. He hadn't even bothered to rake his fingers through his hair after getting out of bed this morning. Tight faded jeans and a tie-dyed T-shirt in a rainbow of bright colors encased his lean frame, and a pair of scuffed leather boots completed the ensemble. Brinker wanted him to blend in. After his walk around campus, down Telegraph Avenue and through People's Park, he concluded that he did.

"My name's Rod Llewellyn," he said.

Annabel repeated the name as though she liked the taste. A breeze stirred the wind chimes hanging from a hook above Annabel's living room window. They were drinking coffee, Annabel from a green mug, Lindsey from a blue one. Annabel sat on a rattan chair, one of four that looked as though they'd spent several seasons on the porch. The low table held a wooden tray with two mugs, orange and yellow, a sugar bowl and creamer, a Thermos, and a square pan of brownies, several missing.

"Would you like some coffee?" Annabel asked. "Claire and Gretchen must be sleeping in this morning. No sign of either of them, and it's almost noon."

"No, thanks," he said. "I'm just here to have a look around the place."

Lindsey refilled her mug. "I heard Gretchen come in about nine."

"Claire was probably out till all hours." The front door opened and Annabel looked over her shoulder. "Speak of the devil. Here's one of the stragglers."

Rod identified the newcomer—Claire Megarris, with her short blond hair. Her sleeveless knit shirt clung to her body, showing off breasts unencumbered by a bra. The shirt was tucked into the elastic waistband of a pair of shiny red-and-white nylon athletic shorts, and her long slim legs stretched to bare feet. Fingernails and toenails were painted bright red.

"Late night?" Annabel asked.

"You're wearing Stanford colors," Lindsey said, referring to Cal's archrival in Palo Alto.

"They're Stanford shorts. Track and field, sweetie. I took 'em off a skinny little guy with a great big javelin." Claire threw back her head and laughed. Then she fixed Rod with a direct gaze. "Who's this?"

"Rod Llewellyn," Annabel said. "Mr. Brinker hired him to keep an eye on us. Mr. Llewellyn, my cousin, Claire Megarris."

"Miss Megarris," he said, with a nod.

A smile teased Claire's mouth. "Oh, that sounds so very formal. How about I call you Rod, and you call me Claire?" She picked up Annabel's green mug and took a sip.

Annoyed, Annabel removed the mug from Claire's hands. "You're always helping yourself."

"Oh, all right." Claire rolled her eyes. "You put too much cream in your coffee anyway. I like mine to bite back." She poured black coffee into the orange mug. "Lindsey made brownies for breakfast." She dug a square from the pan and draped herself over one of the porch chairs, making pleasurable moans as she tore off moist chunks and stuffed them into her mouth, licking gooey chocolate from her fingers. A woman of appetites, Rod thought. She put him in mind of a sleek cat, stretching her long legs out to the sun, washing herself after a meal.

The front door opened and the fourth resident of the house stepped onto the porch. Gretchen froze, staring at Rod. She looked as though she'd had a bad night, and whatever had precipitated it wasn't going to be cured by coffee and brownies. Her red-rimmed eyes invited him to leave.

"I'll have a look around, inside and out," Rod said, taking out the key that fit both the front and back doors. "I'll check the backyard first."

He turned as Claire said, "Gretchen? Sweetie, what's wrong?"

"Doug and I had a fight," Gretchen said, voice ragged.

Time I got out of that conversation, Rod thought. He rounded the corner of the house and walked up the driveway. The thick privet hedge to his left separated this lot from the rooming house. A six-foot-high redwood fence surrounded the backyard. There was a gate wide enough for a car, now secured by a padlock, and a smaller gate with a deadbolt lock. Rod unlocked this, stepping into the backyard, where a detached single garage was used for storage.

Rod walked the perimeter of the yard, checking the padlock on the garage doors and making sure there were no loose boards on the fence. The garden at the back of the yard waited to be turned and planted anew. The roses had been pruned and the canes sprouted new growth above the cuts. He glanced up at the rooming house on the other side of the fence, at the windows of the two second-floor rooms that Max Brinker had rented. His new boss had chosen well. Both the patio and the back stairs were visible from the rooms where the security guards would be staying. A man with a moustache looked down at Rod—Carl, his new partner.

When the house had been converted from a single family home into four apartments, metal stairs had been added to the back, for access to the upstairs hallway as well as a fire escape. A square concrete patio outside the back door held a barbecue grill, picnic table, lawn and lounge chairs. More wind chimes hung outside Annabel Dunlin's bedroom window.

Rod climbed the metal stairs. The curtains of Lindsey Page's bedroom were open, revealing a neatly made double bed with a colorful patchwork quilt, books piled on the nightstand. He unlocked the second-story entrance. Claire's apartment was to his right, Gretchen's to the left. He walked down the inside stairs. The front door was ajar. He heard Gretchen say, "We love each other. I want to get married. He wants to wait until he finishes law school. If I push him he might break it off."

"I'll knock some sense into the guy," Claire said.

"They need to work it out for themselves," Annabel said.

"Give it time. You'll figure things out." Lindsey pushed the door wider, looking startled to see Rod in the hall.

"Sorry," Rod said.

Lindsey unlocked her apartment. "I guess we'll have to get used to it."

Rod stepped out to the porch. Gretchen wiped away tears and turned her head so Rod couldn't see her face. "Everything looks fine," Rod said. "Just make sure the doors are closed and locked when you're inside. I'll be going to class with you on Monday, Miss Dunlin."

She smiled. "Please, call me Annabel. We're going to be spending a lot of time together."

25

THE RESTAURANTS ON Clement Street reflected the diverse demographics of this part of town—Asian, Russian, and everything else. Lindsey entered a Chinese restaurant, its tables covered with pink cloths. The front counter held a cash register and a collection of Phalaenopsis orchids, with pink, white and magenta blossoms like fat butterflies, on tall thin stems. An older woman sat at a corner table, dressed in blue slacks and a beige silk sweater.

"Lily Hsu?" Lindsey asked.

The woman nodded. "Lindsey Page. Finally we meet, after all these years. Please, sit down." Mrs. Hsu reached for the pale green teapot, poured tea into Lindsey's cup and freshened her own.

"I'm glad I located you." Lindsey sat down and picked up the delicate porcelain cup, sipping the hot fragrant brew.

Lily Hsu appeared to be in her seventies, small and fine-boned, with short silver hair brushed back from her wrinkled face. Deep brown eyes regarded Lindsey across the table. "This morning I went to see Annabel. She's getting better." She picked up a menu. "The food is good here. Do you like hot things?"

"I do, but not too hot. What would you recommend?"

Mrs. Hsu pointed out her favorites, advising which entrées were mild or moderately spicy, as opposed to incendiary. Then she beckoned to the server, ordering in Chinese.

"I feel as though I already know you," Mrs. Hsu said. "Your daughter Nina is the same age as Tess. You were a history professor in San Luis Obispo. Then you retired. You live in Berkeley and you write books."

"I don't know anything about you," Lindsey said. "I didn't even know you existed until Annabel mentioned you last week."

"That's the way Annabel wants it." Mrs. Hsu sipped her tea. "Our relationship is a secret. We talk on the phone, we meet for lunch. But no one else knows."

"Why the mystery?" Yet another puzzle, Lindsey thought.

"Annabel feared we might be prevented from seeing one another. This arrangement began when she was still in high school. Things were different then."

That seemed unnecessarily cautious, even for Annabel. But Lindsey recalled Annabel's words from a week ago. "She lost you, and then she found you again."

"In nineteen sixty-seven. The Summer of Love, they called it, those hippies who came to the city." Mrs. Hsu smiled briefly. "Although it wasn't summer. It was spring. Annabel and Claire cut school, to go to the Haight. My husband and I lived there. Annabel saw me coming out of a store and followed me home. I almost didn't recognize her, she'd grown so much. Since then, we have kept in touch."

"How long have you known her?"

"Her whole life. I started working for the Dunlins when Annabel was a baby. Now she has grown children of her own. And I'm an old woman."

The server set two platters and a covered lacquer bowl in the center of the table. Lindsey removed the cover from the bowl and spooned steamed rice onto her plate. Her lunch entrée, a combination of chicken and garlicky eggplant, was supposedly mild, but the spices and peppers brought tears to her eyes. She ate some rice to put out the fire.

"Annabel's mother, what was she like?" Lindsey asked.

Mrs. Hsu wielded chopsticks over her prawns and snow peas. She didn't respond right away, her face guarded, her eyes less welcoming. "Why do you ask?"

"I have a box of Annabel's things," Lindsey said. "Address books, datebooks, file folders. When I was looking for your phone number, I found a folder with photographs and newspaper clippings about Mrs. Dunlin and her death. Annabel kept them all these years. I guess she's curious about her mother, since she died when Annabel was so young. Now I'm curious, too. The photographs and articles tell me Mrs. Dunlin was beautiful and much younger than Mr. Dunlin. She was from a wealthy family in El Salvador."

"Rich people are different." Mrs. Hsu's voice and expression turned vinegary. "Rich people are waited on, hand and foot. That's the way she grew up, in that rich family in El Salvador. She never picked up after herself. I don't think she knew how. She'd always had someone to clean up after her. For the last nine years of her life, it was me." The older woman shrugged. "I got used to it. When you need a job, you get used to lots of things."

Lindsey remembered the things she'd gotten used to, a single mother adapting to the demands of a job while juggling the demands of a child. Unappreciative, unmotivated students, the ones who cut class, didn't do the work, then whined because they got a bad grade. Academic politics, the endless meetings and committees and commitments that ate time and interfered with research and instruction. Turf wars over offices and perks and pecking order. Petulant, sniping, back-stabbing colleagues. The constant search for grant money to do research. No wonder she'd retired early.

"So you took care of Annabel as well, from the time she was a baby."

"Who else was going to take care of that little girl?" Indignation flared in Mrs. Hsu's eyes. "Mr. Dunlin ignored her, because she wasn't a boy. He wanted a son. He didn't get one. When Annabel was two Mrs. Dunlin got pregnant again, then miscarried. She was more interested in clothes and parties. She had a baby because he expected it. She didn't know how to be a mother any more than she knew how to keep house. I took care of Annabel, so they didn't have to pay any attention to her. Unless they needed to show her off. Then they'd dress her up and display her. People like that shouldn't have children. I was Annabel's mother."

People who clean our houses and diaper our children know a lot about us, Lindsey thought, more than we would like them to know. "Thank goodness Annabel had you. But you left at some point."

"Six weeks after Mrs. Dunlin died. They fired me," Mrs. Hsu said. "Him and that sister of his. For negligence. I put a pot roast into the pressure cooker and went out for a visit. The meat boiled dry and burned, set the kitchen cabinets on fire. But it wasn't an accident. I didn't make a mistake like that. There was plenty of water in that pot, and the stove burner was set on low, to simmer. I checked before I left and I was gone half an hour. Someone poured off the water and turned the stove setting to high."

Why start a fire? To provide an excuse to fire Lily Hsu? Why get rid of the housekeeper? Unless… "You were there the day Mrs. Dunlin died," Lindsey said. "What happened?"

Caution erased Mrs. Hsu's resentment. "She fell down the stairs."

"Was there more to it than that?" Lindsey asked. "There's a hint of something in the newspaper clippings. Speculation, questions unanswered."

"Why do you want to stir up old things better left to gather dust?"

"What happened then plays a part in who Annabel is now,"

Lindsey said. "I found other things in that box. Metal wind chimes, with a tag inscribed with Chinese characters. Did you give her those?"

Mrs. Hsu smiled. "For her ninth birthday. She saved them all these years?"

"Her ninth birthday would have been about three months before her mother died. Were you there that day?"

Mrs. Hsu's smile vanished. "When you look into the past, sometimes you find things that are better left there. Careful what you wish for, you might get it. Are you prepared for what you might get?"

"The truth is what I hope to get."

"The truth can be unpleasant. It can hurt you, and other people."

Lindsey thought about her own unpleasant truths. "Believe me, I know. Why would Annabel keep a piece of broken crystal and a little silver pineapple?"

Mrs. Hsu lifted the lid of the teapot, then signaled the server, who brought another teapot, full and steaming. She poured fresh cups for both of them. "Mrs. Dunlin had a collection of pineapples, on a table at the foot of the stairs. Dust catchers. There was a big crystal one." She stopped and compressed her lips. "So Annabel kept the silver one. She must have picked it up when she found..."

Lindsey finished the sentence for her. "The body. Please tell me about that day. Was there something odd about the way Mrs. Dunlin died?"

"Annabel asked me that question many times. I put her off. But she kept asking. Finally I told her." Mrs. Hsu sipped her tea. "I baked almond cookies that morning. Annabel loves my almond cookies."

26

San Francisco, California, April 1961

LILY HSU PUT THE LAST batch of almond cookies into the oven. She set the timer, then washed the bowl and utensils. Outside the kitchen window, a gray sky held a hint of rain. Wind stirred the metal chimes near the back door. Lily switched on the radio. "I guess

I'll have to change my plan," she sang along with Mel Tormé. She put
the teakettle on the stove. When the timer dinged, Lily turned off
the oven and removed the cookies, plump and golden-brown, with
slivered almonds on top.

The teakettle whistled. Lily switched off the burner. She spooned
black tea into a pot and poured boiling water over it, letting the tea
steep until it was good and strong, then she poured herself a cup and
relaxed for a moment, humming along with Rosemary Clooney and
Frank Sinatra. Soon the clothes dryer buzzed, out on the enclosed
back porch. She folded the sheets, stacking them in a wicker basket.
Two doors led out of the kitchen, one to the dining room, another
to the hall, where a door under the stairs led to Mr. Dunlin's study.
Lily balanced the basket on her hip and carried it up the hall. The
pineapple figurines on the little half-moon table at the bottom of the
stairs needed dusting again. She trudged up the stairs and put the
clean sheets away in the linen closet.

Mrs. Dunlin came out of the master bedroom, wearing a gray
linen suit and gray high heels, with a peach silk blouse and pearls.
Her dark hair was pinned into a bun. "I thought you'd gone. You do
the marketing on Friday."

"I'll go soon. Do you need the car?" Lily used Mrs. Dunlin's Ford
for errands.

"Not today. Let me know when you leave." Mrs. Dunlin went
downstairs.

Lily knew from experience the disarray she'd find in the master
bedroom. Mrs. Dunlin rose late and rarely emerged before noon. Lily
brought her a breakfast tray and Mrs. Dunlin sat in bed, drinking coffee and reading the newspaper. Now the tray sat on the unmade bed.
The toast plate was next to the mounded pillows. Crumbs sprinkled
pillowcases and sheets. The cup was on the nightstand, a puddle of
spilled coffee marring the finish. Mrs. Dunlin's nightgown and robe
had been tossed on the carpet near the dressing table. Heaped on
the floor were the blue towels she'd used to dry off after her morning
bath. She'd blotted her lipstick with the napkin. Lily sighed as she
wiped up spilled coffee. She gathered up the breakfast things and set
the tray on the floor. She made the bed, hung the nightgown and

robe in the walk-in closet, collected the damp towels from the bathroom, and replaced them with a mossy green set.

Then she noticed Mrs. Dunlin's suitcase and makeup case on the
chair near the closet door. Both cases were closed, as though packed
and ready to go. On top Lily saw a hat, gloves, and handbag.

Lily frowned, irritated. Was Mrs. Dunlin going away? It would
be just like her to make plans and not tell Lily, who had commitments for the weekend that didn't involve taking care of Annabel.
Tomorrow was her parents' fiftieth anniversary. The whole family was
gathering for a special celebration at a Chinatown restaurant. Lily
had things to do, preparations to make. At times the Dunlins acted
as though the housekeeper didn't have a life, or a family, of her own.

Lily set the tray on top of the wet towels in the basket and carried
them downstairs. Mrs. Dunlin was seated at her desk in the living
room alcove formed by the bay window, pen scratching across paper
as she wrote on pink stationery.

Mrs. Dunlin looked up. "You'll do the marketing now?"

"As soon as I finish with the laundry," Lily said. "Is there something you want?"

Mrs. Dunlin shook her head. "No. There's nothing here I want."

"I saw your suitcase upstairs. Are you going away for the weekend?"

Mrs. Dunlin wrote Mr. Dunlin's name on an envelope. "Just
going away."

"I can't stay with Annabel this weekend," Lily said. "I have family obligations."

"I'm sure Mr. Dunlin will manage. Now go do the marketing."

She's trying to get rid of me, Lily thought as she carried the basket to the kitchen. She wants me out of the house. Why would she
do that?

She stuffed towels into the washing machine on the back porch,
added detergent and turned on the appliance. The radio was still on.
The Mills Brothers sang "Paper Doll" in tight four-part harmony. The
last batch of almond cookies had cooled. Lily put them into a big
round tin. She washed the cookie sheet and Mrs. Dunlin's breakfast things. Then she shifted wet towels from washer to dryer. She

176 · Janet Dawson

checked the grocery list, adding a few items. Mrs. Dunlin gave Lily
money for household expenses every week, crisp greenbacks Lily kept
hidden in a drawer. Now she stuffed money and list into her handbag.
There was something else she was supposed to do. What was it? She
was so distracted these days. She switched off the radio, cutting Tony
Bennett off in mid-refrain, slipped on her jacket and picked up her
handbag, fishing inside for the key ring. Then she remembered. She'd
promised to call her sister before noon and now it was almost one.
Lily picked up the kitchen extension and heard Mrs. Dunlin's voice.

"Gray house, corner of Octavia and Washington, as soon as possible."

Lily quickly hung up. She said she didn't need to use the car,
she thought. Maybe she needs the car after all, and she thinks I've
already left for the grocery store. I should go now. But I promised I'd
call May.

Lily picked up the phone and dialed. "Why are you so late?" her
sister scolded. "I've been standing around waiting for you to call. I
have errands to run."

"Me, too. So talk." Lily was on the phone longer than she expected. After they discussed the anniversary dinner, her sister launched
into a litany of complaints about her husband. "I have to go to the
grocery store," Lily said. It was after one.

I'd better tell her I'm going, Lily thought. She went through the
dining room. Mrs. Dunlin, still at the desk, stood and propped the
envelope against the telephone. Suddenly Lily realized the significance of the suitcase. She's leaving him, leaving Annabel. Lily heard
footsteps coming up the front steps. The cabbie must be here. But no,
a key slid into the lock.

Lily backed into the dining room and slipped behind one of the
double doors. Through the inch-wide gap between door and jamb,
she saw George Dunlin enter the house, dressed in gray pinstripes,
the same shade as his wife's suit. Gray the pair of them, just like the
gray house and the gray foggy day outside. He shut the door and
stared at his wife.

"You're home early," she said. "I wasn't expecting you."

"Obviously not. You'll have to change your plan," he said.

She shook her head. "No, I don't think so."

"So that's it, then. Without a word."

She pointed at the envelope. "I wrote you a letter. Everything I have to say is there."

"Say it, then," he snapped. "You owe me that much."

"I don't owe you anything," she told him.

"Like hell. Don't your marriage vows mean anything to you?"

"This wasn't a marriage, George. It was a financial transaction cementing your business arrangement with my family."

"That's not the only reason."

"Yes, the other clauses in the contract." She stepped away from the desk. "You wanted an ornament to display at social functions. I've done that. You wanted a child. I provided one. I've kept my part of the bargain. No more. It's over."

"You've gotten plenty from this arrangement. My money, my position."

"It's not enough," she said. "It hasn't been a good bargain for either of us. We've shortchanged ourselves, and Annabel. I was never cut out to be a mother and you aren't much of a father. Lily's more of a mother than me."

"You've got some man on the hook or you wouldn't be doing this. Who is he?"

She didn't answer. Instead she walked past him and started up the stairs.

"This conversation isn't over," he said.

"It is for me."

The wind gusted outside. Then the house itself creaked, as it sometimes did. Mr. Dunlin looked around, his eyes cold and furious. Lily shrank back, fear crawling up her spine, afraid to breathe lest she make a sound. Had he seen her cowering behind the dining room door? Could she get away now? He was right there in the hall, just a few feet away.

Mr. Dunlin's right hand closed over the big crystal pineapple, as big as his fist. He started up the stairs. In profile his face looked like a hatchet, ready to strike. Soon he was out of sight.

Eavesdroppers never hear anything good, Lily thought. Poor Annabel. That woman is right. I'm a better mother than she is.

Lily fled. In the detached double garage she pressed the button that opened the garage door. Her hands shook as she got into the sedan and fumbled with the key, taking three tries to start the engine. She shifted into reverse. The Ford shot out of the garage. Brakes squealed, a horn blared. Lily stomped on the brakes, clenched the wheel, and glanced back as a yellow cab whipped past and turned right onto Octavia Street. The cab's horn bleated twice. Lily took a deep breath and shifted the Ford into drive. At the stop sign she realized she'd forgotten to close the garage door. She punched the device on the dashboard, but didn't look back to see if the garage door was closed.

At the store, Lily walked the aisles, taking her time as she filled her cart with groceries. She was reluctant to go back to that house. But she couldn't delay her return forever. She had calmed down, but her heart began pounding again as she loaded sacks into the Ford's trunk. When she arrived at the Dunlin house, police cars with pulsing red lights blocked the street. The garage door was open. A uniformed policeman approached the Ford. "I work at that gray house on the corner. I'm the housekeeper. I went to buy groceries."

"Okay, they'll want to talk to you."

Lily eased the Ford into the garage and got out. Then a big black Cadillac parked at the curb. Mr. Dunlin stared at her as he got out of the passenger seat. His assistant, Mr. Brinker, was at the wheel.

Lily and the policeman carried the groceries into the house and left the sacks on the kitchen counter. The tin of almond cookies she'd baked for Annabel was open. Strange men crowded the house. Someone was taking pictures near the front door.

Lily gasped.

Mrs. Dunlin lay at the bottom of the stairs, blood pooled under her head. The half-moon table had been knocked over. Pineapple figurines scattered the floor. When they told her Annabel was there, Lily rushed through the living room to the study and put her arms around Annabel.

In the living room, Mr. Dunlin, Mrs. Megarris and Mr. Brinker were talking with the police. Then Mr. Dunlin told her to pack Annabel's suitcase. Lily glanced at him, somber in his gray suit. But something wasn't right. He'd changed clothes. Earlier he'd worn gray pinstripes. The suit he wore now was charcoal, almost black, with no pattern. His cold eyes raked over Lily. Had he seen her hiding behind the dining room door?

A tall police inspector wanted to talk with both Lily and Annabel, so Lily led the girl to the kitchen and sat her at the table with a glass of milk and the cookie tin. "Put it from your mind. I don't want you to remember it."

Lily filled the teakettle and put it on the stove. Then she put away the groceries. The tall man, who identified himself as Inspector Niebuhr, walked into the kitchen, accompanied by another man, his partner, Inspector Colluci.

They sat at the table, Lily across from Inspector Niebuhr, with Annabel in between. The little girl hunched over the table, stacking cookies in front of her. The inspector took out a notebook and pen, and asked Lily questions.

"I come to work at seven," Lily said. "I take the California Street cable car from Grant to the end of the line, and walk to the house. This morning I made coffee and took it to Mr. Dunlin in his study. I got Annabel up and dressed, fixed her breakfast, and walked her to school. Mr. Dunlin was gone when I got back. Around ten o'clock I took a breakfast tray up to Mrs. Dunlin. She sleeps late."

Lily pursed her mouth, trying not to show her disapproval of Mrs. Dunlin's lay-abed habits. "I did laundry, sheets. I'm not here weekends and there's always laundry."

Inspector Niebuhr smiled. "Yes, there's always laundry. Especially with a child in the house. Do you fold things as soon as they come out of the dryer? My wife does."

"Yes, right away," Lily said. "It keeps things from wrinkling. Then I baked almond cookies, for Annabel."

"When did you see Mrs. Dunlin again?" Inspector Colluci asked, pacing around the kitchen.

"When I took the clean sheets upstairs to the linen closet. She was all dressed up. She asked if I was going to buy groceries. I do that every Friday. When she went downstairs, I made the bed and cleaned the bathroom. She always leaves towels everywhere. I put out fresh towels and rugs, and took the others downstairs. Mrs. Dunlin was at her desk. She asked again if I was going to buy groceries. I said yes, as soon as I finished the laundry. She said to let her know when I was leaving for the store."

"When was the next time you saw her?" Inspector Colluci asked.

"I went to tell her I was going to do the marketing. I didn't notice the time."

"You left the garage door open," Inspector Niebuhr said.

Lily glanced up. The kitchen door was ajar. So was the study door on the other side of the hall. Mr. Dunlin stood there, scowling. She was frightened. What if he heard? If he hadn't guessed already, he would know she was here when he got home.

Inspector Niebuhr got up and shut the kitchen door. "I guess you didn't mean to leave the garage door open."

"I thought I closed it. Sometimes I push that gadget, but the door doesn't close."

"You didn't finish the laundry either," Inspector Niebuhr said. "You left towels in the dryer. Why didn't you fold them?"

Lily hesitated. "I was running late. I thought I'd fold the towels when I got back. I have so much to do on Fridays."

Should she tell him about Mrs. Dunlin calling for a taxi? But that would lead to more uncomfortable questions, about what else she'd seen and heard.

The kitchen door opened wider and another policeman told them Mr. Dunlin was angry, threatening to make trouble. Rich people always make trouble, Lily thought. These inspectors must be bending some rules.

The two inspectors conferred. Then Inspector Colluci left the kitchen. Inspector Niebuhr sat down. "Hello, Annabel. My name's Gary. I'm a policeman. I'd like to ask you some questions. Will you answer them for me?"

Annabel nodded. Inspector Niebuhr questioned Annabel, probing gently, eliciting information. Why had Mrs. Megarris been here at all? Lily wondered. Why had she gone upstairs? What was she doing up there? And why did she bring those shopping bags? There was something odd about the order of events, and this inspector knew it, too.

"Was it before or after your aunt went upstairs that she talked with the police?" he asked. "How many times did your aunt talk with your father? Once, or twice? One time before she went outside and one time after? Just once?"

"I dunno," Annabel whispered. "Maybe I got it mixed up."

Inspector Colluci opened the kitchen door and told Inspector Niebuhr the body had been taken away and Mr. Dunlin's lawyer was coming soon. Inspector Niebuhr told her to pack Annabel's things so she could stay with Mrs. Megarris.

"I won't go!" Annabel swept her hand across the table and her empty milk glass hit the floor and broke. Inspector Colluci picked up the pieces. "I want to stay with Lily."

"Sometimes we have to do things we don't like," Inspector Niebuhr said. "Will you and Lily show me your room? I'd like that."

In the front hall, a man Lily had never seen before swooped at Inspector Niebuhr like a seagull, pecking him with angry words. Inspector Colluci stepped in front of the man as Lily and Inspector Niebuhr led Annabel up the stairs, where Lily opened the storage closet containing the suitcases. Mrs. Dunlin's suitcase and makeup case were there. That's what Mrs. Megarris was doing upstairs, she thought. She'd unpacked the dead woman's cases and put them away.

Lily shivered. She reached for a small case and shut the closet door. She took Annabel to her room. "What would you like to take with you?" Annabel refused to say anything. Instead she grabbed her teddy bear and hugged it, tears in her eyes. Lily packed the suitcase. Then she reached for the music box her mother had given Annabel on her last birthday. It was a merry-go-round with black-and-white horses under a red-and-yellow canopy that played a tinkling little waltz. Lily led Annabel out to the hallway.

"What's that?" Inspector Niebuhr asked from the master bedroom.

Lily stepped into the room, handing him the merry-go-round. "Annabel's mother gave her this music box."

She glanced at the door leading to the master bath, and frowned. The towels were different from those she'd put out this morning. These were a lighter shade of green. She compressed her lips, willing her face to be blank as she thought about what else Mrs. Megarris had done.

"Is there anything else you want to tell me?" Inspector Niebuhr asked. She shook her head. He turned the key and the music box tinkled in three-quarter time, playing the waltz from *Carousel.*

27

LATER THAT AFTERNOON, in her office, Lindsey lined up the accordion folders she'd found in Pandora's Box. The first held the newspaper clippings about Annabel's mother and her death. She read through them again, with a perspective altered by Lily Hsu's account of what she saw the day Mrs. Dunlin died.

Inside the second folder, Lindsey found a thick stack of papers held together with a metal clip, along with a business card—INSPECTOR GARY NIEBUHR, HOMICIDE. SAN FRANCISCO POLICE DEPARTMENT. Under the phone number on the card, presumably the inspector's office, another number had been inked in blue. A home telephone, perhaps? On the back of the card was a note. *Annabel, call anytime, day or night. Gary Niebuhr.*

Lindsey unclipped the papers and spread them out in front of her. This was a copy of the case file. The first document was the initial police report concerning Mrs. Dunlin's death. The second was the autopsy report. After this came supplemental reports, notes in Niebuhr's distinctive spiky handwriting, as well as some typed memos.

Lindsey opened the third folder. It contained more of the case file, a typewritten account of what Annabel herself had seen, describing how she'd found her mother's body at the foot of the stairs—and her aunt's activities before the police arrived. Next was Lily's account of that day—not the one she'd told the police, but the one Lindsey had just heard.

Then two sketches, one showing the floor plan of the fifth floor of the Dunlin Building, and the other the building's basement parking garage. Annabel's accompanying notes said a door led from her father's corner office to a back hallway, terminating at the freight elevator and the back stairs. Both descended to the basement loading dock and parking garage.

But there were other things hidden in the basement, as Annabel and Claire had discovered one afternoon when she and Claire were thirteen. While the attendant fetched Aunt Rebecca's car, the two cousins darted away, finding rooms at the back of the parking garage, dusty chambers containing the boiler, guts of the heating system, wiring for phones and electricity, and a final resting place for broken chairs, battered desks, and outdated office equipment. Then Annabel opened a door onto a dim passage.

I dare you, Claire had said. Annabel took the dare. Their giggles echoed off the walls as they ran down the corridor. It led to the basement of the building next door, more rooms full of wires and equipment, another freight elevator, another stairwell. Up the stairs they went, to a small lobby and out to the sidewalk.

This was the way her father got out of the building without being seen by anyone, Annabel wrote. He'd gone out the back door of his office, down the back stairs to the parking garage, into the passage to the basement of the building next door. Out on California Street he caught the cable car and rode it all the way to the end of the line, just a few blocks from the house. Then he'd come back the same way.

Annabel hadn't been satisfied with the story told in the newspaper—or by her father and aunt—or even the police file. She'd conducted her own investigation into her mother's death, collecting pieces of the puzzle, fitting them together until she had most of the picture.

Inspector Gary Niebuhr was no longer at either of the phone numbers on the business card. Lindsey called directory assistance and got a number for Human Resources at the San Francisco Police Department. A woman answered the phone.

"I'm trying to locate Inspector Gary Niebuhr." Lindsey spelled the last name. "He was a homicide detective back in nineteen sixty-one."

"Wow, that's before I was born," the woman said, making decades sound like centuries.

"I'm sure he's retired." Lindsey hoped he wasn't dead. "I need to get in touch with him."

The woman put up the privacy roadblock. "I can't give out any personal information."

"But you could get a message to him," Lindsey countered.

"Well…" The woman hesitated. "He worked Homicide, you say? Hold on a minute."

It was longer than a minute and Lindsey wondered if she'd been cut off. Then a man's voice came on the line.

"Inspector Cavenaugh, Homicide. I understand you're looking for Gary Niebuhr. He retired a few years back. Is there something I can help you with?"

"Thanks, but no. I need to talk with him."

"What is this about, ma'am?"

"An old case from nineteen sixty-one. The Inez Dunlin case."

Cavenaugh chuckled. "Way before my time. Guess I can't help you at that."

"Could you get a message to Inspector Niebuhr?" Lindsey gave him her name and phone numbers. "Tell him I'm a friend of Annabel Dunlin." She hung up, hoping for the best.

Now Lindsey knew what Annabel meant, on that evening long ago, after Annabel's father died.

He left the house to me, along with the ghosts, Annabel said.

Is the house haunted? Lindsey asked.

In a manner of speaking.

They were all haunted, by the past, by mistakes and happenstance, by twists and turns of luck, stumbling through the present while ghosts whispered in the shadows.

The doorbell rang. Lindsey went to answer it and found Gretchen on the porch.

"I'm returning your key." Gretchen stepped into the foyer. "How was Ashland?"

"Ashland was fine." Lindsey put the key into her pocket.

"Claire says Nina suddenly moved in with Tess. What happened?"

"I told her who her father is. Now she's mad at me all over again."

"You told her?" Gretchen's voice sharpened. "Why now? This started with Tess wanting to find out about her biological father. You're helping her, so you decided you had to tell Nina the truth."

"That about covers it," Lindsey said.

"Damn it," Gretchen snapped, "Nina is your business. Tess and Annabel aren't. They aren't a research project. Neither is my family. Claire told me you're asking questions about Nat's adoption. Why?"

"Have you ever wondered where Nat came from?" Lindsey asked. "Whether he has family back in El Salvador?"

"Of course. But we're his family now. The past is past."

No, Lindsey thought, the past is always with us, affecting what we do and who we are, haunting us at the most inconvenient times. During that morning's strained meeting, Flor had given Lindsey an ultimatum.

"During the war in El Salvador," Lindsey said, "thousands of children disappeared. There's an ongoing effort to locate missing children and restore them to their families."

Gretchen flushed, the mother lion protecting her cub. "Nat isn't missing. He was abandoned. He has no family in El Salvador. We are his family. We adopted him, legally, fair and square. End of story. I won't listen to any more of this." She slammed the front door on her way out.

She's afraid, Lindsey realized. Claire had boasted that her contacts in El Salvador, the Medranos, had eased the adoption, implying some circumvention of the legal process. Did Gretchen have doubts about the legality of Nat's adoption? The pot's boiling, Lindsey thought. I've turned up the heat and it's splashing over, burning anyone who gets in the way.

The phone rang. When she answered, a man identified himself as Gary Niebuhr. "I understand you want to talk about the Dunlin case. I live in Alameda. You want to meet somewhere or come over here?"

"I'm in Berkeley," Lindsey told him. "I'll come there." He gave her the address. She put the accordion folders into a tote bag and grabbed her purse.

Niebuhr lived in a Victorian-era bungalow. The retired detective was tall. He'd lost most of his hair and what remained was thin and gray.

"Thank you for seeing me, Inspector Niebuhr," Lindsey said.

"I haven't been an inspector for a long time. I was a captain when I retired. Just call me Gary." They sat in the living room and his wife brought them tall glasses of iced tea with lemon. "I don't often get calls about a cold case. How do you know Annabel?"

"We lived in the same house while we were in school at Berkeley," Lindsey said. "Did you keep in touch with her after her mother died?"

"Not exactly," he said. "She came looking for me when she was a teenager. How is she?"

"She had a stroke two months ago. She's in rehab."

"A stroke? You think of an old guy like me having a stroke, not a young woman—well, middle-aged. I know she married that fellow who runs the company now, and they've got some kids. Where is she? I'll visit her."

"I'm sure she'd appreciate that." Lindsey gave him the convalescent hospital address. Then she removed the folders from her bag. "I'm going through some of Annabel's papers, at her daughter's request. I found a copy of the case file you gave her."

"Annabel contacted me when she was a senior in high school," he said. "She wanted information about her mother's death, all the reports, including the autopsy. And she wouldn't take no for an answer."

"She wasn't satisfied with the official ruling of accidental death," Lindsey said.

Niebuhr snorted. "Official ruling be damned. George Dunlin murdered his wife."

28

San Francisco, California, April 1961

SHE MUST HAVE BEEN a looker. Gary Niebuhr gazed at the body on the polished wooden floor. Her head lay in a pool of dark congealing blood. Brown eyes stared unseeing at the ceiling. She wore a gray linen suit and a pink blouse, both stained with blood. Her long slender legs were splayed out in an awkward posture. The corpse wore one shoe, a gray high-heeled pump a shade darker than her suit. Where was the other shoe?

China, metal and glass scattered the floor around the body. Pineapples. People collected the damnedest things. The newel post was another pineapple, smeared with blood. The stairs were covered with a carpet runner. Another shoe lay on its side, a few steps below the second floor landing.

Mulcahy, the uniformed officer who'd been first on the scene, gave the details to Niebuhr and his partner, Aldo Colluci. "Inez Dunlin, thirty-two. Sister-in-law found the body. She's in the living room. Husband's on the way home. There's a housekeeper, Mrs. Lily Hsu, but she's not here."

"Food imports," Colluci said. "The Dunlin Building, downtown. I've seen her picture in the papers. Best-dressed society dame at the symphony opening or some such thing."

"I didn't know you read the society pages, Aldo."

Colluci pointed at the shoe on the stairs. "So she catches her heel on the runner, takes a header, smacks her head on the post, then hits the table? It's damn pineapples everywhere."

"I don't know." Niebuhr looked at the newel post, then the wrecked table that must have stood at the foot of the stairs. He peered at the wall, looking for marks indicating the table hit the wall. He didn't see any. Then he knelt and scrutinized the body, looking for patterns of blood on the clothing, bruises on the skin.

They walked up the stairs for a closer look at the shoe. The heel was caught in a thread that had pulled away from the edge of the carpet runner. "Thread's loose all along here," Colluci said. "Accident waiting to happen."

Niebuhr straightened. "The newel post is on the right and the table's on the left. How does she fall, whack her head on the post, take out the table, and wind up in that position? Angle's wrong. Doesn't feel right. Got a hunch."

"You and your hunches," Colluci said. "This Dunlin guy is

188 • Janet Dawson

plugged in with the mayor. They go to the same parties. If you call this anything but an accident, you're gonna need more than a hunch. You need evidence."

"Give me time. We just got here."

The master bedroom was clean and orderly, with a pristine dressing table and nothing out of place on the chest of drawers or the matching nightstands that bracketed the big bed with its carved oak headboard. Colluci opened the jewelry box and whistled. "Get a load of these baubles, bangles and beads."

Niebuhr glanced at the jewelry, checked the walk-in closet, then walked to the bathroom. It looked freshly scrubbed, from the green, blue and white tile on the floor to the walls and ceiling. The green towels hadn't been used and the matching rugs looked as though no foot had trod on them. "Bathroom's clean as a whistle. Like nobody ever used it."

"That's why they got a housekeeper," Colluci said.

If the woman had been killed up here, there'd be blood. Niebuhr didn't see any. He leaned over the bathtub and ran his fingers around the drain. Dry. He'd need probable cause and a search warrant to dismantle the drain. He didn't have either.

They descended the stairs and headed down the hall. Under the staircase a door on the right, slightly ajar, revealed a desk and bookcases. Opposite this, on the left, a door opened onto a big, old-fashioned kitchen. It was warm back here. The scent of vanilla tickled Niebuhr's nose. The table in the middle of the kitchen held an open round tin filled with cookies, surrounded by crumbs and a glass with a trickle of milk. Surely the housekeeper who had left the master bath and bedroom so tidy wouldn't have left crumbs and a dirty glass on the table. Someone else had been here.

The back door opened onto an enclosed porch with washer and dryer. An oval wicker basket sat on top of the dryer. The washing machine was empty, but the dryer contained blue terry cloth towels.

Colluci went out to the backyard, where a detached double garage opened onto Washington Street. He talked with a uniformed officer at the back gate and returned to the house. "Two-car garage, no cars. They got one of those electric garage gizmos, but somebody forgot to shut the door."

"My guess is, Dunlin has one car and the housekeeper has the other," Niebuhr said. "As soon as they get here, I want to talk with them. I'd like to know where the husband was when this happened."

"Murder?" Colluci shook his head. "Are you nuts? Dunlin has friends at City Hall."

"I see things that don't fit with an accident."

"I don't," Colluci said.

They went back to the entry hall. The medical examiner looked up from the body. "She took a blow to the head. As to what caused it, you'll have to wait for the autopsy for anything more definite."

"Time of death?" Niebuhr asked.

"Same answer, Inspector."

Niebuhr turned to Mulcahy. "The sister-in-law found the body?"

"Mrs. Megarris, yeah. She made the call. She says the little girl, Annabel, was in the hall when she arrived."

"Where are they?"

Mulcahy hooked a thumb over his shoulder, pointing toward the back of the living room. Niebuhr saw the woman first. Mrs. Megarris wore a green suit, matching hat perched on her blond hair. She was in her mid-forties, sharp-featured, her lips pinched together, wringing a handkerchief with her hands. A wide doorway led to the study, where a little girl sat in a big chair. Annabel had untidy dark hair, and she wore a white blouse and plaid skirt, knee socks and black shoes.

"Poor kid," Niebuhr said. "What a thing to come home to. Where's Dunlin? I thought he was on his way."

"That's what she said. She called him after she called the cops."

Niebuhr introduced himself to Mrs. Megarris. "Please tell me what happened."

"Well, I don't know exactly." She raised the handkerchief to her eyes. "I came over to check on Annabel, my niece. She attends the Simpson School a few blocks from here, along with my daughter Claire. They're both nine. Annabel wasn't feeling well. Miss Simpson called me because she couldn't reach my sister-in-law or the housekeeper. I assumed they were out. I drove over to the school. But Annabel had gone without anyone seeing her. I came over here. I have a key. When I opened the front door, I saw my sister-in-law lying there at the bottom of the stairs and Annabel standing and staring." Mrs. Megarris took a deep breath. "I called the police, and then my brother."

Niebuhr made a few notes, covertly watching Annabel, who stared at her aunt as though Mrs. Megarris had told a whopper.

The phone on the desk rang. Niebuhr picked up the receiver. "Dunlin residence." He heard background noise, no voice, then a dial tone. Was the caller expecting Mrs. Dunlin?

"George!" Mrs. Megarris swept past Niebuhr and embraced the tall gray-haired man who'd just entered the house. She put her sleek blond head against his and whispered something in his ear. Words of comfort? Then Mrs. Megarris released her brother and stepped back. Niebuhr got his first good look at the dead woman's husband.

George Dunlin was on the far side of forty, maybe even pushing past fifty. He wore a suit of charcoal gray, tailored for his tall frame. His sharp features echoed those of his sister. He stared at his wife's body. Then he looked at Niebuhr with eyes like chips of ice, faintly blue and devoid of emotion. Shock at the sight of his wife lying dead on the floor in front of him?

"Mr. Dunlin, I'm Inspector Niebuhr, San Francisco Police Department. This is my partner, Inspector Colluci. I'd like to ask you some questions, please."

Dunlin gave him a flinty glare, the "how dare you question me" look. Niebuhr had seen it before, especially with people in Dunlin's tax bracket.

A second man stood next to Dunlin. "What sort of questions?" he asked.

"And you are?" Niebuhr countered.

"Max Brinker, Mr. Dunlin's assistant."

"Routine questions," Niebuhr said. "I'm sure we're all interested in finding out what happened to Mrs. Dunlin."

Just then a uniformed officer brought in the housekeeper, Mrs. Hsu, a small, slender Chinese American woman in a flowered house-

dress. She looked tired and stressed, as though her day had started
early and wouldn't be over until late tonight. When she saw the body,
she gasped. Shock and fright warred on her face, then she reined it in,
masking her emotions.

"Mrs. Hsu, I'm Inspector Niebuhr and this is my partner, Inspector Colluci. We'll ask you some questions later. The little girl's in the
study. Please take her—"

Mrs. Hsu rushed to the study and enveloped the child in her
arms. Annabel buried her head in the folds of Mrs. Hsu's skirt.
Niebuhr waited to see if Dunlin would comfort his daughter, but the
man made no move. "Mrs. Hsu, pack a suitcase for Annabel," he
ordered. "She'll go home with her aunt."

Niebuhr raised his hand. "She's not going anywhere until I talk
with her. Mrs. Hsu, please take Annabel to the kitchen. Wait there
until I'm ready to talk with both of you."

"You're not going to question my daughter," Dunlin snapped, as
the housekeeper took Annabel to the kitchen.

"Like it or not, she's a witness," Niebuhr said. "I need to know
what she saw."

"She's a child. She's had a shock," Dunlin said. "She can't tell
you anything."

Niebuhr looked at his partner, hoping Colluci would back his
play. If Dunlin called his lawyer, questioning the kid could be a
problem.

"It's routine, Mr. Dunlin," Colluci said. "We have to talk to
everybody, to get a clear picture of what happened to your wife."

"It's clear to me she fell down the stairs, and you're trying to
make more of it than there is." Dunlin scowled. "If you're going to
question her, get it over with, then."

"All in good time," Niebuhr said. "When was the last time you
saw your wife?"

"This morning, before I left for work."

"Where's that?"

"I'm president and chief executive officer of the Dunlin
Corporation. We have a building on the corner of California and
Montgomery."

You're an arrogant bastard and I don't much like you, Niebuhr thought, trying hard not to leap to any conclusions. "What time did you leave the house this morning?"

"About eight-thirty."

"Where was your wife at that time?"

"Still in bed. She wasn't a morning person. Her custom was to have breakfast in bed while she read the newspaper."

"Who got your little girl off to school?" Niebuhr asked.

"The housekeeper."

"You drive to work?" Colluci asked.

"Yes." Dunlin crossed his legs and brushed the knife-sharp crease in his dark gray trousers. "The Cadillac outside is mine. My wife and the housekeeper drove the Ford."

"When did you arrive at work?" Niebuhr asked.

"About a quarter to nine. I had meetings much of the day, starting at nine."

"I can vouch for that," Brinker added.

"Did you talk with your wife during the day?" Niebuhr asked.

Dunlin's chilly manner slipped and he showed a flash of impatience. "No, I didn't. See here, Inspector, I don't understand the reason for all these questions."

"I'm trying to establish Mrs. Dunlin's movements during the day," Niebuhr said. "Last night or this morning, did she say anything to you about her plans for today?"

Dunlin's self-control reasserted itself. He shrugged. "Last night she mentioned shopping."

"The housekeeper was using the Ford this afternoon," Niebuhr said.

"I don't pay much attention to the day-to-day running of the household."

"Mrs. Hsu does the marketing on Fridays," Niebuhr said. "And the laundry." Dunlin looked uninterested by this domestic detail. Brinker, on the other hand, stared hard at Niebuhr. "If Mrs. Hsu had the Ford, how would your wife get downtown?"

"A cab, I suppose," Dunlin said.

Niebuhr glanced at Colluci. If Mrs. Dunlin had called a taxi, that would be easy enough to check with the local cab companies. Perhaps one of the neighbors had seen a cab roll up to the house. Of course, it was possible she'd changed her mind about going shopping, although she had certainly dressed for an outing.

"Where were you when you were notified about your wife's death?"

"In a meeting. Mr. Brinker was there, along with several others."

"I called him," Mrs. Megarris said. "After I called the police, of course."

"My secretary informed me that I had an urgent phone call from my sister," Dunlin said. "I left the meeting and took the call in my office. My sister told me my wife had taken a tumble down the stairs, she appeared to be dead, and the police were on their way."

The guy had turned downright voluble, Niebuhr thought. "What time did you get the call from Mrs. Megarris?"

Dunlin and Mrs. Megarris traded looks. Then Dunlin spoke, ir- ritation simmering under his words. "I didn't look at the time, Inspec- tor. I was involved in the meeting, and then shocked by the news that my wife was dead."

"What does it matter what time it was?" Mrs. Megarris broke in.

Brinker stared at her. Niebuhr realized the younger man didn't much like his boss's sister. "I'm not sure of the time either, Inspector," Brinker said. "I was in the meeting with Mr. Dunlin. As soon as we got the call, we headed down to the parking garage."

"We left the office right after my sister called," Dunlin said.

"Did you?" Niebuhr glanced at his watch. "You made it in fifteen minutes this morning. Why did it take you so long to get home?"

Dunlin glared at Niebuhr as though he couldn't believe the in- spector's insolence. Brinker, on the other hand, seemed to be expect- ing the question. "We were delayed at the garage. A delivery truck had pulled up to the loading dock and was blocking Mr. Dunlin's car. The driver had to move the truck."

Dunlin's façade didn't slip much, but when it did, there was a nasty temper underneath. Niebuhr probed further but elicited noth- ing else. Besides, he was eager to talk with the housekeeper. From the sound of it, she was the last person to see Mrs. Dunlin alive. Unless his hunch was correct and the woman had been murdered—by her husband.

"Were you surprised to learn that your daughter was here?" Niebuhr asked.

The role of concerned parent didn't fit Dunlin. "Of course I was. A shock, to find her mother like that. All the more reason she should be taken out of here as soon as possible. This isn't the first time she's cut school. She's going through a rebellious phase. She says she doesn't like school, and wants to be here with—"

"Her mother?"

"The housekeeper," Dunlin said. "She's excessively attached to Mrs. Hsu, in my opinion. There will be changes."

Changing housekeepers or detectives? Niebuhr wondered.

"You didn't need to antagonize the guy," Colluci said as they headed for the kitchen. "We're walking a fine line here. He'll be on the horn to the chief and we'll be off this case."

"I'm doing my job," Niebuhr said.

The kettle on the stove whistled. Mrs. Hsu offered them tea. Colluci shook his head, but Niebuhr nodded. "I would, thanks. It's a cold day." When she handed him a cup, he took a sip. "That's good. Hits the spot. Please sit down, Mrs. Hsu."

"Little pitchers got big ears." Colluci pointed at Annabel, hunched over the table, layering cookies atop one another like round bricks. "Want me to take the kid to the living room?"

Not until he'd had a chance to question her, Niebuhr thought. If he let her out of his sight, back to the living room and her father's control, he wouldn't get the opportunity again. "I think she'll be all right here." Niebuhr and the housekeeper sat down at the table. He turned to a new page in his notebook. "Where do you live, Mrs. Hsu?"

"Waverly Place." She gave him the address, a narrow street, not much more than a back alley, in Chinatown.

"How long have you worked for the Dunlins?"

"Nine years. Since Annabel was a baby." She patted the little girl's shoulder.

He listened as she described that morning's routine. After she'd walked Annabel to school, she'd had a cup of tea. "Then I fixed Mrs.

Dunlin's breakfast. She sleeps late. I took her tray upstairs around ten o'clock."

There was disapproval in the housekeeper's voice. Niebuhr couldn't blame her. Mrs. Hsu probably had a husband and children of her own, but she left her own home early in the morning to get another woman's child off to school while that woman lingered in bed.

"She told me to put the tray on the nightstand. That's all she said. Then I went to Annabel's room. I changed the sheets on her bed and took them downstairs to wash. I do laundry several times a week, but always on Fridays."

Niebuhr smiled. "Do you fold things as soon as they come out of the dryer? My wife does."

Mrs. Hsu nodded. "Yes, right away. It keeps them from wrinkling. Then I made almond cookies. Annabel's favorite."

Colluci looked exasperated. "Let's get back to Mrs. Dunlin. When did you see her again? Did she say anything about her plans for the day?"

"No, she didn't," Mrs. Hsu said. "I saw her when I took the clean sheets upstairs. She asked when I was going grocery shopping. I said, when I finished the laundry. She went downstairs. I made her bed and straightened up the bedroom and bathroom. I put out fresh towels and rugs and took the others downstairs to wash. She was at her desk, in the living room. When I went to tell her I was leaving, she was still there." She hesitated, face guarded. "I didn't see her again, until…"

"What time did you go shopping?" Niebuhr asked.

"I didn't notice the time."

"You left the garage door open," Colluci said. "Guess you didn't notice that, either."

Mrs. Hsu didn't respond. She glanced out to the hall, then she looked down at her hands. Niebuhr got up and walked to the half-open kitchen door. Dunlin stood at the study door. Eavesdropping? His proximity made the housekeeper uneasy. Niebuhr was sure Dunlin was no picnic to work for, but Mrs. Hsu's reaction piqued his curiosity. Was she afraid of Dunlin all the time? Or just now?

Niebuhr shut the door and resumed his seat. "You did leave the garage door open."

"I thought I closed it. Sometimes when I push the button it doesn't close."

"You didn't finish the laundry," Niebuhr said. "You left towels in the dryer. Why didn't you fold them, the way you usually do?"

Her mouth tightened. "I was running late. The dryer wasn't finished and the towels were damp. I still had the groceries to buy. I have so much to do on Fridays."

Niebuhr had a feeling it wasn't like Lily Hsu to deviate from her established routine. Had she rushed out of the Dunlin house in a tearing hurry, propelled by something other than her work load, anxious to get away from something, or someone, she'd seen or heard? But what? Mrs. Hsu hadn't told him everything, he was sure of it.

Mulcahy opened the kitchen door. "They're getting ready to move the body. The husband's spitting nails, doesn't want you talking to the kid. He called his mouthpiece."

Colluci leaned over Niebuhr, his voice low. "Where are you going with this?"

"Stall the husband," Niebuhr said. Mulcahy nodded and left the kitchen. The detectives went out to the porch. "Something's off. The housekeeper's holding back. Dunlin doesn't seem that upset about his wife's death."

"The housekeeper's Chinese," Colluci said. "They seem like they're stonewalling even when they're not. Yeah, the husband doesn't act like he's all that broken up about his dead wife. But that doesn't mean he killed her. Could be all kinds of explanations. Maybe he's the kind that doesn't show his feelings. Maybe he's in shock."

"Or maybe he's just a cold, arrogant bastard."

"Don't let personal get in the way of your job," Colluci warned. "Besides, he's alibied five ways from Sunday. He was at his office all day. This guy Brinker vouches for him, and probably a whole lot of other people, too. End of story."

"He can't have been in meetings the whole time. He could have slipped out."

"How would he get here? The Caddy was parked in the garage. Someone would have noticed him taking it out. You heard Brinker.

There was a truck parked behind the Caddy. It had to be moved before he could come home this afternoon."

"Mrs. Hsu gets to work on the cable car." Niebuhr was thinking out loud. "Dunlin could have hopped on a cable car, right in front of his building."

"Motive and opportunity, Gary. I'm not convinced he had the opportunity. Motive? We don't have one. Why would he kill his wife?"

"I'll talk to the kid now," Niebuhr said.

"What do you think you're going to get from her? She's upset about her mom. You heard Mulcahy. Dunlin's pissed. He's calling his lawyer."

"Distract him. Get a list of people he was with in all those meetings. That will buy me some time to talk with the girl."

"I'll do what I can. Make the most of it."

When Colluci had gone, Niebuhr sat down again. He knew a parent should be with the little girl while he questioned her. But her mother was dead and he had concerns about her father. Besides, he'd already figured out that Lily Hsu was more of a parent to the child than the other adults in this household. He'd been watching Annabel from the corner of his eye as he questioned Mrs. Hsu. The little girl had been carefully layering the cookies row by row, but she'd been listening, absorbing words like a sponge took in water.

"Hello, Annabel. My name's Gary. I'm a policeman. I'd like to ask you some questions. Will you answer them for me?" She nodded. "Why'd you leave school today?"

"I wanted to be home with Lily. I hate that school. I have more fun with Lily. She's teaching me Chinese." Annabel rattled off a few words. "That means, how are you, I am fine." Mrs. Hsu smiled, as Annabel drank some milk and wiped her mouth on her sleeve.

"Very good. So you came home alone?"

"I'm not supposed to. I said I had a tummy ache. The teacher took me to Old Prune Face."

Niebuhr grinned. "Old Prune Face?"

"Miss Simpson, the principal. She called home but there wasn't any answer. Then she called Aunt Rebecca and the line was busy. Miss Simpson said I had to wait. But I sneaked out and came home anyway." Annabel looked pleased with herself at having put one over on Old Prune Face. "The garage door was open. Sometimes it doesn't close, like Lily said. Then she swears in Chinese."

"Does she?" Niebuhr glanced at Mrs. Hsu, amused at the thought of the housekeeper ripping off a few curses. "So you came in the back way. Were both the cars gone?" Annabel nodded. "How did you get inside the house?"

"Lily hides a key under the back stairs. She wasn't here. I had cookies and milk. Then I decided to go upstairs to my room and read. I went out to the hall. Mother's pineapples were on the floor. Some of them were broken." Annabel stopped. Her eyes blinked as she whispered, "Mother was broken, too. She had blood in her hair."

"What happened then?" he asked.

"Aunt Rebecca got here. She grabbed me and took me to Father's study and told me not to move an inch. But I got tired of waiting."

"Waiting for your aunt? What was she doing?"

"She talked on the phone," Annabel said. "To Father. Then Miss Simpson called, looking for me. Aunt Rebecca chewed her out because I wasn't at school. Then Aunt Rebecca talked to the police. They came to the house. But that was after she went upstairs."

"Really? Your aunt went upstairs?" Niebuhr leaned forward. Mrs. Megarris had omitted this information from her statement. "Did you actually see her go upstairs?"

Annabel shook her head. "No. But I heard her walking around. She must have used the bathroom. Water was running."

"How long was she up there?"

"I dunno." Annabel's mouth quivered. "She came downstairs and yelled at me. I cried."

"That wasn't very nice of your aunt, to yell at you," Niebuhr said. "Why did she do that?"

"Because I didn't stay in the study like she told me," Annabel said. "I got up and went to Mother's desk. Then Aunt Rebecca yelled at me. I was scared and I dropped the envelope. The one on Mother's desk, with my father's name on it. Aunt Rebecca put it in a bag when she came downstairs with the shopping bags. I dunno why she brought those with her. Lily keeps bags in the hall closet."

Mrs. Megarris had neglected to mention a number of things. "Was Aunt Rebecca wearing a coat when you first saw her?"

"A raincoat and gloves. She wasn't wearing them when she came back downstairs. She took the shopping bags outside and put them in the trunk of her car."

A picture formed in Niebuhr's mind, of Rebecca Megarris in her raincoat and gloves, upstairs. Cleaning up a crime scene? Removing evidence? What was in those bags, now stashed in her car trunk?

"Aunt Rebecca went outside and came back again," Annabel said. "She was sorry for yelling at me. She talked on the phone, to my father and the police. Then the police came."

"You said she talked to your father and the police," Niebuhr said. "Was that before she went upstairs? Or after?" Annabel looked confused now. If Mrs. Megarris had called the police before going upstairs, the time sequence didn't make sense. Once she'd notified the dispatcher that her sister-in-law was dead, the uniformed officers had arrived a few minutes later, followed by the photographer and the techs. He and Colluci got here about twenty minutes after the uniforms. That was on the record. Rebecca Megarris made one call to the police. But how many times had she called her brother?

"Annabel, this is really important. Did your aunt talk with your father once or twice? One time before she went outside and one time after?"

"I dunno. Maybe I got it mixed up."

Niebuhr hid his disappointment. Was the child confused about the order of things? Was she telling the truth? Or spinning a fanciful yarn? If what Annabel said was true… Big if. Could he take at face value the statement of a nine-year-old girl who'd just said that maybe she got her story mixed up?

Colluci opened the kitchen door. "Okay, you're done. The body's gone. I held Dunlin off as long as I could, but his lawyer just got here. I hope you got something useful."

Niebuhr turned to the housekeeper. "Mrs. Hsu, Mr. Dunlin wanted you to pack some of Annabel's things so she can stay with her aunt."

"I won't go!" Annabel shouted. She swept her hand across the table and the wall of cookies she'd built went flying. The empty glass hit the floor and broke. Colluci picked up the pieces and deposited them on a dishtowel.

"I want to stay with Lily. I won't go."

"Sometimes we have to do things we don't like," Niebuhr said. "This is one of those times. It's temporary. You'll come home when things settle down."

In the hall, the attorney went on the attack, jowls quivering as he wielded a lash of indignation and threats. "The chief will hear about this. You're way over the line, Inspector. You've overstepped the bounds of decency. Grandstanding, trying to make something out of a tragic accident, interrogating a nine-year-old child who's grief-stricken and confused at the loss of her mother."

As far as Niebuhr could see, Annabel was more upset by the prospect of being separated from Lily Hsu. He ignored the lawyer, heading upstairs. On the second floor, Mrs. Hsu let go of Annabel's hand and opened the door to a big storage closet. When she switched on the light, she hesitated and frowned. Then she reached for a small case, turned off the light, and closed the door. She led Annabel to her room.

In the master bedroom Niebuhr looked around one more time, waiting for insights that didn't come. He turned and saw Annabel and Mrs. Hsu in the hallway. The housekeeper carried the suitcase in her right hand and something colorful in her left, a carousel with black-and-white horses under a red-and-yellow canopy.

"What have you got there?"

Mrs. Hsu stepped into the bedroom, handing him the object. "Annabel's music box. Her mother gave it to her. It plays a waltz from a show called *Carousel*." Mrs. Hsu glanced at the bathroom. She frowned, as she had when she'd looked in the closet.

Something was off, Niebuhr was sure of it, and the housekeeper had noticed. "Is there anything else you want to tell me?" he asked, hoping to break through her resistance. She shook her head. He sighed and turned the key on the bottom of the carousel. The music tinkled in three-quarter time.

29

"DUNLIN KILLED HIS WIFE upstairs, probably in the bath-room," Niebuhr said. "Hit her on the head and tossed her body down the stairs to make it look like she fell. He—or Mrs. Megarris—cleaned up the blood, then arranged that shoe on the step, maybe even pulled the thread loose from the carpet runner, so it would look like an accident."

"I had lunch with Lily Hsu this afternoon." Lindsey relayed the details of her conversation with the former housekeeper. "The towels were the wrong color. She noticed it right away. She cleaned the bathroom earlier, and put out green towels. But the towels you saw weren't the right shade of green. They were light green. The towels she put out were darker, moss green. Only the woman who changed those towels would notice the difference. The first set disappeared."

"Into Mrs. Megarris's car," Niebuhr said. "Why didn't Mrs. Hsu tell me this?"

"She was afraid of him," Lindsey said. "He must have noticed the garage door was closed when he arrived—and open when he left. He'd have guessed Mrs. Hsu was in the house. She was terrified. So she kept quiet. When he fired her six weeks later, he gave her a very generous severance payment, a payoff to keep her mouth shut. She also said Dunlin changed clothes after the murder. Mrs. Hsu told me he was wearing light gray pinstripes that morning and charcoal gray that afternoon."

"I know," Niebuhr said. "I talked with the garage attendant, to verify Dunlin's story about a delivery truck parked behind his Cadillac that afternoon. The guy mentioned the two different suits. Dunlin claimed he spilled food on his trousers, put on an extra suit he kept at the office, and sent the stained clothes to the cleaners. I checked that, too. The man who cleaned the suit said the stain was tomato sauce. I think Dunlin changed clothes there at the house and the bloodstained suit left the house with Mrs. Megarris."

"Dunlin sneaked out of the building." Lindsey opened the third folder and pulled out Annabel's sketches. "There's a way to get from the basement to the building next door."

Niebuhr nodded. "He caught the California Street cable car to the end of the line and walked home. After he killed his wife, he reversed the trip. But none of the cable car gripmen remembered him. I couldn't prove it. Dunlin had clout. He was a well-connected businessman with friends in high places, state and local politicians, including the mayor and the chief of police. When a certain homicide inspector started asking questions about his alibi, Dunlin called his friends. With me pulled off the case, Dunlin got the result he'd orchestrated. Accidental death. Case closed. On the books anyway. But not for me. I kept nosing around, whenever I could. Dunlin killed his wife for the oldest reason in the book. She was leaving him for another man. He figured if he couldn't have her, no one else could. I found Mrs. Dunlin's lover, several years later. He told me they'd planned to meet that Friday. She'd take a cab to Union Square, where his car was parked in the garage. They'd drive to Reno, so she could get a divorce. Then on to his new job in New York City, leaving the husband and kid in San Francisco. Motherhood no longer figured into her plans. I got the feeling it never did."

Poor Annabel. Two emotionally distant parents, and only Lily Hsu and her almond cookies for consolation. Even Lily had been taken from her, fired a short time later.

"Mrs. Dunlin didn't show up at the meeting place," Niebuhr said. "Her lover called the house. I answered the phone and he hung up. That made me wonder. That and the crime scene and what Annabel told me. But…" His smile was wry. "Who's going to believe a nine-year-old girl, distraught over the death of her mother?"

"She was more upset at being separated from Lily Hsu," Lindsey said.

"It's a homicide cop's job to speak for the dead. When the cop gets muzzled, the dead don't get justice." Niebuhr rattled the ice cubes in his glass. To Lindsey it sounded like the rattle of old, unquiet bones.

30

LINDSEY WAS EARLY for her lunch appointment with Rod Llewellyn on Wednesday. Right now both he and Claire were occupied with the board meeting. She hoped to see Nina, if her daughter had simmered down enough to talk.

Lindsey's cell phone rang. She looked at the number on the screen. The incoming call was from Flor. Again. Flor had already left two impatient messages, one each on Lindsey's home answering machine and on the cell phone. Lindsey was now past the twenty-four-hour ultimatum Flor had given her. But she wasn't ready to talk with Flor yet. She had to tell Gretchen and Doug about Nat, that someone else had a claim on the child they considered theirs. But first Lindsey had to deal with her own child.

The passenger elevator opened and Nina stepped out, dressed in dark gray slacks and a neon pink shirt. She crossed the marble floor toward the coffee bar in the Dunlin lobby alcove. "Mother? What are you doing here?"

"We've both had a day to cool off," Lindsey said. "We need to talk."

Nina frowned. "It's a bad time. The board meeting—"

"This can't wait." Lindsey touched her daughter's arm. "Putting things off is what got us into this mess in the first place. Please talk to me. Here, outside, anywhere. But let's talk."

"All right," Nina said. "I came down to get a latte."

Progress, however small. "I could use some coffee myself," Lindsey said.

At the coffee bar they ordered lattes. "There's no privacy here," Nina said. "Let's go upstairs." With cups in hand, they walked to the counter staffed by the security guard. Lindsey wrote her name and the time on the check-in sheet and obtained a visitor badge. They took the elevator to the fifth floor and walked to Claire's office, a corner suite. "Ellie, this is my mother, Lindsey Page. This is Claire's regular assistant, Ellie Stern. I'll be covering her desk while she's on leave."

"Nice meeting you." Ellie's belly stuck out in front of her like a medicine ball. "I'm off to my doctor's appointment. Then I'll get lunch and be back by by two. Unless I go into labor."

"When are you due?" Lindsey asked.

"Two weeks. But if Junior decides to show up early, I'm way past ready." Ellie grinned and glanced at Nina. "The board meeting will probably last till noon. You have a lunch date?"

"Yes, with Tess, my roommate," Nina said. "Is it okay to leave?"

"Sure, go ahead. Mrs. Megarris is at the meeting. Sometimes she and Claire have lunch afterwards. If that's the plan today it's not on the calendar. Claire doesn't have any other appointments this afternoon. See you later."

When Ellie had gone, Nina sat down at the desk. "Okay, you wanted to talk."

Lindsey pulled up a chair. "I know you're angry with me. I've made mistakes. Mothers always do. I had my reasons for not telling you who your father is. I thought they were good reasons. I wanted to protect you, from hurt and uncertainty."

"You wanted to protect him."

"Yes, and other people too. He wasn't the only one to consider."

"So you hurt me instead." Anger flickered in Nina's eyes. Then sadness took its place. "I wish you had been honest and open from the start."

"When I made those choices I thought they were the right choices," Lindsey said. "But I was wrong. Nothing in life turns out exactly the way we plan. I didn't mean to hurt you. You might have been hurt even if you had known all along who he is. Because we can't be a family, the three of us. That's the hand we were dealt. We have to play our cards the way they fall."

Nina spread her hands wide in frustration and supplication. "What do I do now?"

"I have to tell him," Lindsey said. "I never did, though I wondered if he guessed. Men have remarkable tunnel vision. Sometimes they can't even see what's staring them in the face."

"What am I supposed to do with my hurt?" Nina's voice wavered. "Just get over it and move on?"

"The alternative is to hang onto your anger for the rest of your life and let it warp everything you do or are."

"The way it has so far?"

"I didn't say that, you did." Lindsey sighed. "I didn't know how to answer your questions about your father. I wondered why I wasn't good enough for you. You've built up a powerful load of resentment. It's colored your life for too long. It's done serious damage to our relationship. Why does this have such power over you? Please tell me so I can understand."

"Sticks and stones can break my bones but words can never hurt me." Nina's voice had a singsong cadence as she repeated the phrase that children learn early. "That's not true. Words hurt. They hurt like hell. They sting and make you cry."

"Words have power only if you grant them power." Even as she spoke, Lindsey recalled the angry words Nina had flung at her in the past. She'd given them power. They still hurt.

"It takes time to learn that," Nina countered.

"Some of us never do."

"Think about how hard it is for a kid."

Lindsey nodded. "Believe it or not, I do remember what that's like."

Nina sighed. "It was okay when I was a kid. We lived with Aunt Emma. Then we moved to the city. You taught at San Francisco State. Back then I didn't think about not having a father. Maybe it was because I was so young. But we were always getting together with other people's families—Gretchen, Annabel, the neighbors. There were adult males in my life who filled that role. Some of my classmates had single parents. It didn't occur to me that there was anything odd about not having a father living with us. Then we moved to San Luis Obispo. I didn't want to go. I felt uprooted."

"You know why I took that job at Cal Poly. Grandpa was sick. We didn't know then what Alzheimer's was, what it does to a person, a family." Lindsey felt again the sadness and frustration of her father's slow deterioration. "He was getting more forgetful, more difficult. I needed to be there. Grandma couldn't manage."

"I know that now," Nina said. "I know how hard it was on you and Grandma. But I was a kid. I hated San Luis Obispo. After San Francisco it was the sticks, the back of beyond. Paso Robles was smaller still. With attitudes to match. You know small towns. School was worse."

"Why didn't you tell me? I could have talked with your teachers or the principal."

"It was a girl in my class," Nina said. "The same class, all the way up through high school. The popular girl, the one who was destined to be prom queen. She was a bitch. She picked on kids like me, the new ones, the kids who were a little bit different. She'd seize on one thing about her victims and torment them. The other kids followed her lead, like a pack of wolves. She called me a bastard. It hurt. I started wondering who my father was, why he wasn't around, why you never married him. I asked questions. You wouldn't answer. I resented you and him. There was this big hole you wouldn't fill. I try to be logical about it. But the emotional part gets me every time."

"I'm sorry. You're my daughter and I love you. Always remember that, no matter what." Lindsey reached for Nina's hand and held it. Nina didn't pull away. Instead, Lindsey felt an answering pressure.

"Tess and I had a long talk last night," Nina said. "She wondered why I'd moved out of your house so abruptly. I told her about our quarrel, but I didn't tell her who my father is. I wasn't ready."

"I'll talk with him. Then the two of you can sort things out on your own."

Voices buzzed in the hall, as though someone had disturbed a beehive. Lindsey looked in the corridor, at people exiting the board room. A man and a woman stopped near the doorway. "Llewellyn replacing Caldwell," the woman said. "Claire won't like that. They shot down everything she proposed. Brinker won this round."

The old dinosaur has teeth, Lindsey thought. So the meeting hadn't gone Claire's way.

The woman whistled the opening bars of "Stormy Weather." She and the man retreated. Claire approached, face like a thundercloud, dark and lowering. Mrs. Megarris was with Claire. Despite the age difference, they looked so much alike, not only the planes and angles of their faces. Mother and daughter wore the same bitter, dissatisfied visage.

I know some of your secrets, Aunt Rebecca. You're an accessory to murder.

Evidently Nina hadn't picked up on Claire's foul mood. "How did the meeting go?" she asked.

The wrong question at the wrong time. Anger flashed in Claire's eyes, quickly masked. She didn't answer Nina, instead addressing Lindsey. "Lindsey. What a surprise. I didn't expect to see you here."

"I was in the city, so I stopped to see Nina. I'm just leaving."

Claire turned to Nina. "Any messages?"

"None. It's quiet. Ellie's gone to her doctor's appointment. I'm planning to meet Tess for lunch. Should I wait until Ellie gets back?"

"No, go ahead," Claire said. "Mother and I are going to chat, then I'll walk her down to the garage." Claire took Mrs. Megarris's arm, steered her into the inner office, and shut the door.

"I don't understand all the ins and outs of the company yet," Nina said. "Claire had some proposals for the board. Sounds like the meeting didn't go the way she'd hoped. She and Mrs. Megarris are probably doing a postmortem." She took out her cell phone and punched some numbers. "Tess, I'm free for lunch now. Meet you on the corner?"

Lindsey glanced at her watch. It was noon, time to meet Rod Llewellyn in the lobby. "I have a lunch date, too. We'll talk later."

They took the elevator downstairs and Nina headed for the street. A tall, dark-haired man waited by the coffee bar. "Lindsey," Rod said. "Good to see you again. It's been a long time."

"I understand you've been elected to the board. Congratulations."

"Word travels fast," he said as they left the building. A cable car went by on California Street, bell clanging. "It's a lot of responsibility. I've got to go back to Houston and wrap up things so I can hand them off to my successor. Give up my apartment there and find a place to live here."

208 · *Janet Dawson*

"Where did you live before? When you were here in the Bay Area."

"North Beach. I've always liked the neighborhood. But it's changed."

"Yes. Everything has."

They walked a few blocks to a restaurant and were shown to a table near the front window. "Let's have some wine to celebrate my promotion," he said. "I like a good Merlot."

"So do I." She scanned the menu. When the server returned with their wine, they both ordered salads.

"Max says you want some background information on the coffee business." He reached for a slice of sourdough. "For a book you're writing."

"That's how it started." Lindsey sipped her wine. "Were you in El Salvador in April of nineteen eighty-nine?"

His lean face turned wary. "Why?"

"I'm interviewing Central American immigrant women for my book," Lindsey said. "One is a woman from El Salvador. In April of nineteen eighty-nine, she lived in a village called San Blas, on the Aragón *finca* in Chalatenango department. Something terrible happened there. I talked with Merle Sefton, the reporter who wrote about it. She saw a tall dark-haired man at the Aragón house and overheard conversation indicating the man was a coffee broker from Dunlin Corporation. It wasn't Hal Norwood. He was in New York that weekend. Was it you?"

Rod tore the bread into smaller pieces. He set the fragments on his plate and met Lindsey's gaze. "Yes. I was there. With Claire."

31

Chalatenango Department, El Salvador, April 1989

THE SOUND JARRED HIM from his after-breakfast somnolence, a short repeating burst, a staccato pattern reminding him of the pneumatic rattle of jackhammers. But he wasn't in the city. He was miles from the nearest town, in a country ravaged by civil war.

Rod Llewellyn set his cup on the railing. "That sounds like gun-fire," he said as his host joined him on the veranda.

"It's just my men," Humberto Aragón said, "practicing at the shooting range. We are involved in a war."

That's exactly why the sound of gunfire disturbs me, Rod thought.

Humberto had close-cropped gray hair and a thickset torso in khaki pants and shirt. "My *finca* is quite large. My family has owned this land for a hundred years. I must defend it from those who would take it away from me. The army can't patrol everywhere, all the time. These rebels try to disrupt agricultural production. I don't intend to let them interfere. So I have my own army."

Rod had heard of these private militias, bought and paid for by wealthy landowners, sometimes with more firepower and equipment than the Salvadoran army. "Have you seen fighting here?"

"We've had our share. There are rebels in the town of Los Árboles." The landowner pointed to the northeast, where mountains rose dark green against the blue sky. "About thirty-five kilometers. Severino assures me the next army offensive will drive them away."

Rod converted thirty-five kilometers to twenty-one miles. He didn't much like the idea of a rebel outpost so close. But the ac-quisition of coffee beans to be shipped back to the United States involved more than correspondence, phone calls, and bills of lading. He also visited coffee plantations, consulting with growers, sampling and tasting the crop. He'd put off this visit to El Salvador, reluc-tant to go into a war zone, though other countries he'd visited in Latin America, Africa and Asia had their share of civil and political unrest. The Dunlin Corporation was always concerned about things that could disrupt production of the crops the company imported—weather, natural disasters, civil strife, labor disputes, and politics. But what mattered above all else was business, the crop itself, not culture, government, or the people who grew it.

El Salvador was a pinpoint on the map, but the country had been a major coffee producer since the mid-nineteenth century, when cof-fee supplanted indigo as the main crop. Coffee flourished on the high, cool hillsides and the growers, the coffee elite, amassed huge fortunes and enormous plantations. This unequal distribution of land led to conflict. In the 1970s, failed efforts at land reform brought increasing violence. The civil war began in earnest in the 1980s, with reports of death squads in the cities and massacres in the countryside, the civilian population caught in the crossfire. At times rebels had controlled whole departments in the north and east. The escalating involvement of the United States provided financial aid to the Salvadoran government and an influx of military advisors to the Salvadoran army, but the fighting went on. The intensity and viciousness of the war gave him pause.

Rod had originally planned a quick visit to El Salvador in late March. Then Claire Megarris, now a junior executive in Marketing, invited herself along, delaying the trip till mid-April. She revised the itinerary to a leisurely jaunt spanning more than a week. Their last stop, a long weekend, was the Aragón *finca*. Rod was annoyed, but Claire was the boss's niece and she had Marketing's blessing. Who was he to argue?

They picked up a rental car at the San Salvador airport and headed west into the region called *Cinturón de Oro*, the belt of gold, a broad agricultural area tucked between the two mountain ranges that crossed El Salvador from east to west. Some of the peaks were dormant volcanoes. In the past the country had been rattled by eruptions that had covered the landscape in ash. Geysers shot up water and steam. Fumaroles emitted smoke and volcanic gases. The by-product of volcanic activity was fertile soil, some of the richest in the country. Cattle grazed and other crops grew, but the major crop was Bourbon Arabica coffee.

Distances didn't look that great on the map, but in many areas the roads were terrible. It took them hours to get from place to place. They drove through verdant countryside, where colorful flowers contrasted with lush green. The land itself was beautiful, but El Salvador's roads were lined with people, whole families of them, dressed in threadbare clothes, trudging along the highways with their meager possessions, looking as though they didn't get enough to eat.

He'd seen poverty before. But the destitution—and the disparity—seemed even more appalling here. They stayed with growers they visited, wealthy men who owned the land and ran the country.

The coffee elite lived in opulent homes, ate from tables laden with food. At each stop Rod felt more disturbed, contrasting the comfortable lives and surroundings of the wealthy planters with those of the peasants who worked in the coffee fields and processing plants. The peasants lived—if you could call it that—in hardscrabble villages, huts clustered on the outskirts of towns, in corners on the vast plantations. Or they had nowhere to live at all, like the people walking along the roads, like troops marching from one camp to another.

"Who are all these people?" he asked early in their journey. "Where are they going?"

"*Campesinos.*" Claire, at the wheel of the rental car, pulled out and passed yet another straggling procession of peasants. "Migrant workers. They move from plantation to plantation, working the coffee crop."

"Isn't there any permanent workforce?"

"Some *campesinos* live in villages on the *fincas*. When there isn't enough work, they move from place to place. It's the custom of the country."

"It's a bad custom."

She flashed him a sideways glance. "We have migrant workers in the United States. How is it any different here?"

"I've never seen migrant workers in the States that looked this beaten down."

"Been to any good slums lately?" she asked. "I understand the ones in Mexico City and Manila are particularly fetid. And how about those *favelas* in Rio? You think I'm hard-hearted? Just practical. I didn't realize you were so naïve, after all these years in the business. We can't do anything about the conditions in this country, things that have existed for a long time. Lighten up. Look around you. The weather is gorgeous. The countryside is beautiful."

Callous was what he'd been thinking, but hard-hearted would do as well for a description. You haven't changed a bit, he thought. He was stung by her accusation of naïveté. Maybe he couldn't do anything about the conditions he saw that left these people in misery, impoverished in body and spirit. But at least he could acknowledge what he saw, like the woman whose eyes met his at a dusty crossroad.

She was young, but hunger and hard living had etched lines on her face. She carried a sleeping toddler on her back. Her skirt had faded to gray, like all the hopes and dreams Rod imagined a young woman would have. She trudged in run-down shoes, moving as though her feet hurt. For a moment she looked directly at Rod, her eyes rimmed with fatigue, black with despair, empty of hope. For Rod, the young woman at the crossroads became the face of poverty in El Salvador.

Watching Claire in action, Rod had to admit she was in her element when it came to socializing with growers. He could talk business over cocktails when necessary, but he was more comfortable one-on-one with a grower, discussing crops, prices, and shipping details.

On Wednesday Rod and Claire arrived in Santa Ana, capital of the department of the same name, and the second largest city in the country, with a colonial flavor, its old buildings fronted by wide streets. The city, ringed by green hills and surrounded by plantations, was the beating heart of El Salvador's coffee production. They visited plantations where coffee was grown and harvested coffee cherries were processed into beans ready for roasting. They were guests for two nights at a landowner's mansion, feted at a lavish dinner.

On Friday, they drove northeast to Chalatenango, the large department along El Salvador's border with Honduras. The Aragón *finca* was located in the southwestern corner of the department, a parcel that contained wide valleys and rolling hills, mountains with timber, and green slopes planted with coffee. The reason for Claire's visit became clear. Severino Aragón, a major in the Salvadoran army, was home. Rod knew from the company grapevine that Claire had an off-and-on relationship with Severino. He felt annoyed all over again as he realized why she'd revised the itinerary. Claire wanted an interlude with her lover.

The Aragón colonial-style house was encircled by a wide first-floor veranda. Balconies opened off second-floor rooms. Humberto had a master suite at the front of the house, the south side, while Claire and Severino were in adjoining rooms on the east side. His own room was at the northwest corner of the house. When he stepped onto the balcony, he had a view of the garden, the outbuildings and the mountains to the north.

The sun was low and the temperature must have been in the eighties. He felt tired and travel-weary, impatient to go home. He stripped off his clothes and took a shower, then dressed again in clean slacks and a shirt. He went downstairs to have a look around. There was no one else in sight, though he heard voices in Spanish coming from the kitchen at the back of the house.

In the living room, one wall held family photographs of Humberto, his wife, and their three children. Severino and the younger son, Roberto, looked like their father, dark and stocky. The daughter, Cristina, and the late Mrs. Aragón were both slender, with honey blond hair. In another picture, a much-younger Humberto linked his arm with a slender, beautiful woman in a white satin gown. The other man in the photograph was Mr. Dunlin. So this was Humberto's younger sister, Annabel's mother.

"My aunt Inés," Severino said as he joined Rod. "I didn't know her very well. I was a baby when she married. I only saw her three times after that, twice when she and George visited El Salvador. Once, when I was ten and Annabel was six, we went to San Francisco. We stayed in a fine hotel on Nob Hill and I rode the cable cars. Come, it's time for dinner."

On Saturday morning, he joined Humberto at breakfast. Plans for the day included visits to several coffee groves and the large processing plant on the *finca*. But it was now past nine, no sign of Claire or Severino. Rod lingered on the veranda, drinking coffee. Finally Claire appeared. She wore her blond hair long these days. She was fiddling with it, fastening it back with barrettes. Her blue eyes glittered and the set of her mouth told him she was in a waspish mood.

"I heard gunfire," Rod said. "Señor Aragón tells me it came from his shooting range. He has a militia."

"All the growers have militias," she said. "It's the custom of the country."

If he'd heard her say that once during this El Salvador trip, he'd heard it a dozen times. He didn't much like the custom of the country. The feeling of disquiet returned. Why take a business trip in the middle of a war zone? He didn't want to get shot by someone simply because he was visiting a coffee plantation.

"I'm sorry to keep you waiting." Severino strolled out onto the veranda. "I always sleep better here at home. There's something about one's own bed."

"We had hoped to get an earlier start," Humberto said. "Have you had breakfast?"

"There's nothing in the dining room. Ana's taken it all away."

"She should have left it out for you and Claire." Humberto called for Ana, a thin middle-aged woman, who scurried from the kitchen. Severino spoke to her in Spanish, ordering coffee and *pan dulce*. She left and reappeared a few moments later with a tray, setting it on a low table. Two Jeeps drove toward the house from the outbuildings and braked to a stop. The occupants wore uniforms in a dull shade of bluish-gray and black boots. They carried semiautomatic weapons.

"Here is Cruz now," Humberto said.

The man at the wheel of the first Jeep got out. Big and broad-shouldered, he had a hard face. A scar extended from the outer corner of his left eye all the way to his chin. His nose looked as though it had been broken a couple of times, and his eyes were cold. Ana gave him a wide berth as she left the veranda. Rod realized she was afraid of Cruz.

Humberto told Cruz that they would be ready to leave on their tour of the *finca* in fifteen minutes. As Cruz returned to the Jeep, Claire poured herself another cup of coffee. "What a plug-ugly. Where did you find him?"

"In a San Salvador jail," Humberto said. "In for assault, I believe."

"You chose wisely," Claire said. "He looks like he's ready to handle any kind of trouble."

Or instigate it, Rod thought.

Severino finished his breakfast and they left on their tour. After visiting groves planted in coffee trees, they headed for Humberto's processing plant, Jeeps speeding over a gravel road along a ridge. The plant was a long low building with a loading dock and several bays, where *campesinos* gathered, awaiting the *patrón* and his visitors. Down the slope Rod saw a village, huts grouped around a small adobe church, and beyond that, a pond held back by an earthen dam.

El Salvador's processing facilities were among the most mechanized in the coffee business. Coffee began fermenting as soon as it was harvested, so it required quick processing. Seeds were separated from the other organic material—a thick, sticky substance known as mucilage, a papery membrane called parchment, and a thin coating called silver skin. During processing, the skin and pulp of the coffee cherries were mechanically removed, and the mucilage was dried. Then threshers removed the parchment, all the while taking care not to contaminate the beans, which would be roasted.

"My *beneficio*, my processing plant, is state-of-the-art." Humberto beamed as he showed Rod the plant. In the background, hovering like ghosts, *campesinos* swept floors, scrubbed and polished mucilage dryers. "Come, I'll show you my latest production figures." The landowner led them toward the office.

An old man carrying a bucket stepped from the shadows. Dirty water splashed on Rod's trousers. "A thousand pardons, Señor," the old man said softly in Spanish, setting the bucket on the floor. "Please forgive me." He offered Rod a cloth to blot the water.

Cruz struck. Blood trickled from the corner of the old man's mouth. "Clumsy fool," Cruz snarled. He drew back his hand for another blow.

"It was an accident." Rod moved between the old man and Cruz, who didn't lower his hand until Humberto barked a command, ordering all the *campesinos* to clear out and go home. Rod gave the cloth to the old man, who pressed it to his bleeding mouth, picked up the bucket, and disappeared.

"It was an accident," Rod said. "Hitting that old man was out of line."

Claire shrugged. "Intimidating peasants is what Cruz is here for. That's the way things are done around here. Come on. Our host wants to show you how much coffee he produces in a year. Isn't that what we came for?"

I did, Rod thought. But not you.

AT dinner Rod picked at the food on his plate as though worrying a scab. Don't get involved. Focus on business and nothing else when dealing with people in other countries and other cultures. Don't get involved in politics, don't form opinions. Don't let personal feelings get in the way of business.

Rod usually didn't get involved. In country after country, he maintained his detachment, ignoring beggars and troops in the streets, the faces of poverty and war. Why was it different in El Salvador? Was it the immediacy of the civil war? The stark disparity between rich and poor was not unique to El Salvador. Why did conditions here, no different from a dozen other countries, bother him so much? It was as though an aching tooth, ignored for too long, had finally abscessed. He recalled the despairing eyes of the young woman he'd seen by the side of the road, so devoid of hope, focused on nothing but basic survival.

"I hope you are enjoying your visit, Señor Llewellyn," Humberto said.

Rod forced himself to lift a fork to his mouth. The steak was excellent, as his host had boasted, beef from Humberto's own herd. Rod swallowed and sipped wine. "During the past week I saw peasants, walking along the roads. Claire tells me they move from place to place, looking for work."

"Coffee needs many hands," Humberto said. "With such a large *finca*, we have much seasonal labor, especially during harvest, and when the trees are being planted. Before World War Two, we had more *campesinos* living on the *finca*. We grew only coffee. But a one-crop economy isn't wise. We learned that during the Depression, when prices sank so low. After the war my father and I diversified, expanding into new crops, like cattle and cotton, which don't require as many workers. We started a cattle ranch in a valley with good water and plenty of grass. When we bought our first herd, I told my father that valley was perfect for cattle. So it was, once we cleared away the village."

"You moved the village so your herd could graze there?" Rod asked.

"Moved it? No, we tore it down."

"How long had the village been there?"

Humberto shrugged. "Since my grandfather's time. It was a lot of work to knock down the houses and church to prepare the land for cattle, but worth it. We have done well with cattle."

Like the Highland clearances in Scotland, Rod thought, crofters cleared from their land when landlords needed more room for sheep to graze. Here it was in modern form. "The people who lost their homes, where did they go?"

Humberto smiled. "Their homes? This is Aragón land, ours to do with as we please. The *campesinos* are here to work, nothing more. They come and go, with the harvest, the custom of our country. These *campesinos* aren't like us. The ruling class, my family and people like me, we're of European stock. The *campesinos*, they're *mestizos*, with the Indian strain, ignorant and lazy. They require a firm hand. Like children, they are simple and easily led. That's why many of them fall prey to Communists."

Rod had heard these sentiments before, expressed over dinner in fancy houses on large estates, spoken by coffee barons and their wives and sons and daughters, all convinced of their innate superiority over the huge population of poor people who did the work. They viewed the *campesinos* as a separate, lesser species. Humberto only voiced the opinions commonly held by the coffee elite.

Now Humberto fumed at the thought of changes to his comfortable status quo. "Land reform, they call it. Theft is what I call it."

Severino reached for his wineglass. "Land reform is dead, Father."

"Dead for now, but for how long? These Communists tried it in the Seventies, and again in the Eighties. They'll keep trying until they're eradicated," Humberto said. "These rebels want to take my land, divide it into parcels and give it to ignorant *campesinos*. My father's legacy to me, and someday to my son, and they want to take it away from me. Ridiculous. I won't tolerate this land grab. They won't take this *finca* that I have built with my own labor."

Rod almost laughed. The only people laboring on the *finca* were the *campesinos* in the coffee groves and at the plant, and the servant here in the house. The estate was a feudal fiefdom, with Humberto as lord and master.

"In my father's day it was different," Humberto said. "Men of his generation knew how to handle Communists. A firm hand and no mercy, like *la Matanza*. That was 'thirty-two. I was a boy, but I remember it well. Communists incited the *campesinos* to revolt. Gangs with machetes swarmed from the mountains and took over towns, murdering government officials and *cafetaleros* like my father. Our neighbor was hacked to death on his own veranda. We were sure our *finca* would be next. We were afraid for our lives, barricaded right here in this house, with guns, even me and my mother. Fortunately the attack never came. The *cafetaleros* formed militias, called the White Guards. Together with the army they put down the uprising."

Put it down hard, Rod recalled from his reading of El Salvador's troubled history. *La Matanza* meant the massacre, not of landowners, but of peasants. In the weeks following the revolt, thousands of *campesinos*, whether they'd participated in the uprising or not, were slaughtered indiscriminately—men, women and children, anyone who looked like an Indian or a peasant, anyone who happened to be carrying a machete. Most historians put the death toll at thirty thousand, a significant percentage of the rural population. *La Matanza* had also set the pattern for how El Salvador's ruling class would respond to future efforts at reform, with fear and repression.

"Again the Communists incite the *campesinos* and we fight a war to keep things under control," Humberto said. "Fortunately your government understands the extent of the danger, especially since the Communists took over Nicaragua. Of course, we have stupid outsiders, like those American women who were killed when they tried to run a roadblock, foolish women mixing in where they don't belong. Communists have even contaminated the church. Priests give their allegiance to the devil instead of God. They deserve to die. We need another bloodletting like *la Matanza*, to purge my country of the evils of Communism that threaten our way of life."

You're getting your bloodletting, Rod thought, if half of what I read is true. Chief among the priests Humberto Aragón excoriated was the late Archbishop Romero, murdered in March of nineteen eighty. The foolish American women were three nuns and a lay worker, killed the same month. The Jesuit University in San Salvador had been bombed repeatedly, in response to the church's increasingly leftist stance. The right-wing death squads operating throughout the country distributed leaflets that read: "Be a patriot, kill a priest."

The man is crazy. How soon can I get out of this place?

Humberto glared at his son. "Now these damned rebels have overrun Los Árboles. I tell the army to clean them out, but to no avail."

"We will retake the town, soon," Severino said.

"I give you an example of the pernicious gall of these Communists," Humberto said. "The shopkeeper Tránsito told me a rebel comes to San Blas, the village near the processing plant, comes to my own *finca* preaching revolution to the *campesinos*. His mother lives in San Blas and shelters him. On my land, in a house I built. How dare she?"

"You should nip that in the bud." Claire poured herself another glass of wine. "Don't let a guerrilla come and go like that. He's scouting for a soft spot on your land, hoping to establish an outpost on your *finca*. Send Cruz and his men up to San Blas to throw a scare into them."

Humberto struck the table with his hand. "By God, you are right. These *campesinos* will know who runs this *finca*."

The French doors were open to the warm night. Rod heard shouts. Something thudded outside, as though a body had come into contact with the wooden planks or railing of the veranda. They pushed their chairs away from the table and walked out onto the veranda.

Cruz had another man backed up against the railing, pummeling his victim with his meaty fists, like a prizefighter moving in for the kill. Other men hovered in the background, silent as they watched Cruz beat the other man. Then the man stumbled and fell to the ground. Cruz kicked him. Humberto ordered Cruz to stop. The bloody, bruised man on the ground moaned. His companions carried him away.

"I am sorry for this disturbance." Humberto turned to his guests with an indulgent smile. "These men, sometimes they drink and get out of hand."

"Obviously you didn't hire Cruz for his social skills." Claire looked amused.

"Just as well," Humberto said. "I doubt that he has any."

Both the Aragóns and Claire laughed. Rod frowned as he followed them back to the dining room, where Ana waited in the doorway. Humberto ordered her to clear the table. She did so, then she returned from the kitchen, carrying a heavy silver coffee service. She poured the dark fragrant brew.

"Coffee, our lifeblood," Humberto said, as silver spoons tinkled against delicate china.

The coffee tasted bitter. Rod set the cup back in the saucer.

ON Sunday after lunch they sat on the veranda outside the dining room. Claire fiddled with her hair, taming long blond strands with barrettes. "I don't know why I let it grow. I swear, I'm going to cut it when I get back."

"I like it long," Severino protested, wrapping one lock around his finger.

Humberto talked of plans for the following day, but Rod wasn't interested in seeing any more Aragón operations. Work was piling up on his desk during his absence. He'd been gone far too long. He was ready to head for San Salvador right now, but he and Claire weren't due to leave the Aragón *finca* until Tuesday morning.

Cruz approached, with a *campesino* who held a straw hat in front of his chest. "That's Tránsito, the shopkeeper from San Blas," Severino said as Claire put her arms above her head and stretched like a lazy cat.

Humberto rose and stepped off the veranda. The *campesino* bowed to Humberto and spoke in a low voice. Humberto glowered and dismissed Tránsito with a wave of his hand. As the shopkeeper trudged away, Humberto snapped, "That rebel is in San Blas right now. He walked into the church this morning. The fools treat him like an honored guest."

"Unacceptable," Severino said. "We must do something. We can't tolerate this."

"Agreed," Claire said. "You've got to slap those people down."

"By God, I will." Humberto turned back to face Cruz. "Go to San Blas, capture this rebel, and bring him back here. I will deal with him.

Let the *campesinos* know I am displeased with them. Do whatever you have to do."

Cruz grinned. He assembled his men on the gravel drive behind the Aragón house, armed with guns and machetes as they climbed into their Jeeps and drove away.

"More coffee, Señor Llewellyn?" Humberto settled into his chair as though nothing had happened.

"No, thanks," Rod told him. "I'm feeling a bit tired. I think I'll lie down."

"Ah, yes, a siesta." Severino grinned as he handed a cup to Claire. His hand tweaked her long blond hair. "A time-honored custom."

Upstairs, Rod splashed cold water on his face and reached for a towel. He had the keys to the rental car. He could head back to San Salvador on his own, get an earlier flight. But the somnolent heat of the afternoon sapped his energy. It was easier to do nothing. He kicked off his shoes, stretched out on the bed, and dozed.

Gunfire. Rod roused himself and went to the balcony. Had he imagined gunfire? No, there it was again. Smoke rose beyond the ridge, black smoke hanging like a funeral pall, turning the setting sun as red as blood.

When the Jeeps returned, Rod rushed downstairs. Humberto, Severino, and Claire were already outside, with Cruz. A smirk twisted Cruz's lips and his eyes held a glittering, sated look. A bloody corpse sprawled in the back of a Jeep. Rod's stomach turned. He tried to make sense of the words ricocheting around him.

"We had to fight, *Patrón*," Cruz said. "The rebels fired on us while we were trying to arrest them. It was quite a battle, but these rebels won't trouble you anymore."

"What's done is done," Humberto said. "But why did you bring the children?"

Children? Now Rod saw them in another Jeep—an infant and a little girl who didn't appear to be hurt. The third child, a little boy, had a cut on his chin.

"They'll fetch a good price," Cruz said.

"You're not going to sell them," Severino snapped.

"The army takes children, too." Cruz had a knowing look on his ugly face. "They sell them to rich Americans who want babies. The major knows this."

Severino shook his head. "I know nothing of the sort."

"You'll do nothing of the sort," Claire said. "Ana! Come out here and help me." The frightened woman came out of the house and did Claire's bidding. Rod held the door open as Claire and Ana carried the children into the kitchen. Ana sat the little girl on the floor and the baby in a basket. Claire deposited the boy in a chair. She grabbed a towel, dampened it at the sink, and wiped the blood from the boy's chin, sending Ana to fetch a first-aid kit. Claire rummaged inside the kit for gauze, scissors, and a small brown bottle. The boy whimpered as Claire cleaned his wound and treated it with salve. She covered the cut with a bandage. "*Pobrecito.* He'll have a scar." She washed and dried her hands, then turned to Ana. "Clean them up and give them something to eat. Then put them to bed. Give them a little brandy if necessary, to help them sleep."

Rod followed Claire out to the veranda. "What are we going to do about this?"

"It's not our concern." The low table outside the dining room held a bottle of brandy and several squat glasses. Claire poured herself a shot and drank the liquor in one swallow. "Humberto and Severino can't be held responsible for Cruz and his men going off the rails."

Rod grabbed her arm. "Those thugs work for Humberto. He's responsible. He told them to go up there and throw a scare into those villagers. Your words, I believe."

Claire shook off his hand and set the glass on the table. "Remember who the Aragóns are. Uncle George's in-laws. Highly respected landowners who've owned this land for generations. Growers who produce a high percentage of the Salvadoran coffee the Dunlin Corporation imports."

Rod stared at her. "More important than dead *campesinos*. Is that what you're saying?"

"Yes, that's what I'm saying." Her words were as cold as her eyes. "Dragging the Aragóns through the mud isn't going to bring those dead *campesinos* back to life. Stay out of this. Run along, go take another nap."

"I'm staying right here."

The Aragóns joined them on the veranda. Humberto sloshed brandy into a glass and raised it to his lips. Claire whispered in Severino's ear and urged him and Humberto into the house through the dining room. Rod followed but Severino barred his way. "Señor Llewellyn, this doesn't concern you. Please give us privacy."

Rod waited until they were inside. Then he walked around the veranda to the windows outside Humberto's office. Now he was reduced to eavesdropping.

Severino's voice was so close that he must have been standing just the other side of the window. "If the damn reporters get wind of this it will be a nightmare."

"We can't afford a scandal," Humberto said. "But how do we control the damage?

"It never happened," Claire said. "Get rid of the village. Bury the bodies and bulldoze all the buildings. That's a man-made pond up there, with an earthen dam. Breach the dam and flood the village. Then it's a lake. You say it's always been a lake."

"So water covers our problem." Humberto sounded relieved. "Excellent. I will have the men start right away."

"It's late," Severino said. "By the time they get back to San Blas it will be dusk. They can't work in the dark without generators and lights."

"It will have to keep until morning, then," Humberto said. "I want them up there at dawn, the bulldozer and every man with a shovel. They must be fast and thorough. We saw the smoke. No doubt others did, too, and will investigate."

By the time the Aragóns and Claire returned, Rod was seated outside the dining room, drinking brandy. He set his glass on the table.

"I've told Ana to prepare a light supper," Humberto said, as though nothing had happened.

Rod stood. "I don't have any appetite. If you'll excuse me." He walked through the dining room and glanced into the kitchen. The children were on the floor near the pantry, nibbling on tortillas, the baby in the basket between them.

Rod went upstairs to his room. He stared at the rental car keys and the small camera he carried with him on visits to growers. A plan took shape in his head.

ROD rose before dawn and dressed in the dark. He slipped keys, camera and film into his jacket pockets. He opened the door and listened. No sounds came from the other bedrooms, but someone moved on the first floor. He went downstairs, every squeak of the boards beneath his feet sounding loud as a thunderclap. Ana stood at the kitchen table, stirring something in a bowl. She gestured at the stove, where a coffeepot sat on the back burner. He shook his head and raised a finger to his lips. In the pantry, he saw the baby in the basket, between two shapes huddled in blankets.

Outside the sun was a faint yellow glow on the horizon. Lights and voices in the outbuildings carried on the cool morning air. Rod didn't have much time. He climbed into the rental car and stuck the key into the ignition. The engine started, the sound explosive to his ears. He expected lights to go on in the house, but nothing happened. Rod put the car in gear and headed down the driveway, without lights. A gravel road led directly to the processing plant and San Blas, the likely route Cruz and his men would take. There was also a dirt road, he recalled from Saturday's tour of the coffee groves. The two roads met near the processing plant. He located the dirt road. The sun crept a bit higher. The blackness on either side of the road became gray.

It was a few kilometers to the plant, then another kilometer to San Blas, over a ridge and down into the village. Rod couldn't see the car's odometer but he guessed he'd traveled a kilometer when he passed the spot where dirt joined gravel, a sharp angle to the right that led back to the house. Last night the idea had been to get to the village, take pictures, and get back before anyone knew he was gone. Now, in the cold light of dawn, Rod saw gaps in his plan. What if he got up to the village and then Cruz and his men arrived? How would he get back? What were the consequences of his impulse, of discovery?

Too late to change his mind. He was at the processing plant.

Buildings loomed at him as the sun spread its pale glow across the landscape. Rod gunned the engine and pointed the car toward San Blas. A Jeep sped straight at him. Rod slammed on the brakes.

Cruz got out of the Jeep, walked to the car, and yanked open the door. He pointed a pistol at Rod. "Get out." Rod complied. Cruz backed him against the car. "I ought to shoot you."

Rod found his voice. "Señor Aragón wouldn't like that."

"He won't like you meddling. You're a nosy American. I should blow off your head. But you're a guest of the *patrón*. That's the only thing saving you. So I won't kill you. Not today."

Rod thought the grinding noise he heard was blood rushing through his own veins, but it was a line of Jeeps and pickup trucks, a bulldozer bringing up the rear. The caravan stopped, blocked by Rod's car and Cruz's Jeep. Cruz shouted orders in Spanish. Two men ran to the vehicles, moving them out of the way. The caravan began to move again, cresting the hill, heading for San Blas.

CLAIRE jingled the car keys in the palm of her hand. "You shouldn't have done this."

"I could say the same for you," Rod said. "You're an accessory after the fact."

"You're being dramatic." Her fingers closed over the keys. She tucked them into her pocket and reached for his camera. "So you were planning to take pictures. Then what? Call the *New York Times*? Drag the Aragóns into a scandal? Humberto is appalled that you would abuse his hospitality."

"I'm appalled by the Aragóns," he said. "By the massacre in San Blas, and your part in it. You suggested they send Cruz to that village. Now you're helping them cover it up."

"You're not going to tell anyone," she said. "People like the Aragóns are the backbone of the coffee business in El Salvador."

"They've built it on the backs of the *campesinos*."

Claire tossed words back at him. "Agricultural production all over the world is built on the backs of cheap labor. It's no different here, or back in California. Who do you think picks lettuce and tomatoes in the Central Valley? This *finca* produces much of the coffee we buy in El Salvador. Any scandal affecting the Aragóns reflects on the company and jeopardizes business. Speaking as the boss's niece and the daughter of one of the major shareholders, I can tell you the family won't like that. Keep your mouth shut. You're in a war zone. You could have an accident. The roads are so bad. And there are soldiers everywhere."

Rod had always known she was ruthless but he'd never imagined the past twenty-four hours. "I want to leave."

Claire shook her head. "Our tickets are for tomorrow evening. I won't stay in a hotel when I'm comfortable here. We'll spend the night here as planned and leave for San Salvador tomorrow."

"Since you have the car keys, I have no choice."

"That's right, you don't. I'm taking those children to an orphanage in San Salvador. They'll have a chance of getting adopted."

"They wouldn't be orphans," he said, "if you and the Aragóns hadn't turned those thugs loose in that village."

Rod was trapped, under house arrest. He refused dinner. He couldn't eat with the others, making conversation while the knowledge of what had happened seethed under the surface of social niceties. Instead he drank brandy on the veranda, as the blood-red sun sank behind the mountains to the west.

Tuesday morning he woke with a wicked hangover. Ana brought him a tray with coffee and pastries. He swallowed aspirin and chased it with strong black coffee. The caffeine cleared his head and settled his stomach. He ate, marveling at how hungry he was. Then he showered, dressed, and packed his suitcase. He couldn't wait to get out of this place, off the Aragón *finca*, out of El Salvador.

He stepped onto the balcony as a Jeep skidded to a stop. Two men hauled someone from the backseat, a woman in faded jeans and a blue shirt, a ballcap on a head of blond curls. Rod rushed downstairs to the hall, where Claire and Severino examined an American passport. In the office the woman slumped in a wooden chair near the desk. Blood stained the woman's jeans leg.

"What's going on?" Rod asked.

"Two people were poking around up at San Blas," Claire said. "One got away. This woman is a reporter." Ana came from the kitchen with a tray holding a pitcher of water, a bowl, and folded cloths. She set the tray on the desk and retreated. Claire entered the office and sat down. She reached for the first-aid kit, cut away the cloth on the woman's leg, then cleaned and bandaged the wound.

Humberto Aragón appeared, swearing in Spanish. He glared at the woman in the chair. "They should have put a bullet in her head and left her for the vultures."

"She speaks Spanish," Severino warned.

Claire put her hand on Humberto's arm and led the way out the back door. Rod remained in the kitchen, straining to hear Claire and the Aragóns.

"Better to kill her and get it over with," Humberto said.

"Too late for that." Severino's voice came in and out, as though he were pacing back and forth along the veranda. "Your coffee broker from Dunlin knows too much."

"I can handle him," Claire said. "The journalist can be handled, too. The rebel she was with will contact other reporters. If she winds up dead, you'll be blamed. Too many people have seen her. Take her to San Salvador."

"Let her go?" Humberto bellowed.

"Have her press credential pulled," Claire said. "Your son-in-law works for the government."

"Call Cristina," Severino said. "She and Francisco have influence."

"They'll make it happen," Claire said. "Severino takes the woman to the airport. She's escorted onto the next available flight out of the country. You're a respected businessman. You can't be blamed if your guards got carried away. Who'll believe her? Her camera is smashed, the film exposed."

"What if she had another roll of film and gave it to the rebel?" Severino asked.

"Showing what?" Claire countered. "A lake? No one knows what happened on Sunday."

"What if someone escaped the village?" Humberto asked.

"It doesn't matter," Claire said. "If the story gets out, it's your word against theirs. She has no proof."

No proof. The words echoed inside Rod's head. He leaned against the wall, trying to decide what to do. Claire's threat reverberated in his mind. He was afraid. Rod Llewellyn could wind up dead in El Salvador.

32

"I NEVER TOLD ANYONE," Rod said. "I'm a coward."

Lindsey struggled with the knowledge that the woman at the Aragón *finca* was Claire. Loss washed over her. She'd always considered Claire a good friend. Now that friendship was broken. "You tried to get up to the village."

"What a paltry effort that was." He pushed away his plate. "I could have told Max. I could have resigned. But I did nothing. Why? Expedience. Inertia. Inaction is comfortable. The moment passed. My indignation evaporated."

The server returned and whisked away plates, offering coffee and dessert. Lindsey shook her head, and Rod asked for the check. He glanced at it and took cash from his wallet.

"Then the massacre at San Blas hit the news," Lindsey said.

"I thought I was off the hook," he said. "Merle Sefton did what I hadn't done, much better than I could have, with photos and eyewitnesses. I thought there would be an outcry, an investigation of the massacre. But there wasn't. If I had talked, would it have made a difference?"

"Who knows?" Lindsey shook her head. "The Aragóns disputed the facts loud enough and long enough to discredit Sefton and her story. The cover-up succeeded."

"Claire was the architect of that cover-up."

"I've known Claire a long time," Lindsey said. "Now it seems I don't know her at all."

"No, you don't," Rod said. "I've seen a side of Claire that you never have, one she's hidden from you and the others. There is a human cost to producing a crop. But the price of coffee shouldn't include death."

"Did Claire say anything about the children?" Lindsey asked. "On the trip back to San Salvador, or after you left them at the orphanage?"

"She seemed taken with the little boy, said she knew someone who needed a boy. I told her she couldn't carry him onto the plane like a souvenir. She said she could, if she greased the right palms."

Claire had done it with more subtlety. She'd set the wheels in motion, then told the Segals about the Salvadoran boy who needed a home and a family. Something he'd already had, until that Sunday when the men with guns had obliterated his village.

"The woman I interviewed is a San Blas survivor," Lindsey said. "Her child was taken that day. He's the little boy with the cut on his chin."

"Dear God, how the past comes back to haunt us. Does she know where he is?"

"She's been looking for years. He was adopted, by a couple here in the United States," Lindsey said. "Why did you agree to talk with me today?"

"Max wondered why you asked about El Salvador in the spring of 'eighty-nine. I knew it had to be about that trip, that incident."

"You're curious. But you also want leverage against Claire, because of the company. I have another agenda, too." Lindsey reached for her handbag, removing the book by Dylan Thomas she'd found in Pandora's Box. She had translated the inscription via computer the night before. "I should have known all along. But it didn't really occur to me until recently, when I found this."

Rod stared at the book, emotions flickering on his face. "Where did you get that?"

"I found it in a box of keepsakes. It contains things that are important to Annabel. A book by a Welsh author, with a Welsh inscription." She opened the book to the flyleaf and pointed at the words written so long ago. "*Cariad* means love. And Rhodri is a popular boy's name in Wales, just as Llewellyn is a common surname. Sometimes when you speak I can just hear it in your voice, a lilt, an accent."

"I left Wales a long time ago." His index finger traced the handwritten letters. "I'm surprised she kept it."

"I'm not. You and Annabel were lovers."

"I'm not sure how it began," he said. "But I remember how it ended."

33

Berkeley, California, Spring 1974

LOUD, URGENT MUSIC PLAYED on the coffeehouse's radio, Steppenwolf on a magic carpet ride. "What are you reading?" Annabel asked.

"*How Green Was My Valley.*" He held up the well-thumbed paperback. "I've read it before, and seen the film."

"Me, too. I love old movies," she said. "I've been trying to place your accent. You do have one. You're Welsh, aren't you? Llewellyn, same as the author of that book."

He smiled and set down the book. "Yes, I'm Welsh, but Richard Llewellyn, the man who wrote this book, wasn't. It's a pseudonym. He was English. I understand he never actually went to Wales, just interviewed people. Still, it's a good book. My people are coal miners, like the characters in this story."

"Is Rod short for Roderick?"

"Rhodri." He pronounced it with a long *o*. "I'm named for my Granddad. In Welsh, 'rhod' means circle and 'rhi' means ruler."

"Circle ruler… How long have you lived in this country?"

"Over ten years, and a citizen for three. You say I've got an accent, but when I go home for a visit, my mother says I sound American. I was born and raised in a village called Cwmgwrach." The name rolled easily from his mouth. She tried to pronounce it and he laughed at the result.

"It sounds like a cat hacking up a hairball," she said.

"You have to be Welsh to say it properly. Cwmgwrach is a tiny speck on the map, in Glamorgan, a county in South Wales. The closest city is called Abertawe in Welsh, Swansea in English. I left when I was eighteen. Didn't want to be a coal miner like my father and brothers. I want to see something of the world."

"So do I." Annabel's eyes took on a faraway glow. "I'd like to see Wales someday. Just travel around and look at the countryside. I'll bet it's beautiful."

"It's grand," Rod said. "We used to go on holiday to Tenby, an old walled town on the southwest coast. And north into the mountains, a town called Brecon."

She leaned closer and he caught the scent of lavender. "I want to visit the places I've read about in books. London, Edinburgh, and Cornwall. The Cotswolds and Yorkminster. Stonehenge and Skye. I've never been farther east than Lake Tahoe." She sounded wistful. "We go there in the summers. The longest trip I ever took was after Claire and I graduated from high school, to Hawaii with Aunt Rebecca. We stayed at the Royal Hawaiian and saw all the sights of Oahu. Claire sneaked out at night to party with the beach boys and score Maui Wowie."

"What about you? Any adventures in the tropics?"

"Me?" She shook her head, gold earrings shimmering against her chestnut hair. "I'd never do anything reckless or daring. I'm the good girl. I sat on the beach and read books about Hawaiian history and culture. That's Annabel, always with her nose in a book."

"Get your nose out of the book and have adventures," he said. "It's time you did. You graduate in May."

"I start grad school in the fall," she said.

"You have the whole summer. June to August you're a free woman. You can see a lot in two months. Just pack a bag and go."

"A free woman." She frowned. "Am I? You don't know my father."

"I know enough. That's why I'm here, isn't it? You're an adult. You can do as you please. As long as you have the time, and the money for a plane ticket."

"I have both," she said. "But I don't have a passport."

"There's a passport office in San Francisco. You have pictures taken, fill out a form, and hand over some cash. Easy as that." He grinned and dangled the names in front of her, like yarn luring a kitten. "The Tower of London, Westminster Abbey, the British Museum, the Tate Gallery. Theatre in the West End, shopping at

Harrod's, afternoon tea at Brown's Hotel, like Agatha Christie. Then Paris. Stroll down the Champs Élysées from the Arc de Triomphe to the Place de la Concorde, then through the Tuileries to the Louvre."

A smile teased the corners of her lips. "I could, couldn't I?"

"Yes, if only you would." The music on the radio changed. Joni Mitchell declared that she was free in Paris, unfettered and alive.

"My father would have a heart attack. Or insist that Claire and Aunt Rebecca go along. With Max Brinker as chaperone. Wouldn't that be a band of merry travelers?" She laughed.

"I'll go along to chaperone," he whispered.

He was falling off a precipice and he didn't care. Did it start then? Or the first day he reported for duty at the house on Hillegass? He only knew he was smitten. He enjoyed keeping an eye on Annabel Dunlin, and not for the reason Max Brinker had hired him.

They finished their coffee. He walked her home, dusk darkening the sky. "So you like films," he said as they turned the corner onto Hillegass Street. "Have you seen any of the new ones?"

"*American Graffiti*," she said. "That was a lot of fun. I love the music. I enjoyed *The Sting*, too. I like comedy, romance and film noir. Old movies from the Thirties and Forties."

"I like the old ones." He gazed at her in the soft wash of light from the street lamp. "There's a film playing in the city Saturday night. Not that old, from nineteen fifty-nine. It's called *Tiger Bay*, takes place in Cardiff. I think you'd like it."

She smiled. "Why, Rod, I'd love to go out with you."

On Saturday he took her to a San Francisco movie house that had seen better days and now eked out its survival showing art films like *Tiger Bay*, a gritty black-and-white drama set in a rough Cardiff dockside neighborhood. They shared popcorn, and when it was gone he set the empty container on the floor and put his arm around her. His heart beat faster when she leaned into him. He turned his head and they kissed.

He accompanied Annabel home from class Wednesday afternoon and she detoured into Cody's Books on Telegraph Avenue. Instead of browsing through fiction, as she often did, she walked straight to the travel section. He hovered at one end of the row, watching while she leafed through the books that lined the shelves. Finally she selected several volumes about Britain, France and Italy.

"I'm planning my escape," she said as they walked back to the house. "I took my application over to the passport office yesterday. While I was in the city I stopped in at a travel agent's office and asked about air fares and train passes. I have lots of brochures. Once I started thinking about all the places I'd like to see it was hard to stop. If I'm going to London and Paris, why not Rome and Florence? I could cover a lot of ground over a summer."

"You could at that. Well, speaking of Italy... That cinema we went to last weekend, it's showing an Italian film this Saturday. Rossellini, *Open City.*"

"I've always wanted to see that. We should have dinner first. At an Italian restaurant, since we're seeing an Italian movie."

"I know a great restaurant, on Russian Hill," he said. "It would be my pleasure to escort you..."

She nodded. "You're supposed to escort me everywhere I go."

He was impatient for Saturday to arrive. His heart quickened when he saw Annabel in a sea-green dress with a matching jacket, made of silk, soft and shiny. The fabric clung to her hips and thighs. The dress's neckline plunged, revealing a few tantalizing inches of her breasts. Her earrings and necklace were made of silver stars.

"What a tiny little out-of-the way place," she said. "The neighborhood's more residential than commercial. How did you find this restaurant?"

"Rambling around." He held the door open for her. "That's how I learn about a city. I get out and walk. Or I ride the bus to see where it goes. I've been exploring San Francisco that way since I arrived."

They were seated in a secluded alcove. Annabel studied the menu. Rod studied her, drinking in every detail. When the waiter returned, pen poised over pad, Rod reluctantly tore his gaze from her and glanced at the menu. "Have you decided?"

She shook her head. "Not quite. Let's have some wine first. That would be lovely."

"I don't know much about wine."

"I'll choose." She examined the wine list and selected a Chardonnay. The waiter returned with the bottle and glasses. He poured their wine and left with their dinner order. Annabel picked up her glass and swirled the pale liquid so that it shimmered. "What shall we drink to?"

To us, he thought, but didn't voice it. He raised his glass. "To your summer adventure."

She smiled and their glasses clinked together. He drank, deciding he liked the taste of the wine. If she chose it, it must be ambrosia.

The waiter reappeared with a cart, several bowls and some implements. With a flourish and a head of romaine, he made a Caesar salad, tossing it before he divided it onto two plates and served it. Then he left them alone.

Annabel speared lettuce with her fork. "I'm making plans for my trip. I'm leaving the first week in June. I'll spend a week in London, then Oxford, Cambridge, and York. Then Edinburgh, Inverness and across to Skye. And back down to Glasgow and Liverpool. Then Wales, of course. And Ireland."

He smiled. "You don't have to see it all in one trip."

"I have to see as much as I can. It might be my only chance."

"You'll have other opportunities to travel. You have your whole life ahead of you."

"My whole life. That's too big a canvas to think of right now. I'll just think about this summer." Her eyes gleamed with excitement. "I'll take the boat train from London to Dover, just like the characters in an Agatha Christie novel, and sail across the channel, then take the train to Paris. I'll explore the Louvre and Notre Dame. Day trips to Chartres Cathedral and Versailles."

"See what I've started," he said, "suggesting you go. You took the ball and now you're running with it."

She smiled. "No, it was always there, the desire. You helped bring it to the surface."

They finished their salads and the waiter brought their entrées. Annabel dusted her pasta with parmesan. Rod cut into his chicken marsala, listening as she talked about her trip. All he could think about as he ate his dinner was that he wouldn't see her for two months.

"When are you going to spring this on your father?" he asked.

"I'll tell him when it's a *fait accompli.*" Annabel touched the napkin to her mouth and pushed away her plate. "When I have my tickets and my passport in hand. Then I'll say, by the way, I'm going to Europe. He won't like it. But I won't let him stop me."

The waiter appeared and removed their dinner plates, offering coffee and the dessert menu. They ordered cappuccino and panna cotta, a creamy pudding with an underlying hint of alcohol.

"Tell me about your apartment, and your ramblings through the city," Annabel said.

"I have this grand little flat above a deli in North Beach. I can see Washington Square from my living room window."

"A view, and food downstairs. What more could you ask?"

Someone to share it with, he thought. He'd always considered himself a loner, content with his solitude, but now he felt a pang of loneliness.

He told her of his forays to the public library, where he checked out books about San Francisco's history. He read about the Gold Rush and the ships abandoned on San Francisco Bay as their crews headed for the mountains in search of treasure, the hulls and masts eventually forming the bones of landfill along the city's waterfront. He'd read about the Barbary Coast saloons and brothels, where barflies and prostitutes drank and caroused, where ruffians shanghaied unsuspecting men for sailors. That part of old San Francisco was gone, leveled by the 1906 earthquake and fire. Out of those ruins rose the Financial District. On his days off, he tramped through the neighborhoods where the historical drama had played out, from the narrow alleys and fascinating shops of Chinatown, the sunny Latin-flavored streets of the Mission District, all the way to the shifting dunes of Ocean Beach.

"I wish I could have seen the Sutro Baths in all their glory," he said. "And that amusement park, Playland at the Beach."

"Playland was wonderful. We went there when I was a kid," Annabel said. "It's a shame they closed it down. At least Laffing Sal is still there, at the Musée Mécanique. That laugh used to frighten me. It's been a long time since I went out to Cliff House and Ocean

Beach." She leaned forward. "I want you to show me the city. The way you discovered it."

"You were born and raised here. Haven't you seen it?"

"My range has been limited, and the past four years in Berkeley, I've focused on my studies. I haven't really explored the city much now that I'm an adult. I want to see it through different eyes. Let's take a field trip, next Saturday. You'll escort me to a museum."

Guarding Annabel made it easy for Rod to spend time with her. They went to the de Young Museum in Golden Gate Park that Saturday, holding hands as they walked through the galleries. Then they had tea at the Japanese Tea Garden and walked to the Conservatory of Flowers. On other excursions, they viewed the ruins of the Sutro Baths and took in an art exhibit at the Palace of the Legion of Honor.

The last week in March was spring break at the university, no classes, so they spent one day visiting the Spanish mission that gave the district its name, and another day wandering through Chinatown. On Friday they went to Fisherman's Wharf, breathing in the aroma of fish and salt air flavored with popcorn and cotton candy. They lunched on crab cocktails from one of the stands crowding the sidewalks outside restaurants fronting the wharves. As the afternoon waned, they headed for North Beach, Rod's neighborhood, and climbed the steep hill to Coit Tower. At the top they watched cars twist and turn their way down Lombard Street's steep one-block curlicue. The sunset streaked the sky with red, pink and purple.

They walked down Telegraph Hill to Washington Square, past the looming towers of Saints Peter and Paul Church. The smell of garlic wafting from a nearby restaurant made Rod hungry. "Where shall we have dinner?"

Annabel squeezed his hand. "There's a deli below your apartment. Let's get sandwiches and eat at your place."

They crossed the square. His building was on Union Street, between Powell and Mason, just off the square. The bell above the door jangled as they entered the deli.

"Oh, they have cannoli," Annabel said. "I love cannoli."

"So do I." Already his mouth watered as he anticipated biting into one of the crisp light shells filled with creamy sweet ricotta.

Mr. DeLucci, his landlord, was behind the counter, talking non-stop as he sliced meat and cheese and constructed their sandwiches. Mrs. DeLucci filled a pink pastry box with an assortment of cannoli and biscotti.

"It's enough food for six people," he said. "Or if we plan to be snowed in."

Annabel laughed. "Snow? In San Francisco? It could happen. Anything can happen."

"No snow in the forecast. The weather will be warm and sunny all weekend."

"All the better for our rambling." She took his hand and they went upstairs to his apartment. He unlocked the door. They put their purchases on the kitchen counter and set the table. Then Annabel opened the front window and leaned out. "You need a window box and some flowers. Hey, I can see the wharf."

"I'll put on some music," he said. Brick-and-board shelves held a few books, his stereo and LPs. He turned on the stereo and stacked LPs on the spindle. The first was a favorite, Dave Brubeck's *Take Five*. They ate dinner, talking and drinking beer. Then he washed the dishes, while Annabel dried and put them away. It felt cozy and domestic, and somehow right, to have her standing next to him in the little kitchen. He made coffee. They sat on the sofa, nibbling cannoli and biscotti, sipping coffee as they talked.

Annabel had ricotta at the corner of her mouth. He wiped it away with a finger. She held his hand against her cheek. He kissed her, finding her mouth much sweeter than the pastry they'd been eating. She pressed closer to him, kissing him back, her own hands tangled in his hair. Before he knew it they were stretched out on the sofa, their bodies molding to one another. His heart pounded as his mouth explored hers and his hands slipped under her shirt and found her breasts.

"I'd better take you home," he said, his voice thick.

She tugged the zipper of his jeans. "I'm going to spend the night with you."

BEGINNINGS and endings, Rod thought.

He and Annabel sat at a table in another coffeehouse, another song in the background, as Carly Simon mused about the way things should be. On this afternoon in late May, unseasonable rain washed the sidewalks of Washington Square and streaked the café's windows. He spoke words filled with hope. But the coffee in his mug tasted bitter.

Annabel sipped her cappuccino, her face grave. "I don't want to get married. Not right now. Maybe later. Maybe never."

He looked out at the pouring rain and longed to recapture the exhilaration of nights in his bed, making love to Annabel, of mornings when he'd awakened with her next to him, her body fitting into the curve of his own, her head pillowed by his arm. The bright sun had poured in through the white curtains, bathing their bodies in its honey glow. Now he felt the gray chill of despair. It didn't matter that he loved her, wanted her, needed her. He should have known that her plans—graduation and grad school, her teaching career, her upcoming trip to Europe—didn't include him.

"Is it marriage you don't like? Or me?"

She shook her head. "Oh, Rod, it isn't you. I love you."

"Then why? I love you. Two people who love each other should be together."

"I have to be myself first," she said. "Before I can be part of a couple."

"I don't understand. You are who you are. Being married doesn't change that."

"Doesn't it? We're changed every time we interact with someone, whether it's a moment or a lifetime." She stared into her coffee. "My parents didn't have much of a marriage."

"Marriage is what you make of it," he said. "It's hard work. I know that. My parents have been together forty years. They've had ups and downs, but they've stayed together, raised a family, built a life together. We love each other. That should be all that matters."

"I'm not sure I'm ready for that commitment," she said. "The only thing I'm certain of is that I have to be Annabel first."

Whatever happened to love conquers all? He was losing her. He felt pain, sharp as a knife in his breast. Could it be over, as quickly as it began? Could it be something as simple and prosaic as skewed timing? Could it be, the same question posed a month or a year from now would garner a different response?

Beginnings and endings, he thought again. A car sped by outside, splashing water from an overflowing gutter onto the sidewalk. Events in the larger world shaped the destinies of mere individuals. His job began in February when a woman was kidnapped from an apartment in Berkeley. It ended in May, when a group of people burned to death in a house in Los Angeles. Patty Hearst was still missing, claiming the name of Tania, professing solidarity with her Symbionese Liberation Army captors, most of whom had died in the shoot-out and fire that followed. Rod hadn't seen the television coverage of the fire but he'd seen the memorial service for the dead SLA members held in Berkeley, just a few blocks from the apartment on Benvenue where the kidnapping took place, another bizarre chapter in the strange story.

At the time, he didn't realize these events also signaled the end of a chapter in his own life. A few days after the Los Angeles incident, he was summoned to headquarters. Max Brinker was phasing out security at the Hillegass Street house.

"Those SLA thugs died in in Los Angeles. Good riddance," Max said. "The danger has passed. Annabel and Claire graduate at the end of the month and start grad school in the fall. They don't want security guards now. Tom's found another job. He gave notice yesterday. Mike will work security at the coffee roasting facility south of Market, and Carl will join us here at headquarters."

Rod didn't know whether he was relieved or anxious. Maybe he could come out in the open with his relationship with Annabel. He didn't like hiding, not being able to talk about the woman he loved. Who was he, an upstart, an employee, to be squiring the boss's daughter?

"Am I out of a job, then?" Rod asked.

"No," Max said. "I've had my eye on you. You're smart, efficient, loyal. You have potential. You can join my staff here at headquarters, if you want to stay in security work. If you're game to try something different, you can take a position that's opening up, out in the field. Learning the business from the ground up. I'd like to send you to Houston. The man in charge there is an old hand. If you're interested in learning, he's a great teacher."

"I don't know what to say." Emotions warred within Rod, thoughts of Annabel mixed with gratitude toward Max.

"Either job, security or Houston, gives you the opportunity to move up the ranks in this company, if a career with the Dunlin Corporation is what you have in mind." Max smiled. "Much as I'd like to have you with me here at headquarters, I'll be honest—the field job offers more potential for advancement. I think you'd be good at it. It means long hours, lots of travel. You should take that into consideration as you make your decision. Sleep on it. Take a couple of days, and then let me know."

Rod left Max's office. If circumstances were different, he'd be interested in the field job, with the opportunity to travel, to learn something new. But he wanted to be near Annabel. If he stayed here and worked at headquarters, he could be. On weekends, the way it was now. But that wasn't really what he wanted. He wanted her with him all the time.

He pushed through the lobby door to the street, taking stock of himself, making his decision. I've saved some money. I have a good job with a future. I've found the woman I love. Annabel and I will get married. After she finishes grad school, she can teach for a while. Then we'll have children.

He pictured the two of them living in a sunny little house, with Annabel's wind chimes hanging from the front porch, roses and children in the back garden. He would propose, and the dream would become reality.

Instead it washed away with the rain. He pleaded with her to reconsider. But she shook her head and left the coffeehouse, walking across Washington Square.

He waited a few days. On Sunday he went to Berkeley. Claire sat on the porch, painting her toenails bright red. Her eyes glittered with barely concealed amusement as Rod asked if Annabel was home.

"She went away for the weekend, down to Carmel. With Hal." With a sly smile, Claire added, "Any message?"

Stunned, Rod left. He had his answer, a harsh one. He saw Max the next morning. "I'll take the job in Houston. I can leave in a couple of days. The sooner the better."

Rod walked back to North Beach and told the DeLuccis his company was transferring him to another location. An APARTMENT FOR RENT sign went up in the deli window that afternoon. It didn't take him long to erase the evidence of his brief occupancy. He gave away most of his things. He was as naked of possessions as he had been when he'd arrived in San Francisco the previous September.

Travel light, he thought. That way it's easier to leave.

He picked up his suitcase and went downstairs to the deli, handing over the key. Mrs. DeLucci insisted he take some cannoli.

Outside, he raised his hand and a cab screeched to a halt. He got in and shut the door. "The airport," he said. The cab sped off down Columbus Avenue.

Rod looked at the pink bakery box tied with string, thinking of Annabel, that night they'd shared cannoli in his apartment, that first night they'd spent together in his bed. Could he ever push that memory from his mind?

The driver was on the freeway now, flying south, radio blasting Steppenwolf. The magic carpet ride was over. When they reached the airport he left the box of cannoli on the backseat.

34

"I TOOK THE JOB, and never looked back," Rod said. "It's ancient history, over and done."

"She kept the book you gave her," Lindsey said.

"Sometimes we hang onto memories and mementos, things from the past. They're like ropes dragging us down." He sighed. "You'll have to ask Annabel why she kept the book."

"I know why. This book isn't the only thing she has to remember you by. Rod, you have a daughter. Tess, Annabel's oldest child."

He stared at her, stunned. "Annabel married in June of 'seventy-four," Lindsey said. "A month after you left. She had a baby early in 'seventy-five."

He struggled to form words. "I was hurt and angry. She'd turned me down. A month later she married Hal. After all she'd said to me about not wanting to get married. So I pushed her out of my mind."

"Did you?" Lindsey asked.

Rod pushed his chair away from the table. "Let's get out of here. I need some air."

Outside they walked toward California Street. "Annabel wanted to be herself first," he said, "instead of part of a couple, someone's wife and mother. All those things she wanted to do. She never got a chance to do them. The trip to Europe, grad school, teaching. Instead she got married. But not to me." He clenched his fists. "I would have married her. If only I'd known, I'd have come back for her. Instead I got angry and wondered why Hal, and not me?"

"She must have found out she was pregnant after you left," Lindsey said. "Hal was here, convenient. Annabel called him the designated suitor. We all did."

They walked toward the corner, reaching it as the light changed from red to green. But Rod stood unmoving at the curb. People eddied around them, out into the crosswalk. He gazed down the hill at the Dunlin Building, on the opposite side of the street.

"I want to meet her," Rod said. "Tess. My daughter. Can you arrange it? She doesn't have to know that I'm her father. Does she have any idea?"

"She knows Hal isn't her father," Lindsey said. "She figured it out, because of the blood-type discrepancy. In fact, that's why I'm involved. She asked for my help. Yes, I can arrange it."

"I would like that very much. A daughter. I'm trying it on to see how it fits. I'd resigned myself to being alone. Call her now, please. I want to meet her."

"She works downtown." Lindsey took her cell phone from her purse and punched the keys. Tess's office line rang, then cycled into voicemail. She left a message asking Tess to return her call. "She must be on the phone, or with a client." Lindsey looked at her watch. "Tess and Nina went to lunch, just before you and I left." Lindsey called Tess's cell phone. Voicemail again. She left another message.

"What's she like?" Rod asked. "My daughter?"

Lindsey tucked her cell phone into her purse. "Tess looks a lot like Annabel. She's serious and quiet. The kind of person who keeps you at arm's length."

"Like Annabel," he said. "Thanks for doing this. I know it must be difficult for you."

Lindsey shrugged. "A favor for Tess."

"That's not what I mean," Rod said. "The other question that went through my mind when I heard Annabel and Hal got married was, why her, and not you?"

Somehow Lindsey wasn't surprised. "You knew that, too?"

"Of course I did. My job was to watch the house and everyone in it. I knew everything that went on that spring. Claire's fling with Carl, my fellow bodyguard. Gretchen's break-up with Doug, how suspicious she was, accusing you of wanting him. Which was ridiculous, because you were involved with Hal. You were in love with him. I thought he loved you."

"No, he didn't." Lindsey looked at a store window and saw the imperfect reflection of a woman with gray hair and wrinkles. Years had gone by, but the emotions were still there. It had been a long time since she'd admitted those feelings, much less spoken them aloud.

"I still love him. As a friend. At least that's what I tell myself," she said. "He did care about me, but he didn't love me. He loves Annabel, and he always has. I've accepted that."

"How did we get to this point?" Rod asked.

"Bad timing." Lindsey pushed back memories. "My daughter Nina is the same age as Tess."

"Does Hal know he's her father?"

"He might. I've never told him. I think Annabel knows. It's a delicate dance we do, the three of us, waltzing around the truth and never singing the lyrics."

35

Berkeley, California, Spring 1974

LINDSEY PUT THE LP on the hi-fi and sang along with Dusty Springfield's how-to guide on getting the man of her dreams. The man in question hadn't figured out how she felt about him. He couldn't see a damn thing even when it was staring him in the face.

I don't need a man, she argued. I don't have to be part of a couple. But it would be nice to snuggle in bed with something besides that teddy bear. Maybe I'll get a cat.

She stirred the chili in the cast-iron pot, tasted it, and added more chili powder. Then she mixed the ingredients for a batch of cornbread and put the pan in the oven to bake. Another lively Friday night in Berkeley. It was spring break. She'd been working on her dissertation research all week, her desk piled with books and papers.

It had been an unsettling day, though it hadn't started out that way. The spring weather was inviting, blue skies and balmy temperature. After breakfast Lindsey carried her coffee to the front porch to read the morning newspaper in comfortable solitude. She looked up as Annabel came outside, dressed in denim. "Where are you off to? You've been gone every day this week."

"San Francisco," Annabel said. "Rambling around, exploring the city."

"You grew up there. I should think you'd know the city pretty well."

Annabel smiled. "But I've never really seen it, not the way I'm seeing it now. Twin Peaks, the Mission District, Chinatown. Today it's Fisherman's Wharf, then North Beach and Coit Tower. I've lived in San Francisco all my life and I've never been to Coit Tower."

"You can have the wharf," Lindsey said. "Tourists and tacky souvenir shops."

Was Annabel exploring the city with Hal? Lindsey wondered, with a stab of unjustified jealousy. On a weekday? Surely not. Hal would be in his office, unless he'd taken some time off. Did Annabel ramble alone? Well, of course not. Annabel and Claire were never really alone these days. The bodyguards were always there, by now so woven into the fabric of their lives that often Lindsey didn't notice them. This morning Rod, the tall one with dark hair and blue eyes, waited at the curb. He opened the passenger side door of his Chevy. Annabel slid into the seat and he got behind the wheel.

Lindsey finished her coffee and newspaper, then went inside and gathered up her laundry. When the wash cycle finished, she took the clothes out to the backyard clothesline. Might as well take advantage of the sunny day. A moment later, she heard a woman's voice cry out. She looked up. Framed in the second-floor window of the rooming house next door, the one occupied by the bodyguards, she saw Claire, her arms around a man's bare torso, her face visible above his shoulder. The man turned, revealing Claire's body. She was naked, her legs wrapped around the man's hips. The man clasped Claire to him, hands splayed across her buttocks, mouth devouring hers. The two figures moved together in the obvious rhythm of sex. Claire cried out again. The man drew back his head and laughed. He had a dark handlebar moustache. Then the couple in the window moved out of view.

Lindsey recognized the man with Claire—Carl, the bodyguard with the luxuriant moustache. It was just like Claire to get involved with one of the bodyguards. It's none of my business, Lindsey thought. She went back to the house. As she unlocked her door, Gretchen came down the stairs, her face red and blotchy. She leaned over Lindsey, fury in her eyes. "Bitch! You're after Doug."

Lindsey stared. "What?"

"You were with him at a café on Telegraph," Gretchen said. "Claire saw you. Why would she tell me that if it wasn't true?"

To get a rise out of you, Lindsey thought. Which she has. "It didn't happen that way."

"You admit you were with him."

"I'm not admitting anything," Lindsey said. "I was having coffee. Doug sat at my table. He wanted to talk. He loves you. But he's not ready to get married. If you keep pressuring him, you'll lose him."

"I don't believe you," Gretchen snapped.

"Why believe Claire, and not me? I am not interested in Doug. I never have been. Now if you'll excuse me, I have work to do."

Lindsey went into her apartment and shut the door, feeling as wrung out as the clothes on the line. Instead of working on her dissertation, she took refuge in housework, mindless labor, listening to records as she scoured sinks, swept and mopped floors, and dusted furniture. After retrieving the clothes from the line and putting them away, she walked to the grocery store. She'd make comfort food— spicy chili, homemade cornbread, and a batch of brownies.

Now, as her unsettling day gave way to twilight, the needle

reached the end of the Dusty Springfield album and clicked rhythmically against the grooves. Lindsey stuck the album back in its sleeve. She flipped through the LPs she stored in a wooden crate, finally settling on Carole King, who sang about the earth moving, and the sky tumbling down. Then someone rang the front door bell.

Lindsey left her apartment and opened the outer door. With a jolt that felt like an earthquake, she saw Hal Norwood. Her heart lifted, though her head told it to stop that nonsense. He wore a dark blue suit. So he had been at the office today. "Hi. Is Annabel here?"

"She went out this morning and she's not back. Was she expecting you?"

"Not really," Hal said. "I've called several times this week. But there's been no answer. I guess she's busy."

Lindsey shivered in the chill evening air. "It's cold out here. Come inside." Hal hesitated. Then he followed her into her warm living room. "Did you and Annabel have a date?"

Hal shrugged. "Not really. I stopped by to see if she was free for dinner. And to talk about a winetasting tomorrow, in Napa. I invited Annabel to go with me. She didn't say no, but she didn't say yes, either." He smiled. "I assumed we had a date. You know what they say about people who assume things."

I assumed Annabel was with you, Lindsey thought. We were both wrong. She's with someone else. I don't know who, but I don't care. The field is clear.

"I guess Annabel's not interested in me," Hal said. "No matter how I try. Perhaps it's time to move on."

She hoped he meant that. If Annabel didn't want him, she did.

The timer dinged. Hal followed Lindsey to the kitchen. "Whatever you're cooking smells wonderful," he said.

"It's just chili and cornbread. Stay for dinner. There's plenty." He said yes, and removed his jacket and tie, hanging them on the back of a chair. Lindsey took two beers from the refrigerator and pried off the caps. She handed one bottle to him.

"Here's to chili, cornbread and beer," he said, clinking his bottle to hers.

The Carole King album had finished playing. Hal walked over to the hi-fi and looked through the albums. A moment later she heard the familiar opening bars of the Beatles's *Sergeant Pepper's Lonely Hearts Club Band.*

Lindsey set the table and made a salad. As she carried bowls of chili to the table, the Beatles pleaded with lovely Rita, meter maid. Give us a wink, she thought. Give me a sign. Give me anything. "It's ready, such as it is."

"I haven't had a home-cooked meal in a while." Hal buttered a square of cornbread and dipped a spoon into his bowl. "Not unless I cook it myself, and I don't cook much. I eat lots of Chinese takeout. This is great."

"Thanks. I'm glad you like it." The chili was spicy hot in her mouth. "I don't go out much, even takeout. Not on a grad student's budget."

"Yeah, I remember those days, when I was working on my master's. How's the dissertation coming along?"

She glanced at her desk. "It's not. I've been wrestling with it all week. I like to think I'm winning. But I haven't been able to concentrate."

"It's spring break. That implies taking a break from your studies."

"Not if you're a doctoral student. It just means the library's less crowded."

"Sounds very nose-to-the-grindstone."

"I have to finish this dissertation and get on with my life. I want to teach at Berkeley."

"What about marriage and a family?" he asked.

"Eventually. Career first, though. What about you? I mean, career-wise, not marriage and family. You went to Penn and got your master's at Wharton School of Business."

"I was lucky to get to college at all, let alone Wharton," he said. "My family doesn't have much money. Good thing I had scholarships and grants. Even those didn't stretch very far. I'm from a little town northeast of Pittsburgh. My father owns an auto parts store. My mother works in the city clerk's office. Neither of them went to college. My folks scrimped and saved, my sisters and I worked, and we all got college scholarships."

"Your family sounds like mine," Lindsey said. "Dad owns a hardware store in Paso Robles, and Mom teaches elementary school. There wasn't much money for things like college, but they started a college fund for me and my brothers, and added to it over the years. I got scholarships, too, and worked part-time jobs, starting with baby-sitting in junior high."

"Same here." Hal chuckled. "Not baby-sitting, unless you count looking after my sisters. I worked in my dad's store. Stocking shelves and running the cash register."

"I've stocked a few shelves myself. Cash register, inventory, ordering. I can even mix paint. We have a lot in common. How did we wind up here, with these rich people?"

"Answered an ad for an accountant." He finished his chili. "How about you?"

"Answered an ad for an apartment."

"Serendipity." He looked at her for a moment. "Your chili's really good. I'd like more." She reached for his bowl at the same time he did. Their hands met and neither of them pulled away. "I'll get it. You want more?" She shook her head. While he was in the kitchen, Lindsey looked at her hand where he'd touched it. Was that a sign? Or was she seeing signposts that didn't exist?

Hal returned to the table. "My family hoped I'd come back to Pennsylvania after I graduated. But I got this job in San Francisco. Which, believe it or not, reminds me of Pittsburgh. I guess it's the hills and the water, the neighborhoods, and the history."

She started a pot of coffee. They washed and dried the dishes. Then they sat on the sofa, drinking coffee with the brownies, listening to music as they talked. He put his arms around her and they kissed. She didn't know it was going to happen. But she hoped it would, and she was glad.

THE next morning she woke up early, nestled next to Hal in bed, watching him sleep as she thought about how much she loved him. He woke up and smiled. After breakfast they drove up to the wine-tasting in the Napa Valley. Late that night, when he brought her home, she drew him toward her bedroom, and they spent another night together.

In so many words that never got said, they didn't talk about their relationship. They went out together and Hal spent many nights in Lindsey's bed. Afterward, she wondered if it had been too precipitous. Maybe the stars were not aligned for romance.

Maybe it was just bad timing. That morning in May was fixed in her memory, like glass etched with acid. She was in the garden, enjoying the sunshine as she cut roses. She inhaled the fragrance of a lush, red blossom, then snipped the stem with shears.

A bikini-clad Claire came out the back door, carrying a towel and bottle of suntan oil. "Heard the latest bombshell? Annabel's getting married. Right after graduation."

Lindsey stared. "What? Annabel's going to Europe this summer."

"I guess that will be her honeymoon."

"But who? Why so sudden?"

"Hal, the designated suitor." Claire pulled petals from a rose and tossed them to the dirt. "Annabel's pregnant. Hence the reason for what my mother calls unseemly haste."

Lindsey froze. For a moment she couldn't breathe. Loss, betrayal and hurt overwhelmed her, suffocated her.

How could he? How could Hal do this to her?

She went back to her apartment and put the roses in the kitchen sink. Blood seeped from her fingers, scratched by thorns. Nausea swept over her. She ran to the bathroom and threw up. She flushed the toilet, dampened a washcloth in cold water, and scrubbed her lips. Tears leaked from her eyes.

How could he? He'd toyed with her, marking time, using her until he obtained his primary objective, the boss's daughter.

All the time he was with me, he must have been with her, too. What a fool I've been.

Nausea hit her again. She leaned over the commode and retched. Nothing came up but bile.

This is crazy. All I had for breakfast was oatmeal.

In the bathroom mirror her face went white. She counted back the days in her mind. Usually she was careful to put in her diaphragm. But not always. At times she let herself be swept away by the passion of the moment, as she had a month ago, making love with Hal on a secluded beach.

Oh, dear God. I can't be pregnant. I just can't.

Morning sickness. She'd heard stories about how awful it could be. And it was. She reeled through the next few days and finally went to a doctor, confirming what she feared. She was pregnant, with Hal's child.

What now? In her head she played a crazy movie of Annabel's wedding ceremony, the part where the minister asked if anyone knew of a reason why this man and this woman shouldn't be joined together in matrimony. She saw herself float down the aisle toward the bridegroom. That fantasy wouldn't play in real life. Hal wanted Annabel. Knowing Lindsey was going to have his child wouldn't change that.

She had to face reality. She wasn't equipped to be a single mother. What about her career? Normally it took three to four years of classes and research to get a doctorate. She'd finished her coursework, but she still had to complete her research and write her dissertation. A baby could derail her plans. It could take years to get her degree. Or she might never complete it.

She could have an abortion. She considered herself a feminist and she'd cheered when abortion became legal. But somehow that decision was easier when made by someone else. This was Hal's child.

What if I never get married? What if I'm alone the rest of my life? What if this is the only child I'll ever have?

"I'll support whatever decision you make," Aunt Emma told her one afternoon as they talked over tea and shortbread.

Lindsey stared into her teacup, then raised her head. "I want to have this baby. It's going to be tough. Mom will have a fit."

"She'll get over it." Emma poured more tea. "It will be tough. But you'll manage. I'm sure of it. Give up the apartment and move in with me, so you won't have to pay rent."

Lindsey nodded. "I can work as a researcher through fall semester. And pick up editing and writing jobs. The baby's not due till February. I'll put away as much money as I can. After I have the baby, I'll get a job. I don't have to have my doctorate to teach, even at the college level. All it takes is planning."

When she drove back to the house on Hillegass Street, Hal was on the porch, talking with Annabel. Lindsey pulled her Volkswagen to the curb and waited until he left. She fought back tears, determined to move ahead and leave the past behind.

36

LINDSEY PUSHED AWAY the memories that lurked around the periphery of her life. If she wasn't careful, those feelings she had buried would emerge. It was pointless to get mired in thoughts of what might have been.

Her cell phone rang. Tess? No, it was Flor's number on the screen. Lindsey let the call go to voicemail. She turned to Rod. "Someone from headquarters is going to come along and wonder why you're here with me, and not back at the office taking over the reins of power."

"Power," Rod said. "How much do you know about the company operations?"

"Very little. When Mr. Dunlin died, Hal became CEO. Simple as that."

"Not quite. There was a lot of upheaval." Rod gazed down California Street at the Dunlin Building as though he could see past the brick façade, to the people inside. "Mrs. Megarris said Hal didn't have enough experience. She wanted the job. She even had support from some board members. Max reminded the board that Dunlin designated Hal as his successor. So Hal was elected CEO. But that wasn't the end of it. Claire was moving up. It was only a matter of time before she joined the board. Claire is her mother's proxy."

"We meet for lunch," Lindsey said. "The four of us, every month or so. Claire talks about her work. Much of what I know about the company is filtered through her. Last week I saw something in the newspaper, about the board vacancy and the direction the company is headed. The article hinted about internal dissension."

"It's a battle for control, Max on one side, Claire on the other, and Hal in the middle."

"You're allied with Max," Lindsey said. "Claire's at odds with him. Gretchen told me she had a candidate for the board vacancy. But you were elected instead. She doesn't like that."

"We don't work well together. El Salvador poisoned our relationship."

"Claire had such an angry look on her face after the meeting this morning. It disturbed me." Lindsey frowned as the pieces fell into place. "Claire is trying to oust Hal so she can take over."

Rod nodded. "Claire thinks she's entitled to the company, as her birthright, because her father started it. She ingested that attitude with her mother's milk. Mrs. Megarris has been feeding that line to Claire since she was a child. Megarris was a lousy businessman and an alcoholic. After Dunlin forced him out, he was dead within the year, leaving Mrs. Megarris with a pile of debts. She had to take charity from her brother and she hated it, resents it to this day. Eventually Dunlin put Mrs. Megarris on the board. But she wasn't grateful to him. As far as she was concerned, he owed her that."

His generosity had less to do with charity and more with self-preservation, Lindsey thought. Mrs. Megarris helped her brother cover up his wife's murder. How many times had she collected on that debt?

"Claire had been scheming for quite some time, according to Max," Rod said, "waiting for a board vacancy so she could engineer the election of someone who's in her pocket. She's done it before, with the woman who's now the general counsel. Another vacancy had to happen sooner or later, given the age of senior management. Then Caldwell decided to retire. Claire saw an opportunity. So did Max. He got me elected instead."

"Claire doesn't like being thwarted," Lindsey said. "She has to get her own way."

"Not this time," Rod said. "She tried to create another vacancy. By eliminating Annabel."

Lindsey winced at his choice of words. "How could she do that?"

"By declaring Annabel incapacitated. Because of the stroke."

"But Annabel's getting better."

"That's good," Rod said. "Because if Annabel is incapacitated after eight weeks, her board seat is declared vacant, as if she had died. There's a provision in the bylaws for replacing an incapacitated director. Claire said, due to the lapse of time since Annabel's stroke and her inability to perform her duties as a member of the board, she should be replaced. Mrs. Megarris seconded her motion and the board voted. Claire lost."

A vote wouldn't stop Claire. She was dead set on her goal, ready to mow down anyone who got in her way. She hadn't been able to eliminate Annabel from the board with a vote. But there were other ways. Lindsey grabbed Rod's arm. "We have to go."

Rod stared at her. "Go? Where? Why?" Then it dawned on him. "Annabel?"

"The look in Claire's eyes after that meeting. Annabel may not be incapacitated. But what if she's dead?" Lindsey stepped off the curb and snared a taxi with a wave of her hand. She gave the driver the address of Annabel's convalescent hospital. The cab sped away from the curb. Rod took out his cell phone. "Max, I'm with Lindsey. She thinks—"

Lindsey took the phone from Rod and spoke directly to Max.

"Claire is going to try to kill Annabel."

37

ANNABEL HAD BEEN IN rehab for several weeks now, speech and movement returning. She had too much time to think, though. Memories she'd kept at bay for years lurked in her mind, waiting to torment her again. Like Mother. Like the spring of 1974.

She didn't want to remember anymore. She wanted to feel like herself again, the Annabel who'd made peace with her life, who didn't think about the past.

I want to go home and sleep in my own bed.

Soon. She glanced at the walker. Yesterday she'd made one lap, all the way to the end of the hall and back. She could talk now, and people understood her, even if she slurred her words.

If it weren't for the visits from her family and friends, she'd go crazy. Tess usually came by after work, easy enough since she lived in the city. Sharon drove in from Marin County in the evening, sometimes with her fiancé, Gil. Adam came when he could get away from school down at Stanford. Lindsey and Gretchen were regular visitors. Annabel was glad Lindsey had been able to get word to Lily, who'd visited yesterday afternoon and promised to return. And of all the surprising things, she'd gotten a phone call from Inspector Niebuhr.

Hal came to see her daily. On a work day, he dropped in before going to the office and again in the evening, before going home. Today he'd arrived just after noon, bringing lunch from a nearby deli. Her bed had been raised to a sitting position. Hal maneuvered the tray in front of her. He reached into a bag he'd set on the floor, took out two plastic containers, and removed the lids. "I got chicken with pesto and prosciutto with melon balls."

Annabel smiled. Steady, reliable Hal, so considerate, so supportive. After all these years she had grown to love him. Their relationship was comfortable, without much passion. It wasn't the way it had been with... No. She tightened her mouth. No more memories.

Annabel tucked a paper napkin into the collar of her bed jacket and clenched her hand around the plastic spoon. She scooped up salad and aimed for her mouth. Salty prosciutto contrasted with the sweet marble-sized balls of honeydew melon and cantaloupe. Juice dribbled from her mouth and she used the napkin to blot it. Hal screwed the tops off two bottles of soda and stuck a straw in hers. "Root beer for me, cream soda for you." Annabel sipped her soda, then picked up her spoon again, digging it into the chicken salad.

Hal unwrapped a sandwich. "Roast beef and cheddar on an onion roll. Want some?" She shook her head.

Annabel ate several mouthfuls of chicken salad without making a mess. That was progress. Movement, speech, the everyday activities that one took for granted, were getting easier. It was certainly an improvement over the previous week, when she'd dumped fruit salad in her lap. Who ever thought she'd be so proud of not spilling her food?

They ate in companionable silence. Hal finished his sandwich and tossed the wrapper into the nearby wastebasket. Then he reached into the bag and brought out a small pink bakery box. He opened the lid, tilting the box with a flourish, to show her the contents. "We had tiramisu last time, so I got cannoli for a change."

Annabel looked at the pastry tubes. She used to like cannoli, but not anymore. It reminded her of a deli in North Beach, a long time ago.

Stop, she told herself.

Someone knocked on the door, then pushed it open. The physical therapist, the tormenter. That's the way Annabel had thought of her at first, when the therapist started the daily round of exercises. Now that she was making progress, she was grateful for the regimen.

"Mr. and Mrs. Norwood," the woman said. "I'm following up after our physical therapy session this morning."

"How's she doing?" Hal asked.

"Pretty good," Annabel said.

The therapist smiled. "Yes, you're doing very well."

Hal squeezed Annabel's hand. "When can she come home?"

"The doctor and I think you're ready," the therapist said. "Now, Mr. Norwood, you said you've had a lift installed on the stairs in your home."

Hal nodded. "And I hired someone to help around the house. We'll get a nurse if you think that's advisable."

"In that case," the therapist said, "you can go home tomorrow, Mrs. Norwood."

"Terrific," Hal said. After the therapist left, he reached for one of the cannoli. "I'm so glad you're coming home. I've missed you. We have plans and schemes. You're supposed to be the mother of the bride in August. Sharon and Gil talked about delaying the wedding, but I told them no. You'll be your old self by then. We can boogie at our daughter's wedding."

"No boogie." Annabel pointed at the walker. "Slow dance."

"It's something to shoot for." Hal grinned.

"Board meeting this morning," she said, carefully enunciating the words. "Tell me."

He hesitated, not saying anything as he fitted the lids on the salad containers. "It was…contentious. Look, I know I've talked about it a lot during my visits. Just to be talking. I wasn't sure how much you were taking in."

"Enough." She fixed him with a stern look. "What happened with Claire?"

He gathered up the remains of lunch and stowed them in the bag. "Max and I have been concerned about Claire's machinations, but it's going to be okay. We elected a new director this morning, Rod Llewellyn, who heads up our Houston operation."

When she heard Rod's name, Annabel's hand tightened on the bedcovers. Hal continued with his account of that morning's board meeting. When he got to the part about Claire's attempt to have Annabel declared incapacitated and replaced as a board member, Annabel felt alarm. What would Claire do now that she'd lost this round?

Hal looked at his watch. "Didn't realize what time it was. I need to get back to the office." He leaned over and kissed her gently. "I love you."

He picked up the shopping bag and left the room. A moment later the housekeeper entered the room, pushing her cart of cleaning supplies. "I'll just be a minute, Mrs. Norwood. I'm going to empty the trash and give that bathroom a once-over."

Annabel lay back against the pillows and let the memories come.

38

San Francisco, California, May 1974

ANNABEL STOOD in Washington Square and watched the bride and groom exit the Church of Saints Peter and Paul. The woman wore a frothy white wedding gown, veil streaming from her hair, laughing as she held up her bouquet of pink roses. Her bridegroom laughed, his hand up to ward off the rice thrown by the spectators. The bride tossed her bouquet high into the air. The newlyweds escaped into the backseat of a white Cadillac, arms around each other as the driver sped off.

Is it as easy as that? Yes, Rod, I'll marry you. He'd take her into his arms and everything would be all right.

It was a Saturday, late spring. North Beach was crowded with people, strolling along the sidewalks, sampling food and coffee in the cafés and delis, stretched out on the grass of Washington Square, faces turned toward the sun. A man and a woman, tourists with cameras looped around their necks, stopped in front of her as they consulted a map and talked about the best route to Coit Tower. She stepped around them and crossed Columbus Avenue. When she reached the deli, she looked up. The curtains were open in Rod's living room.

What am I going to do if he's not home? We left it in such a bad place when he proposed and I turned him down. That was before…I have to talk with him. I do love him.

A bell clanged as a cable car lumbered toward Fisherman's Wharf. Then she saw a sign in the deli's window—FOR RENT, 1 BR, INQUIRE WITHIN.

No. She refused to even consider the thought that pushed into her mind.

Mrs. DeLucci was behind the counter, scooping potato salad into a container. Her husband whistled a jaunty tune as he sliced salami. Annabel waited near a display of olive oil until the customer departed. Mrs. DeLucci smiled at Annabel. "Can I help you?"

"The sign. The apartment for rent."

"It's a nice apartment, one bedroom, furnished, sunny. You can even see the wharf from the living room window. It's available right now."

Available now. She heard the words with dread. "The man who rents that apartment, Rod Llewellyn. Has he moved out?"

Mrs. DeLucci nodded. "Yes. Are you a friend? He didn't tell you he was leaving?"

"No." Annabel hated the look of sympathy in the woman's eyes. "Did he leave a forwarding address? A phone number?"

258 · *Janet Dawson*

The woman shook her head. "His company transferred him to another place. He had to leave right away. We saw him off in a cab, three days ago. Listen, honey, it's none of my business, but—"

Annabel left the deli. She was on Montgomery Street before she realized where she was headed. No one would be at the Dunlin Building on a Saturday, except maybe Max Brinker. He would know where Rod had gone.

The front door was locked. She peered inside and saw a security guard making his rounds. She rapped on the glass. He recognized her and unlocked the door. "Hello, Miss Dunlin. What brings you here on a Saturday?"

"I'm looking for Mr. Brinker."

"You're in luck. He went upstairs about an hour ago."

Max Brinker was at his desk in the security office. "Annabel. What are you doing here?"

"I was in the city...on an errand." The words sounded stiff and awkward. Surely he'd know something was wrong. He always did. But there was some truth to her description. Her errand had come to naught. "I wanted to ask about the security guards. Now that they're no longer needed at the house, what happens to them? Are they still working for the company?"

"Tom got another job. Mike and Carl still work for me."

"What about Rod Llewellyn?" She tried to keep her face blank.

"Rod took a job in our Houston office."

Annabel forced a smile. "They were nice guys. I wish them well."

He looked at her as though he knew there was something else on her mind. "Congratulations on graduating next week. It's a real milestone. You must be pleased."

"I am." She looked at her watch. "I have some shopping to do. Thanks, Mr. Brinker."

"Any time, Annabel."

She walked to the elevator and got onto the car. Her hand slipped on the central panel and she punched three instead of one. The doors opened and she looked out on an empty hallway. She punched the button to close the doors but they stayed open. Off to the right, she saw movement and a tall figure came into view.

"Annabel? Annabel, wait." The elevator doors closed. The car descended again.

On the first floor she crossed the lobby. The security guard let her out. A cable car went by, clanging its bell as it climbed toward Nob Hill. Annabel walked up the steep slope to Powell Street, where two cable car lines intersected. The cable car on the Powell line stopped and picked up passengers. People stood on the steps and clung to railings as the car clanged its bell and began its steep descent to Union Square.

Annabel passed the Fairmont Hotel and the dark sandstone Flood mansion. The mining kings and robber barons of another era had built their palaces atop this hill, only to lose them to forces stronger than their owners. Most had been shaken to rubble and burned to ash during the great 1906 earthquake and fire. But this one had survived. It was now the Pacific Union Club, the exclusive province of latter-day robber barons like her father. On the next block Huntington Park beckoned, a rectangular green oasis. On the other side of Taylor Street stood Grace Cathedral, an Episcopal church modeled on Notre Dame in Paris.

Annabel sat on a park bench and gazed at the round stained glass window above the cathedral's front door. The sidewalks and steps in front of the church were crowded with men in dark suits and women in pastel dresses and hats.

Specters rose, words and images haunting Annabel, memories of her days and nights with Rod. She remembered that last day, when he'd asked her to marry him. She'd turned him down, her refusal signaling the end of their relationship. Now he was gone. Too late. Or was it? Could she contact him? What if he didn't want to hear from her? Maybe he wanted a clean break.

But it wasn't all that clean. There was something left over, something more tangible than Annabel's memories.

Her missed period brought several days of denial. No, it couldn't be true. It was stress, brought on by her approaching graduation and the promise of independence. But her cycle was always regular, just like clockwork. Finally she went to a clinic and confirmed her fears.

I have to figure out what I'm going to do. I'm pregnant. Barely a month along, but pregnant. Rod's gone. I have a decision to make. But it was difficult to focus as conflicting emotions washed over her.

She could have an abortion. It was legal in California, even before the Supreme Court decision called *Roe v. Wade*. She supported that choice in the abstract but when it boiled down to Annabel Dunlin, pregnant and unmarried, making that decision felt very different. Besides, it was Rod's child, the only thing she had left. Did she really want the responsibility of raising another human being for the next twenty years? Panic rose inside her.

Other people have been looking after me for so long. I can barely take care of myself. How can I take care of a baby?

Across the street a long white limousine pulled up to the curb. Four young women in lavender dresses spilled out, accompanied by a little girl wearing a miniature version of their dresses. An older woman in a mauve dress got out, holding a white bouquet with streaming lavender ribbons. Then the bride emerged, in her lacy white gown and flowing veil. The older woman handed her the bouquet. The bride entered the cathedral, three of her bridesmaids holding her train. The fourth bridesmaid remained outside, with the little girl.

Marriage, Annabel thought. Or abortion. My decision. I have to choose.

What would this baby do to all of her dreams and plans? With a pang of regret, she thought about her summer trip to Europe, graduate school, her career plans.

She tried on the idea of an abortion again. Safe, simple, an outpatient procedure, or so she'd heard. No one would know. She could get on with her life. Was it that easy?

The little girl across the street held a white basket tied with ribbons wrapped around the handle. A rose fell from the basket. The girl squatted and picked up the bloom, putting it back in the basket. Then the bridesmaid took the child by the hand and led her into the cathedral.

What if this is the only baby I'll ever have? What if this is my only chance to be a mother? Oh, God, I don't know what to do.

She felt something wet on her cheek and looked up at the sky, blue with wisps of clouds, a gorgeous day in late spring. Surely it couldn't be raining. She wiped her fingers over her cheek and discovered she was crying.

"Annabel?"

She looked up. The man was tall and dark. For a joyous moment she thought it was Rod. There must have been a mistake. He wasn't gone after all.

But it was Hal. He thought the hopeful look on her face was meant for him.

"Didn't you hear me calling you?" he asked. "When the elevator opened on the third floor? When I got outside I saw you walking up the hill, so I followed you. Annabel..." He sat down next to her on the bench. "You're crying. What's wrong?" He pulled a white handkerchief from his pocket.

She took the handkerchief and wiped away tears. He was a nice man, easy to be with, a friend. She needed a friend right now.

"Annabel, what's wrong?" He reached for her hand. "Tell me. I can help."

"I'm pregnant." Oh, damn, just blurt it out.

A shadow brushed over his face. Then it was gone, as quickly as it had come. He squeezed her hand. "We'll get married. Everything will be fine."

She stared at him. He was throwing her a lifeline and still she wasn't sure whether to grab it. "Are you sure you want to take on the responsibility of a child who isn't yours?"

"A child who will be mine. I love you."

"I don't love you, Hal."

"I know that. But we're friends. You like me, I hope. That's a start. If you'd give it...us a chance, love could grow. We could have a good marriage. We could give this baby a wonderful home. Please marry me, Annabel. Let me be the father of your child."

"All the things I want to do," she said. "Travel, graduate school."

He smiled. "We can travel together. Anywhere you want to go. You can start graduate school in the fall, just as you planned. And you can go back after the baby's born."

She leaned back on the bench, feeling calmer as he stroked her hand, listening to his seductive voice. Steady, reliable Hal, so considerate, so supportive. Being with him was comfortable. Maybe he was right. Maybe she'd learn to love him.

She heard the organ booming from Grace Cathedral, the opening bars of Bach's "Jesu, Joy of Man's Desiring." Then she frowned. "What about Lindsey?" she whispered. If he heard her, he gave no sign of it.

39

ANNABEL REACHED FOR the rectangular control attached to the left bed railing. She adjusted the bed's angle downward and lay back against the pillows, thinking about her long-ago plans and dreams. A different road than the one she found herself on now, married to Hal, mother of three children.

She'd graduated from Cal that May of 1974, mortarboard on her head, gown billowing around her as she rushed down the aisle and onto the stage to accept her diploma. Afterwards she suggested eloping to Lake Tahoe, as soon as possible, before she changed her mind about marriage. Hal wanted something more formal, with his own family there to celebrate. Annabel gave in. She owed him that much for solving her problem.

So June brought another ceremony, another journey down an aisle, this one at a slower, more reluctant pace. Annabel wore an unadorned ice blue silk gown, bought off the rack. She couldn't bring herself to wear white.

June, the month for brides and weddings, and most churches had been booked, every weekend, months in advance. There was no big Saturday production, just a small weekday ceremony, late on a summer afternoon, the sun lowering in the west as tendrils of fog threaded their way through the Golden Gate. Annabel and Hal said their vows at Grace Cathedral, their words echoing off the walls and ceiling of the vast, nearly empty sanctuary. The small reception took place afterwards at the nearby Fairmont Hotel, where George Dunlin had arranged for Hal's family to stay.

When she told her father she was getting married, and soon, she wasn't sure of his reaction. He didn't question the sudden wedding and the reason for its haste. Instead he appeared to be pleased. She was marrying the designated suitor, after all. It seemed her father liked steady, reliable Hal. For Hal's sake, and her own, she hoped she would learn to love him.

Had she?

Later that summer, she told her father she was pregnant. She didn't elaborate. He could count to nine, just like anyone else. No doubt he'd assumed she and Hal had slept together before they got married. It was the Seventies, after all. Such things happened all the time. Aunt Rebecca had a knowing look in her eyes. Claire probably told Aunt Rebecca the truth about the baby. Claire would.

What about Lindsey? Hal never answered. Lindsey was gone, living with her aunt. But Annabel wondered. She'd gone ahead with the wedding. No turning back. But the question didn't go away. Did Lindsey mean so little to Hal that he could marry Annabel without a backward glance? Did Lindsey mean so little to Annabel that she could marry Hal even when she didn't love him? And Lindsey was pregnant, according to Claire, with Hal's child.

Had Annabel learned to love Hal? Or had she just gotten used to having him around?

Mr. and Mrs. Hal Norwood went to Maui for their honeymoon. Rod was the only man Annabel had ever slept with. Now it felt strange to share a bed with Hal, to have sex with him, especially with another man's child growing inside her. When they got back from Hawaii, she moved into his two-bedroom flat on Russian Hill, more spacious than her flat in the house on Hillegass Street. It looked like home once she added her own things. Apartment living was fine with Annabel, but Hal wanted a house and a yard, all the trappings of married life. He thought it would be better to make the move before the baby was born. As summer spun into fall, the morning sickness went away. Annabel adjusted to the idea of motherhood and marriage. She and Hal spent weekends in the company of a real estate agent, eventually buying the Noe Valley house. They moved in, designating the smallest bedroom as the nursery.

She signed up for one fall semester graduate course. But as the months passed, her figure thickened and her ankles swelled. She felt uncomfortable and ungainly, awkward and out of place, tired most of the time. Driving from San Francisco to Berkeley, for class and time in the library, got harder and harder. It was difficult to concentrate on classwork, distracted as she was by the move, decorating the house, the physical changes to her body, the fact that she was about to give birth to another human being. She was relieved when the semester was over and she could stay at home and rest.

When Tess was born, Annabel got caught in the web of motherhood—breastfeeding, colic, teething, appointments with the pediatrician, and dirty diapers. Wealth eased the way as much as possible, with a nanny for the baby and domestic help with the cleaning and cooking. It was another eighteen months before she could sign up for a class. Midway through that semester she discovered she was pregnant again, with Sharon. Two babies in four years. It seemed overwhelming. She gave up the idea of acquiring a master's degree. Instead she took the occasional class at San Francisco State.

I did see Paris and London and Rome, she thought. Eventually. Just not on my own.

The irony was that Lindsey had done all the things Annabel hadn't, though burdened with her own pregnancy and child. She'd done it alone, without a husband to support her. When Annabel looked at Hal's daughters—Nina, Lindsey's child, and Sharon, her second child—she saw the resemblance. Surely others could. She knew Lindsey did.

But they were all such good friends, so polite, spending time together, but never really talking about what must be going through their minds, deluding themselves into seeing what they wanted to see, instead of what was really there, caught in their own variations of the devil's bargain.

Then there was Claire. Contrary Claire. Difficult. Contradictory. She'd never trusted Claire. Her cousin could be generous, but you didn't want to get on her bad side. She could be ruthless, capable of deliberate cruelty. When she was good, she was very, very good. And when she was bad, she was horrid.

Speak of the devil, and she appears.

Claire walked into the room and shut the door. Something about her was off, vibrating like a steel wire pulled taut. Much too tight. Tight enough to snap. When she spoke, her voice was rushed and breathless. "We have to talk," Claire said, fingers playing with the clasp on her shoulder bag. "You need to listen to what I have to say. I want you to understand. It's really my company. Your father stole it from mine."

What nonsense. Yet Annabel knew the source. In Claire's feverish words she heard Rebecca's grievances, festering unabated through the years, unmitigated by the favors George Dunlin had doled out. Claire had been hearing this skewed version of the facts her whole life.

"It's my father's legacy to me," Claire said. "I should have been CEO when Uncle George died, but he gave it to Hal instead. Just because Hal married you when you got knocked up. I'm taking it back. I'm almost there. That old bastard Brinker put a crimp in my plans. Guess who they elected to the board this morning? Your lover. Rod Llewellyn."

Annabel felt alarm as words spilled from Claire's mouth, hot as the light in her eyes. Claire moved restlessly about the room, becoming more agitated as she poured out her plans. Rod's election to the board was a temporary setback. There was another way. All she needed was another vacancy on the board. She knew how to create that.

Claire grabbed the metal railing at the foot of Annabel's bed and shook it hard. "Hal doesn't know, does he? That Rod is Tess's father. Maybe it's time he did, now that Rod is back in San Francisco. He came over to the house looking for you."

What was she talking about? He? The house? Then Annabel knew. Rod had come to the house on Hillegass, before he left. And *I wasn't there.*

"You'd gone for a walk. I told him you went away for the weekend, to Carmel with Hal. But it was Lindsey who went to Carmel with Hal that weekend." Claire laughed. "You should have seen the look on Rod's face."

That was the cruelest thing of all. *He came looking for me and didn't find me,* Annabel thought. *A week before I went looking for* him and didn't find him. If only I'd known. I would have gone over to the city that very afternoon and thrown myself in his arms.

Claire left the foot of the bed, talking about the present now, about how simple it was to create a vacancy on the board.

What did she mean? Then Annabel knew.

She means to kill me.

The phone rang. Annabel grabbed the receiver.

"Mom, it's Tess. Just calling to check in. How are you?"

"Claire is here to kill me," Annabel said.

"What? Claire? Mom—"

Claire pulled the phone jack from the wall. Then she grabbed a pillow. Annabel crossed her wrists and forearms over her nose and mouth as the pillow descended onto her face and Claire pushed down. Annabel pushed back. She turned her head and reached for the control on the bed railing, pressing the button that summoned the staff. Surely someone at the nurse's station down the hall would hear the buzzer and see the light flashing outside her door.

Claire pushed the pillow harder onto Annabel's face. Annabel wrapped her fingers around the control and brought it down hard on Claire's head. Claire swore and backed away. The strap of her handbag slipped from her shoulder and fell to the floor with a loud clunk, as though there were something heavy inside. Claire dropped the pillow and picked up her purse.

A nurse entered the room. "Hi, Mrs. Norwood. You rang for assistance? Everything all right in here?"

"She's trying to kill me," Annabel said.

The nurse looked at Annabel in consternation. Then she stared at Claire, at the gun in Claire's hand.

40

AS THE CAB SPED through a yellow light, Lindsey's cell phone rang. It was her daughter. "Nina? Where are you?"

"In a cab, heading for the convalescent hospital. Tess called her mom. Annabel said Claire was trying to kill her. Then the phone went dead. Tess called the cops, and Hal. I don't know what's going on but we'll find out."

"Nina, be careful. I'm on my way to the hospital." Lindsey disconnected the call and relayed the conversation to Rod. "Part of me says I'm overreacting, but the other part—"

"I know what Claire is capable of," Rod said.

"You far better than me," Lindsey said.

"I don't have your emotional investment in being her friend."

It is an investment, Lindsey thought, with a friend, or a lover, letting down one's defenses. The Claire who had been revealed to Lindsey over the past few days wasn't the one Lindsey thought she knew. She tried to quiet her fears as the cab sped west.

"Right at the next intersection," Lindsey told the cabbie, "then pull over in the middle of the block." Rod paid the driver and they got out of the vehicle.

It was midafternoon and construction workers in hard hats were visible inside the shell of the hospital's new wing. The gate securing the temporary chain-link fence was open and a pickup truck had been backed halfway down the sloping driveway that led to the new parking garage. Lindsey and Rod took the elevator to the fifth floor.

Three nurses and a security guard clustered in the hallway, the guard with a cell phone in his hand. "She had a gun," a nurse said. "Then Mrs. Norwood's daughter and another woman came in and she took them. I saw them go into the new wing."

"We've got a hostage situation," the guard said into the phone.

Claire had Nina and Tess. Lindsey spun around. The fire door separating this older building from the new wing was open, the doorway covered with the clear plastic sheet intended to muffle construction sounds and dust. The thick plastic had been pushed aside, revealing a short hallway, and beyond that, a big empty space with support columns. The new section of the fifth floor had not yet been divided into rooms. There would be a stairwell somewhere, with access to the ground level. Had Claire gone this way?

Lindsey saw neon pink—Nina's shirt?—against the gray concrete, someone moving in the new wing. She plunged into the construction zone. Rod followed. Her footsteps echoed on the bare concrete floor. She stopped, getting her bearings, looking for that flash of pink. She heard the voices of construction workers below. To her left, at the rear of the building, was a stairwell. Directly in front of her the elevator shaft was barricaded with a gate. The elevator was stopped on the floor above, cables dropping to the bottom of the shaft. To her right, at the front of the new wing, another stairwell led down to the street. Lindsey ran toward it. The voices below turned agitated. Someone shouted. She couldn't make out the words. Then a construction worker ran up from the landing, cell phone to his ear. "…some crazy woman with a gun…"

Nina! Lindsey looked over the railing and started down the stairs, Rod behind her. As Lindsey reached the fourth floor, she saw Claire, Nina and Tess on the landing between the third and fourth floors. Lindsey took a step down. "You can't do this."

The gun in Claire's hand turned upward, an ugly glint of metal. "Of course I can. Don't push your luck, Lindsey."

Lindsey took another step down, turning so she could see Rod on the fourth floor landing. His hand slipped into his pocket, reaching for his cell phone.

Claire pointed the gun at Tess. "Get your hands where I can see them, Rod. Or I'll kill your bastard right here and now."

Rod stopped and raised both hands. Tess stared at him, comprehension dawning. "You're my father?"

"Yes." He looked at Claire. "Lindsey knows about El Salvador. I told her everything."

"I warned you," Claire said. "Did you know Hal is your father, Nina?"

"Of course I do," Nina snapped. "Is that your big surprise?"

"The police are on their way." Lindsey took another step toward Claire. She wasn't really brave or foolhardy. But she had to get to her daughter. "You think you'll go down these stairs and out to the street, but it's impossible. Any minute now we'll hear sirens."

"Keep walking." Claire brandished the gun at Nina and Tess.

Lindsey glanced over the railing. Construction workers gathered at the bottom of the stairwell, talking, gesturing, pointing up. Then she heard Hal's voice, calling Tess's name as he ran up the stairs.

The gunshot was deafening, echoing off the stairwell walls. Lindsey clapped her hands over her ears and huddled against the railing. Nina and Tess had dropped, on the landing between the floors. Was the slug ricocheting around the stairwell? No, it had found its target. Red blossomed on Hal's shoulder. He collapsed on the third-floor landing.

"Daddy!" Tess scrambled down the stairs and cradled Hal's head in her lap. Nina moved to follow but Claire put the gun to Nina's head, forcing her up the stairs and out onto the fourth floor. Rod ran down the stairs past Hal and Tess, onto the third floor. Sirens wailed in the distance.

Lindsey ran up the stairs, to the fourth floor. Claire headed for the other stairs at the back of the new wing. She was halfway there, Nina in front of her. Just as she passed the elevator shaft, Rod stepped out of the back stairwell. Claire raised the gun and fired. Rod darted out of sight. Nina ran to hide behind the thick columns at the back of the elevator shaft. Lindsey did the same. She clasped Nina to her, as tightly as Nina held her.

"You're safe," Lindsey said, tears streaming down her face.

"We're not out of this yet," Nina said.

The sirens were louder, closer, then they stopped. Lindsey peered around the columns. Claire headed for the fire door that would take her to the fourth floor of the existing hospital. But the door was locked. She doubled back toward the construction elevator, toward the columns where Lindsey and Nina were hiding. Claire jabbed at the elevator controls. There was a loud grinding sound, then a steady mechanical hum. The elevator descended, slowly, as Claire wrenched open the barrier gate. The elevator stopped with a jerk, still five or six feet above the floor, as though someone below had cut off the power. Voices echoed in the front stairwell. When Claire turned toward the sound, Lindsey grabbed Nina's hand.

"Now," Lindsey whispered.

They ran. Lindsey heard the gun roar. She hugged Nina as they slipped into the stairwell.

But where was Rod?

He was in front of the elevator shaft, towering over Claire, reaching for her hands. They struggled for the gun and it fired again. Then Rod backed away, gun in hand.

Blood stained Claire's chest. She fell. Lindsey ran to her, dropped to her knees, reached for Claire's hand. But Claire pulled away, hissing words that Lindsey couldn't understand. The angry hot light dimmed in Claire's blue eyes.

41

BIG BLACK TYPE SPREAD across the front page of the *Chronicle*, Claire's picture visible above the fold. Rod looked up from the newspapers on the gift shop counter as Lindsey crossed the medical center lobby. "We've been to see Hal," he said. "Max will be along soon. Then we're off to the Hall of Justice. Another session with lawyers and police."

"Will they charge you?"

"I don't know. Max and the lawyers are working on it. Mrs. Megarris has been telling everyone I murdered her daughter." He shook his head. "But it wasn't like that. We were struggling and the gun went off. Our daughters are safe. That's all that matters. Tess and I had a long talk last night. Awkward as hell, at first. Having a grown daughter takes getting used to."

"Have you talked with Annabel?" Lindsey asked.

"Not yet. But I will. She's home now."

"I know. I'm planning to see her later."

"I thought I'd give her a few days to settle in." Then he shook his head again. "No, that's not true. I'm the one who needs a few days to work up to it."

"I know what you mean," she said.

Rod's hand touched her shoulder. "Hal?"

"Yes. I'm not sure what I'm going to say to him."

The doors of the nearby elevator opened and Max stepped out. He looked tired. "How are you, Lindsey?"

"As well as can be expected. I'm avoiding the press and the phone. I suppose the furor will settle down eventually."

"I certainly hope so." Max ran his hand through what was left of his hair. "Everything's in turmoil at the office. Damn reporters in front of the building, sticking cameras and microphones in people's faces as they come out of the lobby. We need to have an emergency board meeting. But it's difficult when the CEO's in the hospital because an executive vice president tried to kill him and his wife."

"Then got killed herself," Rod said. "With another executive quite possibly facing charges for his part in her death."

"Not if I can help it," Max growled. "I've still got some clout in this town."

Lindsey took the elevator up to Hal's private room. He lay in a hospital bed, surrounded by flowers from well-wishers, face pale above the blue gown covering his bandaged shoulder. He opened his eyes and smiled. "Lindsey. Come in."

She walked into the room and stood with her hands on the back of a chair that had been pulled up close to his bed. "Were you asleep?"

"Just drifting. Max and Rod were here, a little while ago." He pressed a button and raised the bed, so that he was in a sitting position. "Annabel's home."

"Yes, I know. How are you?"

"I'm okay. A little sore. Doctor's going to cut me loose in a day or so. And you?"

"Me? I'm tired. Like I've been running a marathon. I've been having trouble sleeping."

Hal grinned. "Not me. Good drugs." His smile vanished. "Are you okay, really?"

"There's something I need to say." Lindsey glanced at her hands, marked with old scars. Then she looked into his eyes. "It doesn't hurt anymore. It's like having a thorn stuck in my hand. I spent years worrying about how much it would hurt if I pulled out the thorn. It would have been better to experience the pain all at once instead of avoiding it, letting it fester."

"I thought we were going to have this conversation a long time ago," Hal said.

"You know Nina's your daughter?"

"I figured it out. I'm not completely clueless. However, I'm just

272 · Janet Dawson

as good as you are at avoiding unpleasant truths." Hal shifted and
winced. He raised his right hand and dropped it. "Would you please
straighten these pillows? Whenever I reach for them, my shoulder
hurts and I don't want to ring for the nurse."

She adjusted the pillows. His hair, once so dark and thick, was
now mostly gray, getting thin on top. "How's that?"

"Fine. Thanks." He looked troubled. "Why didn't you tell me
Nina was my child?"

"Would it have made any difference? What would you have
done? Cancelled your wedding and eloped with me?"

"I don't know. I found out you were pregnant a couple of weeks
after Annabel and I got back from our honeymoon. Claire let it slip.
By accident, or so I thought at the time."

"Claire, who I thought was my friend," Lindsey said. "She told
me Annabel was pregnant, and you were going to marry her. Told
me, so she could amuse herself with my reaction. I thought Tess was
your child. I felt used, angry. You were fond of me, nothing more. You
enjoyed my company for a time. Annabel wasn't available. So I let
you into my life, my bed. It was more than just physical attraction.
I loved you. Though you'd never given me any reason to think that
you had the slightest interest in me. You simply took what I offered."

"Lindsey—"

She raised her hand. "No, let me say it. I've been avoiding it for
too long. Time I got it all out in the open."

"Don't take all the blame," Hal said. "Leave some for me. I
shouldn't have led you on like that. No matter how upset I felt about
Annabel ignoring me. When she told me she was pregnant, all I
could think was, finally, she needs me. I can be there for her. I didn't
think about you. Not until I realized you were carrying my child.
Then I felt guilty. I waited for you to say something. You didn't. I
should have. But there I was, with Annabel, her baby on the way, me
feeling responsible for both of them. It was easier to avoid the issue
of you and Nina."

"You love Annabel," Lindsey said. "You always have. At some
point I stopped feeling sorry for myself and moved on. I thought I
could be so civilized, adult and modern. I could have my child, live

my life and ignore the hurt. That worked for a long time. But something happened, triggering all these memories. It must have started last year, when Aunt Emma died and left me her house. I moved back to Berkeley. Then Annabel had that stroke. More memories. The realization that we're all older. The next milestone could be death. Then Tess asked me to help find her birth father."

"She told me. It was a shock. I didn't know who Tess's father was. It didn't matter, then or now. I've always thought of her as my daughter."

"Tess's question brought me up short," Lindsey said. "I had a certain view of the past. But if you weren't her father, my version of the truth wasn't true after all. I dug deeper, and realized I didn't really know the people I thought I knew."

Hal took her hand. "I'm so sorry. I never meant to hurt you. But I did. I just didn't think."

"I didn't think either. I just felt. I have a little bit of you. My daughter. Our daughter. She's been upset with me for years, because I wouldn't tell her who her father is. I finally did, a few days ago. She's still upset with me."

"As soon as I get out of this damn bed, I'll talk with her," he said. "I have a lot of talking to do, with several people."

"Me, too. One of them lives at your house."

WIND chimes hung from a hook on the porch of the ghost gray house on Octavia Street. Tess opened the front door and waved Lindsey into the foyer. An electronic lift with a seat and railings had been installed on the stairs.

"I took time off work to look after Mother," Tess said. "And Dad…Hal…when he comes home."

"Good. You'll have your hands full," Lindsey said. Annabel stood in the doorway, hands on the grips of a bright red walker with four fat rubber wheels. "Snazzy walker."

"Adam picked it out. All it needs are racing stripes."

"It's good to see you up." Lindsey put her arms around her friend.

"Good to be home," Annabel said when Lindsey released her. "We'll have tea."

"Coming right up," Tess said. "Sandwiches, too. I've been making lunch." She walked down the hall toward the kitchen.

Annabel turned her walker in a wide circle and led the way to the living room. In the years Annabel and Hal had lived in the Dunlin house in Pacific Heights, the alcove formed by the bay window had always served as a reading room, furnished with a comfortable wing-back chair upholstered in blue flowered fabric, a matching ottoman, a small table and a lamp. The windowsills held an assortment of African violets with lush pink-and-purple blooms and thick velvety leaves.

"Your mother's desk was in that alcove," Lindsey said.

Annabel settled into a recliner near the fireplace and flipped up the footrest. "He got rid of it. Got rid of all her things. After he killed her. That's what my father left me. That and his company. What do I have to remember my mother by? The carousel music box she gave me for my ninth birthday. A silver pineapple and a shard of crystal. The files you read. Tess's box is full of ghost stories."

"Like this house," Lindsey said. "I remember what you said, just after your father died. That he left this house to you, with all the ghosts."

"I've banished a few, over the years. But not all."

Tess pushed a tea trolley into the living room. She positioned it next to Annabel's chair. "Are we fancy, or what? I made that chicken salad myself." The trolley held all the accoutrements of afternoon tea: a china pot, two cups, silverware, sugar bowl and creamer. A two-tiered milk-glass serving plate held small square sandwiches and round cookies, each with slivered almonds in the middle.

"Are these Lily's famous almond cookies?" Lindsey asked.

Annabel smiled. "Yes. She brought them this morning."

Tess poured two cups of tea. Lindsey caught a whiff of bergamot from the freshly brewed Earl Grey. "Do you want anything in your tea, Lindsey?"

"No, thanks."

Tess reached for the sugar bowl. "Mother likes sugar and milk." She added both to Annabel's cup. "I'll be in the kitchen if you need anything."

Lindsey popped a cookie into her mouth, tasting almonds. "Ah, they are good."

Annabel raised her teacup, her hand shaking a little. She steadied it with the other hand and took a sip. Then she set it on the tea trolley and reached for a cookie. "It's more than that. These cookies are full of memories of feeling warm and cared-for. No matter how lonely I got, Lily was there, stirring up a batch of almond cookies, just for me."

"I'm glad I was able to get in touch with her. It took me a while to figure out your doodles in your old address books."

Annabel finished the cookie and brushed the crumbs from her hands. "I needed a code. When I was younger, I thought my father and my aunt would prevent me from seeing Lily. Especially after they fired her. When I convinced her to tell me what she saw the day my mother died, I was sure they'd retaliate. So our visits have been a secret between the two of us." She picked up her cup. "My mother is an old ghost. We need to talk about more recent ghosts."

"You and Rod." Lindsey took one of the sandwiches.

"That, too. You and Hal." Annabel took a deep breath. "I'm sorry I took him away from you. I didn't love him, and you did."

Lindsey's feelings were still close to the surface after her conversation with Hal. "That's water under the bridge."

"Is it?"

Their eyes met, over things too long unsaid. Lindsey nodded. "Yes, it finally is. I loved him. But I don't anymore."

"I felt guilty," Annabel said. "I did think about you, briefly. But not for very long. I'm a coward. I don't have your courage, the guts to see it all through in spite of detours, like an unwanted pregnancy and single motherhood. You went on and didn't look back."

"I went on because I had no choice," Lindsey said. "And I did look back. I wasted a lot of time wondering what might have been. Then I realized second-guessing was a luxury I couldn't afford. I had to support myself, and Nina. I realized something else, that Hal loved you. He never felt that way about me. But I couldn't figure out why you married him. You'd never given any indication of having feelings for him. Then I thought you'd hidden them, out of rebellion against

276 · Janet Dawson

your father and the whole designated suitor joke. I never dreamed Tess wasn't his child. All those feelings and questions came back. So I agreed to help Tess, even though I hadn't told Nina that Hal is her father. Which he knew, as I discovered when I talked with him this morning."

Annabel took another sip of her tea. "Why did I marry Hal? I was afraid. I took the first life raft that floated by. Hal loves me. I've grown to love him. He's a good husband and father."

"Maybe things turned out the way they were supposed to."

"Why the hell did it have to be such a rocky road?" Annabel asked. "With so many damned detours?"

"So we could learn from it?" Lindsey reached for another sandwich. "Things will never be the way they were."

"When Tess told me she knew Hal wasn't her father, I thought, good, time she knew. Now she does. Now she has to deal with the feelings. I hope she'll work it out."

"Nina was so angry with me," Lindsey said. "For so many years. She'll have to figure things out for herself. Hal would love to have a relationship with her. He already does, since we've been friends for so long, ever since the girls were born."

"A long time to be keeping secrets," Annabel said. "Papering over the truth with polite smiles. Rod and Hal and…"

"Claire?" Lindsey asked.

"Yes. Claire." They sipped their tea in silence. "I knew from an early age Claire was off kilter," Annabel said. "She could be kind one minute, cold and manipulative the next. She was sick. And evil. But Gretchen won't see it that way. She has a blind spot where Claire is concerned. Have you talked with her yet?"

Lindsey shook her head. "That's my next stop. I must tell her and Doug something about Nat. It won't be easy." She told Annabel what she had learned about Nat's parentage and Claire's part in the events that took place so long ago in a remote village in El Salvador.

"Gretchen will be angry," Annabel said. "She's always been ambivalent about you."

"I know. It has to do with Doug. She once accused me of trying to steal him. She's never said anything to me, but she wonders if

Nina is Doug's child. I'm sure Claire planted that seed. I see suspicion in Gretchen's eyes sometimes, when she looks at my daughter. That's a bitter pill, since Gretchen can't have children of her own. Now I'm going to tell her that her adopted son has a mother living, right here in the Bay Area."

"Ghost stories." Annabel looked around her living room, as though she saw a different cast of characters gathered there, on a long-ago April afternoon.

The ghosts in Lindsey's mind roved farther, across the bay to Berkeley, across the sea to El Salvador. "The ghosts of the past come back to haunt us. Self-doubt, guilt, old hurts we hang onto, even though they don't do us any good. Sometimes it's hard to let go of those ghosts." She reached for the teapot, intending to pour another cup for each of them. But the ceramic felt cool. "The water's cold. I'll get a warm-up."

She went through the study to the door, across the back hallway to the kitchen. Tess wasn't there. The door leading to the porch was open and so was the outer door to the backyard. Lindsey switched on the burner under the teakettle and stood there, thinking about watched pots that didn't boil. She heard footsteps on the back stairs. Tess entered the kitchen with a basket, looped on one arm.

"Mom's roses are spectacular this year. Look at these. Aren't they gorgeous?" Tess set the basket on the counter and filled a vase with water.

Lindsey reached for a rose with coral petals and a heavenly scent. A thorn pricked her finger and she saw a sharp little spine embedded in her flesh. She pulled out the thorn. Then she turned on the faucet and rinsed away the blood.

42

WHEN LINDSEY RETURNED to Berkeley later that afternoon, Nina was on the front porch. "I'm out of a job," she said. "It's just as well. Things are in a mess. No one knows what's going to happen to the company. The head of Human Resources says she'll put me to

278 · Janet Dawson

work in another department for the time being. But I don't know if I can be there."

"You can move back here until you find another job." Lindsey unlocked the door and they went inside.

"Tess doesn't want me to move. Besides, she's staying temporarily with Annabel, now that she's home."

"I know. I was just there." Lindsey reached for Nina's hand.

Nina didn't pull away. Instead she squeezed her mother's hand. "Mom… I thought about what you said. You're right. I've held onto that anger long enough. I have to move past it and see if I can establish a relationship with Hal…with my father."

"I saw him this morning, at the hospital," Lindsey said. "He knows you're his daughter. He kept his distance because he thought it was better to do so. He wants to talk with you. You'll sort it out, the two of you."

"Life's strange, isn't it?" Nina sighed. "How about I make some coffee?"

Lindsey shook her head. "There's something I have to do. I've been dreading it. But I can't put it off any longer." She relayed the story of Nat, El Salvador, Claire's involvement, and Flor. "On Tuesday, Flor gave me an ultimatum, twenty-four hours. I promised to talk with Gretchen and Doug yesterday. I went over that deadline and then I didn't answer Flor's calls. When I called her this morning, Flor was very angry with me. I told her I was overtaken by events. And I was. But that's only partly true. I kept thinking I'd find the right time to tell Gretchen and Doug. But there's never going to be a right time. I can't put it off any longer."

"I'll go with you," Nina said

Together they walked to Gretchen's house. Nat and Amy, home from school, greeted them at the door and motioned them into the hallway. "You want to talk with Mom?" Nat asked. "She's been hoping you'd call or stop by."

"Both your mom and your dad," she said. "I saw his car in the drive."

"Yeah. Dad took time off work to be with Mom. She's really upset about Claire."

Amy shouldered her pink backpack and turned to her brother. "I'm going over to Polly's house to work on our history project. Her mom invited me for dinner. I asked Mom a couple of days ago and she said I could."

"Okay," Nat said. "I don't want you walking home alone after dark, even if it's just a couple of blocks. You call me and I'll come get you."

"Okay. You're a good brother. I take back everything I said about you." She stood on tiptoe and hugged him.

"Yeah, right. Till the next time." He patted her on the back and watched her leave. He shut the door. "Mom's out on the patio. Dad's in the kitchen."

Doug was making tea for Gretchen. "She found out about Claire in the worst possible way. She'd switched on the TV in here to watch the local news while she fixed dinner."

"How awful," Lindsey said. "I would have called. But the police, the questions…by the time I got out of there, it was late."

"She hardly slept last night. Couldn't stop crying," Doug said. "I decided I'd better stay home today. The press coverage is bad enough. But I should have screened her calls, incoming and outgoing. Gretchen called Claire's mother. I don't know what Mrs. Megarris said to her, but that just made it worse."

"I can imagine." Lindsey knew what Rebecca Megarris had been saying, to the police, the press, anyone who would listen. Claire's mother was grief-stricken and angry about her daughter's death, making excuses for Claire, spewing venom and threats of legal action. In Gretchen, Mrs. Megarris found a sympathetic ear.

Lindsey and Nina declined Doug's offer of tea, and followed him out to the patio, where Gretchen huddled in a chair, a shawl over her shoulders. She had dark circles under her reddened eyes, her hands twisting a handkerchief. "Where have you been?" Gretchen demanded. "Why didn't you come over? I called you, at home, on your cell phone, and got voicemail."

"With the police." Lindsey sat down. "Today I've been to the city, to see Hal and Annabel. They're fine."

"Claire's dead." Tears leaked from Gretchen's eyes. "We'll never see her again. One of my dearest friends in the world. I couldn't be-lieve it. Even when I heard it on the news. How could they say such horrible things about Claire? It's not true, any of it. It's all lies. I can't believe it. I won't."

"I'm sorry," Lindsey said. "I know Claire was your friend. But it's true. She tried to kill Annabel. Then she shot Hal. I saw her do it."

Gretchen waved away the mug of tea Doug offered. "No. You'll never convince me of that. It's a horrible mistake."

"I didn't really come here to talk about Claire. Not how she died, anyway. I have something to tell you. It involves Claire. It's about Nat. And El Salvador."

Lindsey told the tale as best she could. What pain she caused them, these two friends. Doug wiped tears on his sleeve. Gretchen's eyes went wide with shock. She rose from the chair, lunging at Lind-sey. Nina moved between the two women as Doug grabbed Gretchen and wrapped his arms around her, holding her close.

"How could you do this to me?" Gretchen cried. "How could you do this with your meddling? Why can't you mind your own business? I'll never speak to you again."

"Cut it out, Mom."

Nat's voice sliced like a knife through Gretchen's tirade. He'd been hanging back, listening. Now he walked over to face her, no longer a teenager, instead a thoughtful, steady young man, like the man in the picture Flor had shown Lindsey, her first husband, Atena-cio, Efraín's father...Nat's father.

Gretchen's voice shook. "I am your mom."

"Of course you are," Nat said. "Dad's my dad. I love both of you."

"We love you, son," Doug said. "No matter what."

Nat took a deep breath. "Yes, I'm your son. But I had another mom and dad, before. I always knew I was adopted. I always won-dered who I really am and where I came from."

Gretchen sobbed. "The people at the orphanage told us you didn't have anyone. That's all we knew. It doesn't matter where you came from. We loved you the moment we saw you. You're our little boy."

"I know that, Mom. But there was a time before the orphanage.

When I was someone else's little boy." A shadow passed over Nat's face. "I remember things."

"Because you heard Lindsey talking about El Salvador," Gretchen said.

Nat shook his head. "No, Mom. I do remember. Maybe I always did and it was under the surface." He closed his eyes and opened them again. "Sometimes I have dreams. A big black crow swoops down from the sky and snatches me from my mother."

Gretchen dropped to the chair as though her legs had been knocked from under her. "Why didn't you tell us, son?" Doug asked.

Nat shrugged. "I don't know. I felt, like, maybe it was disloyal of me to bring it up. On weekends, my buddies and me, we'd hop on BART and go over to San Francisco, check out the neighborhoods. One Saturday afternoon we were hanging out in the Mission District. We went into this Salvadoran place. This lady was cooking something on a grill, a *pupusa*. The smell and the sound of it sizzling made my mouth water. The funny thing was, I knew how it tasted, even before I put it in my mouth. I remembered this woman, cooking *pupusas* over an open fire. She'd tear off a corner and give it to me." He smiled. "My mother?"

Lindsey nodded. "What else do you remember?"

"A man who smelled like coffee," Nat said. "He rode me around on his shoulders. A house on a hill. Not really much of a house. More like a one-room cabin. An old lady. A store. A church." He frowned. "Guns. I remember guns. People with blood all over them." Nat stroked the scar on his chin. "Running up the hill, to get away from those men with guns. My mother was carrying me. But we fell. I cut my chin on some broken glass. I cried and she tried to shush me. A lady with gold hair put a bandage on it. That was Claire, wasn't it?"

"Yes," Lindsey said. "She took you to San Salvador and left you at the orphanage. She arranged for you to be adopted, by Gretchen and Doug."

"I guess that was a good thing," Nat said. "Coming out of a bad thing. I'll have to think about that. My birth father. What was his name?"

"Atenacio Guzmán."

"He was killed that day," Nat said, his voice flat. He shook off the memory. "I kept going over to the Mission District. I couldn't get enough of those *pupusas*. The lady that runs the place, she and her husband came to the States during the civil war. I told her what I remembered. She said there was this organization looking for missing kids from El Salvador. I looked it up on the Internet. I didn't know if anyone was looking for me. But I wondered. Then I read about that UC Berkeley database, where they were doing DNA testing, hoping to link people whose kids were missing with adopted kids here in the States. I thought about looking for my birth parents. But I didn't. Maybe I was afraid of what I might find out. Afraid of hurting people who love me. I felt...torn. Like I belonged in two places at once. I didn't know how Mom and Dad would react. Well, maybe I did. So I was missing and now I'm found. My birth mother's here, in the East Bay?"

"She lives in Oakland," Lindsey said. "Her name is Flor Cooper. She's remarried, with two children. She saw you at the Berkeley Farmers Market and is sure you're her son. You look like your birth father. And there's that scar on your chin."

Nat ran a finger over the scar. "My birth name, what's that?"

"Efraín Guzmán," Lindsey said.

"Efraín Guzmán." He repeated the name several times, tasting it as he had tasted the *pupusa*. "I want to see her."

"I don't want to lose you." Gretchen stood and flung her arms around Nat. "I don't want you to leave me."

"You're not going to lose me," Nat said, hugging her. He stepped back. "I'm grown up now. I'm graduating from high school and going away to college. I am leaving home. That's part of life. But it's not forever. I'll be back." He turned to Lindsey. "I'd like to see my birth mother. Will you take me to her? Now?"

BEFORE they left Berkeley, Lindsey called Flor. "I'm coming over. With Efraín."

"I'm scared," Nat said, when they were in the car.

Lindsey reached for his hand. "So is she. But she'll be so proud of you. You've grown into a fine young man."

"It'll be okay," Nina said. "You'll have two families. What an adventure."

Flor stood on the front porch of her home in the Fruitvale district. Her husband and children waited with her. Nat walked toward her, staring at her face.

"*Mamá?*"

"*M'ijo, m'ijo.*" Flor rushed down the steps and flung her arms around her son. "*Mi corazón, mi precioso.*"

At first Nat hesitated. Then he wrapped his arms around her, holding her close.

The two children ran toward their mother, eyes wide, curious and frightened at the same time. Flor's husband followed them and patted his wife on the shoulder. Flor released her son and reached for her husband's hand.

"This is your stepfather," she said. "My husband, Tony. Your brother, Michael. Your sister, Antonia." She smiled, beaming like the sun. "This is my son, Efraín."

Tony's eyes were moist as he took Nat's hand. "Welcome home, son. Your mom's been hoping and praying for so long that she'd find you. Seems like a dream come true."

"Yeah, I know." Nat knelt so that he was eye-level with the younger children. "You can call me Nat for short. Because I'm used to Nat." He looked up at Flor. "Okay?"

Flor nodded. "Nat. It's fine."

"I have another sister," Nat said. "Her name's Amy. She's eleven. Maybe you guys can meet her sometime. She loves cats. We have a cat named Moby."

"We got a cat named Tigger." Michael tugged on Nat's arm. "We'll show you."

Nat stood and Flor smiled. "You look like your father. Come. I'll show you a picture of him." As Nat, Tony and the children entered the house, Flor said, "Lindsey, you and your daughter, you come, too."

Lindsey shook her head. "We don't want to intrude. Go, enjoy your reunion with your son."

"I have something for you. I will be right back." Flor went into the house and returned a moment later, holding out the pillowcases

she had been embroidering all these weeks, with their border of flowers—roses and pansies and daffodils, meticulously stitched in jewel-
bright red, purple and yellow.

"You were making those for a friend," Lindsey said.

Flor smiled. "You are my friend. Even though I doubted you for a
while. You returned my son to me. That's a better gift than anything
I can give you."

"*Muchas gracias.*" Lindsey took the pillowcases, the white fabric
stiff against her hands. Flor said good-bye and went back into the
house.

Lindsey's vision blurred as tears streamed from her eyes. All the
secrets were out now. Pandora's Box was empty of everything, except
hope.

"Mom." Nina put her arms around Lindsey. They stood there for
a moment, then Nina stepped back and smiled. "Come on. Let's go
home."

◆

MORE MYSTERIES
FROM PERSEVERANCE PRESS
🕵 *For the New Golden Age* 🕵

ALBERT A. BELL, JR.
PLINY THE YOUNGER SERIES
Death in the Ashes *(forthcoming)*
ISBN 978-1-56474-532-3

JON L. BREEN
Eye of God
ISBN 978-1-880284-89-6

TAFFY CANNON
ROXANNE PRESCOTT SERIES
Guns and Roses
*Agatha and Macavity awards
nominee, Best Novel*
ISBN 978-1-880284-34-6

Blood Matters
ISBN 978-1-880284-86-5

Open Season on Lawyers
ISBN 978-1-880284-51-3

Paradise Lost
ISBN 978-1-880284-80-3

LAURA CRUM
GAIL MCCARTHY SERIES
Moonblind
ISBN 978-1-880284-90-2

Chasing Cans
ISBN 978-1-880284-94-0

Going, Gone
ISBN 978-1-880284-98-8

Barnstorming
ISBN 978-1-56474-508-8

JEANNE M. DAMS
HILDA JOHANSSON SERIES
Crimson Snow
ISBN 978-1-880284-79-7

Indigo Christmas
ISBN 978-1-880284-95-7

Murder in Burnt Orange
ISBN 978-1-56474-503-3

JANET DAWSON
JERI HOWARD SERIES
Bit Player
Golden Nugget Award nominee
ISBN 978-1-56474-494-4

What You Wish For
ISBN 978-1-56474-518-7

Death Rides the Zephyr
(forthcoming)
ISBN 978-1-56474-530-9

KATHY LYNN EMERSON
LADY APPLETON SERIES
**Face Down Below
the Banqueting House**
ISBN 978-1-880284-71-1

**Face Down Beside
St. Anne's Well**
ISBN 978-1-880284-82-7

Face Down O'er the Border
ISBN 978-1-880284-91-9

ELAINE FLINN
MOLLY DOYLE SERIES
Deadly Vintage
ISBN 978-1-880284-87-2

SARA HOSKINSON FROMMER
JOAN SPENCER SERIES
Her Brother's Keeper
(forthcoming)
ISBN 978-1-56474-525-5

HAL GLATZER
KATY GREEN SERIES
Too Dead To Swing
ISBN 978-1-880284-53-7

A Fugue in Hell's Kitchen
ISBN 978-1-880284-70-4

The Last Full Measure
ISBN 978-1-880284-84-1

MARGARET GRACE
MINIATURE SERIES
Mix-up in Miniature
ISBN 978-1-56474-510-1

WENDY HORNSBY
MAGGIE MACGOWEN SERIES
In the Guise of Mercy
ISBN 978-1-56474-482-1

The Paramour's Daughter
ISBN 978-1-56474-496-8

The Hanging
ISBN 978-1-56474-526-2

DIANA KILLIAN
POETIC DEATH SERIES
Docketful of Poesy
ISBN 978-1-880284-97-1

J.B. REINSTEIN

JANET LAPIERRE
PORT SILVA SERIES
Baby Mine
ISBN 978-1-880284-32-2

Keepers
Shamus Award nominee, Best
Paperback Original
ISBN 978-1-880284-44-5

Death Duties
ISBN 978-1-880284-74-2

Family Business
ISBN 978-1-880284-85-8

Run a Crooked Mile
ISBN 978-1-880284-88-9

HAILEY LIND
ART LOVER'S SERIES
Arsenic and Old Paint
ISBN 978-1-56474-490-6

LEV RAPHAEL
NICK HOFFMAN SERIES
Tropic of Murder
ISBN 978-1-880284-68-1

Hot Rocks
ISBN 978-1-880284-83-4

LORA ROBERTS
BRIDGET MONTROSE SERIES
Another Fine Mess
ISBN 978-1-880284-54-4

SHERLOCK HOLMES SERIES
The Affair of the
Incognito Tenant
ISBN 978-1-880284-67-4

REBECCA ROTHENBERG
BOTANICAL SERIES
The Tumbleweed Murders
(completed by Taffy Cannon)
ISBN 978-1-880284-43-8

SHEILA SIMONSON
LATOUCHE COUNTY SERIES
Buffalo Bill's Defunct
WILLA Award, Best Original
Softcover Fiction
ISBN 978-1-880284-96-4

An Old Chaos
ISBN 978-1-880284-99-5

Beyond Confusion *(forthcoming)*
ISBN 978-1-56474-519-4

LEA WAIT
SHADOWS ANTIQUES SERIES
Shadows of a Down East
Summer
ISBN 978-1-56474-497-5

Shadows on a Cape Cod
Wedding *(forthcoming)*
ISBN 978-1-56474-531-6

ERIC WRIGHT
JOE BARLEY SERIES
The Kidnapping of Rosie Dawn
Barry Award, Best Paperback
Original. Edgar, Ellis, and Anthony
awards nominee
ISBN 978-1-880284-40-7

NANCY MEANS WRIGHT
MARY WOLLSTONECRAFT SERIES
Midnight Fires
ISBN 978-1-56474-488-3

The Nightmare
ISBN 978-1-56474-509-5

REFERENCE/
MYSTERY WRITING

KATHY LYNN EMERSON
How To Write Killer
Historical Mysteries:
The Art and Adventure of
Sleuthing Through the Past
Agatha Award, Best Nonfiction.
Anthony and Macavity awards
nominee.
ISBN 978-1-880284-92-6

CAROLYN WHEAT
How To Write Killer Fiction:
The Funhouse of Mystery & the
Roller Coaster of Suspense
ISBN 978-1-880284-62-9

**Available from your local bookstore or from
Perseverance Press/John Daniel & Co. at (800) 662-8351
or www.danielpublishing.com/perseverance.**